the Inventor's Companion

ARIEL TACHNA

Dreamspinner Press

Published by
Dreamspinner Press
4760 Preston Road
Suite 244-149
Frisco, TX 75034
http://www.dreamspinnerpress.com/

The Inventor's Companion
Copyright © 2011 by Ariel Tachna

Cover Art by Anne Cain   annecain.art@gmail.com
Cover Design by Mara McKennen

ISBN: 978-1-61581-822-8

Printed in the United States of America
First Edition
March, 2011

eBook edition available
eBook ISBN: 978-1-61581-823-5

To the men
who have inspired my muses
since I first laid eyes on them.

GABRIEL BLACKSTONE adjusted his collar, the formal leather jacket uncomfortable in its unfamiliarity. In his workshop, he rarely wore anything over his shirtsleeves, and at home alone he wore even less, especially in the heat of the summer. His assistants and friends, Caleb Deahl and Andrew Lambert, had gone in together and purchased an evening out for him as a birthday present, though, so he had to make himself presentable. The gentlemen's club where he was supposed to meet his companion for the evening was one of the most exacting in town, only allowing members to enter unless special arrangements were made. Gabriel had no idea how Caleb and Andrew had made those arrangements, but they were quite clear about where Gabriel was to go, so he had replaced his old breeches with fresh ones and dug out his cravat and coat, even going so far as to don a hat. He doubted he would wear it for long in this heat, but it gave him an air of respectability as he waited for the mechanized hansom that would bear him to his destination. The coach arrived in a whoosh of steam, making Gabriel wish he had left on the goggles he wore in his lab. Instead he shielded his eyes with his hand to protect them from the cinders as he gave the address to the driver and climbed inside.

The coach resembled a horse-drawn carriage, but a large engine took the place of the unpredictable animal, making the contraption dependable regardless of weather or traffic. Unsurprisingly, it had almost entirely replaced horse-drawn carriages except for the aristocrats who considered the horses a sign of their wealth. Gabriel envied the man who had invented the mechanical conveyance. He was surely a rich man because of it.

Gabriel wasn't ready to retire just yet, but he was ready to have one of his inventions catch on enough to keep his workshop running instead of having to worry each month where he would find the funds to pay Andrew and Caleb or to buy the supplies he needed for his work. He'd enjoyed small successes here and there, but nothing big. As the coach carried him toward his destination, his mind shifted to the project in the basement of his workshop. Not even Caleb and Andrew knew about it yet. A flying chair that would allow people to travel short or long distances without having to sit in traffic or wait for a train. He was sure, if he could make it work, that it would be the discovery that made his name in the world. The Blackstone chair. Unfortunately he lacked the money he needed to invest in all the tools and supplies he would need to make an engine powerful enough to carry a person but light enough that its own weight would not hold it down. It worked in theory, but he had not completed a prototype yet, and no one would fund an idea as radical as this one based on theory, not without a big-name inventor behind it, anyway.

A rap on the roof of the hansom drew Gabriel from his musings. They had arrived at the club. Fighting with his collar once more, Gabriel descended and paid the driver. At the club's entrance, a burly man, clearly a guardian of the gate for all his formal attire, barred the door. "Your name?"

Gabriel might have taken offense at the lack of honorific, but the quality of his clothes proclaimed him to be part of the merchant caste even if the scales tattooed on the web of skin between his thumb and forefinger did not. Only the aristocracy escaped the process of being marked, their status in life proclaimed each time they shook hands.

They always shook hands.

"Gabriel Blackstone. I was told you were expecting me."

The guardian scowled but checked his records, eventually opening the door to let Gabriel in. "Mind your manners. There's quality folk inside."

Gabriel did bristle at that comment. Although he did not have the wealth or social status of an aristocrat, he knew how to behave in society. "Mind your own," he snapped. He pushed past the guardian, ignoring the increasing grumbles. He might not be an aristocrat, but he had the right to be here. His friends had paid for this evening, and Gabriel refused to let a lout like that stop him from enjoying every part of it.

His righteous indignation fizzled out when he caught sight of the other patrons of the club. Unlike him, they all wore silk and linen instead of leather and cotton. Even more strikingly, many of them wore gloves. Despite knowing he had bathed and laundered his clothes, Gabriel suddenly felt grimy next to their polished elegance. He almost retreated, his earlier determination aside, when a soft, smooth hand clasped his. "Mister Blackstone, I presume?"

Gabriel turned to see who had spoken his name, wondering as he did how anyone here would know him. He found the most beautiful man he had ever laid eyes on. "Yes, I'm Blackstone," he choked out, not sure how he could make his voice work when every bit of his mind was taken with the vision in front of him. His companion had pitch-black hair, pulled back into a long queue that fell below his collarbone as it lay across his shoulder. The locks contrasted sharply with fair skin that seemed never to have seen the sun. His eyes were the color of the dark chocolate Gabriel could rarely afford.

"I'm Lucio," the other man said, his grip changing so that he shook Gabriel's hand. "Your companion for the evening."

Automatically Gabriel glanced down to where their hands met, catching sight of the tell-tale fan on Lucio's hand.

"It's a pleasure to meet you," Gabriel said, his mind reeling as he took in the number of ribs in the fan. Lucio was not merely pleasure caste. If Gabriel had counted correctly, he was the highest echelon of companion. Gabriel nearly flinched at the thought of what Caleb and Andrew must have paid to secure Lucio's presence at the club.

"Perhaps we could find our table?" Lucio suggested smoothly. "We would draw less attention that way."

Gabriel trailed along behind Lucio, his eyes raking over the companion's body now that the beauty of the man's face was denied to him. Lucio was almost as tall as Gabriel, but his lithe form gave him a much slighter appearance. His costume, nearly as elegant as that of the aristocrats who surrounded them, clung to his body in a way the other men's clothing did not, highlighting the line of his back and the curve of his legs most provocatively. Lucio's coquettish glance over his shoulder suggested he knew exactly the effect his appearance had on Gabriel, which pricked the inventor's pride enough to want to be contrary. He would enjoy the evening and the companion's company, but he would treat the other man as a friend or a colleague rather than as a body in which to take his ease.

"I hope you don't mind," Lucio said as he took a seat at the table in a private lounge, sprawling elegantly in the chair, "but I took the liberty of ordering a light repast for us. I was not sure you were familiar with the offerings."

Lucio's cultured tones bespoke an educated upbringing, everything but the fan on his hand giving the impression that he was one of the aristocracy. For a man who had more than once denounced the idiocy of the caste system to his friends, Gabriel found the illusion disturbingly arousing. Before Gabriel could reply, a server approached with a bottle of wine. He showed the label to Lucio, who nodded his approval. The sommelier opened the bottle and poured a small amount into Lucio's glass for him to taste. The companion sniffed delicately and sipped the wine. "Would you care to taste it as well?" he asked Gabriel.

"If it pleases your discerning palate, I'm sure it will be to my taste," Gabriel said, not willing to show his ignorance in this setting. His clothes and the tattoo on his hand set him apart badly enough as it was.

Lucio nodded to the sommelier, who filled Gabriel's glass before topping off Lucio's. He left the bottle on the table and discreetly withdrew. Gabriel picked up the goblet and sipped at the wine as he had seen Lucio do, trying not to make a fool of himself. The flavor of the wine rippled over his tongue and up into his sinuses, filling his head with its richness, far more complex and potent than the liquor he was accustomed to drinking. He managed not to choke as he swallowed, approaching the next sip more cautiously.

"I understand you're an inventor, Mister Blackstone," Lucio said when Gabriel had recovered. "I've always been fascinated by machines."

Gabriel almost scoffed at the blatant fawning, but he stopped himself with the firm reminder that Lucio had not chosen his lot in life any more than Gabriel himself had and that being a companion did not make Lucio unintelligent. "It is a fascinating field," Gabriel agreed. "The new inventions over the past twenty years alone have changed the world as we know it."

"It always amazes me when I think of the amenities our parents had to do without," Lucio said enthusiastically. "I can't imagine not having steam to heat my bath in the morning."

Gabriel nearly choked on his wine again at the evidence of the luxury Lucio clearly enjoyed. Gabriel's own bath had no such heat. He still warmed his water in pails over the fire and poured them by hand into his copper tub.

"It is an improvement indeed," Gabriel agreed, trying not to imagine Lucio reclining in a marble tub, steam rising around his face and dampening his hair. He wondered cynically if the comment had been intended to summon just that thought, but Lucio's face bore no guile. "I cannot imagine working by candlelight."

"Such a prosaic example for an inventor," Lucio chided flirtatiously. "Give me a better example, something you have contributed to our technological revolution."

"My contributions have been small," Gabriel demurred. "You have probably never seen them."

"Don't be modest," Lucio insisted, leaning forward and taking Gabriel's hand in his own, his thumb stroking the lines that crossed Gabriel's palm.

The jolt of lust was undoubtedly what the companion had intended, reminding Gabriel where they were and why. Drawing his hand back, he shook his head. "Enough about me. Tell me about yourself instead."

Lucio's eyebrows jumped in surprise, making Gabriel wonder if no one had ever asked before. "I am a companion. What more is there to say?"

"You are fascinated by machines," Gabriel said. "I'm sure that isn't true of every companion, or if it is, perhaps I should have sought one out before."

"Most are not," Lucio said after a long moment, "unless perhaps they are out to dinner with an inventor and are not sure what else to talk about."

"Then it was simply a ploy to draw me out?" Gabriel asked, frowning at the idea of being deceived.

"No," Lucio replied quickly, reaching for Gabriel's hand again, "but it is the kind of gambit we are taught so we might be pleasing company to our guests for the evening. It was felicitous that our interests coincided and I needed no ulterior motive to bring it up."

That could be as much a lie as the rest, Gabriel knew, but he sensed honesty in Lucio's words. Either the companion was telling the truth, or he was even better trained than Gabriel had imagined. The one saving grace in the entire conversation was Lucio's willingness to admit to his wiles. Surely he would have hesitated to do so were he using them on Gabriel. Then again....

This was why Gabriel had always refused to hire a companion. He couldn't trust a word any of them said. He prided himself on being a plain-spoken man, and their pretty ways were more than he could tolerate.

They were interrupted by the arrival of the first course of their dinner, a thin soup the color of the rich earth. The server placed the dishes in front of the two men and retired without saying a word. "What is this?" Gabriel asked.

"It's onion soup," Lucio said before he tasted it. Gabriel watched in fascination as the companion's eyes closed and a look of bliss crossed his face. Gabriel's gut clenched at the idea of seeing that look again in more intimate settings. He pushed the thought aside. He had already decided not to take advantage of the companion's charms. He did not need release so badly that he would take it meaninglessly in the potentially unwilling body of the man across the table from him. Lucio might have been born into the pleasure caste, barely one step above servants, but that did not mean Gabriel had to demean him that way. Looking at the quality of Lucio's clothes, the elegance of his coiffure, Gabriel saw little to suggest any lack in Lucio's life, certainly nothing compared to the way Gabriel lived. Lucio might not have had a choice in his profession, but he had clearly thrived at it. Even so, Gabriel would not take that choice from him tonight.

Pushing all thought of desire from his mind, Gabriel tasted the soup, surprised at the richness of the thin broth. In his experience, clear broth, even one as dark as this one, was as bland and tasteless as a meal came, but this was different. Gabriel had no idea why, but his tongue proclaimed the truth of the situation with great delight. "This is wonderful," he said, determined to converse with Lucio as he would with any equal. "What other delights do you have in store for me?"

The moment the words were out of his mouth, Gabriel cursed silently. He had just handed Lucio the perfect opening to bring up the more carnal aspect of the evening. Lucio let the opportunity pass, smiling simply before replying, "The chef here is excellent, as you've already seen. He has a salad, a fish course, a lamb dish, and then dessert. I prefer lamb to beef or pork. I hope you don't mind."

"Not at all," Gabriel said, though in truth, he had only tasted lamb a few times in his life, the meat being out of his reach given his current financial situation. "It will be a lovely treat."

Lucio shifted slightly on the chair, drawing Gabriel's eyes back to his body. "I hope the rest of the evening will be a treat as well."

Gabriel looked away, uncomfortable with the suddenly suggestive mood of the companion's voice and stance. "I'm sure it will be," he said, his voice tight. "I rarely have an evening out."

"What makes tonight special?" Lucio asked, the seduction gone again as quickly as it had appeared.

"It's my birthday," Gabriel admitted softly. "My assistants arranged our meeting as a gift."

Lucio smiled and leaned forward. "I like the idea of being your birthday present."

Gabriel looked up sharply. "I don't. I don't like the idea of anything being forced on you."

Lucio laughed. "Do I look like I'm being forced? No one is standing here with a gun to my head. No one is threatening to hurt my mother or my sister in order to make me be here. I have earned enough status to choose which new guests I accept. If I had not wanted to be here, someone else would have come in my place. Your friends did not ask for me by name."

Gabriel's eyes narrowed. Lucio's words made sense, but he was a companion. He had already admitted to transforming himself in order to please his client. This could be one more example of that. "Why?"

"Why what?" Lucio asked, finishing his soup and pushing it aside. He rose from the chair and approached Gabriel.

"Why would you accept an inventor as a guest when you are obviously used to much better?" Gabriel rasped, resisting the urge to reach for Lucio.

"Because I was intrigued," Lucio replied, his hands resting on the back of Gabriel's chair so they brushed the inventor's shoulder blades lightly as he bent forward, his breath stirring the fine hairs on Gabriel's neck as he spoke. "I've never met an inventor before because rarely can they afford me. Your friends were very specific in what they wanted for you, which I found intriguing, and I decided I wanted to be the one to deliver it. I haven't been disappointed at all. I hope you haven't either."

Gabriel swallowed against a suddenly dry mouth. He told himself this was one more line, but his body didn't care. He caught all the signals Lucio was sending out, and he yearned for that contact. Only the knowledge that it was bought and paid for held him back. He would never be able to face his friends at the Caste Equality movement if he gave in. "I haven't," he croaked. "I should finish my soup. I'm sure the server will be back soon to clear the table and bring the next course."

Fortunately Lucio backed off, resuming his seat and easing the intensity of his approach. Almost as if on cue, the door opened, and the server came back in, setting down the salad Lucio had promised and clearing the used dishes. Gabriel regretted not finishing his soup, but the salad looked equally enticing. He nudged the greens with his fork, trying to decide what else was in the salad.

"It's cranberries, walnuts, bleu cheese, and a light dressing," Lucio said before taking a bite.

Gabriel nodded and ate, determined to finish this course rather than be distracted by Lucio's charms. Lucio seemed to sense his new mood, letting him eat without conversation. Only when Gabriel had finished did Lucio resume their earlier discussion as if the moments in between had never occurred. "You didn't tell me what you were working on, Mister Blackstone. I truly am interested."

Gabriel hesitated, deciding after a moment that it couldn't hurt to tell Lucio some of the public projects he was working on. If he kept the flying chair to himself, it was because he hadn't told anyone about it yet. "I have a patron who has always wanted a pet but is allergic to their fur," he said. "He has commissioned a mechanical dog that he can activate when he wants companionship and turn off when he's out of town or when having a live animal would be inconvenient."

Lucio bit back a laugh. "How very... practical of him."

"Self-indulgent is more like it," Gabriel muttered, "but he's paying me, and I can't afford to turn down the commission."

"Is it going well?" Lucio asked.

"Well enough, I suppose," Gabriel said with a shrug. "The challenge is making all the parts move together in something that approaches natural movement. I've built a prototype, but its movements are still awkward. Too awkward for my client."

"It sounds like challenging work even if the result will be less than groundbreaking," Lucio said.

"It pays the bills," Gabriel replied. "At this point I'm grateful for that. I have another project I'm working on, but I don't have a sponsor for it, and that means it always gets pushed aside."

Lucio nodded. "Money does seem to rule the world. Even among the aristocrats who pretend to be above all that, money determines who enters where, as much as the lack of mark on their hands."

"At least that's honest," Gabriel said. "No matter how much money I make, there will be doors closed to me because I have a tattoo. The same is surely true for you."

"It depends," Lucio said. "If I am on the arm of a wealthy aristocrat, his status is enough to gain me entrance. On my own, I imagine even more doors would be closed to me than to you."

"You were able to gain us entrance here," Gabriel pointed out. "I could not have done that alone."

"Point taken," Lucio replied, "but I'm known here because of the number of guests I have entertained. I neglected to mention when I made our reservation that you were merchant caste. They assumed you were an aristocrat, and I didn't correct them."

Gabriel laughed. Perhaps there was a bit of revolutionary inside Lucio after all. "I think I like you."

THE words struck a surprising chord inside Lucio. He had never cared if his guests liked him. His job wasn't to make them like him. His job was to bed them—although there was rarely a bed involved—and send them away satisfied. Even internally, he couldn't seem to avoid the euphemisms his trainers had insisted he use lest he offend the delicate sensibilities of the aristocrats. Never mind that many of the aristocrats cursed regularly and volubly as they fucked him over the table or the couch or whatever surface was closest. He couldn't be the one who talked that way. Glancing at the man sitting across the table from him now, Lucio suspected he could be as free with his speech as he wanted without offending his guest, except that for once, Lucio actually cared what his guest thought because for once, his guest seemed to care about him. Not in any deep sense—Lucio wasn't naïve—but enough to ask if his interest in machines was genuine, enough to ask about Lucio's own interests.

That had never happened before, and it was enough to intrigue the companion. To hide his unease, he flipped open the fan he carried in defense against the heat, the bamboo ribs providing a veil between his emotions and the man seated across the table from him.

Everything about this guest was at odds with the men and women Lucio was used to entertaining. His clothes were rough rather than elegant; his hair was shaggy, as if someone had hacked at it with a knife, rather than perfectly coiffed. His skin was ruddy, evidence of time spent outdoors, rather than pale as fashion dictated. His hands, when Lucio had touched them, were callused with work rather than smooth and soft, making Lucio wonder what they would feel like on his skin. Would the rough edges rasp over sensitive places, adding to what pleasure he drew from his encounters with his guests? He shivered at the prospect, his determination to seduce the man across from him growing with each passing second. At first, it had been a professional challenge: he'd never left a guest unsatisfied. It had become more than that as they talked, everything about Mister Blackstone appealing to him. He had learned at an early age to feign pleasure even when he felt nothing. If he ever convinced the inventor to touch him, he suspected he wouldn't be faking anything.

"I think I like you too," Lucio replied belatedly. "I've never had a guest like you before."

"Never had a guest from the merchant caste?"

The bitterness in the words hurt, all the more because they were true. Lucio's handlers had groomed him from an early age to cater to the aristocracy, recognizing that he had the physical attributes to appeal to the upper caste. "I've never had a guest who resisted me," Lucio countered, for that was far more important to him than the tattoo on the inventor's hand. "It makes me wonder why you're here."

"I'm here because my friends wanted to give me a birthday present," Mister Blackstone replied. "I don't want to waste their generosity."

"I'm part of that generosity," Lucio pointed out, the continued reluctance intriguing him. He reached up and loosened the tie holding his hair in its queue, shaking his head slightly so his hair would fall about his shoulders. "Any way you want. All you have to do is tell me what you desire. Or better yet, show me."

A knock on the door interrupted them, the server returning with the next course. Lucio hid his impatience behind a practiced mask of manners, only the speed of the waving fan giving away his annoyance, but he wanted the server gone, the meal finished, so he could apply his skills to breaking down the reserve he sensed in his guest. "What is it you desire?"

Mister Blackstone ate several bites of his fish before he finally looked up, his startlingly blue eyes piercing Lucio. "I want to enjoy a good meal with a beautiful man in a place that would normally be closed to me. I want to go home tonight smiling because I took pleasure in your conversation. I want to remember tonight as the one time I will be allowed into the aristocrats' world."

"No one has ever wanted me only for my conversation," Lucio said before he could censor the words. "They usually have more... concrete desires."

"Their loss is my gain."

The phrase was familiar, of course, but the words made no sense to Lucio in this context. "How do you figure that? What could you possibly gain from our conversation that would outweigh the pleasure they take in my body?"

Mister Blackstone smiled, revealing slightly uneven teeth, another little imperfection the aristocracy would never have allowed. It only added to the inventor's attractiveness now in Lucio's eyes. "They're all the same to you. They blur together unless one is particularly generous or particularly cruel, I would think. You meet them at the agreed-upon location, perhaps you spend a certain amount of time pretending it is more than a business transaction, and then you take your clothes off and let them fuck you or who knows what else. Then you go home, a little richer maybe, but no more interested in them than you were when you arrived."

Every word was true. "You haven't answered my question," Lucio said huskily.

The smile widened. "I'll go home tonight knowing you'll remember me because I was different," the inventor continued. "You won't think of me as yet another man who used your body for his own release. You'll remember me as the one who didn't. The one who asked for something else instead. And because you'll remember me at all, I'll have gained something none of them ever will."

Lucio wanted to deny that he would remember this evening as anything special, but it would be a lie, and he couldn't bring himself to say the words. Mister Blackstone had treated him differently than his other guests did from the moment they met. He had seen the flicker of interest, but rather than pawing at him, Mister Blackstone had maintained a respectful distance, treating Lucio with respect and consideration. He couldn't help but wonder if that would carry over into the sexual arena as well. He shivered again at the thought of someone actually caring about his pleasure rather than simply taking their own.

"I see your point," he said, his voice low now out of true desire rather than any artifice. Out of his element, he turned his attention back to the crisp, flaky fish on his plate, letting the silence stretch between them in a way he would never have done with his aristocratic guests. They expected to be entertained the entire time they were in Lucio's company, either by his wit or by his body. Lucio had become an expert at both, but Mister Blackstone did not seem to expect entertainment. Lucio's company was enough.

He barely tasted the food that crossed his tongue as his mind raced. Growing up in the pleasure palace, he had listened to the older companions talk about their experiences. The women dreamed sometimes of finding a single guest, someone who would buy their contract and take them away from the communal quarters and the life of entertaining whoever had the money to pay for their time for the night or the day. Lucio had always scoffed at that, not because it didn't happen. It actually happened often enough not to be noteworthy to anyone but the companion whose contract was purchased. His disdain had come from the sense that it wouldn't matter if he was serving one person or many. He was still a companion, the fan on his hand guaranteeing he would always be viewed as less than those around him. At least in the pleasure palace, he had gained a certain status and could pick and choose new guests, although refusing a repeat client was more problematic unless the guest had been truly abusive. If someone bought his contract, he would have no say in his life, no choice in his guests.

Suddenly, though, he could envision a situation in which being with only one person would not be a hardship. If that person treated him with the consideration Mister Blackstone had shown this evening, leaving the pleasure palace might not be such a terrible thing. He shook his head at himself. Mister Blackstone was a poor inventor by his own admission. He would never be able to afford his own companion, even without taking into consideration the exorbitant cost of Lucio's contract.

"Tell me about your friends, the ones who gave you this evening as a gift," he said, suddenly needing the distraction of conversation. He could not allow his fanciful thoughts to raise hopes that would never be fulfilled.

"Caleb Deahl and Andrew Lambert," the inventor said after a moment. "They're my assistants in the lab."

"Have you known them for long?"

"For about ten years," Mister Blackstone replied. "We went to school together, but I was the one whose final project garnered enough attention and prize money to be able to open a workshop. They both accepted immediately when I offered them jobs. That was six years ago, and I haven't regretted it for a moment. They work as hard as I do and share their ideas as freely as if they were partners in the lab."

"Why aren't they?" Lucio asked. "If they truly do the work you say they do."

"Because they would have to invest in the lab, and they don't have the funds to do that now any more than they did six years ago," Mister Blackstone replied. "They choose to spend their salaries differently than I have done."

"Apparently," Lucio said with a grin, "since they bought you such a generous present."

The moment the words were out of his mouth, Lucio regretted them. Talking about his friends, Mister Blackstone had relaxed, his face becoming more animated, but the reminder of the business transaction that had led to Lucio's presence here shut all that off as surely as if Lucio had closed a steam valve.

"They have always been generous to a fault," Mister Blackstone said, standing. "I've taken enough of your time already. I will take my leave now and let you return home."

"Don't go," Lucio said, catching the inventor's hand again in his own. "I didn't mean to offend you. I'm used to dealing with people who understand and accept, even prefer, the fact that my presence at their table was bought and paid for. There is no ambiguity for them. They pay my fee, and I give them what they want. I don't know how to act with you because you don't see this evening that way. You've defied my expectations from the moment I first saw you, and I keep making mistakes because of it. I can't change what I am, Mister Blackstone, any more than you can, but I can try to forget the money that changed hands and simply enjoy your company. If you'll give me another chance?"

"You can start by calling me Gabriel," the inventor said slowly. "No one calls me Mister Blackstone. Even my patrons just call me Blackstone."

"Then sit down, Gabriel," Lucio urged, rolling the name on his tongue. A thrill shot through him at the illicitness of addressing a guest so informally. His handlers would be horrified if they knew. Somehow he doubted Mister Blackstone—Gabriel—would complain. "We haven't finished dinner yet, and I promise the dessert is worth waiting for."

Gabriel sat down slowly, picking up his fork and finishing the remaining bites of fish. When he was done, he looked at Lucio. "Put your hair back in its queue. You wouldn't wear it down like that if you were having dinner with friends."

The request surprised Lucio, but he obeyed, tying his hair back in a messier queue than earlier since he had no brush or mirror to make sure every strand lay smoothly. "I would, actually," he said when he was done, "because the only friends I have dinner with are other companions like myself, and when we are alone, we spend as little time on our appearances as decency will allow, since we must spend so much time on the way we look when we go out."

Gabriel did not reply, making Lucio sigh.

"You say you want to talk with me without guise or guile, but then you shy away from the things I say when I am open about myself," he said. "You cannot have it both ways, Gabriel. I can be the perfect dinner companion, never making any reference to what I am or what I do, or I can be myself. The choice is yours, but you must choose."

"It bothers me to think of your life as a companion," Gabriel said slowly, "but I would rather have your honesty. I may not like what I hear, but at least I will know it's the truth."

Lucio took his time replying. He was tempted to promise Gabriel he would always speak the truth around him, but it seemed like such an empty promise to make when they would never see each other again after tonight. He would go back to his gilt palace and Gabriel would go back to his lab and the evening would be nothing but a precious memory for him and a time to forget for Gabriel. He wanted to give Gabriel more than that somehow. "Ask me something, then," he said. "Something truly personal, and I'll tell you the truth in all its brutal reality. Something so you know *I* am answering, not the trained companion."

The silence lasted so long Lucio thought Gabriel wouldn't take his offer, but finally, in a voice so soft Lucio had to strain to hear it, he asked, "How old were you when you had your first guest?"

"Sixteen," Lucio replied. "Late for a companion, honestly, but the couple who paid for that right saw me when I was much younger and selected me then. They waited until the night of my sixteenth birthday to redeem the chip that gave them the right to take my virginity."

Gabriel shuddered visibly. "Thank you for telling me the truth."

Lucio had the irrational desire to comfort Gabriel. Unable to stop himself, he stroked the back of the inventor's hand. "It wasn't awful, you know. They took their time with me, and the wife actually took the time to stroke me to completion while her husband bedded me."

"You say that like it's a rare treat," Gabriel said.

Lucio laughed, the sound bitter even to his own ears. "Why do you think I remember it? It's the only time in eight years anyone has bothered to see to my pleasure. I'm a companion, Gabriel. My job is to pleasure my guests. My own release is unimportant."

"It wouldn't be for me."

Lucio nearly begged then, the need to feel those work-roughened hands on his body almost more than he could bear, but he had little enough dignity as it was. He wasn't willing to give it up for a man he barely knew. "Words are cheap."

Gabriel was on his feet immediately, pulling Lucio to standing. Lucio's eyes closed in anticipation of whatever his guest intended when the server's knock on the door ended the embrace. Lucio did curse this time, the hiss of breath releasing none of the tension brewing inside him, but he took his seat again and waited for the braised lamb he had praised so highly earlier. The moment the door closed behind the club staff, Lucio rose again, tugging on Gabriel's hand, but Gabriel resisted. Lucio tugged harder until Gabriel jerked his hand away.

"No, I won't treat you that way."

"What way?" Lucio demanded.

"Like chattel."

Lucio's face tightened. "Then stop blowing hot and cold. If you don't want me, that's fine, but don't toy with me."

"It has nothing to do with what I want," Gabriel insisted, his face tortured as he looked at Lucio. "I'd love nothing better than to spread you out on this table and feast on you until they kicked us out because the club was closing, but I wouldn't be able to live with myself tomorrow if I did."

"Why not?" Lucio asked seriously. "Everyone else does."

"Because it would be as meaningless as what everyone else does," Gabriel replied, "and I won't be that man. I've never paid for sex, and I won't start now, even if I'm not the one who paid for it. I can't do that, Lucio, but I'm only human, and you are temptation incarnate. Forgive me if I have trouble resisting."

"I don't want you to resist," Lucio whispered. "For the first time in my career, I can say that with all honesty rather than saying it because it's what I think my guest wants to hear, and I'm saying it to a man who won't believe me and won't act on it even if he does."

"I'm sorry," Gabriel said. "I wish I could give you what you want, but even if I believe you—and I want to believe you—it doesn't make it right."

"And you always do what's right?"

"I always try to do what's right," Gabriel replied. "Eat your lamb. It's getting cold."

The meat was as tender as ever, but it tasted like dust in Lucio's mouth. The chocolate mousse arrived, and Lucio ate it mechanically, lost in a fantasy where Gabriel finally gave in and spread the creamy dessert all over Lucio's body before licking it off. Guests had indulged that way before, but usually it was an annoyance to clean up after they left so he wouldn't ruin his clothes rather than a titillation. He knew it wouldn't be that way with Gabriel, except that Gabriel would never suggest it and would probably be horrified if Lucio did.

The staff cleared the dessert, leaving coffee on a warmer by the fire. Lucio was at a loss, not at all sure how to proceed since he couldn't do what he usually did and seduce his guest. When Gabriel rose to leave, Lucio let him don his hat again and start for the door. It would be better for everyone to let the evening end and put it behind him where it belonged.

One hand on the door, Gabriel turned back. "Thank you for an enjoyable evening. It was the nicest birthday dinner I've ever had."

The words broke Lucio's resolve. His guests never thanked him. They had paid for him. He didn't merit that consideration in their eyes. "Wait," Lucio said, rising and coming to Gabriel's side. "Dinner was your friends' gift to you. This is mine."

Before Gabriel could pull away, Lucio rose to his toes and pressed their mouths together. Gabriel's lips parted, an enticement Lucio could not resist, his tongue surging forward to taste. Gabriel's arms went around him, pulling him close with a strength that left Lucio yearning for more. He would be content with the kiss, though. He would have to be, because he suddenly did not want to sully the memory of the evening with anything more. Drawing away slowly, he rested his hand against Gabriel's cheek. "One more way in which you will be special in my memories."

"What do you mean?" Gabriel asked.

Lucio opened the door and urged Gabriel through. "I don't kiss my guests. Ever."

GABRIEL was already hard at work in his lab the next morning when Caleb and Andrew arrived. He scowled at them through the protective goggles he wore as he tinkered with the gears on the mechanical dog, trying to improve its range of motion.

"Did you enjoy your evening?" Caleb asked as he took off his jacket and donned the leather smock he wore to protect his clothes from cinders, shavings, and grease.

"Well enough," Gabriel replied shortly, "although you could have gotten me something smaller and saved your funds to invest in the lab so you'd be partners rather than employees. It would have been a far more prudent use of your money."

"You're the one whose job it is to be prudent," Andrew replied. "We like being hired help. It means we don't have to take any responsibility for anything other than our work. Nobody but you comes to us looking for anything."

"Then invest it in something else," Gabriel said, "so you have it against the day you can't work anymore or the day the lab can't pay you. Last night was an unnecessary extravagance."

"But was it an enjoyable one?"

"Dinner was very good," Gabriel replied, not willing to talk about Lucio even with his two closest friends.

"Details, man, details," Andrew scolded. "What was the club like?"

"Very elegant, very reserved," Gabriel said, trying to recreate the image in words. "The guardian at the door didn't want to let me in. I'm afraid I wasn't up to the standards of the usual clientele. The interior was done in dark wood, not as dark as the mahogany we use sometimes. Maybe cherry. I didn't have a lot of time to look at it."

"I'd hope not," Caleb joked. "If you were looking at the wood, I'd wonder about the companion we paid for too."

Gabriel pulled his goggles off, frustrated at his friends' casual attitude. "We spent most of the evening in a private salon where we had a delicious dinner. Fortunately no one expected me to order since I wouldn't have known where to begin. I'm not sure I've ever eaten a better meal."

"Gabriel, you're killing us here," Andrew burst out. "Tell us about the companion. Was he as perfect as they're reputed to be?"

"He isn't an animal to be judged on his conformation," Gabriel snapped. "He's a person just like you or me, and he deserves the respect of not being talked about like he's too stupid to understand or too vapid to care."

Andrew looked at Caleb. "He must have been beyond perfection."

Caleb grinned. "And Gabriel was too noble to fuck him the way he expected. I wonder what he made of that."

Gabriel knew, but he wasn't about to share those details with his friends. He had come home from his rendezvous with Lucio and brought himself off to the memory of holding the companion in his arms, of tasting the hint of chocolate on his lips as Lucio kissed him. The dark eyes and curved mouth had haunted his dreams all through the night, taunting him with what he could have had if only he had fewer scruples.

"Get to work, you two," Gabriel growled instead, stalking toward the back of the workshop and the stairs into the basement. They could fight with the mechanical dog for awhile. Gabriel needed the solace of working on his dream. He could hear them bickering in typical fashion as he descended the rickety wooden staircase to his own personal haven. He almost shouted back at them to leave Lucio out of their discussions, but that would only give them more reason to talk.

He pulled the tarp off the engine he was working on, studying it carefully as he tried to visualize the steps he would need to follow in order to complete it in such small scale, but still with enough power to do its job effectively. He had just pulled his measuring tape from his utility belt when the creak of the stairs alerted him to someone else's presence. Twitching the tarp back into place, he turned to see which of his assistants had joined him.

"What are you hiding back there, Gabriel?"

"Nothing, Caleb," Gabriel replied slowly. "Did you need something?"

Caleb sighed audibly. "Whatever it is, you know Andrew and I will help you with it, no questions asked, no explanations needed."

"I know," Gabriel said, and he did. He just wasn't ready to share quite yet. "Was there something else?"

"I wanted to apologize if we offended you somehow just now," Caleb said. "We didn't mean to."

Gabriel slumped onto the stool at the workbench that held the plans for his flying chair. Pushing them aside, he motioned for Caleb to take the other stool. "How would you feel if I came in and told you today that you wouldn't get anything to eat unless you went with a random stranger and let that person have their way with your body?"

"You wouldn't do that!" Caleb protested.

"No, I wouldn't," Gabriel agreed, "and not just because I can't with the scales tattooed on your hand. If you had a different tattoo, that's what your life would be. Have you ever really thought about it from the other side of the coin? Have you ever tried to imagine what their lives are like?"

"But they're companions," Caleb said, "pleasure slaves. It's all they know."

"Because it's all they're allowed to know," Gabriel explained, running a hand through his shaggy hair. "What if one of them wanted to be an inventor instead of a companion? What if one of them has an idea that would revolutionize our world but he can't create it because he doesn't have access to the tools or the training to make it a reality?"

"They don't think about things like that," Caleb insisted. "Their only concern is what color looks best on them and whether a garment is flattering."

"You don't know that," Gabriel all but shouted, thinking of his conversation with Lucio and how the companion had marveled over machines. "Have you ever actually asked a companion if he has any interests outside of his job?"

"I've never had a companion, as you well know," Caleb reminded Gabriel. "You're the only one in this lab who's had that privilege."

"Well, I did ask him," Gabriel said quietly, "and he said two things. He said I was the first person who had ever asked, and he said that he had always wished he could learn more about machines."

"He said that to flatter you," Caleb said immediately. "You know you can't believe a word a companion says. Even I know that."

Gabriel knew it too, but Lucio had been different. He'd never convince Caleb of that fact, but Gabriel was certain of it. Why else would Lucio have shared such an intimate memory with him? Why else would Lucio have kissed him so sweetly before they parted without pressing for more? He might not be able to convince Caleb of his belief in Lucio's honesty, but the entire evening had only added to Gabriel's conviction.

"That isn't the point," Gabriel said, going back to the part of the argument he thought he could win. "The point is that he could have been interested in any number of things if he'd been given the opportunity. He's a companion because of an accident of birth, not because he couldn't have been something else. The entire caste system is based on flawed logic."

"That's dangerous talk, Gabriel," Caleb warned, drawing back from Gabriel's earnestness. "The kind that gets people thrown in jail or beaten in dark alleys."

"Which is why it's all the more important to keep saying it," Gabriel said. "The Caste Equality party has a candidate for the legislature. If enough people vote for him, we'll finally have a representative who sees things with more open eyes. I've met the man, Caleb. He's a brilliant speaker. He'll bring people around."

"If he lives long enough to take his seat," Caleb said. "The aristocrats won't put up with it."

"They won't have a choice," Gabriel insisted. "They can't kill or imprison all of us. They wouldn't have food on their tables or heat in their houses if it weren't for us. They don't see it that way, but they will."

"And who's going to pay us in the meantime?" Caleb demanded. "Your pleasure slave? Because I'm pretty sure he has even less money than we do."

"Don't be vulgar," Gabriel snapped. "He doesn't deserve your scorn."

"He doesn't deserve your adoration."

"This isn't about him," Gabriel insisted. "It's about the entire system, about the fact that we didn't have a choice any more than he did. About the inherent unfairness of a mark on our hands determining our position in life. What if you'd wanted to be a farmer instead of an assistant inventor?"

"I'm perfectly happy as an assistant inventor," Caleb said. "We just had that conversation upstairs when you were yelling at us for spending money on your birthday instead of investing in the lab."

Gabriel rolled his eyes. "Never mind. Get back to work. I'll be upstairs in a few minutes, but think about what I said, please. This is important."

"I'm going," Caleb said, standing up, "but I want you to remember something too. Whatever it is you're working on under that tarp, you know Andrew and I will help you with it in any way we can and support whatever use you decide to put it to. I may not see the urgency for change that you do, but I am your friend. Whatever you need, if it's in my power to help you with it, you know I will."

"I know," Gabriel said, "but right now, I need to do this by myself."

EXHAUSTED, Gabriel climbed into bed, staring at the plain whitewashed ceiling and walls and wondering where Lucio was and what he was doing. He had lost track of the number of times he'd caught himself thinking about the companion over the course of the day. Each time, he firmly ordered his mind back to business with the stern reminder that Lucio was a companion, and an expensive one at that, and that any fantasies were doomed to end in disappointment. His orders had yet to work.

Even with the windows open, the room in the attic of the building that also housed the lab was stifling. Gabriel was tempted to drag his mattress to the basement where he might have some hope of a hint of coolness, but the basement smelled of machine oil and metal shavings, not exactly conducive to peaceful sleeping either. With a sigh, Gabriel reached for the fan he kept by the bed, the prosaic item making him think once more of Lucio and the mark that proclaimed his status to the world. Gabriel had no idea what Lucio's lodgings would look like compared to his own, but if the quality of Lucio's clothes and his comment about heated water for his bath were any indication, the companion would have far more comforts than Gabriel's own shabby garret. He sighed, hating his inability to push the companion from his thoughts. After everything he had said about respecting Lucio as a person and not wanting to treat him differently because of his caste, Gabriel was doing exactly that in his mind.

He had relived the kiss over and over, the sensation of Lucio's lips capturing his own, taking control for that swift, sweet moment before he pulled away. Gabriel had let him pull away, determined to be different in Lucio's eyes, but now, alone in his room, he imagined a different conclusion to the evening. In his dreams, Lucio was not a companion whose time had been purchased but rather an equal, a merchant like himself or someone of a different but equal caste, someone free to be with Gabriel of his own choosing rather than because of a financial transaction. In his dreams, the kiss was not goodbye; it was the prelude to a night of sensual lovemaking. He peeled away the layers of fine clothes to discover the lines of muscle hinted at by the cut of Lucio's garments. Lucio moved willingly to facilitate his disrobing, returning the favor until Gabriel's plain garb fell away, leaving them both gloriously naked. Their bodies brushed together, Gabriel's work-scarred hands dark against Lucio's pale skin, Lucio's hair dark next to Gabriel's reddish-brown mane. Their lips met again and again, the taste of Lucio's mouth too great an intoxication to ignore even to explore other delights.

Lucio's hands moved with practiced ease, but the thought did nothing to disturb Gabriel because he knew Lucio had chosen to be with him here and now. The past didn't matter. The future remained to be written. There was only this moment, and in this moment, Lucio was his as fully and completely as possible.

Gabriel's hand shunted over his cock as he imagined the feeling of Lucio pushing him back onto the bed and moving over him, straddling him so he could continue the kiss, his hands roaming over Gabriel's chest and down to his groin. He thrust up into his fist, wishing it were Lucio's hand that surrounded him. As he quivered in the throes of an unexpected climax, he summoned the image of Lucio's face as he had taken the first spoonful of onion soup.

With a groan, Gabriel rolled to his side, wiping his sticky hand on sheets that would need to be washed far sooner than usual if he continued at this pace. This was the third time he had brought himself off to thoughts of Lucio in the twenty-four hours since he had left the companion.

The sheen of sweat covering his body did nothing to help cool him in the still air, and the damp sheets suddenly chafed against his skin. He rose again from bed and turned on the faucet, one of the few luxuries he had in his apartment. He splashed the cool water over his face, hoping to restore some of his composure, but it did little to help. Heedless of his nudity, he moved to the window and stared out into the night sky, the stars partially obscured by the smoke from the city's factories that never fully cleared. He had to stop obsessing over Lucio this way. He was no lovesick schoolboy to pine over an unattainable man. He had known what Lucio was from the moment they met, and no amount of wishing on his part could change that. His political activism might change it in time, but not in the next weeks or months. By the time any meaningful change did occur, Lucio would surely have forgotten about the odd inventor who refused to even bed him.

He snorted bitterly. It wouldn't take weeks or months for Lucio to forget him. The companion made his living selling his body. He had probably bedded three or four guests since leaving Gabriel last night. Gabriel had no more claim on Lucio's thoughts than he did on his body, and he never would, because he couldn't afford to buy another evening with the companion even if his scruples would allow it. This was all self-indulgent nonsense brought on by a night that should never have been and a loneliness that had no one to blame but himself.

He slammed his fist into the window sash, pain radiating sharply enough up his arm to shock him out of his self-pity. He made his living with his hands. If he injured them, he would be dependent on Caleb and Andrew until they healed. Cradling the sore limb against his chest, he flexed his fingers carefully to make sure none of them were broken. He could move them all, albeit gingerly. "Grow the fuck up, Blackstone," he muttered, forcing himself to go back to bed.

He stared at the ceiling, listening to the ticking of the clock next to his bed for another several hours before he finally gave in to his exhaustion. Even then, thoughts of Lucio followed him into his dreams.

"Gabriel!"

Gabriel turned, searching for the voice that called his name. Lucio leaned out of the window of a hansom much like the one that had borne Gabriel to their rendezvous. "Lucio. What are you doing here?"

"You have to help me," Lucio pleaded. "The handlers... they're trying to send me to the bed of the most notorious aristocrat in the city. If he doesn't kill me, he'll surely maim me so badly I'll never be able to work again."

"What do you want me to do?" Gabriel asked, heart clenching at the thought of Lucio being hurt.

"You're the inventor. Figure it out."

Before Gabriel could reply, Lucio disappeared in a thick fog. Moments later, the mist parted to a very different scene. Lucio crouched naked on a blanket, his attention on the body of a faceless man beneath him. "Lucio!"

The companion's head turned. "What do you want, merchant?"

"You asked for my help," Gabriel reminded him.

Lucio laughed scornfully. "Are you offering to suck me off while he fucks me? Because that's the only thing you could do to help me at the moment."

Gabriel recoiled as if slapped. "But you said...."

"And you believed me? I'm a trained companion. I'll say whatever it takes to make my guests happy. Now if you don't mind, I'm a little busy at the moment. Come back when you can afford me."

The mist closed over the scene again, leaving Gabriel reeling as he struggled to assimilate the two different sides of the companion. Mocking laughter followed him out of the dream.

"THERE you are, Lucio. I looked for you last night, but you hadn't gotten home when I left."

Lucio looked up and smiled as his best friend joined him in the garden. Like him, Cressida wore as little as possible against the heat, a swath of fabric that barely covered her breasts and loose, diaphanous pants over her legs. He counted himself fortunate that he could do without the chest covering. More than once, he had considered doing without the pants, but while modesty was an impossible virtue among their caste, the handlers required they keep their genitals covered any time they left their private rooms.

"And I left this morning before you woke up, lazy chit," he teased, swinging his legs to the side so she could sit at the foot of the chaise longue he had reclined on. Night had fallen, but it brought no hint of coolness, making Lucio wonder when autumn would arrive. The gas lamps hissed and flickered around them, providing enough light for Lucio to watch his friend's face for her reaction to his teasing.

"So tell me about him," Cressida prompted.

"Which him?" Lucio replied, although he knew exactly who she was talking about. "I've entertained four guests since the last time we talked."

"Only four?" Cressida teased. "And you accuse me of being lazy! The merchant, you twit. The new guest."

Lucio smiled. "It was interesting."

Cressida smacked his thigh lightly with the fan she used to create a breeze on hot, still summer nights like this one. "Details, Lucio. What did he look like? What was he wearing? Was he as uncouth as they say merchants are?"

"He was a perfect gentleman," Lucio replied immediately, "even if I could tell he was out of his depth. He was far kinder to me than most guests ever think to be."

His words trailed off, his thoughts drifting back to the evening spent with Gabriel. That he had bedded three guests since then did not matter. That was a typical day's work. Gabriel had been anything but typical.

Cressida smacked him again, drawing his attention back to the present. "What did he look like?"

"About my height," Lucio said, remembering what it had felt like to stand close to Gabriel and look into his eyes. "Perhaps a little taller. I did not have to look up at him when we were close. Broader than I am, but not heavy. Wide shoulders, a solid frame." What he had felt of it, anyway, in the few seconds he had pressed against its length as they kissed. Far less than he would have usually known, but far more powerful in his memory because of it.

"Well dressed?" Cressida interrupted.

"For a merchant, I would think so," Lucio replied. "He wore leather breeches and a leather coat, but they were well made, and his shirt was clean and his cravat tied neatly, if not in the latest fashion. He was presentable."

"Was he handsome?"

"He had reddish-brown hair, probably lightened by the sun because his skin was darkened by it as well," Lucio replied, skirting the question. If he spoke in too much detail, Cressida would realize Gabriel had made more of an impression on him than he cared to admit. The novelty of being with someone from the merchant caste would excuse the attention he paid to certain details, but he had to keep his enthusiasm in check. "Not obscenely so, but enough to mark him as working class even before I shook his hand and saw the scales. And blue eyes. The lightest blue eyes I think I've ever seen."

"How many guests actually let you look them in the eye?" Cressida retorted. "Most of them want you on your hands and knees the entire time, either sucking them or with your ass in the air so they can fuck you."

"Don't be vulgar, Cressida," Lucio chided, reaching out to tug on a lock of her waist-length hair. "It's unattractive."

"You don't care," Cressida replied, tucking the lock of hair he had pulled back into the disorderly pile of curls atop her head. "My manners are as pretty as the next companion's with a guest, but I don't see any reason to mince words with you. Did he take his time with you before he fucked you?"

"He didn't 'fuck me' as you so crudely put it," Lucio said, although it hadn't been from lack of trying on Lucio's part. He felt a fresh flush of desire at the memory of the kiss and what it had done to his body. As often as he had sex, he rarely cared about the acts themselves one way or the other. He completed them to the best of his ability and the satisfaction of his customers, but they held little interest for him outside of his work. And then he had kissed Gabriel.

"He paid that much money for a night with a companion and settled for having you suck him off?" Cressida asked, her surprise clear in her voice. "How much money does he have? Most of the aristocrats won't even settle for that if they'd paid for a whole evening."

"His friends paid for the evening as a birthday present," Lucio explained. "He probably has no idea what it actually cost. He's working on a mechanical dog for an aristocrat who's allergic to pets but wants a dog. It sounded fascinating."

"You and your machines," Cressida said with a shake of her head. "I swear if they wouldn't lock you in your room for getting your hands dirty, you'd have taken apart every contraption in the place to see how it works."

Lucio shrugged. "They're interesting. I want to know how they work."

"It should have made for some interesting dinner conversation if nothing else," Cressida agreed. "He did let you eat dinner, didn't he?"

"Cressida, he's an inventor, not a barbarian!" Lucio said in exasperation. "He was very kind and very considerate. He treated me like he would a friend instead of a convenience. It was... nice. I'd take him as a guest again in a moment."

"You aren't falling for him, are you?" Cressida asked, eyes narrowing. "You know that's never a good idea."

"Of course I'm not falling for him," Lucio replied automatically, even as he acknowledged how easy it would be to fall for the only person outside the walls of the pleasure palace who had ever showed any interest in him as a human being. "I spent one evening with him. I hardly know him well enough to fall for him, and since he's a poor inventor, I doubt I'll ever see him again, anyway."

"But you would if he asked for you again?" Cressida pressed.

"Of course," Lucio said. "As I said, he was kind to me. How was your night and day?"

Cressida let him change the subject, thankfully. "Not too bad," she replied. "My guest last night was a repeat. She wanted to ride my face while I played with her breasts. This afternoon was someone I hadn't met before, although it was clear he knew what to expect from a companion.

He took me on a carriage ride—with a real horse, if you can believe it—out into the country. It's been ages since I left the city. I'd forgotten what fresh air smelled like. He had me dance for him until he was all worked up. I thought I'd actually get a good ride out of it, but he decided he wanted my ass instead of my cunt. It seems he has a fear of getting a companion pregnant, and so while he always asks for a female companion because he likes breasts, he only takes them from the back. I know you like it up the ass, but for me it was disappointing all around."

Lucio made sympathetic noises, well familiar with Cressida's perennial complaint. A child born to a female companion would join the pleasure caste regardless of who the father was. Some aristocrats didn't care, but many did not want even a by-blow of theirs in the lower castes. Some of those solved the problem by requesting male companions. Others chose to find their release in the female companions' mouths or on their skin or in their rear passages. Cressida liked the latter least of all.

"You didn't give me details of what your merchant did to you," Cressida said suddenly, coming back to the topic Lucio most wanted to avoid. He knew how shocked she would be if he admitted to kissing Gabriel, especially if she found out he had initiated the contact.

"Nothing special," Lucio said. He justified the words by reminding himself that Gabriel had, in fact, done nothing to him.

"He didn't hurt you, did he?" Cressida demanded, reaching for the waistband of his thin pants and tugging at them. "Turn around so I can make sure you aren't injured."

Lucio knew she would not find anything, but he shifted and let her pull the cloth away because she would not be satisfied until she had seen for herself that his rosette was the same light pink as always. He accepted her worry for him, knowing she had been close to a companion who had died from internal bleeding a few years ago after a guest used him roughly. He hissed as she probed at the pucker with her fingers, but it was from the stimulation, not from any pain.

Apparently satisfied with what she saw, she patted the curve of his cheek lightly and pulled his pants back into place. "You're not hurt," she agreed. "If you don't want to share with me, that's your business, I guess, but please, Lucio. Don't romanticize your encounter, whatever it entailed. You know you'll never see him again. Even if he got a taste for having a companion, he'll find someone more affordable. You're too expensive for a merchant's wallet."

"I won't, Cressi," he promised, "and I know you hate it when your guests take you from behind, but at least you don't have to worry about a baby this time."

"I take precautions," Cressida said.

"I know, but they only work some of the time," Lucio said, thinking of the washes the women used after they'd bedded a male guest to clean the seed from their bodies. He found it refreshing enough to use sometimes, too, especially if he did not have time for a long bath between guests. Even the guests who, unlike Gabriel, saw him only as a convenient receptacle for their lust did not want to find evidence of someone having been there before them, and they tipped better when nothing shattered their illusions.

Lucio had the wild thought of using some of that money to invest in Gabriel's lab, but while the money and gifts his guests gave him directly—and some of them were quite generous—were his, the handlers controlled closely how he spent it. He could buy all the trinkets he wanted, but that kind of investment would never be allowed. They'd see it as getting ideas above his station.

"What are you thinking about so intently?" Cressida asked.

"What bauble to buy next," Lucio replied, wondering suddenly if he would be allowed to use his money to buy one of Gabriel's machines.

"You don't need more baubles," Cressida scolded. "You're beautiful enough as it is."

"At least if I spend the money on something, I have something I can keep," Lucio reminded her. "It's not like I have to spend it on food or clothes."

"The rest of us don't have that problem," Cressida teased. "We don't get tipped the way you do."

Lucio shrugged, knowing his guests were among the most generous in their pleasure palace. There were other palaces in the city, and he knew little of what went on in any of them, but he was certainly the wealthiest companion in his own corner of the world. For all the good it did him.

"What would you like?" he asked. "Tell me what I can buy for you and I will."

Cressida smiled at him sadly. "Even you can't afford what I want. Don't stay up too late. I'm sure you have a busy day tomorrow as well."

Lucio watched her walk inside, her fan twitching against the heat. He wished it would be cooler inside, but even the thick walls of the pleasure palace only held the heat in once it got this hot. He couldn't stay outside, however. The biting insects were starting to swarm around the lights, and he'd lose guests—or at least tips—if he entertained them covered in welts from insect stings.

Gabriel wouldn't mind, he thought rebelliously as he walked inside, but Gabriel wasn't on the next day's schedule, and if what the inventor had implied about his finances was accurate, Gabriel wouldn't ever be on his schedule again. Lucio found the thought oddly sad because he had enjoyed their conversation. Closing his eyes, he let himself imagine Gabriel's workshop, although he was sure none of the details were correct given his inexperience with such venues. He could see the inventor surrounded by tools and parts, his leather jacket tossed aside as he tinkered with this gear and that valve. In his dream world, Lucio joined the inventor at the table, picking up a tool and handing it to him before picking up a different one and setting to work on his own portion of the project. They worked in comfortable silence except for the occasional request to pass a wrench or a screwdriver. In his fantasy no one yelled at Lucio for getting his hands or his clothes dirty. No one cared that he broke a fingernail and smeared grease all over his face when he wiped the sweat from his brow in the heat. No one chided him for sweating in the first place or ushered him into the bath so he would smell sweet for his next customer. In his imagination he didn't have to worry about entertaining guests because the mark on his hand had changed to a set of scales and he was Gabriel's partner. They spent their days together working on inventions that would amaze all of polite society and their evenings in easy conversation over dinner. When dinner was over, they retired each to their own bed for a night of uninterrupted rest. Perhaps a time would come when they chose to share a bed, but it would be something they had both chosen, an act of giving rather than the given that sex was in Lucio's current profession.

Reminding himself that he would never know that life, Lucio stripped out of his thin trousers, tossing them on a chair for later. He turned the lever on the windows, opening them as wide as they would go, grateful that the mesh across the window protected him from the night insects while still allowing any hint of a breeze to enter.

He climbed into bed, picking up his own fan and waving it in front of his face. It helped while he was awake, but eventually sleep would overtake him and he would spend the night tossing and turning because he could not get comfortable. He wished he had a fan that would keep working even after he fell asleep. As his eyes closed, he had the fleeting thought that he should ask Gabriel to make one for him.

"I THINK I did it!"

Gabriel's shout brought Caleb and Andrew running in from the other room of the workshop. "Look," Gabriel said, activating the control mechanism on the mechanical dog. The creature lifted his head, looked around, and stood slowly, as if stretching. Gabriel pushed another control on the dog's leash, and the dog walked to his side, tail wagging. "What do you think?"

"I think you've done it," Andrew agreed. "So what are you going to do now?"

"Take it to Lord Stuart and see if it meets his approval," Gabriel replied.

"That's not what I meant," Andrew said. "What project are you going to start on next?"

"That will depend on whether Lord Stuart has another commission for me," Gabriel said. "If he does, I'll start on that. We can't afford to lose his patronage if he's still willing to give it to us."

"He'll be willing," Caleb said confidently. "You've done amazing work on that dog."

"But that doesn't mean he has another project in mind right now," Gabriel reminded them, "and while the gold from the dog will pay off our outstanding debts, it won't keep us solvent indefinitely. I need another paying project."

"Take some of that money and do something for yourself," Caleb urged. "I know you want the debts paid off, but you can't deprive yourself forever. Splurge on a fancy dinner. Buy an evening with a companion. Do something just for you."

"That's a waste," Gabriel insisted, pointedly not thinking about Lucio and the evening they had spent together almost a month before. Even if he could bring his conscience to accept it, he doubted he could afford another evening with the man unless Lord Stuart was far more generous with his bonus than the agreed-upon price. The aristocrat had always tipped Gabriel when he completed a project, but usually only a few extra coins. Certainly not enough to buy an evening with as expensive a companion as Lucio undoubtedly was. Gabriel had not let himself ask how much Caleb and Andrew had paid for Lucio's time, but any price was too high when Gabriel resented the custom of companions being rented out. If only he could stop thinking about the other man. Lucio's casual acceptance of his life bothered Gabriel nearly as much as his desire for the companion did. More than once, he had considered approaching the other supporters of the Caste Equality movement with the idea of buying and freeing Lucio, but he feared their reaction. They had so much work to do even for the merchant caste and others that Gabriel doubted they would be willing to spend that kind of money on a companion who might not have any interest in escaping his station. Perhaps if Gabriel had thought to ask... but he had not and he would not, because to raise Lucio's hopes only to have them dashed by a refusal would be beyond cruel.

"What?" Gabriel said, looking at Caleb and Andrew in confusion when they burst out laughing.

"You've been standing there staring at the blank wall for five minutes," Andrew said. "You sure you don't want to know where we hired that companion?"

On impulse, Gabriel nodded.

Caleb's eyebrows jumped, but he gave the information. "We went to the pleasure palace on Mayfair Place," he said, "and asked about prices. For the entire evening—seven until three—we paid one hundred gold coins, but he quoted less expensive rates for shorter amounts of time, starting at fifteen coins for an hour."

Gabriel's stomach churned at the waste of money given that he had spent less than half the paid-for time in Lucio's company, but he was sure the handlers wouldn't let him take the balance of it now. Fifteen gold, while extravagant, was not totally outside Gabriel's reach. If Lord Stuart was generous, Gabriel could perhaps find a way to see Lucio again. They could go for a walk in one of the parks outside the city where they could escape the heat for a short time. They would lose a portion of their hour to getting there and back, unless Gabriel stipulated that Lucio meet him there. He didn't know if he would be allowed to do that, but even if they rode out in a hansom cab together, they could still talk.

He could almost hear Caleb and Andrew scoffing at him for paying that kind of money for an hour with a companion and then doing nothing but talking, but it was his money. If he was going to waste it, he'd be the one to decide how.

"THIS is exceptional work, Blackstone," Lord Stuart boomed as he watched the mechanical dog walk around the room at Gabriel's command. "I am holding a ball on Friday to celebrate my niece's birthday. I will introduce my new pet to society then. You should attend. My Roxie will make quite a stir. You could perhaps gain another commission or some additional patronage from among my guests."

"I couldn't possibly do that," Gabriel demurred. "I don't belong at an aristocratic party. I'm a merchant."

"Times are changing," Lord Stuart disagreed, "and men like you will be at the forefront of that change."

"You sound as if you welcome it," Gabriel said slowly, thinking of his friends in the Caste Equality party and their frustration at not finding any of the aristocracy willing to help them.

"We've gotten inbred in the upper echelon of society," Lord Stuart said. "We need fresh blood. While I'm not a proponent of abandoning all propriety, I see only good in allowing men of merit to mingle with us."

"I have nothing better than this to wear," Gabriel protested. "I would be a laughing stock, as would you for inviting me."

"I suspected you might say that," Lord Stuart replied, "so I have summoned my tailor. He will take your measure today and have a suit ready for you by Thursday."

Gabriel felt his face flush with embarrassment. "I can't afford a new suit. I have debts and employees to pay." He did not mention his hope of seeing Lucio again. The practice of purchasing companions was common among the aristocracy, but it was not something anyone discussed.

"That is why I summoned *my* tailor," Lord Stuart countered. "You have made me very, very happy with my new friend. I would like to be of some benefit to you as well."

Gabriel hesitated still. Lord Stuart's introduction could indeed provide him commissions or sponsors whose gold would give him the leisure to research his flying chair. He knew how to be polite, but the etiquette of the highest caste was far more complex than the simple good manners his parents had taught him. "If I commit some gaffe that ruins the evening for everyone? That would be a poor way to repay your generosity."

"Stop protesting, Blackstone," Lord Stuart insisted. "I will take care of everything, including making sure you have a guide for the evening. Do you prefer male or female companionship?"

"Male," Gabriel replied honestly.

Lord Stuart nodded. "I shall find a woman to guide you, then. Don't misunderstand. I am not judging you, for it is a preference I share, but you will be less distracted with a woman on your arm than a man."

"I had noticed there was no Lady Stuart," Gabriel observed, trying to quiet his reeling emotions as the full extent of Lord Stuart's implications sank in.

Lord Stuart shook his head and rapped Gabriel's knuckles with the black fan he carried. "Such questions will not pass in polite society," the aristocrat warned. "I am not offended because I buried my wife many years ago, but you must not ask a person directly unless you know them far better than you know me."

"This is why it is a bad idea."

"Nonsense. I know the perfect young woman to make sure you behave yourself in the public eye on Friday. She has accompanied my nieces and nephews to a variety of events and has a much better head on her shoulders than those flibbertigibbets, despite the fan on her hand. She has far more to lose, I suppose."

Gabriel started to shake his head again.

"Don't worry. She'll know exactly what to expect of the evening, and it won't be your amorous attention," Lord Stuart said. "My tailor is in the music room. He gets impatient if I keep him waiting for too long. Come."

Lord Stuart led Gabriel into the music room where a short, portly man waited for them. "Blackstone, this is Banks, my tailor. Banks, I want Blackstone attired for my niece's ball on Friday. A black suit, I think, since he won't want to draw too much attention to himself, unlike those young popinjays today. He's interested in finding a patron, not in attracting a wife."

"You'll want him to see your barber as well, then," Banks muttered, taking out his tape measure. "Down to your undergarments, Blackstone. I can't fit you properly over those rags you're wearing."

Gabriel bristled at the slur, but he held his tongue. Even if Friday night did not garner any new clients for him, he could not afford to alienate Lord Stuart. Uncomfortable, he stripped down to the thin shirt and short pants he wore beneath his leathers. Fortunately they were in decent repair, but he knew they were not the quality the other two men would wear. Banks clucked disapprovingly but refrained from any more comments as he measured the breadth of Gabriel's shoulders and chest and the length of his arms and inseam. "At least he's a well-built man," Banks said to Lord Stuart. "He'll wear an evening suit well."

"I suspect he would wear anything well," Lord Stuart said. The tone of his voice made Gabriel look at him sharply. "Don't worry, Blackstone. I don't have designs on your person, but I'm not blind. I can appreciate a handsome, well-made man when I see one. Properly attired, you will draw many an eye on Friday night, male and female alike."

"I am looking for an investor, not a…." He paused, not sure what word to use that would be clear without possibly offending his patron. He could not talk to the aristocrat the same way he talked to Caleb and Andrew.

"You have no interest in matters of the heart," Lord Stuart agreed. "While it aggrieves me to say so, the size of your purse should discourage any of the eligible ladies who might have an eye to marriage, and the gentlemen would prefer a polished companion on their arm. We are a superbly shallow group, I'm afraid."

Gabriel opened his mouth to be polite and to help himself ignore the tailor as he continued to poke and prod and measure, but Lord Stuart interrupted him. "Don't argue. Even my new pet is a perfect example. I wanted a dog, but I can't keep a live one. Instead of accepting that with grace, I'll have given the others a new reason to shake their heads at daffy old Lord Ian."

Banks interrupted to take his leave.

"You know," Gabriel began slowly as he started to dress again, "there is a group—"

"The Caste Equality party," Lord Stuart interrupted. "I've heard of them, but I mustn't put my nieces and nephews at risk by inquiring more about them."

"I would be happy to bring you as much information as you would like," Gabriel offered, buttoning his shirt. "Anonymously, of course."

Lord Stuart looked at him speculatively. "We'll see how Friday goes and then we'll talk again. Equality is more than a word to bandy about."

"It is," Gabriel agreed, pulling on his jacket, "but until we're allowed a chance, we can hardly prove ourselves worthy of it."

"Friday is your chance."

GABRIEL strode down the street, weaving in and out of the hansoms stuck in the traffic jam that embroiled the center of the city, mind reeling with everything Lord Stuart had said—and not said—that afternoon. He was nervous about the ball on Friday, especially about the companion Lord Stuart had promised to provide. Gabriel had been uncomfortable enough alone with Lucio. The idea of spending an evening with a companion on his arm with all of society watching only made him more nervous. Everyone would look at him and think he had money to spare, something that would hardly encourage investment, although it wouldn't preclude a commission. More than that, his conscience nagged at him for accepting the situation. Lord Stuart saw nothing wrong with it, in fact considered he was doing Gabriel a service, but he was an aristocrat. They thought nothing of having companions by their side or in their beds. Gabriel could not be so sanguine, especially not after talking to Lucio. He tried to console himself with the memory that Lucio had a thought in his head besides sex. Perhaps the girl would be the same. Gabriel had known plenty of intelligent women in school. This one could be more like them than like the vacuous aristocratic daughters who sometimes came into his workshop with their fathers or brothers.

His money purse jingled with gold for once as he walked, the bonus from Lord Stuart even more than he had hoped for. He would be able to pay off his debts as well as pay Caleb and Andrew the money he owed them from last month's salary. His thoughts drifted to Lucio, as they were wont to do any time Gabriel let them wander. With the bonus and the prospect of more commissions from among Lord Stuart's guests on Friday, the possibility of seeing Lucio again no longer seemed like such an extravagance. The companion had haunted his sleeping thoughts even if he managed to push thoughts of him aside during the day. Gabriel had given up calling himself a fool and had decided to simply accept his obsession. He wouldn't spend the money on another evening with Lucio, even if he had that much left once he was done clearing his debts, because his conscience wouldn't allow it, but nothing could stop him from dreaming and perhaps contemplating an afternoon in the park. Of course, in his dreams, Lucio was more than a companion. Lucio was the partner he had always hoped to find. Gabriel knew that wasn't realistic for too many reasons to count, but most especially because he knew the kind of societal change that would allow such a relationship was still many years away. The best he could hope for would be to purchase Lucio's contract from his handlers and install Lucio as his private companion, but even that was hardly realistic given the price of such a contract and Gabriel's current financial situation. Not even with all the gold in his purse could he afford such a thing.

He would be far better off looking for a partner among the merchant caste or perhaps a serious investor at the ball on Friday, someone perhaps with the business skills to help him turn his research into something profitable for once instead of being required to take frivolous commissions in order to stay afloat.

Movement caught his eye in the coach to his left. He paused, sure his eyes were playing tricks on him when he caught sight of Lucio in the conveyance, his back to the direction of travel so that he seemed to be looking right at Gabriel. Gabriel froze as he stared in the window, having convinced himself that he would never see Lucio again despite the gold in his purse. The companion was even more beautiful than Gabriel remembered, the pale blue of his afternoon jacket perfect for his complexion. His hair was pulled back in its queue just as it had been the night they met, but Gabriel thought Lucio looked tired. He took a thoughtless step toward the cab, breath catching in his throat as Lucio leaned forward. Before Gabriel could call out a greeting, Lucio reached out to someone else in the coach, his hand cradling the other person's cheek exactly as he had done with Gabriel as he kissed him.

Gabriel recoiled as if struck at the sight of Lucio touching the beautiful, dark-haired woman so tenderly. Despite his first reaction to Lucio, he had believed the companion was telling him the truth when he spoke of not kissing his clients, but that gesture was too practiced, seeing it now from the outside, to be anything but a common one. "Fool," he muttered to himself. "Stupid, lovesick fool. Forget about him and get back to work."

He stumbled blindly the rest of the way back to his workshop. Caleb and Andrew had already departed for the day, leaving the building silent and empty in their wake. Gabriel was almost glad of it because he wouldn't have been able to hide his turmoil from his friends, and he had no desire to explain the illusions he had been harboring where the accursed companion was concerned.

Tossing his money purse on his bed, Gabriel flung open the window, grateful he had done the framing himself or else he might have torn it off its hinges completely. He stared up at the darkening sky, clouds gusting across his line of sight between his building and the next as a storm worked its way toward the city. Gabriel hoped it stormed like mad. Maybe it would break the heat and give him some relief from his dreams.

His stomach roiled as he imagined Lucio in the arms of the woman he had seen in the coach. He had not gotten a good look at her, only enough to know she had long, dark hair, pale skin, and a perfect profile: all marks of an aristocrat. He found it all too easy to picture the companion in her bed, lavishing pleasure on her body with his hands and mouth, pleasure that Gabriel desperately wanted for himself. He had pointedly refused to think of Lucio with other people, though he knew that was naïve given the companion's role in society, but he had told himself such encounters were meaningless compared to the tender caress and the kiss he and Lucio had shared. He had even started to believe it until he had seen that same tender gesture bestowed on another.

"You should have known he was lying," he scolded himself, bile rising in his throat. "You should have known he was too good to be true, and instead you've sunk so low that you were considering compromising your values to see him again. You were nothing to him except maybe an easier night than usual since you didn't have him on his knees within minutes of meeting him. He's no different than any other companion, willing to say whatever it takes to keep a customer happy. Forget about him. You have bigger things to worry about, like not making a fool of yourself on Friday night at Lord Stuart's party."

Thunder boomed outside, a prelude to the storm to follow. Gabriel shut the window against the drops that quickly became a downpour. Rain pounded on the roof as he prepared for bed, but the moment his eyes closed, the image of Lucio leaning in to kiss him again assailed him. He tried to turn his head, to reject the kiss, but Lucio's eyes haunted him, begging him to accept the gift for everything it represented.

Sleep came finally, but dreams of Lucio in the arms of other men tortured Gabriel all night long.

"WELL, damn," Lucio muttered as the skies opened and rain descended in sheets. He closed the windows quickly, not wanting to ruin his suit or Cressida's dress. Their wardrobes were provided as long as they didn't damage them. Replacement or repair costs came out of their tips.

"Now whose language needs monitoring?" Cressida teased. "We're going to get soaked when we get to the palace anyway."

"Maybe it will have stopped by then," Lucio said hopefully, his eyes darting back to the quickly emptying sidewalks. He had started studying faces in the crowded streets over the past month, not in any real hope of seeing Gabriel again—in a city of two million or more he didn't trust fate to be so kind—but because Gabriel had opened his eyes to a new world, showing him that manners could be found outside the aristocracy and that class did not equate with caste. He had never been treated as well as he had been by the inventor, a merchant with a tattoo on his hand, albeit a different one than Lucio's.

Cressida had tried cajoling details from him a few more times since that night, but Lucio had refused to budge. He did not want anything to tarnish his memory, and he suspected Cressida's opinion of his foolishness in harboring even fond memories would do far more than tarnish it. She would never understand the impulse that had led him to offer Gabriel a kiss. His first kiss. None of his guests had ever wanted that from him, just as none of them had ever wanted his cock. They wanted his hands or his mouth on them, his ass around them, but they had no interest in a true connection. That was what Gabriel had offered him, and as the inventor had predicted, that was why he caught himself at odd moments searching for the shaggy reddish-brown head in a crowd. He thought he'd caught a glimpse of Gabriel as he and Cressida sat stuck in traffic, but it had to have been his imagination. He had given in to Cressida's cajoling after that, sparring with her verbally until the rain started moments ago.

"Where are you?"

Cressida's voice broke into his reverie.

"I'm right here," Lucio said. "Where else would I be?"

"I don't know," Cressida replied, "but only your body is here. Your thoughts are far away from me. Where do you go when you stare out into space that way?"

To a world where I am free to love and be loved, Lucio thought sadly. He knew better than to let himself dream of such things. Even if he were to find someone to purchase his contract so he could escape from his current life, he would still not be free. "To another world," he said simply.

"It must be a happy one," Cressida said wistfully. "You have such a look of bliss on your face when you get lost in your thoughts. I'm not sure I've ever been to such a place, even in my head."

"Don't turn maudlin on me, Cressi," Lucio scolded. "We might have finished work for the afternoon, but I'd be willing to bet we'll have new orders awaiting us when we get home. Time for a wash and to change our clothes, and we'll be off to another dinner or party and another guest to delight with our sparkling wit and effervescent personalities."

Cressida glared at him. "I'm tired," she said finally. "I don't dare admit it lest they decide I'm not good for anything now but breeding my replacements, but I am tired. I can't entertain four or five or six guests a day like I used to. I start to lose patience with them, with their demands and needs and their callous disregard for me."

Lucio reached for Cressida's hand, stroking it as he had earlier stroked her cheek. "I know, Cressi. I know. I don't know what the solution is, but I know how you feel. Just remember that if you give in to it, you'll lose everything. You're too young to be relegated to the breeding barns. And… and what would I do without you to keep me sane?"

"You'd be fine," Cressida said. "You're always fine. Even when I know you're not, you're fine."

Lucio did not know how to respond to that. More than once, he had insisted he was indeed fine when he was tired or annoyed or even hurt so that he wouldn't upset his friend. It seemed those times had come back to haunt him. "What if I told you I wasn't fine?"

Cressida looked at him sharply. "What are you talking about?"

Lucio glanced toward the ceiling of the coach as if to make sure no one else could hear him. "Ever since the night I met the merchant," Lucio confided, "I haven't been able to think of anyone but him. I smile and laugh and pretend when I'm with my guests, but it's even more mechanical now than it was before. I don't want their hands on me. I don't want their cocks in me. I want them all to go away and leave me alone because they aren't him."

"What did he do to you?" Cressida asked. "What could he possibly have done to you that would make you feel this way? It was an evening, and not a long one at that."

Lucio took a deep breath. "He kissed me."

"He what?" Cressida exclaimed.

"He kissed me," Lucio repeated, knowing it was a lie. "He didn't know any better. He'd never been with a companion before and had no idea what would be acceptable and what wouldn't. He spent the evening talking to me like no one else ever has and when it came time to part, he kissed me."

Cressida's mouth opened and closed again, but nothing came out. Finally she said, "So what does it feel like?"

Lucio's heart fluttered as he remembered heatedly what it felt like to have Gabriel's mouth pressed against his, the flavor of dessert on his tongue. "Like nothing else anyone has ever done to me. The rest... it's sexual, but that's it. I learned to separate it from who I am long before I ever saw my first guests, but this... there's no separating it from anything. He put his tongue in my mouth, which was incredible enough, but then he invited me to do the same. I tasted him as he had tasted me, and it was like nothing else. I think if I could kiss him one more time, I could die a happy man."

Cressida's fan rapped sharply across Lucio's knuckles. "No talk of dying!" she snapped. "I won't have it. You aren't to leave me, do you understand?"

Lucio leaned his forehead against hers. "I understand. I won't leave you. No matter what happens, I'll find a way to stay with you."

"Even if your merchant finds a way to buy your contract?"

"He's a merchant, Cressida. He couldn't afford to buy an evening with me—his friends had to pay for it. He won't be able to buy my contract," Lucio said reassuringly. "And you assume he wants to. He was horrified by the idea of my being a companion, of being unable to choose the path of my life, as if he'd had any more choice in his life. Even if he could buy my contract, I don't think he would because he wouldn't feel right about owning it."

"He sounds like the perfect man," Cressida chuckled.

Lucio laughed in reply, lightening the mood in the coach. "Except for the fact that he has absolutely no idea how to act in society. I'd be fed up with him in a matter of days because I'd always have to be teaching him things."

Cressida shook her head. "You keep telling yourself that. It will make the fact that we're home easier to bear."

They raced from the coach to the entrance of the pleasure palace, but by the time they gained entrance, they were both soaked to the skin. Lucio gave Cressida one last smile as they parted to change clothes and prepare for their evenings. He treasured the moments like the carriage ride when they could be alone together and truly talk. Even with the secrets he kept from her—one fewer after today—she was his confidant, his best friend, his touchstone. He could always count on her to understand and support him, even when he concocted a hare-brained scheme likely to land them both in trouble. He'd learned his lesson in recent years, but she had been his willing accomplice in their youth.

With a sigh, he opened the door to his private rooms, grateful he had the status to provide a certain level of luxury. He stripped off his suit, hanging it over the rack to dry, and clad in nothing but translucent silk underwear, he sat at his desk to see if the handlers had added anything to his calendar. When he left that afternoon, his schedule had been blessedly empty for the evening, giving him a chance for a much-needed rest.

A gilt invitation sat on top of his calendar. Opening it, he read the invitation to a birthday ball in honor of Lord Ian's niece to be held on Friday evening. At the bottom, Lord Ian had added a handwritten note indicating he desired Lucio's company at his side for the evening and in his bed for the night. Lucio looked at his calendar and saw that the handlers had already marked out his other appointments for that evening. Whatever Lord Ian had offered, it was enough to risk upsetting Lucio's other guests. He shook his head. That was their worry. His worry was what to wear to such a ball—and with such an invitation—on such short notice. Sighing, he went to his closet to see what could be found. The handlers might have rearranged his schedule, but they would not be happy if he demanded a new outfit at the price a tailor would charge for the rush. Lucio was tempted to insist just to be difficult, but he did not want to endanger his position in the pleasure palace by being too particular too often. He had enough other things to worry about as it was.

He was still thumbing through suits, trying to remember which ones Lord Ian had seen and which he hadn't—without going back and consulting his calendar—when the door opened behind him. "Lucio?"

"In the closet," Lucio called back. "What is it, Cressida?"

"Apparently I am going to a ball on Friday evening."

"A ball?" Lucio said absently. "Whose ball?"

"Lord Ian Stuart's."

Lucio spun around, heedless of his near nudity. "What did you say?"

"Lord Ian Stuart's," Cressida repeated. "You know, the elderly gentleman who sometimes buys your time."

"I know who you're talking about," Lucio said. "I want to know why you're invited to his ball when he sent me an invitation to both the ball and his bed."

Cressida grinned. "It seems I'm to play chaperone and guide to a protégé of his," she drawled. "One Mister Gabriel Blackstone, inventor."

Lucio's throat tightened as his heart sank into his stomach. "No."

"What?" Cressida said, surprised. "What are you talking about?"

"You can't," Lucio said, his voice a harsh whisper. "You can't have him. He's mine. He's *my* inventor." *My dream.*

Cressida's eyes widened as she stared at Lucio. "You mean this is the same man who kissed you?"

Lucio nodded. "Please, Cressida," he begged. "As you love me, don't do this."

Cressida crossed to his side, enfolding him in perfumed arms. "Relax, Lucio. Lord Stuart was very clear. He wants me to make sure Mister Blackstone doesn't embarrass himself in society during the ball. He wants me to act as his guide, nothing more. His instructions specifically say that Mister Blackstone prefers male companionship in more intimate surrounds and that my only job is to look pretty on his arm." Her hand closed around Lucio's bicep as she led him toward the bed. "I think you've been telling me tales. You shouldn't be bothered by this. We pass guests between us and the other companions all the time. What's going on?"

Lucio shook his head, trying to come to terms with everything Cressida had just revealed. Gabriel would be at the ball on Friday night, the same one Lucio would be attending, but Lucio would be there as Lord Ian's companion and Cressida would spend the evening on Gabriel's arm. If it had been another client, he would have begged her, bribed her, offered her anything to change places with him, but Lord Ian had no interest in women since his wife died. He would never accept such a substitution, and Lucio did not dare anger him by disregarding the invitation. At least the gentleman had always been kind to him, including him in any balls or dinners before bedding him. He even had a certain affection for Lord Ian. The man was a fine conversationalist, entertaining Lucio even as he was entertained by him. If it had not been for the difference in their ages, Lucio might have tried to convince Lord Ian to purchase his contract, but he did not want to be at the mercy of Lord Ian's heirs when the old man died. He had met a few of them, and they were not all their uncle's equal.

His racing thoughts swirled back around to the reason for his discomposure. Gabriel. Gabriel would be at the ball on Friday and Lucio would barely be in a position to speak to him in passing, much less in private the way his heart ached to do. He needed to know if he had imagined what could be between them or if there was some hope.

"You have to help me," he said, grabbing Cressida's hand in his. "I must speak with Gabriel Friday night."

"And how am I to do that when I'll be at the ball and you'll be heaven knows where?" Cressida demanded.

"I'll be at the ball as well," Lucio said, producing his invitation.

"At Lord Stuart's side," Cressida reminded him sharply. "You can't seriously be considering.... Lucio, that's beyond stupid!"

"I don't want to fuck him," Lucio retorted. "I just want to talk to him for a few minutes. I need to know if I've built him up in my mind beyond reality. I need to know if I dreamt the magic of that night. A few minutes' conversation will do. You can even stay in the room if you promise not to listen in."

"You're risking Lord Stuart's patronage and the anger of an influential aristocrat directed at both of us," Cressida reminded him. "If he finds out and takes exception, he could have us both reduced to streetwalkers with a snap of his fingers."

"Then we'll have to make sure he doesn't find out," Lucio said with a confidence he did not entirely feel. "He's the host of the party. He'll have to do his duty to all the grandes dames and lords. Even if he wanted to, he won't be able to hang on my arm every second. When he's otherwise occupied, I can simply join you and Gabriel. No one would look askance at me seeking out another companion when I am otherwise unoccupied, and the three of us will retire to a quiet alcove where I can have a word with Gabriel."

"You make it sound simple," Cressida accused, "when you know it will be anything but."

"Please, Cressi," Lucio begged. "Tell me you'll help me."

Cressida sighed. "I'll help you, but you'll owe me even if no one finds out what we've done. And if they do, you'll owe me even more."

"Whatever you want," Lucio swore. "If it's within my power to give it to you, it's yours."

Cressida frowned. "This means too much to you. You can't get attached this way. He can't even make his own arrangements. If what you said is true, this is the second time someone else has paid for him to have a companion for an evening."

"It's not like that," Lucio insisted. "It's not whether he could pay, but his insistence that it's wrong to pay us and then require us to do anything the other person wants. He feels like that's unfair to us."

"And yet he kissed you," Cressida pointed out. "Something you've never done with anyone else, unless there's something you haven't told me. How is that respecting your desires?"

"I kissed him." Lucio's voice was almost too soft to be heard, but Cressida figured it out, her hand falling from his arm.

"You didn't."

Lucio nodded, not looking up at her. "He had been so kind to me, so courteous, asking about my interests, insisting I tell him the truth and not what I thought he wanted to hear." He looked up finally, his eyes prickling as he took a deep breath. "For an evening, I got to be me. Me. Not the polished, practiced companion everyone sees, but me. The same person sitting here with you. I got to have dinner with an interesting, handsome man and be myself, and all he asked of me was my honesty. Do you know what he said before he left?" Cressida shook her head. "He thanked me for the most enjoyable birthday dinner he'd ever had. He thanked me, Cressida. No one has ever thanked me for anything. They find their release in my mouth or my ass or on my body somewhere, and they leave like I'm something too unclean for them to look at once their lust is sated. But not him. He thanked me for spending the evening with him. I couldn't let him go without giving him something in return. A kiss was all I had."

"All right," Cressida said after a long silence. "I'll help you, but you have to promise me you'll be careful. Lord Stuart may not be young anymore, but that simply means he's learned all the tricks. I've only met him a few times, when I was with his nieces or nephews, but he strikes me as a sharp old man. I don't want to see you hurt."

"I'll be careful," Lucio said. "I'll be discreet, and I'll guard my heart, but I have to know if I imagined the chemistry between us."

GABRIEL plucked at the sleeve of his evening jacket, sure he looked like an absolute fool in his new finery. He had no real idea what he'd expected when Lord Stuart discussed arranging an evening suit for him, but it was certainly nothing as elaborate as what he now wore. The trousers, while better quality than anything he owned, were nothing too shocking with their high waist and flat front. He had not even needed the suspenders to keep them up. The shirt, likewise, was of similar cut to what he was used to, the high collar allowing for any manner of cravat to be worn with it. That was where the resemblance to his normal attire ended. The jacket was close-fitted across his shoulders and open in the front, despite the buttons on either side. Long tails hung down almost to Gabriel's knees in the back, but the front barely brushed the top of his trousers, making him feel as if he were halfway undressed, accustomed as he was to wearing a full leather frock coat that came down to his upper thighs. He might have been able to live with that were it not for the pale blue waistcoat easily visible between the open halves of the tailcoat. The color was eerily close to the color of his eyes, making him wonder who had spent so much time studying his face, Lord Stuart or the tailor. Neither thought did anything to ease his nerves. The gloves and top hat only rounded out his misery. He was used to wearing a hat, although not one so tall or formal, but the gloves stymied him. He knew aristocratic gentlemen wore them, but he was not and would never be an aristocrat, and he was already nervous enough about being laughed out of Lord Stuart's drawing room without misrepresenting himself by covering his tattoo.

A knock at the door startled Gabriel into looking at the clock. Eight o'clock. His own personal witching hour. Setting his jaw determinedly and pulling on his gloves, he opened the door. "Mister Blackstone?"

"Yes."

"Your coach is waiting, sir. I've already picked up the lady," the driver said with a touch to his cap.

"Thank you," Gabriel said, locking the door and following the driver to the mechanical coach. The man held the door so Gabriel could enter, shutting it behind him and leaving him enclosed in perfumed shadows.

"Don't forget to tip him," a female voice advised softly. "We'll have a much more pleasant ride for your generosity."

Gabriel fumbled in his pocket for a coin, offering it to the driver through the window. "Thank you, Miss...." He realized he didn't know his companion's name.

"I'm Cressida," she said, her face still hidden by shadows. "You needn't call me Miss."

"Thank you, Miss Cressida," Gabriel said. She might claim not to need the honorific, but Gabriel's mother, rest her soul, would have his head on a platter if she thought for a moment he'd been less than polite to a woman of any station.

"Well, aren't you a polite one?" Cressida said with a sultry laugh. She leaned forward so Gabriel got his first glimpse of her in the dim interior.

Her hair was every bit as dark as Lucio's, pulled up in a disheveled chignon with long curls falling on either side of her neck. Gabriel knew the look was calculated to put all manner of illicit thoughts in the minds of all who saw her. Gabriel suspected it was very effective. In the dim light, he could not decide if her dress was dark blue or purple, but either way, it was the height of the latest fashion, long and slender with little to hide the curvaceous lines of her body. Only the daring neckline proclaimed her profession. Even uninterested in female companionship, Gabriel could see she was stunning. "My mother taught me to always respect a lady."

"Your mother wasn't talking about me," Cressida replied candidly. "Tell me a little about yourself, Mister Blackstone. Have you been out in society much?"

"Only to visit the patrons of my workshop," Gabriel answered honestly. "I have no idea what to expect tonight."

"And have you spent much time with other companions?" she pressed.

Gabriel shook his head. "Only once," he said. His voice softened as he spoke. He knew it, hated it given what he had seen, but he could not dismiss Lucio from his head. "But it was a private dinner. I have no idea what to expect tonight, other than what Lord Stuart told me."

"And what did Lord Stuart tell you?" Cressida asked. "I don't want there to be problems tonight because we have differing expectations of the evening."

"He told me you would be my guide," Gabriel said. "My chaperone, really, to make sure I don't make a fool of myself or him over the course of the evening. What did he tell you?"

"The exact same thing," Cressida replied. "He also said he expected you would have little or no interest in my person."

Gabriel hoped the shadows hid the flush he could feel staining his cheeks. "You have to know you are a beautiful woman," he said slowly, "but you are indeed a woman, and I prefer my bed partners to be somewhat more masculine."

"Did you tell Lord Stuart that?" Cressida asked.

Gabriel nodded and then realized she might not have seen him. "I did, but he said I risked being distracted by the company of a man, whereas you would be an able guide without being a distraction."

"We shall see if he is right," Cressida agreed. "Well then, since you have no experience to guide you, I will stay at your side as much as I am permitted, my hand on your arm. If I squeeze once, you would do well to change the course of the conversation. If I squeeze twice, you would do well to end the conversation entirely. The ball is in honor of Lord Stuart's niece, so I expect the guests to be primarily young men and girls of her acquaintance and then Lord Stuart's peers to keep him company, but that doesn't mean they are all equally worthy acquaintances."

"I'm the one likely to be considered unworthy," Gabriel reminded her. "I'm the one with scales on my hand."

"But you will be wearing gloves. They will not know unless you tell them or unless Lord Stuart does," Cressida reminded him.

"He invited me because he wants to share my success in creating a new toy for him," Gabriel explained. "He wants to help me find new patrons. He will tell them."

"Then the two squeezes will be for those whose purses are too empty to be of interest to you," Cressida said. "If they cannot afford your services, they are of no interest to you, correct?"

"As patrons, no," Gabriel agreed, "but that doesn't mean they are not interesting as people."

"You aren't there to make friends," Cressida said bluntly. "You are there to attract attention to your skills and your workshop. If they cannot afford your services, they are of no interest to you. Trust me in this. I may know nothing of machines, but I do know something of business. After all, even on your arm, I might attract a guest for a later evening."

Gabriel hated the reminder of her profession, but he could no more change it than he could change Lucio's. "You are the second companion—and I have only known two—who was startlingly forthright about the nature of your life. I had not expected as much, either time."

"Perhaps it is your attitude that brings it out in us," Cressida suggested. "We sense your basic goodness and straightforwardness and respond in kind."

"I hope that is so," Gabriel said, "because I appreciate honesty above all else."

"It is a rare trait in the circles we will move in this evening," Cressida warned. "Believe only a quarter of what they say until you see the color of their gold, and only half after that. If they can take advantage of you, they will, because they will see you as less than they are."

"In their eyes, we are less," Gabriel reminded her.

"I know how they see me," Cressida said, her face betraying her sadness even in the dim light, "but we shall have to make them see your worth this evening. Trust me a little and I can make you shine, Mister Blackstone. I promise you won't regret having me on your arm tonight."

Gabriel smiled, hoping to coax a smile from her in return. "I will be the envy of every man in the room," he assured her, "because no other lady will hold a candle to you."

"Ah, but they all know they can have me for the right price," Cressida sighed, "and that takes all the mystery away. However alluring I try to be, they know I am available to the highest bidder."

"Not tonight," Gabriel said. "Tonight you are mine, and I will not share. Unless you want me to, of course."

Cressida's smile was sweet as she looked at him. "No, I don't think I want you to. I think I like the idea of being off the market for once."

"If I had my way, none of you would be on the market ever again," Gabriel confided, "but that is beyond my ability to arrange. We'll have to settle for one evening instead."

"I look forward to it," Cressida said. "We're here. The driver will open the door and lower the steps. Descend and then turn and offer me your hand so I can step down."

Gabriel followed Cressida's instructions, descending the steps slowly and turning to offer his hand. He could feel eyes on his back, though he did not turn to see, keeping his gaze focused entirely on the entrance to the coach and the woman about to appear. The top of Cressida's head appeared first as she gathered her skirts about her so she wouldn't trip. Gabriel caught the slightest hint of a narrow shoe as her foot found the first step and thought he heard a gasp behind him as the rest of her appeared and she straightened, pausing momentarily for effect. He had to admit his earlier assessment in the carriage had done her an injustice. Standing as she was, the dress fell in understated, elegant lines highlighting her slender waist, finely boned hips, and generous bosom. She lifted the fan that had hung limply from her wrist and opened it, holding it modestly in front of her décolletage and face as she joined him on the pavement. He offered her his arm without being prompted.

"Very pretty manners," she said, her voice barely above a whisper. "When we go inside, give the butler your hat, but keep your gloves. The gentlemen may remove them for dinner, but they will want them for the dancing."

Gabriel blanched and nearly missed a step. "I don't know how to dance," he confided, his voice as soft as hers.

"Then we shall hold court instead," Cressida said, nothing in her manner betraying any dismay at Gabriel's announcement.

As Cressida had foreseen, a servant waited just inside the door to collect Gabriel's hat. He saw the lady in front of them remove her cloak as well, but Cressida was not wearing one. "No cloak?" he said softly.

"It is too hot for one, and I have no need to pretend a modesty I do not feel," she explained. "We must greet our host and his family. Shake the gentlemen's hands and bow over the ladies'."

Lord Stuart stood at the head of the receiving line, shaking Gabriel's hand heartily and leaning forward to kiss Cressida's cheek. Gabriel started to draw her away protectively, but she squeezed his arm once, silently signaling him to leave well enough alone. He subsided, not wanting to alienate the one definitely friendly person in the room.

"Blackstone, this is my niece, Miss Patricia Stuart," Lord Stuart said, introducing Gabriel to the girl standing next to him. "Patricia, Mister Blackstone is the inventor who made Roxie for me."

"Oh, sir," the young lady, whose pale, gauzy dress proclaimed her to be unmarried and in the market for a husband, exclaimed. "I am so taken with my uncle's new pet. You are a genius, I'm quite certain."

"It was the least I could do for such a kind man as your uncle," Gabriel replied uncomfortably, bowing over the gloved hand and catching a whiff of highly floral perfume. The scent nearly made him choke. He was glad Cressida had chosen a less cloying fragrance.

Miss Stuart tittered on for another minute before Lord Stuart drew her attention away to greet the next guest. Cressida provided the introductions the rest of the way down the receiving line, easing Gabriel's way with a grace he envied.

"Thank you, Miss Cressida," he said again when they had greeted the last of the family. "I would certainly have floundered without you by my side."

"The evening is young, Mister Blackstone," Cressida said with a flirtatious grin. "If we are not to dance, then we should find a couch or settee where we can hold court as quickly as possible before they are all gone."

Gabriel's superior height let him see over some of the sea of heads. He caught sight of an empty couch near an unlit fireplace. "Over there," he said, stopping himself before he could point.

"Lead the way," Cressida directed. "I am at your beck and call tonight."

"Oh, no," Gabriel replied, wending his way through the crowd. "I am at yours. You have to keep me on the straight and narrow."

Cressida laughed. "This may be the first time I've ever been asked to do that! I tend to be more of a corrupting influence than a stabilizing one."

"That isn't what Lord Stuart said," Gabriel told her. "He assured me you were quite the positive influence on his nieces and nephews and that you had far more sense than the lot of them."

Cressida looked at him in surprise. "That's news to me. Then again, I've known for some time that he has a soft spot for those of my caste."

They reached the couch and Cressida took a seat, spreading her skirts around her to best show off her dress and her figure. She patted the seat next to her when Gabriel hesitated. "If another lady joins us, you will cede your seat to her, of course," she counseled, "but while we are the only ones here, you may sit at my side."

"And if another gentleman joins us?" Gabriel asks.

"In that case, you would rise and speak with him without offering him your seat," Cressida replied. "After all, I am *your* companion for the night, not his."

"Even if he outranks me?" Gabriel asked, fully aware that everyone in the room outranked him.

"Yes," Cressida said. "As I said, I am yours tonight, and his rank doesn't change that. Now, sit here and look out at the crush as if it were the most fascinating thing you've ever seen."

"That's how we're supposed to pass the time?" Gabriel asked incredulously.

"Unless you're interested in courting one of the debutantes or you want to flirt with one of the matrons looking to cheat on her husband with someone other than a companion, then yes, that's how you're supposed to pass the time," Cressida replied.

"What if I were interested in convincing one of the husbands to cheat on his wife?" Gabriel joked.

"Do you see someone you like?" Cressida asked, her voice sharper than Gabriel could explain.

"No," he replied immediately. "I was simply curious if it was an option."

"Everything is an option if you have the wit and courage to arrange it," Cressida answered. "You are here. Did you need more proof of that?"

"I'm here because Lord Stuart insisted."

"You're here because Lord Stuart believes you deserve to be here," Cressida disagreed, "and that's a very different thing."

"So what do we do now?" Gabriel asked. "No one here knows me. Will anyone even come up to us without an introduction?"

"That's where I come in, once again," Cressida said. "I have spent enough time in aristocratic circles to be your *entrée* into society. Their curiosity will make them wonder who the man is at my side, the man they don't know but who can afford my presence, and then they will use our prior acquaintance to obtain an introduction. It will be up to you to keep their interest once I have introduced you."

Before Cressida could say any more, her predictions played out, a gentleman of a certain age approaching and bowing over Cressida's hand in courtly fashion. "What a delight to see you here, my dear," the man said, "and with someone I haven't had the good fortune to meet. You will be so kind, won't you?"

"Of course," Cressida said with a pretty smile. Having seen her real smile, Gabriel had no trouble as pegging it as fake, the awareness alerting him to her opinion of the other man. "Lord John Nowden, may I introduce Mister Gabriel Blackstone, one of the great minds of our time? Lord Stuart owes him a great debt of gratitude."

Gabriel managed to smother a laugh at Cressida's exaggeration, standing and offering his hand to the aristocrat as if he spent all his time rubbing elbows with the notables. He was surprised she knew his first name when he had not thought to introduce himself fully, but he assumed Lord Stuart had given her that detail. "Pleased to meet you, Lord Nowden," Gabriel said. "Miss Cressida is generous with her praise."

"So what is this debt Stuart owes you?" Lord Nowden said without preamble. Gabriel bristled at the affront to Cressida, but he knew where companions stood in the eyes of men like Lord Nowden. It was one more reason to resent them.

"He plans to share my invention tonight," Gabriel said, not wanting to steal Lord Stuart's thunder. "I'm sure he will unveil it when he feels the time is right."

"So you take commissions, then?" Lord Nowden asked.

"On occasion," Gabriel replied, not wanting to seem overly eager. He might not like the man, but he would not refuse the offer of a job if it came his way.

Lord Nowden nodded sharply. "I will keep that in mind. My wife has been after me to arrange some improvements to our home. I shall be getting your details from Stuart."

Gabriel tipped his head. "I look forward to speaking with you again."

"Now see," Cressida said softly when Gabriel sat back down after Lord Nowden left. "That wasn't so bad, was it?"

"My hands are shaking and my palms are sweating inside my gloves," Gabriel whispered. "I can't do this all night."

"It won't be all night," Cressida promised. "As soon as the dancing begins, we can circulate, perhaps even step outside onto the terrace for a breath of fresh air, if there is such a thing in the city this time of year. The longest part of any ball is waiting for everyone to arrive."

Gabriel hoped she was right. Falling back on her earlier advice, he stared out at the crowd, not making eye contact so as not to attract the wrong kind of attention, but studying how the gentlemen stood and moved, hoping he could emulate them well enough not to make a fool of himself at dinner. His eyes passed over a familiar dark head almost without seeing it when his heart clenched.

Lucio was here.

CRESSIDA must have noticed his distress because her hand closed around his bicep. "Mister Blackstone?" When Gabriel did not reply, she squeezed a bit. "Gabriel? What's wrong?"

The liberty she had taken with his name shook Gabriel from his daze, trying to reconcile the vision across the room from him with the dreams that had haunted his sleep for the past month. "Nothing," he said with a firm shake of his head. "I thought I saw someone I knew. I must have been mistaken."

"Who did you think you saw?" Cressida's voice was so soft Gabriel could barely hear her. He turned toward her, tipping his head closer to hers, uncaring of the image they presented to society.

"What?"

"Who did you think you saw?" she repeated.

Gabriel swallowed a couple of times, not sure why he was tempted to confide in the woman at his side. Yes, she had been incredibly kind to him in the time they had spent together so far, making sure he would not make a fool of himself, but that did not mean he needed to spill his deepest secret to her, one he had not even shared with his own best friend. "No one important," he said, hoping to put her off track. "I thought I caught a glimpse of the other companion I visited with a month ago, but I'm sure I was mistaken."

"Would you like to see him again?" Cressida asked, the tone of her voice enough to make Gabriel look at her sharply. Her gaze brooked no dissimulation.

"I thought I would," Gabriel said finally, "but now I'm not sure. The reality can't possibly compare to my imaginings, can it?"

"I'm sure it doesn't matter anyway," Cressida said with a shrug. "The only other companion here tonight is Lucio, and he is here as Lord Stuart's guest. He's the most sought-after companion in the palace where I live. I'm sure that isn't who you were looking for."

Gabriel gasped at the words, both at the knowledge that Lucio was indeed as elite as Gabriel had feared and at the realization that his eyes had not tricked him. He could not stop the flinch at the image of Lucio in Lord Stuart's bed, but he pushed the thought aside. However much he might dream otherwise, Lucio was not and would never be his. He had to accept that and move on. "Actually it is," he admitted softly, "but it doesn't matter. If he's here with Lord Stuart, he won't have time for the likes of me. He'll have forgotten me by now. He must see many guests far more interesting than me."

Cressida's hand ran the length of Gabriel's arm. "I can't speak for Lucio, but I can't think of a guest in recent memory who was nearly as interesting as you." She paused for so long that Gabriel breathed a sigh of relief, thinking she had let the topic of Lucio slide, when she squeezed his arm again. "He wants to see you."

"What?" Gabriel exclaimed, his voice rising to the point that it drew the attention of several of the people standing nearby.

Cressida hushed him with the rap of her fan across his hand. "Softly now, or it won't matter what any of us want. He was most unhappy when he learned I would be the one to escort you tonight while he was tied to Lord Stuart's side. I wasn't going to say anything, but I think I see why he feels the way he does."

"How does he feel?"

Cressida shook her head. "That's for him to say or not to say, but I will do my part in giving you the chance to ask him." She caught Gabriel's chin with her fan, tipping it up so their gazes met. "Listen to me carefully, Mister Blackstone. Lucio is important to me, possibly the most important person in the world as far as I'm concerned. If you are toying with him, I will do everything in my not inconsiderable power to ruin you."

Words caught in Gabriel's throat at the fierce tone of her voice, the tight expression on her face. He took her hand in his, rubbing his thumb over her gloved knuckles. "I can't predict the future," he said after a moment, "but I would never deliberately hurt him. Is it possible, here at the ball, for us to speak?"

"He cannot approach us openly," Cressida replied, "but there are more ways than one to skin a cat. Place your trust in me and we will see what can be done."

Gabriel tried to relax again at Cressida's side, to look suitably bored with the comings and goings around him rather than clinging to Cressida's hand while he waited to see what she could do to arrange a discreet meeting with Lucio. Given that she had promised not to leave his side, he had little faith it would work, but it increased his determination to use a portion of his earnings from Lord Stuart to purchase some time alone where he and Lucio could truly talk without having to worry about others overhearing. If Cressida was right….

If Cressida was right, his fondest wish over the past month had come true. He had made enough of an impression on Lucio to remain in his thoughts despite the relatively short time they had spent together and the innocence of what had passed between them. He scanned the room reflexively, trying to find Lucio's dark head among the sea of guests. Finally he caught sight of the companion lounging against the far wall, his finger running along the top of the fan.

"He wants to meet with you," Cressida murmured at his side.

"How can you tell?" Gabriel asked.

"Men," Cressida muttered. "Do they teach you nothing? See the way he holds his fan? He is asking for a meeting. It is too soon to slip away yet. After dinner perhaps, around ten, I think."

"If you think that is best," Gabriel replied, "but how will he know?"

"Leave that to me," Cressida replied. "I will tell him what he needs to know." Carefully she opened her fan until ten of the ribs showed. Gabriel glanced from her hands to Lucio, who opened the fan and then shut it sharply. "He says you are cruel."

"You were the one who said we should wait," Gabriel protested, keeping his voice soft.

"I will tell him you are sorry," Cressida promised, closing her fan and lowering her eyes as she drew the closed fan across her face.

Gabriel studied her closely before returning his gaze to Lucio. Slowly, deliberately, he shut the fan that had been half open. Beside Gabriel, Cressida gasped. "What did he say?" Gabriel asked.

Cressida shook her head.

"What did he say?" Gabriel pressed.

"He asked for a kiss," Cressida whispered.

Gabriel's heart pounded in his chest as he remembered the first time he and Lucio had met and the kiss that had left him floundering for days. To be able to have that again, without fear this time, was a lure Gabriel knew he would not be able to resist. All thought of seeing Lucio in the carriage with the unknown woman disappeared. Only the possibility of knowing the tempting taste of Lucio's mouth again remained.

"Anything he wants."

Cressida hesitated a moment longer before resting her fan against her right cheek.

A slow smile crossed Lucio's face. He met Gabriel's eyes and held his gaze for several long seconds before turning away at the sound of his name.

"Did you and Lucio develop those signals between you?" Gabriel asked when he could no longer see Lucio clearly.

Cressida rolled her eyes. "You truly are ignorant of society's ways, aren't you?" she asked. "Look around and watch carefully. From the youngest debutante to the most fashionable matron, you'll see them using the same signals. Even with the freedoms they enjoy, there is so much they are not allowed to say, at least not in public, so they flirt and set up rendezvous and cuckold their husbands all with a flick of their fans. The men will all deny they carry a fan so they can reply to the lady of their choice, but what use is a fan in the winter?"

"I had no idea," Gabriel murmured, studying the occupants of the room with much greater interest.

Cressida rolled her eyes behind his back.

"See Miss Partridge over there in the pink monstrosity she calls a dress," Cressida said without looking in the girl's direction. "Her parents want her to marry Mister Mority, but she has her heart set on Mister Adams. She has been trying for weeks to engineer a scene in which society catches her in a compromising position with the beau of her choice. Her parents seem determined to keep that from happening until after she is married according to their plans."

"Why can she not marry Mister Adams?" Gabriel asked.

"Because while he has no tattoo, he also has no money," Cressida said bluntly, "and Miss Partridge's parents are nothing if not avaricious. Nothing short of a scandal will force their hand, and so she is determined to arrange one."

Gabriel shook his head. Such machinations made him glad he was a simple inventor, so far below the interest of the men and women in the room that he barely merited their interest. All the better to slip away unnoticed so he could meet with Lucio at the agreed-upon time. The gong sounded to announce dinner, putting an end to Gabriel's ramblings.

"GOOD evening, ladies and gentlemen," Lord Ian boomed as his guests made their way into the dining room for the meal. "I've taken the liberty of shaking up the seating a bit for the evening, so our guest of honor is not stuck at my side surrounded by my friends and cronies instead of free to laugh and talk with her own friends, as well she should on her birthday. I'm sure you'll all bear the rearrangements with good grace and help me celebrate my lovely niece this evening."

The guests applauded politely, although Lucio thought he read disgruntlement on some of the faces of those displaced to allow the younger crew to sit near the head of the table. As always, Lord Ian's foibles would be excused because he was rich as Croesus and eccentric as daVinci.

Lucio moved to the place to the left of the head of the table where he knew Lord Ian would have placed him for dinner. The matrons would shake their heads and whisper behind their fans, but Lord Ian had never cared for their gossip, preferring to keep Lucio close enough to hand to be entertained by him during the evening. After all, what was the purpose of purchasing a companion if not to be entertained in all manner of ways?

Lucio caught sight of Gabriel's shaggy head as he and Cressida made their way into the dining room, looking for the place cards that indicated their seats. To Lucio's surprise, they were seated mid-table. Before Lucio could question that any further, Lord Ian appeared at his side, a hand running discreetly down Lucio's back. "Come, take your seat, Lucio. We mustn't block the way for those still in the hall."

Lucio moved to stand behind his chair, not taking his seat yet, but out of the way. He watched with interest as Lord Ian moved around the table, speaking with people, soothing ruffled feathers, and generally ensuring a pleasant evening for everyone. When the aristocrat reached the place where Gabriel and Cressida stood, he put a hand on Gabriel's shoulder, making Lucio bristle, even as he told himself that was ridiculous. "We have another special guest this evening, although he has refused to let me seat him as highly at the table as he is in my esteem. I'd like to introduce to you Mister Gabriel Blackstone, the inventor of my new pet, Roxie. For those of you who haven't met my little canine companion yet, I'm sure you'll see her before the evening is over. Either way, I'm honored that

Mister Blackstone agreed to join us this evening. I hope you'll all help me make him feel welcome."

"Thank you, Lord Stuart," Gabriel said, his voice sounding shaky to Lucio's ear.

Lucio suppressed a smile. As rich as Croesus and as eccentric as daVinci. He had no idea what the rest of the meal would bring, but he was certain he wouldn't be bored.

Gabriel was too far down the table for Lucio to join in the conversation that started almost as soon as Lord Ian pulled out his niece's chair for her to be seated, the other aristocrats following suit, but Lucio could tell the inventor was in high demand.

"You seem as fascinated by my guest as everyone else," Lord Ian murmured at Lucio's side. "Should I be jealous?"

"Of course not," Lucio said quickly, perhaps a little too quickly. "Unless you are far more generous with him than you are with me"—he stroked the back of Lord Ian's hand to soften his words—"he wouldn't be able to afford me, anyway."

Lord Ian tutted and turned his hand over, squeezing Lucio's fingers gently. "I'm more than generous with you, pretty boy, and well you know it. I suspect you're right about Blackstone's fortunes, although perhaps tonight will change that for the better."

Lucio felt an unexpected spurt of resentment at Lord Ian's epithet for him. Lord Ian had called him "pretty boy" from the first time they met, a few weeks after Lucio was first presented to society. Until now, Lucio had always found it endearing, a sign that the older man cared for him in some small way. Now it only served to remind him of his place in society, far more constrained than he wished it were. He would never be worthy of Gabriel's true regard because he would never be anything more than a rich man's plaything.

Lord Ian's hand caressing his thigh beneath the table only underscored that, adding to the bundle of nerves in Lucio's stomach. Often Lord Ian would purchase his time simply to have enjoyable company for the evening, sending Lucio on his way with nothing more than a pat on the head and a grope or two, but tonight appeared to be one of those nights when the aristocrat wanted more. Lucio had no idea how he would pretend any enthusiasm for bed sport with his thoughts so focused on Gabriel. He considered canceling their assignation, but that thought tore at him as well. He had built his evening with Gabriel up in his mind to such proportions that it eclipsed everything else. He had told himself repeatedly not to make such a gargantuan mistake, but he kept remembering their kiss. Lord Ian didn't even try to kiss Lucio, and Lucio felt closer to him than to any of his other clients.

He summoned a smile, hoping Lord Ian would not see the difference, and stroked his guest's leg in return, his fingers stopping shy of the older man's groin. He wanted to tantalize, not scandalize. Before Lord Ian could do more than send Lucio a lustful glance, one of the other dinner guests called his name, drawing his attention away, much to Lucio's relief. He turned to the lady sitting on the other side, a woman he did not know, and engaged her in polite conversation, hoping Lord Ian's attention would remain elsewhere.

A few moments later, Lucio felt a hand stroking his hair. He smiled politely to the lady and excused himself, giving his attention back to Lord Ian. Lucio had never thought anything of the casual way his guests touched him—they all did it, and nobody thought anything of it—but now, knowing Gabriel could be watching, Lucio resented even that rare, innocent touch. He knew it could be worse. Lord Ian could have groped his ass instead of stroking his hair, but even that gesture bespoke the assumption that Lucio was his to do with as he pleased, an assumption he would never make with another aristocrat. Men didn't touch their wives in public, much less anyone else, but no one hesitated to touch a companion any way they pleased. While it happened to Lucio less often than to others, Cressida frequently commented about a guest groping her breasts in public, occasionally even complaining that her guest had pulled down her bodice for the titillation of others.

Lucio barely resisted the urge to look down the table and see if Gabriel had noticed. He hoped Cressida had managed to keep the inventor distracted, but he could do nothing about it one way or another at the moment. Lord Ian had purchased him for the evening, and nothing could change that fact, no matter how much Lucio wished he could switch places with Cressida. He knew without a doubt that Cressida was not suffering the humiliation of unwelcome caresses. Gabriel had not taken advantage of Lucio even in private and knowing how willing Lucio would have been. He would not touch Cressida in any but the most innocent ways in public. Lucio would bet money on it.

"Are you enjoying yourself?" Lord Ian asked, his hand lingering on Lucio's face.

"Of course," Lucio said, not tipping his head into the caress as he would have done previously. He couldn't change Lord Ian's actions, but he could control his own. "You always throw the most interesting parties."

Lord Ian chuckled. "Mixing up the seating or inviting a merchant or both?"

Lucio summoned a smile. "Both, of course. I wouldn't venture to guess which was the more daring choice."

Lord Ian laughed and tugged at Lucio's ear. "You make me happy, pretty boy. I shall have to think of a way to reward you once we are alone tonight. Be thinking about what you would like. I am feeling magnanimous."

"Being at your side is more than reward enough," Lucio replied automatically, his training kicking in and keeping the conversation going as his mind shied away from the thought of being alone with Lord Ian later. The man was a reasonably considerate bed partner, far more caring than most of Lucio's guests, but he was still an aristocrat intent on finding his own pleasure without a thought to Lucio beyond making sure he did not inflict pain on the companion. Lucio wondered how Lord Ian would react if he asked for something for his own pleasure, but he knew he would not give voice to the thought. Aristocrats did not think in terms of a companion's pleasure, only in terms of their own. He risked a glance down the table to where Gabriel was engaged in conversation with the people around him.

One more way in which the inventor was different.

GABRIEL thought dinner would never end. The food was excellent, he was sure, but he hardly tasted a bite between trying to field the questions of the people around him concerning his work and his nearly obsessive need to keep Lucio in his line of vision. Lord Stuart touched the companion almost constantly with a casual possessiveness and blatant disregard for Lucio's self-respect that made Gabriel want to scream at the older man to open his eyes and see what he was doing. The empty seat at the foot of the table where Lord Stuart's wife would have sat were she still alive was proof that the man possessed finer sensibilities, but none of them seemed to come into play where Lucio was concerned.

When they finally rose from the table, Cressida pulled Gabriel aside. "What is wrong with you?" she demanded. "You could barely finish a sentence at dinner, and I know you are more conversational than that. I spent the hour before dinner chatting with you quite comfortably."

"How can Lord Stuart call himself a gentleman, the way he was pawing Lucio during dinner?" Gabriel replied softly. "I couldn't stop thinking about it."

Cressida sighed in resignation. "There will be a few minutes of milling about before the ball begins and we can keep our meeting with Lucio. Walk with me out on the terrace where we might catch a breath of fresh air and perhaps find a moment of privacy."

Gabriel nodded and guided her through the throng of people to the terrace that stretched along the back of the house, stone steps leading down into a manicured garden. When they were alone, Cressida released Gabriel's arm and leaned against the ornate balustrade. "I don't know if I can make you understand what our lives are like. No one cares for our dignity, our self-respect. Nothing Lord Stuart did tonight, however much it seems to bother you, came even close to what our 'guests' feel perfectly entitled to do to us with all of society looking on. Short of stripping him naked and bedding him on the dinner table, I'm not sure Lord Stuart could have done anything to Lucio his peers would consider objectionable, and even then they might have cheered him on."

"They don't treat each other that way," Gabriel protested.

"No, they don't," Cressida agreed, "but we aren't aristocrats. We're companions whose only purpose in their lives is to provide them pleasure. When I was young and ignorant, I complained to one of my guests that I had not found fulfillment. Do you know what he told me? He told me not to bother him with that because companions were incapable of finding release. That's why we were companions. We needed the constant stimulation of sexual contact, but we couldn't find release."

"That's ridiculous," Gabriel said. "Your body is no different than any other woman's, is it?"

Cressida shook her head. "Not at all, but they don't care enough to find out. They use us for their release and send us home to find our pleasure at our own hands if we can. We don't rate at all in their minds. Lucio always tells me they're as much a product of their upbringing as we are, but I think he does them too much credit."

"I can't imagine treating someone, anyone, that way," Gabriel said with a shake of his head.

"I know," Cressida said, "and that's why Lucio can't get you out of his head. I laughed at him when he first told me about your birthday dinner. No one could be as perfect as he described you as being." She paused and reached for Gabriel's hand. "I'm not laughing anymore."

"I'm far from perfect," Gabriel denied, flushing at the unexpected praise. "I would hardly call showing a little consideration perfect."

"I tried to talk Lucio out of his infatuation," Cressida continued as if Gabriel had not spoken. "I told him not to get his hopes up, not to expect to see you again. He nodded and said all the right things, but I've seen the change in him over the past month. I came tonight with the intention of warning you off, but I can't do it. I've watched the way you watch him, and you look at him with the same starry look in your eyes that he gets when he talks about you. I still think you're both fools setting yourself up for nothing but heartbreak and misery, but I'll do what I can to help."

"Unless you know a way I can get him out of there, I don't know what you can really do," Gabriel said sadly.

"You buy his contract," Cressida said bluntly. "The only other way out of the pleasure palaces is death."

Gabriel laughed bitterly. "We'll both be dead before I have the money for that. I don't know what it would cost, but I can barely afford an hour with him."

"You must tell him that," Cressida said urgently.

"No, I couldn't," Gabriel demurred, squirming with embarrassment at revealing the true depth of his poverty to a companion so used to being surrounded by wealth.

"You must," Cressida insisted. "He's built you up as a savior in his mind. He needs to know the truth so he can go forward with no illusions. Have you thought about this, Gabriel? He earns his livelihood by bedding the highest bidder. You and I will leave here tonight, and he will go upstairs with Lord Stuart and probably not come home before lunch tomorrow. No part of him can belong completely to you. Can you really live with that?"

"I have no choice, do I?" Gabriel asked, the words cutting him like knives. "I can't afford to purchase his contract."

"You can walk away now," Cressida said. "You can go inside with me, meet Lucio wherever he can arrange, and tell him you can't do it. That you can't afford him and you can't live with the reality of his life. You can let him go. If you don't, you'll have to live with that reality, and you'll have to keep living with it because if you start this relationship with him, whatever that might look like, and then you end it because of who he is, it will kill him. He puts on a careless façade, but I know his heart—I may be the only one who does—and he is ready to put it on the line if you can deal with all the rest of his life."

Gabriel had no reply for that, only nodding slowly to let her know he had heard her. Even knowing it would be considered rude, he pulled away from her, walking slowly to the far end of the terrace. He had teased Lucio with the idea that he wanted to be the one the companion remembered, but he had not expected—not really—that it would work. Apparently it had.

His thoughts flashed back to the woman in the carriage and the same tender gesture Lucio had used with both her and with him. Turning sharply, he studied Cressida's features. Even in the few hours they had known one another, her influence and importance to Lucio had been obvious. Perhaps.... "Did you and Lucio share a coach home on Monday afternoon, not long before the rain started?"

"What are you talking about?" Cressida asked.

"I saw Lucio on Monday in a coach with a woman," Gabriel said, aware he was not making any sense to her, but he needed to know. "Was that you with him?"

"Yes, but why?" Cressida said.

Gabriel let out a sigh of relief. "Because I saw him touch your cheek, the same way he touched mine before he kissed me. I thought he was with a guest, and it angered me that he had lied to me, but if he was with you, it wasn't a lie."

"I don't know what he told you," Cressida said, "but I don't think he has it in him to lie to you. To everyone else, undoubtedly, but you have been different from the moment your name first appeared in front of him, and you only seem to add to that as time goes on. Are you ready to go find him?"

Gabriel was pretty sure he wasn't ready, but he had the opportunity now to meet Lucio on even ground without any exchange of money between them. If ever there was a time to speak frankly about matters between them, this was it, when Lucio had no reason to say what he thought Gabriel wanted to hear and felt no pressure to make an offer he wasn't comfortable making, when Gabriel had no guilt over being at Lucio's side and no reason to refuse a heartfelt offer. "I suppose we should go inside," he agreed. "I wouldn't want him to think I'd forgotten him."

"You are a good man, Gabriel Blackstone," Cressida said as they walked back into the crowded ballroom. "Maybe too good."

LUCIO couldn't stop the surge of jealousy when he caught sight of Cressida and Gabriel walking back into the salon from the terrace. He knew Cressida was only hired to help Gabriel navigate the evening and that she wouldn't go beyond the terms of the contract even if Gabriel had asked, but he was the only one who knew those terms. Everyone else in the room would assume that Gabriel had found a private place and bedded her. Even knowing it wasn't true, even knowing Gabriel had undoubtedly treated Cressida with the same consideration he had shown Lucio, the knowing looks on the aristocrats' faces grated on Lucio's nerves. He wanted to shout that Gabriel would never treat Cressida so poorly. If he did decide to bed her, he would take her to an actual bed and treat her like a lady. No one would believe that any more than they would believe

Gabriel hadn't bedded her in the first place. He sighed, keeping his fan up to hide his sour expression.

He watched the ebb and flow of the guests invited only to the ball rather than the dinner beforehand, biding his time before they could slip away. He had been at Lord Ian's often enough to be familiar with the house and the grounds, but he doubted Gabriel or Cressida had the same degree of familiarity. The folly in the gardens would be ideal, but it was rather remote, and he wasn't sure how long he dared absent himself from the ball. A few minutes could be excused by his need to visit the retiring room, but not the time it would take to get out to the folly and back. Not while he was Lord Ian's guest. He debated using the conservatory, but it was a frequent trysting place for Lord Ian's niece. Lucio had no idea if she had a beau at the moment, much less if she would try to slip away from her own ball, but he did not think it was a risk worth taking. That left the library or the music room, which lay on opposite ends of the house. Lucio would see which door he could slip out more easily and make his decision from there.

Lord Ian entered the ballroom with his niece on his arm, calling for everyone's attention. The musicians struck up the notes of a lively waltz, and Lord Ian and his niece opened the ball, suggesting to Lucio that the girl did not have a chosen partner at the moment. That could make the conservatory an option again, but he would see how the evening went. He didn't dare disappear immediately, sure Lord Ian would seek his company after the dance.

The moment the music ended, everyone applauded. Lord Ian offered his niece's hand to the next gentleman on her dance card and opened the floor to the rest of the guests. The musicians began the next set, and as predicted, Lord Ian made a beeline for Lucio's side. "Not dancing tonight, pretty boy?" Lord Ian asked.

"I did not want to commit myself to anyone else when you might have need of me, my Lord," Lucio replied with a coquettish smile. "After all, I am here to serve you this evening."

"Don't I know it," Lord Ian replied, running a finger down the center of Lucio's chest. "I also know that I won't be free of this nonsense for hours yet, so if you wish to dance, you should feel free, or if you prefer to wander the grounds and take some air, make yourself at home. Just don't go too far in case I find a few free moments."

"Thank you, my Lord," Lucio said, trying not to reveal his glee at being given leave to wander at will. "I will take advantage of your generosity. It has grown quite warm in here, and I would not smell of sweat later if it can be avoided. I know you prefer a more fragrant companion in your bed."

"Such talk," Lord Ian scolded with a wink. "If I didn't know better, I would think you were trying to seduce me."

Lucio lowered his eyes and lifted his fan modestly. "My Lord," he flirted, "I hope you will not think too poorly of me."

"You are too pretty for your own good, pretty boy," Lord Ian said with a pat to Lucio's rear. "Go enjoy yourself. I will find you later."

Lucio took the words as permission, offering Lord Ian a short bow before withdrawing toward the nearest door. Glancing back with his hand on the knob, he sought Cressida with his eyes, his fan open in his right hand, shielding all but his eyes. *Follow me.* She nodded, her fan touching her right cheek. It was all the confirmation Lucio needed. He slipped through the door into the cool, dim hallway. He passed the conservatory, wondering once more if he should try it as a meeting place, but the sound of laughter from within dissuaded him. That left the music room at the end of the hall. Making sure no one was watching, he went inside, leaving the door open a crack so he could hear Cressida's and Gabriel's approach. Cressida had seen which direction he went when he left, but there was more than one room along this corridor. He would have to signal them when they were able to slip away.

"WHAT are we waiting for?" Gabriel whispered sharply the moment Lucio moved toward the door. "Shouldn't we follow him?"

"And tell the entire ball we are joining him?" Cressida replied. "No, we will wait until a seemly time has passed and then we will stroll leisurely that way. If you can bring yourself to act suggestively in my regard, it will add to the illusion that we are sneaking away because you cannot bring yourself to wait for my services any longer."

"But—"

"No buts," Cressida said. "Whether you do anything or not, whether we stand here or leave, they are thinking it. All you're doing is deflecting their interest from Lucio's departure before ours."

Gabriel warred with his conscience, but he certainly did not want anyone, particularly Lord Stuart, guessing the true nature of his assignation. "So what do you suggest? Nothing too obvious, because I wouldn't do that even if I were interested in you."

"But they would," Cressida reminded him. "You saw the way Lord Stuart acted with Lucio. The simplest thing would be to drop your hand to my back, or perhaps a little lower, and escort me out that way instead of with me on your arm."

"You won't be offended?"

Cressida turned and smiled sweetly at Gabriel. "I won't be offended. I may be sorry you aren't interested in me, but I won't be offended. We've waited long enough. We can go now."

Taking a deep breath and trying to convince himself no one was watching, Gabriel let Cressida's hand fall from his arm and placed his hand on her back, just above the swell of her buttocks, far lower than he would ever have dared without her permission. He could swear her posture changed at the touch, everything about her demeanor suddenly becoming more inviting. If he had not known it was a ruse to cover their meeting with Lucio, he would have sworn she was welcoming his advances, if not actively trying to seduce him. Urging her forward, he guided her toward the door Lucio had taken, reminding himself that the subterfuge was necessary in order to grant him the meeting he had dreamt of for the past month.

He breathed a sigh of relief when the door to the ballroom shut behind them, leaving them enclosed in near darkness, only one gas sconce at the far end of the hallway illuminating the corridor. Gabriel peered into the gloom, counting at least four doors. "How will we know where he went?"

At that moment, Lucio's head appeared through the last doorway.

"He'll let us know," Cressida said unnecessarily, preceding Gabriel down the hall and into the music room. She waited on the threshold as Gabriel came in. Lucio had retreated to the other side of the room, twisting his hands in front of him.

"Hello, Lucio," Gabriel said, his voice barely loud enough to carry across the room.

Gabriel could see Lucio's mouth move, but he couldn't hear the reply. He took a couple of steps toward the companion, his stomach tied in knots as he tried to think of what to say. "How are you?"

"I'm well, thank you," Lucio replied, but Gabriel couldn't decide if it was truly an honest answer or if the companion had replied out of habit. "And you?"

"Now that I'm here with you."

"Enough, you two," Cressida scolded from the doorway. "You both have been dreaming of this moment, and now that it's here, you're acting like virginal schoolboys, something I know neither of you have been for a number of years. I'm going to step outside to keep watch and give you a little privacy. You don't know when you'll next have this chance. Don't waste it!"

THE door shut behind Cressida with an audible click. Lucio took a deep breath and steeled himself for the coming conversation. "I don't quite know what to say," he admitted. "Usually when I sneak off like this, it's because my guest wants the titillation of bedding me where we could be caught at any time."

Gabriel flinched visibly, even from across the room. "Don't say things like that. I have a hard enough time dealing with your profession without you throwing it in my face."

Lucio frowned. "I can't change what I am, Gabriel. You know that. You've known that from the moment we met. If all you're going to do is criticize me, maybe it's better if I leave."

"No, wait," Gabriel said, his hand reaching toward Lucio. "Don't go, please. I don't like it, and I'll never like it, but I don't blame you for it. I do, however, wish it could be different."

Lucio shrugged. "If I had a coin for every time I wished things could be different, I'd have enough gold to buy my contract, but it doesn't work that way. This is who I am and this is what I do. You're the only person who's ever treated me differently. I can't get you out of my head."

The admission unrooted Gabriel's feet from the floor. He crossed to Lucio's side, taking the companion's hand in his. "I haven't been able to stop thinking of you either."

The words thrilled Lucio to his core. Perhaps they could find a way forward despite the obstacles in their path. "You promised me a kiss," he said, squeezing Gabriel's hand gently. "Will you keep your promise?"

"I always keep my promises."

Lucio's eyes closed in anticipation as Gabriel leaned toward him. Without his sight, he could not guess when their lips would meet. The initial touch was so soft that Lucio thought at first he had imagined it, but he could feel the rush of Gabriel's breath against his face. Slightly chapped lips brushed across his cheek and then over his lips, disappearing before Lucio could react, only to reappear on one of his eyelids, the bridge of his nose, and then the other eye. His eyes fluttered open, lips parted. "Please, Gabriel," he whispered. "Kiss me properly."

"I am," Gabriel said, his voice husky and low, sending tendrils of arousal through Lucio's body. He knew what it was to feel desire, but for the first time, it was more than just a physical ache. He wanted Gabriel's closeness far more than he wanted any carnal release.

"How do you do this to me?" Lucio gasped. "How do you make me want things I thought I'd put aside years ago?"

Gabriel smiled and stroked Lucio's cheek, the rough edges of a healing cut rasping along the smooth skin. "Because I'm offering them to you," he said simply. "I don't have any money to speak of. Lord Stuart bought me a proper suit so I could attend tonight and paid for Cressida's presence at my side so I wouldn't make a fool of myself and of him. I have no idea how we will manage to see each other since I doubt this kind of fortuitous circumstance will repeat itself very often, but what I have, I offer to you freely."

"What do you have?" Lucio asked with bated breath, hoping he knew.

"My kindness, my consideration, my respect, and my devotion," Gabriel replied. "Call me a fool if you must, but with a kiss and your honesty, you have mesmerized me. I want the chance to know more, but I don't know how to make it a reality."

"You are here tonight to seek new commissions, correct?" Lucio asked, an idea forming in his head.

"Yes, why?"

Lucio smiled. "Because it so happens that I need a few things, and I'm quite certain only you can provide them. I think it fitting that I use the gold my guests give me to make sure we have another opportunity to be together. What do you say? Will you make the machines I ask you to make?"

Gabriel hesitated.

"It isn't charity, Gabriel," Lucio said, fairly certain he knew the reasons behind the other man's silence. "The gold is mine to spend as I please, within reason, at least, and I truly could use a mechanical fan that would provide a breeze in my room all night. I could go elsewhere and commission it, but then someone else would get my money, and we wouldn't have a chance to meet." He laid his hand on Gabriel's cheek, the same gesture that had worked so well the first time they met. "I want to see your workshop. I want to see the machines and the tools and maybe learn something while I'm there. I can't purchase my own contract, but I can find ways to give you as much of my gold as possible so that perhaps one day you can purchase it, and we can be together without resorting to subterfuge."

A knock forced them apart. A moment later, Cressida appeared. "Lucio, Lord Stuart is looking for you. Say your goodbyes quickly before he comes this way."

"Say you'll let me visit you," Lucio pleaded, pressing tender kisses to Gabriel's jaw. "Say you'll give us this chance."

"Very well," Gabriel agreed, catching Lucio's cheek with his hand and kissing him thoroughly. Lucio moaned softly, melting into the suddenly torrid embrace. He needed more, but he could not let Lord Ian catch them this way.

He pulled away, stroking Gabriel's cheek one more time. "I will do my duty tonight, but tomorrow I will come to you, or Sunday at the latest if you will see me on your day of rest."

"My door will always be open for you," Gabriel promised.

Lucio smiled sadly and started toward the door. He turned back with his hand on the knob. "I cannot change what they do to my body, but I will never kiss anyone but you."

THE door closed, then reopened a moment later. Gabriel looked up hopefully, but Cressida came through the door, not Lucio. "You don't have to talk to me," she said softly. "You don't have to look at me or acknowledge me in any way, but it will look exceedingly odd if I stand in the hall alone."

"It's fine," Gabriel said. "We probably shouldn't linger anyway."

"Yes, we should," Cressida disagreed. "We haven't been gone long enough for anything to have happened, and you don't want Lord Stuart associating your disappearance and reappearance with Lucio's. That could be bad for both of you."

"As bad as knowing Lucio is somewhere doing who knows what with Lord Stuart?" Gabriel asked bitterly.

"Stop right there," Cressida scolded sharply. "You cannot do this. You cannot make it so that he can't do his job. If you have any respect for him, you must leave him that because without it, he will lose all status within the pleasure palace, and his life will become a living hell if that happens. The handlers know he is valuable and so they take care of him, protect him, but I have seen what happens to companions who have lost their value. They get sent to the aristocrats who enjoy inflicting pain, and when they return, they don't always get the care they need because they can't afford to pay for it themselves. Don't condemn Lucio to that with your irrational jealousy."

"Irrational?" Gabriel repeated. "I hardly think it's irrational to be bothered by the fact that he could kiss me so sweetly and then go off to another man's bed."

"It is irrational," Cressida insisted, "because you knew before you ever met him what he was, and you knew before you walked in here tonight what you would have to face if you wanted to see him again. You cannot have it both ways unless you have a fortune hidden away somewhere."

"So what do I do? Pretend that it doesn't bother me?" Gabriel asked.

"That's exactly what you do," Cressida said. "You never make any reference to him being a companion. You never ask if he's been with a guest or how many he's been with when he comes to you. You treat the moments you do have as the blessings they are and forget that anything else exists, because the moments you do have together will be unlike anything he shares with anyone else. That's what you have to hold onto."

"You heard what he said," Gabriel said, thinking of Lucio's parting promise.

"I did," Cressida admitted, "but I didn't need to hear the words to know he was thinking it. I already told you I know his heart like no one else. He wants you, and he wants far more than a few stolen hours. This will be hard enough for you both. Your jealousy will only ruin the time you do have together."

"I'll do my best," Gabriel promised, although he had no idea what he would do with the rancor roiling inside him. "I don't want to lose him, and I certainly don't want anything to happen to him."

"Do you have someone you trust to talk to?" Cressida asked. "Someone you can spill all the frustration to so that when you're with Lucio, you can focus on him?"

Gabriel thought of Caleb and Andrew, but he was not sure they would understand. His friends at the Caste Equality party would understand even less because he would suddenly be buying into a system they opposed if he spent money so he could see Lucio. "Not really."

"Find someone," Cressida advised. "You can't keep all this inside you and expect it not to overflow onto Lucio."

As if finding someone would be that easy. His thoughts turned to his assistants again. They might not understand, but maybe Caleb would be willing to listen. He'd probably tell Gabriel he was a fool, but he'd listen. "Maybe my assistant," he said finally. "We've been friends for a long time."

"Find someone," Cressida repeated. "Now, enough time has passed that we can return safely to the ball. It wouldn't hurt if you could manage to look smugly satisfied."

"Trying to add to your reputation?" Gabriel teased.

"Do you blame me?" Cressida asked. "All I have is my reputation. If the aristocrats begin to think I'm not capable of servicing them, I'll be sent to the breeding barns until I'm too old to have children. I'd rather not have that happen, if it's all the same to you."

Gabriel shuddered. Just the words made him want to scream at the injustice of it, former companions being forced to bear children so a new generation of companions could grow up in the same conditions. "I'll do my best."

Cressida poked him with her fan. "Think of kissing Lucio. Think of the fact that Lucio wanted you to kiss him. That should make you as smug as you can be."

"And then I'll think of him with Lord Stuart."

Cressida's hand cracked hard across Gabriel's cheek. "How many times do I have to tell you that what he does with Lord Stuart or any other guest doesn't matter? He doesn't care about any of them. They bed him and they send him on his way. Forget about being smug. The others can think what they like. I can't be seen with you right now."

She was gone before Gabriel could call her back. He cradled his stinging cheek in his hand, the gesture so close to the one Lucio had used that his heart ached. "Stupid, lovesick fool," he muttered, but his voice sounded weak, even to him. He buried his face in his hands and tried to find a way out of this predicament. He wanted Lucio with a desperation that defied measure, and that meant accepting his profession. Now if he could only figure out how to do it.

LUCIO lingered in the retiring room, pressing a cool cloth to his lips in the hope of reducing the telltale puffiness from Lord Ian having fucked his mouth in the library. Lucio almost wished the aristocrat had ordered him to drop his trousers and bend over. At least then, Lucio would still have the taste of Gabriel's mouth on his tongue instead of the salty bitterness of Lord Ian's cock. He hated the thought that Gabriel would look at him and know what had happened. He didn't care about what anyone else thought. They all saw him as the same convenience that Lord Ian considered him. Gabriel, though, was different. He wasn't a convenience to Gabriel. He was…. He didn't really know what he was, but he knew it was different. His stomach turned, bile rising in his throat as he worried over Gabriel's reaction. He couldn't change his life. The tattoo on his hand preordained his role in society, but he feared the implications of the mark would drive a wedge between Gabriel and himself that nothing could overcome.

Would Gabriel even want to see him again after having Lucio's life rubbed in his face so cruelly? Even if the inventor did not figure out the exact nature of his tryst with Lord Ian, he would have to be beyond naïve not to realize that something sexual had occurred. He moved the cloth away from his lips. The swelling had gone down some. He only hoped it was enough because he could not stay in here forever, and he had no doubt Gabriel would be waiting somewhere in the ballroom for him to return. They wouldn't be able to speak again, but Lucio could perhaps send him a message of apology and devotion with Cressida's help. Taking a deep breath, he steeled himself for the knowing looks of the aristocracy and the pain he feared to see in Gabriel's eyes.

No one even glanced his way when he reentered the ballroom. Lucio looked around as surreptitiously as possible, hoping to catch a glimpse of Cressida or Gabriel in the crowd, but the crush stymied him. He would simply have to circulate and hope to stumble across them that way. More than one hand, male and female, groped at him as he wandered the rooms, the press of bodies enough to hide the trespasses. Lucio stifled a sigh. Always in the past he had sought the owners of those transgressing hands to offer a suggestive smile. He might be at the ball as Lord Ian's companion, but that was only for one night. Tomorrow night, the night after, and the one after that, he would need guests to earn his living. Now, though, the touches only annoyed him. He kept his gaze forward, not reacting at all to even the more obvious impositions. Only when he found his way blocked did he meet the person's gaze. He recognized Lady Merydith, although he had never been her companion. "You're getting airs above your station," the lady said bluntly, "cutting people who are your betters when they're trying to get your attention."

"If anyone desires my attention, they have but to call my name," Lucio said, his heart racing beneath his calm façade. He didn't want to make a scene that would spoil Lord Ian's ball.

"You're a companion," she scoffed, sliding a hand beneath the open placket of his jacket and pinching his nipple tightly. "All it should take to get your attention is a touch of an aristocrat's hand. Do I have your attention now?"

"Yes, m'lady," Lucio replied, trying not to grimace at the painful touch. Most of the aristocrats he entertained cared nothing for his pleasure but likewise did not wish to cause him pain. Every so often, though, he would have a guest who delighted in making him cry out in other ways.

"Good," she said, her hand sliding down to the flat front of his breeches. She squeezed his cock until he hissed. "Yes, very good. I shall be seeing you again soon. Lord Stuart is undoubtedly far too gentle with you. You need a lesson in manners."

"As you say, m'lady," Lucio said, his voice as even as he could make it with her fingers still digging into his sensitive flesh. He would put her off as long as he could with the handlers, claiming prior commitments, but he recognized the determination in her face. It might be better to get it over with so he didn't have to live in fear of what she would do when she finally did purchase his time.

She released him. "Think twice about cutting anyone else tonight. I'll be watching, and I'll make you regret every slight I see."

Lucio did not dignify the comment with a reply, but he forced himself to act as he always had before for the rest of the ball. If Gabriel saw him, it might complicate matters in that arena, but Lady Merydith was a far more real threat. If she hurt him badly, he could lose guests who wanted him for his perfect body. The handlers would charge an extra fee for any damage, but that wouldn't restore Lucio's looks.

"You are quite the coquet tonight," Lord Ian commented when he encountered Lucio in the crowd some time later.

"I am what I am," Lucio replied simply, although he would have been anything else at the moment if he'd had the choice. "I may smile at them, but they know I am yours for the night. You are the envy of everyone in the room because while they might look, might even touch, only you will get to possess."

"If you keep saying things like that, I shall have no choice but to whisk you away again," Lord Ian teased. "Is that what you want, pretty boy?"

"I live to serve," Lucio said, hiding his increasing resentment. He knew he would spend the night in Lord Ian's bed, but at least then Gabriel would have left and would not be around to see it.

"And I am so fortunate that you do," Lord Ian agreed. "I think I shall keep you on my arm for awhile, to remind everyone that you *are* mine tonight. Some of them have gotten a little too friendly with you on my coin. Come, let us mingle."

11

GABRIEL returned to the ballroom feeling more than a little lost without Cressida on his arm. She had been his guide, his touchstone all evening, and now she was nowhere in sight. He wondered if he should search for her, but she had made her opinion of him very clear and he didn't want to force his presence on her unwanted. Even worse was the knowledge that somewhere in the house, Lucio was with Lord Stuart doing who knew what manner of things. Things Gabriel wished he were the one doing with Lucio, if he was honest. They had done nothing more than kiss, and Gabriel intended to keep it that way until he was sure he could live with this new reality. It would be hard enough to walk away after the two intoxicating kisses they had shared. If they shared more, he was not sure he would ever be able to walk away, even if his resentment of Lucio's life became more than he could bear.

Rounding the corner into a room set up with tables for whist and bridge, Gabriel came face to face with Lord Stuart, Lucio on his arm. Gabriel was sure his eyes were wild as he tried to decide where to look. He wanted to devour Lucio with his gaze, but he feared his expression would give too much away, especially when he caught sight of Lucio's swollen lips. Fortunately, Lord Stuart claimed his attention. "Are you enjoying your evening so far, Blackstone?"

"I am, my Lord," Gabriel said. "It has proved most… educational."

Lord Stuart laughed. "I'm not sure that's a word I'd use to describe a ball. Ah, but I am remiss in my manners. Mister Blackstone, my companion for the evening. Lucio, Mister Gabriel Blackstone, inventor extraordinaire."

"It's a pleasure to meet you, Mister Blackstone," Lucio said, extending his hand for Gabriel to shake. Even with two layers of cloth between them, the contract sent sparks along Gabriel's arm, making Gabriel want to feel that touch again on his bare skin. "Lord Stuart has regaled me with tales of his new pet. I might have to impose on you to listen to a few of my own ideas."

"Another time," Lord Stuart interjected, his good-natured smile remaining in place.

"Of course," Lucio said smoothly.

"You seem to have lost your companion, Blackstone," Lord Stuart added. "Did you wear out our lovely Cressida?"

"No, of course not," Gabriel stuttered. "She... she stepped out for a moment."

"Perhaps you should find her," Lucio suggested. "Not all aristocrats are as noble as Lord Stuart. It would be a shame if some harm befell her because she had strayed from your side."

Gabriel's eyes widened. "Surely not here at a ball."

Lucio shrugged. "Some people see an unattached companion and have no care for their dignity."

"Did someone importune you while you wandered without me?" Lord Stuart asked. Gabriel fumed inwardly that the aristocrat had the right to ask the question burning inside Gabriel, but at least he would be able to hear Lucio's answer.

"Of course not," Lucio replied, "but you introduced me at dinner as your companion for the evening. Cressida did not receive such an introduction, either as your companion or as Mister Blackstone's. Anyone who has not seen them together could easily believe she was here in search of a guest for the evening, and there are some who would not believe her when she said otherwise. They have not bothered me tonight, but I have a long memory."

Lord Stuart frowned. "You will tell me after my guests have departed who they are and I will see they are no longer welcome in my salon. For now, however, I think Lucio speaks wisely, Blackstone. Find your companion and keep her close for the rest of the evening."

Gabriel bowed slightly and withdrew, concern for Cressida weighing heavily on his conscience. He did not care for her the way he did for Lucio, but she had been charming and indeed had helped him significantly. He owed her more than to let her be accosted because he had angered her. He had to fight not to look back over his shoulder as Lord Stuart and Lucio went the other way.

As he searched for Cressida, he mulled over Lucio's apparent ability to separate their public and private interactions. He had sensed none of the interest that had been so apparent in private as they spoke just now. If he didn't know better, he would swear he had spoken to two different men.

Lucio had seemed perfectly content on Lord Stuart's arm, his mouth showing signs of recent activity, signs Gabriel's tender kisses had surely not caused. It was disturbingly easy to imagine Lucio on his knees, the perfect bow of his lips opening to accept a hard cock. Anger swirled inside him again, but he tamped it down, trying to follow Cressida's advice and stop torturing himself with thoughts of Lucio with other men.

He made his way through the main ballroom as well as the drawing room, where the ladies sat fanning themselves when the crush in the ballroom became overwhelming, but he saw no sign of Cressida. He had nearly given up when he caught sight of the train of a purple dress disappearing onto the terrace. Swiftly he followed her, catching her as she started to descend into the garden below. "Are you sure you should wander alone?"

"What do you care?" Cressida snapped.

"I don't want you to be hurt," Gabriel said. "I would never forgive myself if any harm befell you because I had made you angry with me."

"But you don't care about the harm you'll do to Lucio with your attitude," Cressida retorted.

"Please, Miss Cressida," Gabriel said. "Can you at least accept that it will take me some time to grow accustomed to the idea?"

"Don't call me Miss Cressida," she ordered. "It feels like you're making fun of me. I'm simply Cressida, a worthless companion."

"You aren't worthless," Gabriel disagreed. "I can't argue about the companion part, but you aren't worthless. You couldn't defend Lucio the way you do if you were worthless."

"For all the good it did either of us," Cressida muttered. "I slapped you."

"I deserved it."

"That won't matter if you report me," Cressida said. "I'll be ruined."

"I'm hardly going to report you when doing so would endanger Lucio as well, given what we were talking about when it happened," Gabriel reminded her.

"They wouldn't care what we were talking about. A word from you and I would be banned from ever working as a companion again," Cressida said.

"They won't hear it from me," Gabriel promised. "Who would help me if I did something that awful?"

"Really?" Cressida said, her face hopeful. "You won't tell?"

"I won't tell," Gabriel promised. "Will you help me again? Not with Lucio. You've done more than enough there already. Will you help me finish out the evening on a positive note? I suddenly have the need to earn a great deal of money."

Cressida looked at him consideringly, the silence stretching so long Gabriel feared she would say no. "Yes, I'll help you."

"WHERE are you going, pretty boy?"

Lucio froze in the process of leaving Lord Ian's bed. "I had thought to fetch a damp cloth so we do not soil the bedding."

"Don't bother," Lord Ian said, tugging on Lucio's hand until he returned to the bed. "I can think of more interesting ways for you to clean me up, and by the time you're done with that, I'll be ready to get you dirty all over again. Besides, I like the idea of my spunk leaking out of your pert little ass. It means you're mine for tonight."

Lucio let Lord Ian guide his head to the softened shaft and obediently licked and sucked it clean. He could feel the stickiness between his thighs as the older man had described, but while the thought and Lucio's actions appeared to be rousing the aristocrat for another round, the entire situation left Lucio cold. He could handle the sex—he'd been having sex for a living for eight years—but most of the time his guests didn't bother to pretend it was anything more than a business transaction for him and a momentary pleasure for them. They didn't bother with a bed or with any niceties other than enough lubrication to keep from hurting him when they penetrated him. They spilled inside him, pulled out and got dressed, and left him to put himself back together in peace. Even Lord Ian rarely took more time with him than that, although he was more affectionate and teasing with Lucio than most of the aristocrats who bedded him. Something was different tonight—besides the fact that Lord Ian had purchased not only his evening but the entire night as well—but Lucio didn't know what, and he didn't like that at all.

He lifted his head when he had licked every drop of semen from Lord Ian's cock, balls, and belly, waiting to see what his guest wanted next. Lord Ian sat up, plumping the pillows behind his back. "Come sit on my lap," he directed. He reached for a small vial on the table next to the bed and poured yellow powder from it into the glass of wine he had carried up with him. "We will talk for a few minutes while the saffron does its work, and then I shall show you what real bed sport feels like."

Lucio kept a neutral expression at Lord Ian's reference to the popular aphrodisiac. Lucio had no idea if the powder worked, but it would not matter as long as Lord Ian believed it. Straddling his guest's lap, he positioned the half-hard cock at his entrance and worked it inside him until he was seated against Lord Ian's groin. The position, rare as it was, for his guests usually preferred the anonymity of taking him from behind, let him study his guest's features. In his late fifties, Lord Ian remained hale and hearty, his face only lightly lined beneath its shock of white hair. His body had none of the paunch that so plagued many older aristocrats, giving him the appearance of a much younger man. Lucio had always considered himself fortunate to have the patronage of the handsome, generous man, but now he felt all the indignity of his station as Lord Ian toyed with his nipples idly.

"Did you enjoy the ball?" Lord Ian asked, shifting on the bed slightly, the movement stirring his slowly hardening cock in Lucio's passage.

"I did," Lucio replied, not entirely sure where the conversation was going. "I always enjoy the chance to be on your arm."

"Yet you seemed distracted tonight," Lord Ian pressed, his fingers pinching a little more deliberately. "Your body was here with me, but I'm not so sure your mind was. Did someone else catch your eye?"

"No one could hold a candle to you tonight," Lucio lied, hoping he sounded convincing. "If I seemed distracted, I was merely wondering how Cressida was enjoying her evening. We have been friends for a long time, as I'm sure you know."

"I do know," Lord Ian said, his hands settling on Lucio's hips and encouraging him to move. "That's one of the reasons why I selected her for tonight. That, and I thought she would be a good guide for Blackstone. Did you have a chance to speak with him at all?"

"Only when you introduced us," Lucio replied, his cheeks burning as the memory of Gabriel's kiss assailed him. He only hoped the dim light of the gas lamp flickering on the other side of the room would hide the color or that Lord Ian would attribute it to arousal rather than to embarrassment. His thigh muscles burned as he rode Lord Ian's cock slowly. It was easier when it was hard and fast because it was over quickly. Lucio could see the signs of arousal in Lord Ian's dilated pupils and tightening nipples as well as feel it in the cock lengthening inside him, but the desire was nowhere near a fever pitch yet, and the aristocrat seemed in no hurry to speed things along, leaving Lucio to pant through the aching muscles and hope Lord

Ian would find the apparent signs of his own interest arousing rather than off-putting.

"That's a shame," Lord Ian said, his voice rough. "He is quite an interesting man for a merchant."

"He would have to be for you to invite him to a ball," Lucio said, wishing Lord Ian would change the subject. The last thing he wanted was to have Gabriel on his mind while bedding another man. Thinking about him was equal parts pain and pleasure in the best of circumstances. Thinking about him while pleasuring anyone else was pure torture. He forced his mind back to the business at hand and how to arouse Lord Ian's desire faster. He squeezed his internal muscles as he rose and fell on the impaling shaft, winning a slight hiss from the older man. Bending forward slightly, he applied his lips to the roseate nipples peeking through the dusting of silver hair on Lord Ian's chest. The position did not provide quite as much stimulation to Lord Ian's erection, but hopefully the attention to the taut buds would more than make up for that.

"Enough," Lord Ian said after a few minutes of the new position. "Hands and knees now."

Lucio hid a sigh of relief, moving as directed and spreading his legs wide so his stretched hole was easily visible. When Lord Ian did not immediately penetrate him, he reached behind him and spread his cheeks in blatant encouragement.

"Dirty boy," Lord Ian scolded, "trying to tempt me." He pushed Lucio's hands aside, slapping his buttocks just hard enough to sting. It wasn't a new sensation. Lucio had been trained to accept all manner of pleasure and pain from his clients, but it was the first time Lord Ian had treated him this way. He buried his face in the bedcovers and wriggled as he had been taught, the gesture suggesting either pain or a request for more, whichever the guest wanted it to mean. Lord Ian's slaps didn't hurt like some of his guests' spankings had done, but they added to his sense of degradation. He had no idea why Lord Ian was punishing him tonight, but he wasn't about to ask and suggest a guilty conscience.

About the time the repetition of blows moved from light stings to painful prickling, Lord Ian stopped, parting Lucio's cheeks and plunging inside, pounding into Lucio roughly. The companion grunted into the quilt but made no move to reposition himself more comfortably. The sooner Lord Ian found his release, the sooner Lucio could perhaps rest. A few moments later, he felt the hot flood of Lord Ian's ejaculation inside him. Lord Ian pulled out immediately, his hand resting heavily on Lucio's backside. "Don't move yet, pretty boy. I want to enjoy the sight of you for a little longer before I rest."

Lucio bit back a groan of frustration at the humiliation of being put on display this way. He bit down the anger that roiled within him. Lord Ian was not treating him any worse than he had been treated a hundred times. He had simply come to expect better treatment from the man. He could feel the sticky fluid running down his legs, leaving him feeling dirty. He shuddered to think of what Gabriel would think if he could see Lucio now.

"You can't possibly be cold, pretty boy," Lord Ian said. "It's as hot in here as everywhere else."

"Merely anticipating what else you have planned for me tonight, my Lord," Lucio lied, the words as bitter as they were practiced.

"I'm sure I can think of something," Lord Ian replied, running his fingers up Lucio's crease and teasing around his hole, "but first we will rest. I don't have to return you until noon tomorrow. That's plenty of time for a few more rounds. I shall send you back well used this time."

"It shall be as you desire, my Lord." Lucio did not take the comment about resting as permission to move. He had no desire to endure another spanking or to be reported for disobedience.

"You cannot rest like that. Lie here beside me," Lord Ian directed. "And what did I tell you about calling me 'my Lord' in private?"

"You said I should call you Lord Ian," Lucio said, moving to put his head on the other pillow. He would not sleep, needing to be ready for whatever Lord Ian demanded, but he would at least be more comfortable this way.

"And yet you persist with the 'my Lords' tonight," Lord Ian chided. "Should I punish you again?"

"If it pleases you, Lord Ian," Lucio forced himself to say, hoping the aristocrat would let it pass. His buttocks still stung from the earlier spanking, and while he knew he could endure another if he had to, he preferred to avoid it if possible.

"Not tonight," Lord Ian said after a moment. "You should rest now because I intend to make good use of you later."

Lucio closed his eyes, pretending to sleep. Within seconds, slumber had overtaken him.

Lord Ian stroked the black hair back from Lucio's sweaty brow. "You deserve better than this, pretty boy. I only wish I knew what that was."

THE sun had been up for several hours already, but Gabriel had yet to make it out of his bedroom and downstairs to the workshop. He should have spent the quiet hours alone working on his flying chair, but his mind and heart were elsewhere, focused on Lucio as they had been from the moment he caught sight of the companion at Lord Stuart's ball the night before. His heart ached whenever he thought of that pale, beatific face framed by black curls, so elegant, almost too perfect to be true. He licked his lips, imagining he could still taste the freshness of Lucio's mouth against his, except Lucio's mouth wouldn't taste fresh this morning. It would taste like Lord Stuart because no one could have such a beautiful companion in his bed all night long and not take advantage of those full, beautiful lips.

Gabriel had promised Cressida he would not obsess over Lucio's profession, over the things they could not control, and he hoped it would be easier when it was nameless men and women doing things to Lucio's body, but Lord Stuart was a known quantity, and it was all too easy to imagine the aristocrat doing to Lucio all the things Gabriel wished he had the right to do.

"Gabriel?"

Caleb's voice brought Gabriel out of his musings. He hadn't even heard the door to the workshop open, but clearly his friend had arrived. Taking a deep breath and pushing aside thoughts of Lucio and what he was doing at the moment, Gabriel descended the stairs to the showroom of their workshop. "Good morning, Caleb."

"I think you made an impression last night," Caleb said.

Gabriel frowned. "What makes you say that? You weren't there."

Caleb held up a handful of cards. "These were all in the basket inside our mail slot this morning. It's barely even ten and we already have—" he paused to count "—twelve invitations for you to call."

Gabriel plucked one of the cards from Caleb's hand, turning it over. *Lord Bicksley requests you call at your earliest convenience.* He selected another one. *Lady Palmer requests your presence at tea on Tuesday to discuss a commission.*

"I had no idea," he murmured as he continued to read. "I mean, I spoke with a number of people, but I had no idea they were so serious about the possibility of buying things from us."

"Apparently Lord Stuart is a trendsetter," Caleb said with a shrug. "What kinds of things were they asking about? More dogs?"

"No one else mentioned a pet, although that would be a lot easier the second time around since we know how to do it now," Gabriel said. "Mostly it was things like fans to cool the room, mechanical lifts, and other such things. Nothing terribly difficult, at least not that they mentioned last night. I suppose I should start sorting these and figure out when I can call on them all."

"You'll need a calendar if this keeps up," Caleb teased. "Just make sure your newfound social life doesn't keep you from doing your job here in the lab."

"You're welcome to do the visiting for me," Gabriel offered. Having Cressida at his side had helped last night, but he would not have her assistance as he attended future teas and salons. He only hoped his potential clients would forgive any gaffes he committed. "I can stay here and work."

"Oh, no," Caleb said with an emphatic shake of his head. "You're the darling of society, not me. I'll go take an inventory of our supplies so we can see what we have and what we'll need to start making fans and lifts."

Gabriel followed Caleb into the other room even as another card fell through the mail slot into the basket. He ignored it for the moment, Cressida's advice about finding a friend to talk to echoing in his head. He only wished he knew how to raise the subject with Caleb when his friend saw nothing wrong with Lucio's life and would call Gabriel a fool for wanting more than a few purchased hours with the companion in his bed. "Am I a fool to wish I hadn't gone last night?"

"What?" Caleb said. "What are you talking about?"

"All the attention. I feel like I'm in a fishbowl, surrounded by people staring in at me. I don't want to be a curiosity." Gabriel struggled to explain the sense of being out of place. "Everyone was polite to me last night, but I was terribly uncomfortable the entire time, always worried I'd make some unforgivable mistake."

"You obviously didn't, or they wouldn't be summoning you now," Caleb pointed out. "What was it like, anyway?"

"Everything was larger than life," Gabriel said. "The men's suits made the one Lord Stuart purchased for me look plain, and the ladies' dresses came in every color of the rainbow. I've never seen so many jewels in one place. I thought the ballroom was crowded before dinner, but the meal did give me a chance to talk to the people around me for more than a minute or two. Then after dinner, more people arrived until it was almost impossible to walk from one room to another. I understand now why they call them crushes."

"And your companion?" Caleb asked.

"She was a lovely woman who made sure I didn't embarrass myself," Gabriel said, smiling a little as he thought of Cressida.

"And you didn't take advantage of her charms any more than you did the first companion you met," Caleb said with a knowing shake of his head. "Sometimes I think your priorities are all backward, Gabe. You need to live a little."

"Lord Stuart didn't hire Cressida to entertain me," Gabriel insisted. "He hired her to keep me from making a fool of myself. She did her job admirably since, as you pointed out, we are flooded with requests this morning."

"Have you thought any more about hiring a companion for yourself?" Caleb asked. "I've given up trying to get you to look for a lover, but you're human still, the last time I checked. You have needs that aren't being met, and that isn't healthy. I was talking to Bernard the other day, and he said new medical research suggests that a man of our age should have an orgasm at least twice a week to keep everything cleared out and in good working order."

Gabriel sighed. They had met Bernard Headley, doctor of medicine, when they opened up shop. Perhaps five years older than Gabriel and his friends, the doctor had been quick to welcome them to the neighborhood and to provide medical services when they injured themselves in the workshop. Over time, he had become nearly as close a friend as Caleb and Andrew. "And so because Bernard says so, you now think I should hire a companion to see to my needs. Where, exactly, am I supposed to get fifteen gold twice a week?"

Caleb gestured to the pile of cards. "I'm sure your new friends will pay you that and more. They're aristocrats. They have money to burn. You can charge them whatever you like, and they'll pay it."

"That doesn't mean I should overcharge them," Gabriel protested. "If they realize I'm doing that, they could take their business elsewhere and tell others to do the same."

"I'm not suggesting you gouge them," Caleb said. "Just add a little extra. If they ask about the difference of a coin or five, you can remind them that they're paying for top quality and sometimes that means paying top price."

Gabriel was unconvinced, but he didn't argue. He would be the one setting the prices, after all, not Caleb, so he would charge what he knew was fair and hope it was enough to pay for some of Lucio's time. Lucio had promised to visit on his own time to commission his own project, but Gabriel wouldn't hold his breath for that. He didn't doubt Lucio's sincerity, but he wasn't sure the handlers would accept that use of Lucio's tips.

He went back into the outer room and started sorting the cards between those that had specific times mentioned and those that simply requested his presence or had no note at all. He looked down at his stained leathers and wondered how much his new popularity would cost him in terms of clothes. Lord Stuart had paid for his evening suit, but that would hardly be appropriate to wear to an afternoon tea. He could wear the good leather coat and breeches he had worn the night he met Lucio, but it would not be long before everyone recognized that as well. He sighed, feeling like he was banging his head against a wall. He needed money to be fashionable, but he wouldn't have that money until he'd completed at least a few commissions. His thoughts turned to the tip Lord Stuart had given him, which he had set aside to use in buying an hour of Lucio's time. With that gold, he could get at least two new waistcoats and probably a jacket as well.

Heart falling, he called to Caleb in the other room. "I'm going out for a few minutes. I need to see how soon Reading can get me some new clothes. If I have to go out in society, I'd better look the part."

"I'll mind the shop," Caleb said, coming back into the room. "Andrew will be here soon as well and can finish the inventory." He paused, staring at Gabriel intently. "Are you all right? You have the oddest look on your face."

"It's nothing," Gabriel said, trying to smooth his expression. "I'd planned to use the tip Lord Stuart gave me for something other than clothes, but they'll be a far better investment than what I'd intended."

"You were going to use the tip to see the companion again, weren't you?" Caleb asked.

"It doesn't matter now," Gabriel said, summoning a smile. "I can't go calling in my faded leathers, so a visit to the pleasure palaces will have to wait until we've impressed a few more aristocrats."

He didn't wait for Caleb's reply. The last thing he wanted was pity.

LUCIO stood in the center of his bedroom, so tired he could barely even make himself undress. With a sigh, he pulled at his cravat, knowing he would sleep more easily if he bathed before he rested. He did not even turn around when the door opened behind him.

"You reek of sex," Cressida said bluntly. "How many times did he use you?"

Lucio continued stripping, uncaring of Cressida's presence. He didn't have anything she hadn't seen a thousand times or more. "Including having me fellate him during the ball? Six, I think, and he didn't let me clean up in between."

"He isn't a young man anymore. How did he manage that?" Cressida asked curiously.

Lucio shrugged and pulled off his shirt. "He was taking saffron off and on. He may have taken other things as well."

He bent to remove his shoes, groaning as the motion pulled at muscles overused the night before.

"Are you hurt?" Cressida asked.

"Just stiff and a little raw," Lucio replied, kicking off his trousers and padding naked to the bathroom. Cressida followed behind him. "He isn't a small man, and after the ball was over, he wasn't interested in my mouth."

Lucio turned the water on hard, stepping into the tub and sighing as the hot water eased his sore muscles. "Would you be a doll, Cressida, and get some of the lemon wash you use? I seem to be out, and I really need to feel clean right now."

"I'll be right back," Cressida said, leaning over to press a kiss to his forehead before disappearing back out the door. Lucio sighed again, scrubbing at his face with his hands, the scent of Lord Ian's musk assailing him from having stroked the aristocrat to climax all over his chest this morning. Grimacing, he reached for the soap, rubbing his hands together until they were covered with foam and all hint of any scent but the soap was gone. He would scrub the rest of his body the same way in a few minutes, but he needed to relax first. He had, to his surprise, fallen asleep in Lord Ian's bed, but he had not slept well, unaccustomed as he was to having another body in bed next to him. Each time Lord Ian moved in his sleep, it had startled Lucio awake, fear gripping him that the aristocrat wanted something he was not ready to give.

Lucio scratched absently at the dried semen on his skin, watching it flake off into the water. Feeling suddenly dirty again, he grabbed a washrag and attacked the remnants of Lord Ian's passion, wanting to erase every sign of their intercourse.

"Easy does it," Cressida scolded, coming back into the room. "Don't rub yourself raw. You won't please any guests that way."

"I don't care," Lucio said, but Cressida tugged the rag from his hand before he could resume his scrubbing.

"Don't say that," Cressida warned. "I know last night must have been miserable for you, wanting to be with Gabriel and being forced to stay at Lord Stuart's side, but you can't go down that road. You can't stop doing your job. If you can't please the aristocrats like Lord Stuart, they'll send you to the breeding barns, or use you for the clients who like to break their toys. You don't have to enjoy it, but you have to do it."

Lucio winced as she cleaned his buttocks, the skin tender from the spanking the night before and from all of Lord Ian's attentions. "Did he spank you?" Cressida asked sympathetically.

Lucio nodded. "He said I was being a naughty boy, tempting him to fuck me." He snorted. "Like I'd have anything to do with him or any of the others if I had a choice. Sometimes I think the real lure of having someone buy your contract is simply knowing you'll only have to have sex as often as your owner can get it up rather than as often as the handlers can rent you out."

"I know," Cressida said sympathetically, "but you wouldn't want that to happen now anyway because if you had a single owner, you wouldn't have any chance of slipping away to see Gabriel."

"Did he find you last night?" Lucio asked.

Cressida nodded. "He did, and he was very kind in spite of my temper."

Lucio raised an eyebrow. "What did you say to him?"

She flushed. "It wasn't what I said, but what I did."

"What did you do?" Lucio asked, curious despite the sudden niggle of jealousy. Surely Cressida wouldn't have done anything sexual knowing how Lucio felt about Gabriel.

"I slapped him."

"You did what?" Lucio demanded, turning to face her. "What possessed you to do such a stupid thing? You could be severely punished for that."

"I know," Cressida said. "I knew it the minute I did it, but he made me so angry. I reacted instead of thinking."

"What did he say?"

Cressida paused for a moment. "I'm not sure I should tell you. You're already blue enough this morning without me adding to it."

Lucio's face fell. "He doesn't want to see me again."

"No, it's not that," Cressida exclaimed. "He was jealous of Lord Stuart, even after promising me earlier he could live with the reality of your life. I kept telling him to focus on the good things, like the fact that you had kissed him, instead of on things he couldn't change, and he kept going back to the fact that you were with Lord Stuart. I lost my temper. He found me later, I guess after you saw him, and promised me he'd stop acting like a fool. He was very much in demand the rest of the evening, so perhaps he'll soon have the funds to visit with you."

"I wasn't planning on making him wait," Lucio admitted, reaching for the lemon wash she had brought and using it to rinse his stinging passage so he would feel as clean on the inside as he finally did on the outside. "I have money to spend as much as the next person. I don't see why I can't commission something as well, and since it must be done to my exacting specifications, I'm sure it will require me to visit his workshop several times."

Cressida laughed. "You are a devious one, paying him so he can pay for you."

Lucio rose from the bath and wrapped a drying sheet around him. Reaching up to his ear, he removed the fob Lord Ian had given him that morning. "And if I were to happen to lose this or some other bauble at the same time, that would be even more money in his pocket that he could put toward paying for my time."

"How much do you have saved up in gold and jewels?" Cressida asked. "If you have enough and can smuggle it to him, he could use it to buy your contract."

"I don't have that much," Lucio said, "but I'll give him every coin I have if he thinks he can raise the rest."

"It won't happen overnight," Cressida said thoughtfully, "but as many people as approached him last night, it might not be as impossible as it seemed before. What is on your calendar for today?"

"Nothing, I hope," Lucio said. "I'm honestly not sure I could stand another cock inside me yet."

"Not even Gabriel's?" Cressida teased.

Lucio scowled at her. "I don't want him to think of me that way," he said after a few moments. "I want him to see me as more than a body to use for his release."

"He does," Cressida promised. "You didn't see him last night. I'm not saying he doesn't want to bed you because he wouldn't have been so jealous if he didn't, but he won't ever use you the way the guests do because he sees you as so much more than a companion."

13

A NAP and a hot meal having done much to restore Lucio's usual good humor, he lingered over dressing, trying to choose the perfect outfit for calling upon an inventor to commission a mechanical fan. He wanted to blend in so Gabriel's friends would not immediately peg him as a companion and dismiss him if Gabriel wasn't there, but he also wanted to look his best in case Gabriel was there. He settled on a pair of fawn-colored linen trousers, not too tight but cut to be flattering, and a conservative gray vest beneath his frock coat. He would probably still be out of place given the leather Gabriel had worn their first evening together, but at least his choice of clothes would not immediately proclaim him a companion. He was still fiddling with his cravat when Cressida appeared in his doorway, already dressed in eveningwear. "Going out?" she asked.

"So are you, it would appear," Lucio observed.

"I suspect I am the main course at Lord McAllister's orgy tonight," she replied. "There is nothing like being fucked repeatedly for hours on end."

"Maybe his Lordship will keep you for himself," Lucio said. "You certainly look beautiful enough that he might not want to share."

"All of my appointments for tomorrow have been taken off my calendar," Cressida said with a shake of her head. "They know I'll be too sore to work tomorrow."

"I'm sorry," Lucio said. "Try to relax and make the best of it. Come let me know when you get back, even if you have to wake me. I want to know you're home safely."

"I will," Cressida promised. "You be careful as well."

"I'm not doing anything dangerous," Lucio assured her, "merely going to commission my fan. If it goes well, I'll buy one for you as well."

The look Cressida gave him suggested she thought he was underestimating the danger, but he didn't argue with her. He didn't want to think about what might happen if the handlers began to suspect he wanted more from Gabriel than his inventions. He would worry about that later. For now, he had a fan to order and hopefully an inventor to impress. Deciding he had done all he could with his appearance, he walked out with Cressida, informing the handlers of his intentions and his expected time of return. If they were surprised at the amount of time he said he would be gone, they did not say, nor did they insist he return earlier.

Lucio hailed a hansom, waving goodbye to Cressida as they went in opposite directions, Cressida toward the posh section of town while Lucio's mechanical cab turned toward the less desirable part of the city. The trip took longer than Lucio had anticipated, making him worry the workshop would already be closed for the night, but when the cab finally reached his destination, lights still blazed through the open windows. Breathing a sigh of relief, Lucio paid the driver and knocked at the door.

A man Lucio didn't recognize opened the door. "Can I help you, sir?"

"I was hoping Mister Blackstone was in," Lucio said. "I met him last night at Lord Stuart's ball and wanted to speak with him about a commission."

"You're in luck," the blond man said. "He just stepped back in. I'll fetch him if you'd like to take a seat."

The man indicated a rickety wooden chair covered in dust. "I'll stand."

The blond shrugged as if to say it was Lucio's choice to be uncomfortable and disappeared into the back room. Left alone, Lucio took the opportunity to study the workshop. The rough-hewn display cases held a few completed items, but it was quickly obvious to Lucio that this was not the heart of the business. Gabriel might discuss business across the heavy oak counter, but he worked somewhere else.

"How can I help you, Mister... Lucio!"

Lucio looked up and smiled tentatively. "I told you I'd come."

"Caleb didn't tell me it was you."

"I didn't give my name," Lucio explained. "I wasn't sure what you'd told your friends, and, well, I really do want to see about having you make something for me. Otherwise the handlers will get suspicious if I keep coming back here."

"Come in the back," Gabriel said, lifting a section of the counter so Lucio could pass through. "We can talk about the commission where we'll be more comfortable."

"And you'll show me your lab?"

Gabriel laughed. "You didn't come to see me. You only wanted to see my machines."

Lucio blanched. "No, of course not," he babbled. "Forget I even mentioned—"

"Lucio, stop," Gabriel interrupted, catching Lucio's hand before he could go through the door into the work area of the shop. "I was teasing. But even if I wasn't, I'm not a guest, remember? You don't have to say things just to please me."

"It's such an ingrained habit," Lucio admitted, not sure how to act if he couldn't fall back on his training. "I don't know any other way to be."

"Talk to me the way you talk to Cressida," Gabriel suggested.

Lucio was pretty sure that figured high on the list of bad ideas. Gabriel almost certainly did not want to know the kind of intimate details Lucio shared with Cressida without thought, but he nodded, not wanting to argue about his profession during the few stolen minutes they had together.

The back room of the workshop was far more what Lucio expected: bits of wire and pipe, gears and levers scattered around the room, partially completed projects on every surface. Besides the blond, another dark-haired man worked at one of the benches. Lucio assumed they must be Deahl and Lambert, Gabriel's friends and employees. He did not press for an introduction, not sure he wanted to hear whatever story Gabriel would concoct to explain his presence.

Gabriel led him through the workshop to a third, much smaller room with a plain wooden table, four chairs, a cast-iron stove, and a few cabinets. He shut the door behind them, leaving the other men in the workshop. The moment the door shut, Gabriel opened his arms. Lucio moved into them without hesitation, his mouth tilting up for a kiss that Gabriel was quick to give him. "Every time you leave me, I worry I'll never feel this again," Gabriel whispered, his lips brushing Lucio's as he spoke.

"If I had the choice, I wouldn't walk away," Lucio said, pulling back to read Gabriel's gaze. "Perhaps I shouldn't tell you this, but I spent all of last night wishing I was with you. I hated myself for doing it because I felt like I sullied our time together by thinking of you when I was with someone else, but my thoughts kept wandering back to you."

Gabriel's face darkened, but he pulled Lucio back into his arms, holding him close. "If thinking of me keeps you safe and sane, then it will make me a happy man indeed. Was… was Lord Stuart good to you?"

Lucio shrugged, not wanting to talk about the aristocrat or any other guest when he was in Gabriel's arms. "No better or worse than anyone else."

"Some day," Gabriel swore, "when you trust me, when you're ready, I'll show you how a man treats a lover. I'll kiss and caress and love you until you go out of your mind with it, but only when you're ready."

Lucio smiled sadly. "You do realize that day may never come, don't you? I spend so much time having sex that the moments of peace are far more enjoyable than anything they do to me."

"I'd have to be dead not to be roused by your closeness," Gabriel replied, "but I'm not some rutting animal, incapable of control. Nothing will ever happen between us that you don't want as fully as I do. You are *not* a convenience to me. If that means all we ever do is kiss, so be it. I will see to my other needs myself."

Lucio had a sudden flash of stroking Gabriel to completion and realized with surprise that the thought was not as neutral or repulsive as such thoughts usually were. He wasn't ready to act on that impulse just yet, but it gave him hope that someday he would be. For now, he would revel in the freedom to kiss Gabriel without worrying about being called away. Gabriel tasted slightly of coffee, making Lucio wonder if he shared a taste for the bitter drink that was sometimes all that kept Lucio going through a long day or night.

"Gabriel?"

Lucio felt like cursing the interruption, but it would do no good. He rested his head against Gabriel's neck. "What have you told them about me?"

"Just a minute, Caleb," Gabriel called through the door. "Nothing. They wouldn't understand and would tell me to fuck you out of my system and be done with it. They aren't bad men. They don't see the shades of gray the way I do. I'm not ashamed of you, so if you want me to go in there and tell them who you are and how I feel about you, I will."

Lucio shook his head. "No, that's fine. I'm content to simply be another customer as far as they're concerned. I really do want that mechanical fan we talked about last night."

"Then we should call Caleb and Andrew in here to discuss it with us. They couldn't run a business to save their lives, but they are creative, hard-working inventors. They will have suggestions to make, and if they don't now, they certainly will when we start working on it."

Lucio nodded. "Would you mind if I stayed here while you tell them whatever you choose to tell them about who I am? I'd rather not hear their reactions."

Gabriel kissed Lucio again. "If they can't treat you as a person rather than a companion, they'll stay out there. I won't have you belittled in my home."

"You live here too?"

"Upstairs. Someday, when you're ready, I'll show it to you."

Lucio paced the kitchen nervously as he waited for Gabriel to return with Deahl and Lambert or to return and say they wouldn't accept him. He hated how nervous he was when all his life he had refused to let the opinions of others touch him. He could hear voices in the other room, but not what they were saying. Nobody seemed to be yelling, though, and that was a good sign.

Gabriel had been gone so long that Lucio started to worry he wouldn't come back when the door to the kitchen swung open again and all three men walked in, sitting down at the table with an ease that suggested they often sat here, to talk or eat or simply be together. Lucio slipped into the extra chair, fortunately next to Gabriel, and waited.

"Caleb Deahl, Andrew Lambert," Gabriel said, indicating the two men in turn, "meet Lucio. Lucio, my friends and employees." He reached for Lucio's hand and squeezed gently. "And the reason we met in the first place."

"Nice to meet you," Lucio said, offering his hand. He had no idea if they would take his hand or reject the advance. As the lower caste, he was expected to offer. It was up to them to decide. Not that he had really given Gabriel the chance to reject him when they first met, but he knew Gabriel would not have even if he had approached him more typically. Deahl—the blond—didn't hesitate, although he did dust his hand on his trousers first. Lambert—the brunet—looked a little more skeptical, but he followed Deahl's lead, shaking Lucio's hand in turn.

"Gabriel says you want a fan," Deahl said, getting directly down to business. Lucio nodded, a little intimidated by the gruff demeanor. Deahl was not a guest to be cajoled or seduced out of his bad mood, which left Lucio slightly unsure how to proceed.

"What size room is it for?" Lambert asked, drawing Lucio's attention.

Lucio looked around the kitchen, trying to compare it to his bedroom. "Perhaps half again the size of this room," he said after a moment, "but definitely smaller than either of the other two rooms in the workshop."

"If you can give us exact measurements, it will help us make sure the fan can adequately circulate the air in the whole room," Gabriel explained. "Your estimation is enough to get us started, but the more details we have, the better the end result will be."

"I'll measure them as soon as I get home and bring them back within a day or two," Lucio promised, trying to remember what was on his calendar for the next few days.

"Where would you want to put it?" Deahl asked. "Are you thinking in front of a window or would you rather have it near your bed?"

"We could design a window mount for it," Gabriel said, getting excited. The sight sent tingles through Lucio's body. This, for the first time, was the real Gabriel, confident in his abilities, stretching his mind. "How many windows do you have in your room?"

"Two," Lucio said. "Why?"

Gabriel didn't seem to hear the question, jotting down notes on a piece of paper. "If we set it so it blows out instead of in, it could pull air in from the other window and cool the entire room that way."

Lambert shook his head. "That'll only work if the windows are on opposite sides of the room. If they're closer than that, it'll just cool the space between them and not the bed." He looked at Lucio expectantly.

"They're on the same wall," Lucio said. "There's a few feet between them, but not a lot."

Gabriel pushed the paper toward Lucio. "Sketch out a floor plan of your room. It doesn't have to be exactly to scale, but just to give us an idea where everything is. Include doorways, windows, and anything that generally doesn't move or that you don't want to move, like your bed or a desk or anything like that."

Lucio took the quill and dipped it in the ink, picturing the relative dimensions of his room and trying to transmit them accurately to the paper. He added the door to the corridor and the door to the bathing area as well as the two windows along the outside wall. He sketched in his bed and desk, with a notation that it could be moved if necessary. He added his armoire on the wall next to the door to the bathing area. "Everything else is small enough to be moved if needed," he said, pushing the paper back to the three inventors.

They studied the drawing for a few minutes before Deahl spoke up. "If Lucio wants a window mount, we could put it here and it would blow toward his bed, but it wouldn't cool the area around the desk very well. If we made it a little smaller and portable, he could put it by this window when he was in bed and at the other window when he was at his desk."

"If it were portable, I could even take it with me if I went to sit in the garden," Lucio said excitedly. "Is that an option?"

"It won't be portable like a hand fan," Gabriel warned, his smile warm, "but in theory you could carry it outside with you, yes."

Deahl and Lambert lingered a few minutes longer, discussing technical details that quickly surpassed Lucio's understanding. He wanted to learn, but now was not the time to bother them with explaining things. He could ask Gabriel later, perhaps. He suspected Gabriel would be more willing to help him understand anyway. Finally, Deahl and Lambert rose. "We'll leave you to discuss price while we get started. If you'll get us the measurements of the room as soon as you can, we'll have it done sooner."

Lucio nodded as they left, the door swinging shut behind them. "That went better than I feared."

"They're good men," Gabriel repeated. "They don't always think things through the way I wish they would, but they're good men. For what you're asking, I'd usually charge forty gold, but since it's for you—"

"Since it's for me, you'll charge fifty-five," Lucio interrupted.

Gabriel's eyes widened. "That wasn't what I was going to say."

"I know it wasn't," Lucio answered, opening his money pouch and pouring the coins into his hand, "but it's what I'm going to pay you. That way you have enough extra to visit with me sometime as well." He reached in his pocket and pulled out the fob, handing it to Gabriel. "And you'll put this in a safe place."

"What's this for?" Gabriel asked, looking from the jewel in his hand back to Lucio.

"My guests give me trinkets sometimes," Lucio said. "I can sell them for gold, but I don't need much, honestly, and they often give me gold as well. No one will miss a piece of jewelry or two or more. I can't buy my own contract, and I can't refuse to accept guests unless someone else buys my contract, but I can give you everything I have in the hope that one day you'll be able to buy it for me."

Gabriel shook his head automatically. "But I don't want to own your contract."

Lucio's face fell. "I thought—"

Gabriel cut his words off with a deep kiss. "I want you. I want to be with you in every way possible, but I don't want to own you."

Lucio relaxed a little, realizing Gabriel wasn't rejecting him. "Our society doesn't work that way. Unless you can live with sharing me for the rest of our lives, you will have to buy my contract. I wish there were a way to be together like we are now, without money between us, but that isn't possible. I have all this gold, all this jewelry that my guests have given me. Can't you appreciate the irony of using that to buy my freedom from them forever?"

14

GABRIEL did see the irony in Lucio's proposition. He just hated that it still resulted in Lucio being owned. "I don't know if I'll ever like the idea," he said slowly, "but the alternative is even worse, so I guess I'll find a way to live with it." He reached for the companion, pulling Lucio onto his lap. "I swear, if I succeed in buying your contract, the first thing I'm going to do after you're safely away from the pleasure palace is tear it to shreds so we don't have it between us."

Lucio smiled and kissed Gabriel sweetly. "The contract is unimportant. You have shown me that you don't see me that way. I don't know how much it will take to pay it off nor, honestly, do I know how much I have. I will bring a few pieces at a time for you to keep safe until we have enough."

"It may not be as long as I'd feared," Gabriel said, thinking of the pile of cards on his dresser upstairs. "Lord Stuart's gambit last night worked. I have dozens of aristocrats wanting inventions with my name on them. It will take time to complete them all, but at least it will be gold in my pocket. Gold that I can save to help you."

"As long as you use a bit of it to visit me when I can't come to visit you," Lucio said.

Gabriel flinched at the suggestion. "I hate this. I hate having money exchange hands so we can be together."

"I know," Lucio said soothingly, stroking Gabriel's hair, "but I can only be so demanding with my requirements for the fan and whatever other inventions we come up with for me to buy, and you have other commissions, real ones, so you can't spend all your time on gadgets for me. There may be weeks when I have no excuse to visit your workshop, and without a plausible reason, they probably won't let me leave, so the only choice is for you to come to me, and that requires payment."

"As long as you will not think less of me or of yourself because I have bought your time," Gabriel said slowly, tipping his head into the reassuring caress. He wanted to return the gesture, but Lucio's comment about not wanting to be touched echoed in his mind. He settled for closing his arms around the companion's waist and holding him close. Lucio smelled of lemon and sandalwood and a scent Gabriel didn't recognize. He nuzzled Lucio's neck, trying to get a better idea of what it was. Lucio shifted on his lap, a gasp escaping his lips. Pulling back, Gabriel looked worriedly at Lucio, but the look on the other man's face was one of wonder and desire.

"How do you make me want things I gave up on years ago?" Lucio whispered, awe coloring his voice.

"I don't know," Gabriel replied, "but tell me what you want and I will give it to you if it's within my power."

"Right now?" Lucio said. "Right now I want to sit here in your arms and kiss you and forget for a few minutes that I have to go back to the pleasure palace."

"You can sit here for as long as you want," Gabriel swore, his arms tightening around Lucio's waist.

"Then I would never move," Lucio promised, "but the handlers would come looking for me, and if they found us like this, they would never let me return. They might still let you buy my time, but a visit like this one, where we are truly free to be ourselves, would never happen again."

"Then we must make the best of the time we do have," Gabriel said, resolutely pushing aside the thought of Lucio returning home. "Do you want to see the rest of the lab?"

"There's more?" Lucio asked.

"The basement," Gabriel said. "It's nothing fancy, not even as nice as the main room, but it's where I'm working on my special project. I haven't even told Caleb and Andrew about it. Would you like to see it?"

"I'd love to!" Lucio said, jumping up.

Gabriel opened the door to the basement and grabbed a lantern so they could see. He kept saying he would install gas lights down there as well, but he hadn't taken the time yet. He led the way down the rickety steps, Lucio on his heels. When they reached the ground, Gabriel hung the lantern on a hook in the overhead beams and pulled back the tarp covering his pet project. The chair's arms and back had been reinforced and a belt added to hold the person in place. Between the wooden legs, a small engine rested on the floor.

"Explain it to me," Lucio requested.

"At the moment there's nothing to explain," Gabriel said, a little embarrassed at the lack of progress on the project, "but if I can get the engine both small enough and powerful enough, it will power a set of propellers above the chair and a set behind the chair, the combination of which would allow the chair to fly. The problem is the size of the engine compared to the size of the chair."

"That engine doesn't look too big," Lucio said, stepping closer and kneeling down next to the chair.

"It isn't," Gabriel agreed, "but neither is it powerful enough to lift anything more than the chair at the moment. If even a small child sat in it, the chair would stay stuck to the ground." He pointed to an engine across the room. "That's the size I would need to make the chair lift a grown man given the current configurations, and it's far too large to fit under a chair."

"So what are you going to do?" Lucio asked.

"Try to make the small engine more powerful and change the configuration of the chair so it requires less power to lift," Gabriel said. "I work on it in my spare time, but since I don't have a buyer or a sponsor for it, I can't afford to set aside my paying projects to work on this one."

"Have you mentioned it to Lord Stuart?" Lucio asked. "He is fascinated by your work. He mentioned it to me several times last night."

Gabriel flinched at the reference to Lucio's most recent client. He had spent too long that morning obsessing over Lucio in Lord Stuart's bed to be sanguine about the reference now. "No, I haven't spoken with His Lordship about anything other than the commissions he has given me."

"And now you're angry with me," Lucio said with a sigh. "Perhaps it's time I returned home. All we'll do is hurt each other if I stay."

Gabriel hated the thought of Lucio leaving, but the companion was right. Every topic of conversation seemed to lead them back to the same point of contention between them. "I want you to visit again," Gabriel said, "but I don't know how to handle this yet, and I know I'm not handling it well. Maybe by the next time we see each other, I'll be better in control of myself."

"I'll show myself out, then."

Gabriel nodded and watched as Lucio started up the stairs, shoulders slumped. Lucio's foot was on the top tread when something in Gabriel snapped. He bounded for the stairs, taking them two at a time and catching Lucio in his arms as the companion neared the kitchen table. He spun Lucio around so their lips met in a passionate frenzy. Lucio squirmed in

Gabriel's tight embrace, making him fear he had trespassed, but when he loosened his grip, Lucio's arms went around him, holding him close as the kiss continued. Gabriel buried his hands in Lucio's hair, carding his fingers through the silky strands. "Don't leave me," he begged, breaking the kiss.

Lucio buried his face against Gabriel's neck with a sob. "I don't want to, but I can't stay. They'll come looking for me, and the punishment if I break the rules will not be a pleasant one. Please, Gabriel, dearest Gabriel, don't make this harder than it is. Let me go back with the memory of your kisses on my lips rather than the sound of harsh words in my ears."

Gabriel took a deep breath and nodded again. "Give me one more kiss, then, to hold us until you can sneak away again."

Lucio pressed his mouth to Gabriel's, the soft lips parting so sweetly that Gabriel couldn't help but delve between them, exploring every inch of Lucio's mouth, thrilling at the thought that no one else had ever tasted Lucio this way. They might have used him in every way possible, but they had never cherished him the way Gabriel did now.

Finally they broke apart to breathe.

"If I haven't come to you by Wednesday evening, buy an hour or more of my time for Thursday," Lucio pleaded. "Don't make me go longer than that."

"I don't know if I can wait that long," Gabriel said hoarsely, "but I'll have to, or I'll spend all the money I make on you now rather than saving it for your contract."

"Thursday," Lucio said firmly. "Wait until then because I might be able to get away sooner. I didn't check my calendar before I came so I don't know what my schedule looks like."

"No hour is too early or too late," Gabriel said. "I live upstairs. The front door locks securely, but if you come around to the back, there's a latchkey that you can use if I don't answer right away."

"I'll do my best," Lucio promised. "I don't want to wait that long to see you either if I have a choice. Now, walk me to the door and wait with me while I hail a cab so I can wave goodbye to you as I leave."

Gabriel followed Lucio back through the workshop, past Caleb and Andrew who kept their eyes studiously on the projects in front of them, and out to the street. It took a few minutes to find a hansom for hire. Gabriel handed Lucio inside and lifted a hand as the cab pulled away from the curb, taking Lucio away from him. With a sigh, he turned and trudged inside.

Caleb called his name as he walked back through the workshop into the kitchen, but Gabriel didn't answer, pulling open the cabinet and taking out a bottle of whisky. He poured several fingers into a glass with shaking hands and tossed back as much as he could in one swallow, hissing at the burn. He slumped down at the table, head in his hands, and wondered for the hundredth time what he thought he was doing.

He heard the door open, then the cabinet door, and a loud thunk as a glass hit the table next to his. "So you want to tell me why we're drinking at… six o'clock in the evening?"

"You saw why," Gabriel said, not bothering to look up.

"No," Caleb said, "I'm pretty sure what I saw was a reason to be over the moon, not falling down drunk."

Gabriel looked up at that, his expression incredulous. "What are you talking about? You aren't blind, and I know you aren't stupid. You know who Lucio is. What he is."

"So?" Caleb challenged. "What does it matter? I saw the way he looked at you. Nobody's ever looked at *me* that way. Andrew doesn't look at me that way."

"What way?" Gabriel asked suspiciously.

"Like you were his every wish come true and more," Caleb replied. "Don't tell me you didn't see it."

Gabriel shook his head. "I didn't see it."

Caleb was on his feet in an instant, cuffing Gabriel's head roughly. "I ought to take you out back and thrash you into next week. If I do that, though, you won't tell me what's going on. And start at the beginning because this is clearly not a short story."

Gabriel sighed and took another sip of his whisky. If he was going to bare his soul to Caleb, he had a feeling he'd need it.

"Lucio is the companion you and Andrew hired for my birthday," Gabriel began, not sure he could put into words the progression of events and emotions that had led to this moment and the bottle of whisky. "I told you then that he was different."

"And I told you then to forget about him," Caleb agreed. "You obviously didn't listen."

"I tried," Gabriel said, "but I kept coming back to him, thinking about him."

"I know you didn't see him again," Caleb said. "So what's he doing here now?"

"He was at Lord Stuart's ball last night," Gabriel explained. "He's close friends with the companion Lord Stuart hired for me, and she helped arrange a few moments for us to talk. It seems his thoughts have been as unruly as mine."

"I can see why you'd be attracted to him," Caleb said. "He's probably the most beautiful thing I've ever seen, but you aren't talking about simple attraction here, are you?"

Gabriel shook his head. "You talked with him while he was here. He isn't some vapid companion with more hair than brains. He's an intelligent, thoughtful man who could fit in here with the right education."

"He certainly seemed interested in the conversation," Caleb agreed. "So what's the problem?"

"The problem is that he's a companion," Gabriel said bitterly, pouring another shot of whisky and downing it against the pain in his heart at having to say those words. "The problem is that he spent last night in Lord Stuart's bed and who knows where he'll spend tonight or tomorrow or tomorrow night. All I know is that it won't be with me."

Caleb nodded. "I can see that being a little... unsettling, but I'll bet he doesn't look at any of them the way he looked at you today. If you're going to be with him, Gabe, you're going to have to separate his body from the rest of him. You're going to have to accept that his body doesn't belong to him, much less to you, and you're going to have to live with that."

"How?" Gabriel demanded, reaching for the bottle again. Caleb caught it, wrestling with him for a moment before Gabriel wrenched it away and poured yet another glass. "How am I supposed to do that when all I want to do is tuck him away upstairs and never let anyone else touch him again?"

"I haven't the foggiest idea," Caleb replied cheerfully, "but until you do, you'd better get damn good at pretending you've figured it out. Your boy doesn't seem like the kind to put up with any shit. He might be a little more patient with you because he's obviously crazy about you, but he isn't going to be happy about you harping on his caste for long, not when he can't change it."

"I know," Gabriel said sadly. "We argued about it today before he left. Why do you think I'm drinking?"

"I think you're drinking because you're due a little self-indulgence," Caleb said, "but I know the solution isn't in that bottle. It's in you figuring out whether you care for him enough to overlook what can't be changed and cherish what time you can have together." He poured another measure of whisky into Gabriel's glass and topped off his own. "And the three of us working our fingers to the bone to earn the money to get him out."

Gabriel's eyes flew to Caleb's face. "What?"

"Andrew and I talked about it while you and Lucio were in here discussing price or whatever you were talking about," Caleb said, lifting the glass to Gabriel in silent salute. "You have been so good to us over the years, making sure we always had enough to eat and money for a place to stay, even when you probably didn't, taking out loans to be able to pay us on time when we hadn't sold enough in the month to cover all the expenses. You didn't make a big deal of it. You just looked out for us. Now it's our turn. Take every commission the pansy aristocrats offer you, and make them pay a percentage up front. We'll work the hours it takes to get it done and the money in your pocket so you can bring Lucio home as soon as possible. You just have to keep from fucking things up until we have the money."

"Thank you," Gabriel said, his voice catching in his throat. He had not really expected his friends to understand his new obsession when he could barely understand it himself. To have their full support was more than he had imagined possible. "Reading said he'd have a suit ready for me in time to start calling on the aristocrats on Monday. I'll have to hope they're as interested when it comes time to talk money as they were last night."

"That's the spirit," Caleb said. "Andrew, come have some whisky. We're toasting Gabriel's future."

Andrew appeared through the doorway. "Did you talk him out of his mood?"

"Probably not," Caleb replied, "but I told him we'd do what it took to help him out."

Andrew fetched a third glass and sloshed a finger's width of the amber liquid into his glass. "To the future."

Gabriel looked back and forth between his friends, gratitude tightening his throat. He lifted his glass, touching it to each of theirs in turn. Suddenly life didn't seem quite so bleak. "To the future."

15

WHEN Wednesday afternoon came with no sign of a visit from Lucio, Gabriel steeled himself for a visit to the pleasure palace on Mayfair Place. The gold in his purse seemed far heavier than it should have, and he could not bring himself to give the hansom driver the actual address, instead directing the man to leave him one street over. The sky bore no sign of impending rain, so he could walk the distance and save himself the knowing looks. He wore his new suit, hoping the handlers would be more willing to deal with him if he looked closer to an aristocrat than a poor merchant. They had allowed Caleb and Andrew to purchase Lucio's evening as a birthday present to him, and Gabriel knew neither Caleb nor Andrew had a fancy suit, but Gabriel wondered if the handlers hadn't taken advantage of his friends' ignorance. Gabriel hadn't asked Lucio how much an hour with him would normally cost because he hadn't wanted to bring up the issue of money again, but he hoped the handlers would be willing to negotiate. He had enough money in his pouch for two hours at the rate Caleb and Andrew had quoted for him. He intended to haggle that into three hours instead.

"Can I help you, sir?" a man asked from behind a counter when Gabriel entered the pleasure palace.

"I'd like to hire a companion for a few hours tomorrow afternoon or Friday at the latest," Gabriel said, everything inside him squirming at the thought of what he was doing. He squelched the nerves, reminding himself that the money wouldn't change what he and Lucio shared. It would simply allow them to share it.

"Male or female?" the man asked, opening a large register.

"Lucio," Gabriel said, hoping his voice conveyed his determination. He would haggle over price, but not over the identity of his chosen companion.

The clerk's eyebrows lifted. "Have you purchased Lucio's time before?"

"He was given to me as a birthday present about a month ago," Gabriel replied. "I very much enjoyed him and want to see him again."

"You do realize he's our most expensive companion," the clerk said. "I'm sure we could find someone else more within your means."

"Are you implying my gold isn't as good as the next man's?" Gabriel challenged. "What is his rate?"

"Twenty gold an hour," the clerk replied.

"That isn't what you told my friends," Gabriel replied. "I may be a merchant, but I'm not ignorant and I'm not unimportant. I'm sure Lord Stuart would be most interested to hear you tried to overcharge his protégé. Or perhaps you would rather I tell Lord Bicksley or maybe Lady Palmer. I visited with both of them this week. If they thought you were falsely inflating your prices, they might decide to take their patronage elsewhere. I know this isn't the only pleasure palace in the city."

The clerk blanched at the threat. Gabriel hid a smile. He was quite sure Lord Stuart had not intended this when he had offered Gabriel his patronage, but Gabriel would take it. Anything to let him see Lucio. "Perhaps we could discuss the price," the clerk said. "If you were willing to mention to your friends the quality of service you received."

"I'm sure I could bring it up," Gabriel said, knowing he never would. "For the right price."

The clerk's eyes narrowed. "Lucio has some time free tomorrow afternoon," he said after a moment. "A cancellation."

Gabriel suspected that was a lie as well, but it gave him another edge in the negotiations. "Then I'm sure you'll be happy to fill that time with something profitable. After all, any gold would be better than none. Three hours for thirty gold."

"That's ridiculous!" the clerk exclaimed. "I'd barely sell my least expensive companion for that price."

"Ah, but if you don't sell his time for that price, he won't be earning any money during that time," Gabriel reminded the clerk. "Isn't thirty gold better than nothing?"

"Someone else might come in and wish to buy him," the clerk insisted.

"Really?" Gabriel asked. "At"—he glanced at his watch—"six o'clock on Wednesday night, you think someone else will come in looking to hire him on such short notice?" He turned as if to leave. "It's your choice, of course, but my gold is a sure thing."

"Wait," the clerk called, drawing Gabriel back to the counter. "We couldn't make a habit of selling him at that price, but perhaps this once...."

"I will be sure to mention your excellent service when I call on Lord Stuart tomorrow morning," Gabriel inserted smoothly, hoping the lie wouldn't show on his face. He had no idea when he would next see Lord Stuart, but the name dropping had worked before.

"Very well," the clerk said, "he is yours from two to five tomorrow. Will you come to fetch him?"

With three hours instead of just two, Gabriel did not mind having the carriage ride out to Nicholasville to share with Lucio. "I will be here promptly at two. Make sure he is ready. I will add any time I have to wait for him to the time I bring him back."

"He will be ready," the clerk promised. "Your name, sir, so I can put it on his schedule."

"Blackstone," Gabriel replied.

"And how shall he be attired?" the clerk asked.

"For an afternoon in the country," Gabriel said, hating the thought that even Lucio's dress was dictated by his guests.

"I'll make a note of it," the clerk said. "Any other requests?"

Gabriel had no idea what else he might request so he simply shook his head and counted out the coins for the clerk. As he stepped back onto the street, he felt like everyone was staring at him, knowing what he had just arranged. It didn't matter that he had no intention of doing anything more than sharing a hopefully pleasant afternoon with Lucio. They would imagine all manner of depravity.

He hailed a cab and climbed inside, wondering how soon Lucio would know that he had kept his promise to arrange a meeting if Lucio could not find a way to visit him. He had no real concept of what Lucio's life was like beyond the fact that the right to his body was bought and sold like so much livestock. Even a trained companion couldn't have sex all the time, making Gabriel wonder how Lucio filled his free time and if he had other friends at the pleasure palace besides Cressida.

He hoped, wherever Lucio was, he was thinking of Gabriel as Gabriel was thinking of him.

GABRIEL arrived back at Mayfair Place at exactly two o'clock the next afternoon, striding through the door to the pleasure palace with far more confidence than he actually felt. He had left the fancy suit at home, far more comfortable in his leather coat and breeches. The clerk—a different one from the day before—glared at him, but Lucio saw him and rose from his seat, greeting him with a slight bow. "Mister Blackstone."

"Lucio," Gabriel said, returning the bow. He did not acknowledge the clerk in any way since Lucio did not either. "Our carriage awaits."

They walked back outside and climbed into the mechanical carriage, careful to keep an appropriate distance between them. "The Beagle and Swallow in Nicholasville," Gabriel ordered the driver before he shut the door, enclosing himself and Lucio in the relative privacy of the cab.

"Are we really going to Nicholasville?" Lucio asked, eyes alight.

"I thought you might enjoy the outing," Gabriel said. "There's an inn there where we can have tea or coffee before we head back later this afternoon, and we can walk in the park for a bit. We might even see some deer."

"That would be lovely," Lucio said, taking Gabriel's hand in his. "I missed you this week."

"I missed you too," Gabriel said, putting his arm around Lucio's shoulders and pulling him closer. "It was a busy week, but I kept hoping you would find time to call."

"I'm sorry," Lucio said. "I wanted to, but I never seemed to have enough time to get across town, see you, and get back before I had another engagement."

Gabriel's heart twinged, but he refused to let it show on his face. He had promised Caleb—not to mention Lucio—that he would focus on the time they had together, not on the times they were apart.

"So what kept you so busy?" Lucio asked, distracting Gabriel from his painful thoughts.

"Visiting all the different aristocrats who want my attention thanks to Lord Stuart," Gabriel replied. "I've probably called on twenty people in the last three days, and every one of them has wanted something."

Lucio smiled. "That's wonderful news. What kinds of inventions do they have you working on?"

"Most of them didn't have anything in particular so much as they wanted to have something by me to brag about," Gabriel admitted. "I've talked quite a few people into fans this week. Caleb and Andrew have made great strides on yours. With the measurements of your room, we can have it done in a matter of a few days."

Lucio's smile widened. "Then I shall have to forget to give them to you so I can visit you this weekend when I have some free time. If you finish a fan before then, give it to one of the aristocrats. Once one of them has it, they'll all want one and you'll be so busy with orders you won't have time for me."

"I'll always have time for you," Gabriel swore, his arm tightening around Lucio. "Don't even joke about something like that."

Lucio soothed Gabriel with a gentle kiss. "I was teasing. I'm sorry if I offended you."

"I'm not offended," Gabriel said, stroking Lucio's cheek. "I don't like to see you belittle yourself. That's all."

"I know my own worth," Lucio replied, his voice steady.

Gabriel shook his head. "No, you know what society thinks your worth is. You are far more precious to me than any amount of gold or jewels."

"Oh, that reminds me," Lucio said, reaching in his pocket and pulling out a watch chain. "You should take this back with you and add it to your collection. Given that you specified an afternoon in the country, I couldn't really wear much of anything else, but they won't question a watch chain."

Gabriel took the chain and slid it carefully into an interior pocket of his jacket, making sure to button it securely closed. "I suppose we could have dinner together sometimes so you could wear more formal clothes," he mused aloud.

"You don't have to do that," Lucio said. "We can do whatever you want. I'll find ways to smuggle things out."

"This isn't about me," Gabriel reminded Lucio. "It's about both of us and what we both want."

"What I want is to see you," Lucio said, pressing tender kisses to Gabriel's cheek and jaw. "As long as we're together, I don't care where we go or what we do. We could sit at your kitchen table and I would be happy."

"The clerk yesterday didn't ask specifically where we were going, but I didn't want to give him my address so they wouldn't question it when you came to visit me," Gabriel explained, "and I thought an afternoon in the country would be nice. Something courting couples would do."

"Is that what we are?" Lucio asked, his voice suddenly shy.

"That's exactly what we are," Gabriel replied. "Despite how we met, despite your profession, that's what we are and what we will be until you are ready for us to be more."

Lucio threw his arms around Gabriel, holding him so tightly that Gabriel could barely breathe. He didn't protest, simply pulling Lucio onto his lap so they could embrace more comfortably. When Lucio lifted his head finally, his lashes were wet with tears. "Are you crying?" Gabriel asked.

"Tears of joy," Lucio whispered. "The handlers made sure we were educated thoroughly as children so we could entertain our guests appropriately. I read all the same books as aristocratic children, the ones that paint a picture of familial happiness and romance. As I grew older, I realized I would never have those things because I was a companion and no one would ever look to me for anything more than momentary pleasure. I made my peace with that eventually because I had no real choice in the matter. Whether I railed against my fate or accepted it, I couldn't change it so I learned to live with it. 'When I was a child…' and all that. You've given me back those dreams."

"I would give you back all your dreams if it were in my power," Gabriel replied, moved nearly to tears himself at the heartfelt words.

"You already have," Lucio said, wiping at his eyes. "It would be so easy to fall in love with you, but I'm afraid, too."

"Why are you afraid?" Gabriel asked, his heart pounding frantically in his chest.

"Because if I gave you my heart and you changed your mind, I think it would kill me," Lucio replied. "I gave up on my childish dreams. I put aside those hopes. I can live with that if I don't let them revive, but I'm not sure I would survive having them destroyed a second time."

"Then I shall have to take care not to let anything damage them," Gabriel said. The carriage rolled to a stop in front of the Beagle and Swallow Inn. "We're here. Let's go for a stroll."

Lucio's smile was luminous. "I'd like that."

THEY walked largely in silence, fingers twined together. Gabriel's thoughts raced with everything Lucio had revealed in the carriage. He could scarcely credit the words, but he knew Lucio had not lied to him, not about something like that. Every time he thought of Lucio's confession, his heart rate picked up, leaving him feeling giddy. This was not some casual affair for Lucio, some diversion to pass the time between regular clients. This was for real.

He glanced at Lucio from the corner of his eye as they walked, taking in the relaxed posture and carefree smile. All the artifice and attempts at seduction from their first meeting, all the secrecy and guile from their hasty meeting at Lord Stuart's ball, all the poise and composure from Lucio's visit to the workshop, were gone, leaving behind what Gabriel suspected was finally and truly the real Lucio. Gabriel thought it made him even more beautiful, even more desirable, than before. Whatever came of their relationship—and Gabriel finally dared hope they could make something of it—he would treasure this memory as something he knew no one but perhaps Cressida would ever see. He did not mind sharing Lucio with her because he recognized the way she looked at Lucio. He suspected he looked at Caleb and Andrew the same way. He only hoped Cressida would be willing to include him into her protective circle because Gabriel had every intention of being part of Lucio's life now.

He didn't delude himself that it would be easy or that Lucio's declaration would take away all the obstacles facing them. As much as he wanted to push the rest of the world aside for the afternoon, they were not a young couple whose only concern was whether their parents would agree to their marriage. The challenges along their path would be far more difficult to overcome. They weren't young debutants barely out of the schoolroom, though, with no thought in their heads other than making an advantageous match. They had already proven they could find ways to be together despite the forces that contrived to keep them apart. They would simply have to continue that way until they could gather the money to allow them to be together permanently.

The chiming of the town's church bells recalled Gabriel finally to their surroundings and his plans for the rest of the afternoon. "Shall we go into the inn? We can have tea before we return to town."

Lucio smiled. "Yes, that would be most refreshing."

Gabriel couldn't resist, glancing around to make sure they were alone before kissing Lucio softly. "Keep your hand tucked in my arm so they cannot see your tattoo. For another hour, we can be that courting couple out for an afternoon stroll."

16

THE private parlor in the inn was not nearly as formal or fancy as the inns Lucio had frequented in the city, but he didn't care. He was blessedly alone with Gabriel once the servants had brought tea and cakes and disappeared. His skin still tingled from holding Gabriel's hand during their walk, but even more than that, his heart swelled with joy. He had admitted his fears and hopes to Gabriel and had not been ridiculed for them. Instead Gabriel had pulled him closer, held him tighter, and made him feel cherished.

"So do you suppose the other courting couples who come here sit at the table like proper ladies and gentlemen?" Lucio said with a smile as he glanced toward the couch near the empty fireplace.

"No," Gabriel said, returning Lucio's smile. "I think they snuggle together on that couch and take advantage of the privacy the room affords them."

Lowering his eyes modestly, Lucio moved to the couch, perching on the edge, hands clasped tightly on his lap, giving every impression of a sweet young thing in over his head, wanting every experience but nervous about it as well.

As Lucio had hoped, Gabriel set aside his cup of tea and joined him on the couch, reaching for his hands. "Are you really that nervous?" Gabriel asked.

"A little," Lucio replied honestly. "I can play any role my guests want me to, and I've played them all dozens of times, but this isn't a role. This means something and that makes it frightening."

Gabriel squeezed his hand, tilting his chin upward. "You don't have to be nervous with me. I won't ever do something you don't want."

"But that's the part that makes me nervous," Lucio struggled to explain. "I don't know how to act with you because this is different from everything else. If you started giving me orders, telling me to do things to you, I'd know exactly how to act, but I'm as inexperienced with this as any virginal debutante."

"I know," Gabriel assured him. "You're not the only one in danger of falling in love, and that's the part of you that snared me from the moment I realized it was there."

Lucio's heart leapt at the words, and he threw his arms around Gabriel's neck. Gabriel tugged at his hips, lifting him so he sat across the inventor's thighs, snuggled closely together. Lucio looked down into the blue eyes, seeing his own nascent emotions reflected in the expressive depths. Feeling emboldened by their mutual declarations, he kissed Gabriel hungrily before lifting his head to ask, "What else do you suppose courting couples do as they sit on this couch, alone for a few precious minutes?"

Gabriel's arms shifted around Lucio's waist, his forearm brushing over Lucio's cock, which had reacted to Gabriel's nearness. The accidental touch surprised a gasp from Lucio's lips, the simple brush through layers of fabric far more arousing than anything his guests had ever done to him.

"I think it depends on the couple," Gabriel replied honestly. "I think some of them sit and talk while others fondle each other through their clothes and still others make passionate love."

Lucio's breath caught in his throat, his body aching with sudden need. He shifted on Gabriel's lap, feeling the other man's reaction as well. He recognized the feelings of desire from his earliest days as a companion, when the naïve part of him hoped he could find fulfillment despite the disregard of his guests, but he had put those dreams aside along with all the others. Now, suddenly, those feelings and hopes came rushing back. "And which will we do?" he asked, his voice husky not from any artifice but from true desire this time.

"Close your eyes," Gabriel said. Lucio complied immediately, his pulse skittering with anticipation. Callused fingers brushed across Lucio's cheekbones and then over his forehead, Gabriel's other arm strong and steadying behind Lucio's back. "I want you to feel what I'm doing to you. Me. Not anyone else. And I want you to react in any way that feels right. Don't pretend with me. If you like something, I want to know about it, but I don't want you to react because you think you should like something. I want to know what makes your body feel good, what makes *you* feel good."

"I... I don't even know," Lucio whispered, his voice cracking with the overwhelming upsurge of emotion. He started to open his eyes, but Gabriel's fingers trailed over the lids.

"Keep your eyes closed. Focus on what you're feeling, not on me or my reactions," Gabriel reminded him. "This is all about you."

Nothing in Lucio's life had ever been all about him. The realization that Gabriel meant what he said brought a soft sob to Lucio's throat. Gabriel soothed it away with a tender kiss and the brush of his fingers down the smooth skin of Lucio's neck. The tips, nicked and scarred by work, caught against his sensitive flesh, another layer of sensation that no aristocrat's hands had ever delivered. That sent a shiver down Lucio's spine, raising gooseflesh all over his body. "Good?" Gabriel verified.

"Very good," Lucio whispered in reply.

Gabriel's slightly chapped lips replaced his fingers on Lucio's offered throat, licking and nibbling enough to tantalize but not enough to mark. Lucio shivered again, wondering where the wicked fingers would land next. The answer came moments later as they started across the palm of his hand and stroked over the inner face of his wrist. "Yes," Lucio hissed, relaxing even more against Gabriel's supporting arm. "No one's ever...."

"Because no one has ever cared the way I care," Gabriel replied, finding Lucio's lips for a kiss.

Lucio could hardly argue with that when no one besides Cressida had cared for him at all, and Cressida had no more interest in sex than Lucio did until Gabriel touched him. Then again, he wasn't sure what this was, but it bore no resemblance to any sex he'd ever had. "More."

"What do you want?" Gabriel asked, lifting his head. "What would make you feel best?"

"I don't know," Lucio said. "I've never been allowed to find out."

"Then we'll find out together," Gabriel promised, his fingers moving up Lucio's arm and sliding beneath the placket of his jacket. His palm spread across Lucio's chest directly above his heart.

Lucio knew many of his guests liked having their nipples caressed or licked or even bitten, but he had never cared one way or another. When Gabriel's hand kneaded the muscle of his chest, Lucio finally understood. Every touch to his nipple, indirect though it was, went straight to his aching cock, making him gasp and squirm on Gabriel's lap. "More," Lucio moaned, "please."

Gabriel didn't reply in words, but his fingers found the sensitive nub, rubbing it through the cloth until Lucio whimpered in his arms. "Too much," Lucio said finally, opening his eyes. "I feel like I'm flying, like I'm going to lose control."

"So lose control," Gabriel said, the smug satisfaction in his voice its own revelation for Lucio. "I want to know I can make you come undone in my arms."

Lucio shook his head, afraid of surrendering the last, untouched part of himself. To his surprise, Gabriel did not insist, his hand sliding down Lucio's side to his hip instead.

"Then if I shouldn't do that, perhaps you would like this instead." His hand started stroking up and down Lucio's thighs, starting at his knees and ending just shy of his aching cock before sliding back toward his knees again. Without thinking, Lucio parted his legs, the action as instinctual as it was learned. Gabriel's hand moved to the inner face of one leg, pausing when the back of his hand brushed Lucio's other leg. "Open your eyes," he prompted.

Lucio's eyes fluttered opened, but it was a struggle to focus on Gabriel's face. "Do you want me to keep going?" Gabriel asked. "I want to slide my hand higher, slip it beneath your waistband and stroke until you fall apart in my arms. I want to see what you look like with your face contorted with pleasure. I want to know what sounds you make when you come. But I only want it if you want it too."

Lucio's belly tightened at the decadent words. It was so easy to imagine what Gabriel had described. He had let countless men and women strip his clothes away, but it had always been for their pleasure, never for his own. "You won't let me go?"

Gabriel's arm tightened around Lucio's shoulders. "Never. Say the word, and we'll leave right now. We'll go south and keep going until we're so far away no one will know or care who we are."

"You know we'd never escape," Lucio said even as he longed to do exactly as Gabriel offered. "I'm too valuable to them." He took a deep breath and unfastened the top button of his trousers. "Do it. I want to know what it feels like."

Lucio smiled at the hitch of Gabriel's breath. He had learned long ago the signs of arousal in his guests. To see it now in his—dare he think it— his lover sent fresh arousal through his body. Gabriel's nimble fingers finished unbuttoning him, opening his trousers but making no effort to push them off. Instead his hand caressed Lucio's belly the way it had earlier caressed his chest, back and forth, kneading lightly, until Lucio pushed his hips upward, asking for more. Only then did Gabriel work his way beneath cloth to find bare skin.

Lucio trembled, the heat of Gabriel's hard palm against him reminding him of the physical side of what they were doing, but he forced his mind away from the lessons he had endured on the right way to touch, to arouse, to linger, and simply enjoyed being touched for his own pleasure for the first time. His eyes closed as Gabriel's fingers found the tip of his cock, exploring it with tender care, leaving Lucio trembling. No one had ever touched him this way, like he was the most precious treasure in the world. His organ jumped beneath the touch, spurting fluid. He trembled when Gabriel released his erection for a moment to lift his hand to his lips and lick his fingers clean.

"Delicious."

Lucio's cheeks flamed. Gabriel had done nothing to him that he hadn't done hundreds of times to his guests, but Gabriel's actions were not coldly calculated for effect. Gabriel touched him, tasted him, whispered praise in his ear because he wanted to, because he meant it. When the work-rough hand closed around his cock again, Lucio bucked up into the caress, desperate suddenly with need. Gabriel's arm tightened around his shoulders, supporting him easily as his other hand moved in time with Lucio's eager thrusts, the calluses on his palm providing almost more stimulation than Lucio could stand. "Come for me," Gabriel whispered in his ear. "Let go."

Lucio convulsed in Gabriel's arms, his body obeying the guttural command. Gabriel's hand kept moving, prolonging Lucio's pleasure until the aftershocks faded and he lay limp in the inventor's grasp. His eyes fluttered open, seeking Gabriel's gaze. "I never knew...."

Gabriel smiled and kissed him. "Now you do."

Lucio smiled in return. "Now that I do, I shall be insatiably demanding," he warned, feeling free to flirt with Gabriel as himself finally. "Every time I see you, I shall want some new experience, some new pleasure at your hands."

"It will be my pleasure to oblige," Gabriel promised.

"What can I do to return the favor?" Lucio asked, shifting on Gabriel's lap so he would have access to the other man's body.

To his surprise, Gabriel caught his hands, lifting them to his lips and kissing them tenderly. "You can finish your tea and sit next to me in the carriage on our way back to town. You can allow me the knowledge that no one else has ever seen your face replete the way I have."

"I will do all that gladly," Lucio said, "but after you took such good care of me—"

Gabriel shook his head. "Everyone takes pleasure from you, from your body. I wanted to give it instead."

"You did," Lucio promised. "You must know that you did."

Gabriel chuckled. "The proof of it is all over my hand. Now put yourself back together so we don't scandalize the servants."

Lucio caught Gabriel's hand, lifting it to his mouth and licking at the sticky fingers, a fresh tendril of desire curling through his stomach at the thought of performing this gesture for a lover rather than for a guest. At that close range, he could see the fine lines of scars on Gabriel's knuckles, testament to the way he made his living. Lucio licked every one of them clean. When he had finished with every inch of skin, he released Gabriel's hand and rose, straightening his clothes slowly, hoping Gabriel would call him back over and stop him. He had never been like this. He had acted like this, but it had always been an act. Now it was for real.

Gabriel didn't call him back, though, so he finished dressing, feeling his hands beginning to tremble as the reality of what he'd done—allowed Gabriel to do—sank in. He had broken every tenet handed to him by every experienced companion he had ever talked to. Every one of them had told him repeatedly not to fall in love with a guest, even if that guest wanted to buy or bought his contract. They all swore no one could ever love a companion, no matter what he or she said. No one would ever see past the ingrained infidelity, the practiced ways, the too-intimate knowledge of everything sexual. People fucked companions. They loved sweet, innocent virgins.

Lucio had never had any problem remembering that before because he had only ever been fucked. His guests called it by more genteel names, but that's what it had always been up until now. Gabriel had not only not fucked him; Gabriel had set aside his own pleasure in favor of Lucio's. He would bet every piece of gold he owned that this was what making love felt like instead of the meaningless rutting he had always known in the past. Composure deserting him, he reached for Gabriel, needing the reassurance of loving arms around him.

Gabriel obliged instantly, enfolding Lucio in a snug embrace, rocking him gently as he fought the trembling and fear. "It's all right," Gabriel whispered soothingly. "Whatever it is, it's all right."

Lucio lifted his head to meet Gabriel's eyes. He could feel tears welling in his eyes and hoped they wouldn't spill over, but he felt like his heart was breaking. "It isn't all right," Lucio said. "We have to go back to town, and I have to meet Lord Endicott at his club. He'll bend me over the arm of a couch or the back of a chair and he'll fuck me like all the rest and I'll spend the entire time sick with the knowledge that I'm betraying you, that I'm letting him use me for his cheap pleasure."

"You aren't 'letting' him do it," Gabriel said. "You didn't ask him to hire you and while you might ask him to bed you because it's what he expects, it's not you saying it, not really. It's an act. You didn't ask to be a companion any more than I asked to be a merchant or Lord Endicott asked to be an aristocrat. It happened. And it will be all right. You'll do your job because you have to, and I'll go home and do mine so I can sell as many of those damn fans as possible and earn the money to buy your contract. And when you crawl into your own bed tonight, you'll close your eyes and you'll focus on what it felt like to have my hand on you instead of Lord Endicott's. You'll remember what it felt like to have me loving you instead of him using you. And you'll fall asleep with a smile on your face. Maybe this weekend you can visit me at the workshop again and we can make another memory for you to treasure, but until then, you'll hold onto this one and you'll remember that I don't care what they do to your body as long as your kisses are mine."

"Do you really mean that?" Lucio asked, brushing at the tears that had escaped during Gabriel's impassioned speech.

"I really mean it," Gabriel said, his voice so strong with conviction that Lucio had to believe him. Gabriel pulled a handkerchief from his pocket, dabbing at Lucio's eyes. "Pull yourself together now. I want to remember you smiling along with the vision of you lost in pleasure rather than your face wet with tears."

Lucio took a deep breath and summoned a smile. "Better?"

"Much better," Gabriel said, kissing him softly, "but we should go soon or you'll be late getting back. I don't want to get you in trouble."

There wouldn't be trouble as long as Lucio wasn't late for his next guest, but he didn't argue with Gabriel. Drawing out the moment, while tempting, would only make it harder for him to climb out of the carriage when they reached Mayfair Place and the pleasure palace. He took another deep breath and stepped out of Gabriel's embrace. "Let's get this over with, then."

Gabriel caught Lucio's hand. "Say the word."

Gabriel didn't finish the sentence, but Lucio understood. He shook his head, too afraid of the consequences of fleeing to take that risk now. He knew of only one companion who had ever tried to run away, and she was the one who was given to all the guests who didn't care what state their companion was in when they returned her. If he could hold out long enough, Gabriel would be able to buy his contract and it wouldn't matter. He just had to hold out that long.

17

GABRIEL kept his face serene and his touch light and loving all the way back to town through force of will alone. He wanted to knock on the roof of the cab and tell the driver to turn around and take them south, away from the capital, but it would make no difference. Laws were laws, and without a contract to prove Lucio was his, they would never be safe on the run. His desire had faded with Lucio's revelation of his evening schedule, not because Gabriel wanted him any less, but because Lucio's distress had driven out all thought of anything but comforting the other man. The knowledge that after setting Lucio down in Mayfair Place he would soon be in the arms of another man turned Gabriel's stomach, but he pushed the thought aside. He could not change it, and he had promised he would not make Lucio's job harder than it already was.

Lucio was pliant in his arms, apparently having taken Gabriel's words to heart. He snuggled in Gabriel's arms and nuzzled Gabriel's jaw, so clearly starved for affection that Gabriel could not resist giving it in abundance. Lucio returned it ten-fold, stroking and cuddling and generally reminding Gabriel of an overenthusiastic puppy. It eased his mind somewhat because he seriously doubted Lucio ever let himself be this genuine, this needy with his guests. Like Lucio's kisses, this side of the companion was only for him. He only hoped it would be enough to sustain him until he could buy Lucio's contract and have every facet of this gem of a man to himself.

Watching Lucio pull his façade back into place as they neared Mayfair Place nearly broke Gabriel. He wanted the sweet, innocent young man of the afternoon back, not the polished, carefree companion. Only Lucio leaning in for a kiss before he stepped out of the carriage stopped Gabriel from begging him not to go. He stayed where he was until Lucio disappeared inside without a backward glance before calling his address up to the driver. He hoped Lucio managed to come see him this weekend because he didn't know how long he could wait to hold him again.

"How was your date?" Caleb joked when Gabriel walked back into the lab. Gabriel scowled at him, pulling off his frock coat and grabbing a leather apron to put in its place. He grabbed a pair of protective goggles and started to work on the next engine for a fan, needing to vent his frustrations on something.

"That bad?" Andrew quipped, but Gabriel didn't even look up. He simply pounded harder on the gear that had gotten bent and was causing the mechanism to stick.

"That good, I suspect," Caleb said in answer to Andrew's question. "That's why he's beating on unsuspecting engines."

"Don't you two have work to do?" Gabriel snapped, not wanting to listen to his friends speculate on his time with Lucio. It was too precious to share even with them.

"Not so much as to keep us from talking while we do it," Andrew replied lightly.

"Then talk about something else," Gabriel growled. "I don't want to hear it."

"That good," Caleb repeated.

With a roar, Gabriel dropped the hammer in his hand, charging Caleb and forcing him against the far wall. "I said drop it."

"Did you finally give in and fuck him?" Caleb goaded.

That was the final straw. Gabriel reared back, his fist cocked, with every intention of punching his best friend. Andrew's hand caught his, wrenching it behind his back. "I wouldn't do that if I were you. You might regret it tomorrow."

Gabriel struggled, but he couldn't break Andrew's grip, especially when Caleb grabbed his other arm. "Talk to us, Gabriel," Caleb insisted. "You don't have to tell us what you did. Just tell us what's going on in your head."

Gabriel shook off Andrew's hand. "I'm fine. I'm not going to hit him. We went to Nicholasville to walk in the woods. It was the most peaceful afternoon I've had in a long time. The forest smelled so fresh compared to town, and nobody knew us or cared who we were, so nobody searched for our tattoos or made judgments because Lucio is a companion. We didn't have to play any roles. We could just be together."

"I can see that being pretty enjoyable," Andrew agreed, taking a step back now that Gabriel had calmed down, "but that isn't why you swung at Caleb."

"We had tea," Gabriel said, reddening as he remembered what else they had done, how Lucio had flushed and babbled in his passion. How his face looked when he came. "And then it was time to come home, and I had to watch the relaxed lover of the afternoon disappear behind the mask of the companion, and I had to watch the man I'm falling in love with walk into the pleasure palace knowing he would spend the evening in someone else's arms."

He held up his hands as if to ward off an incipient smack at the scowl on Caleb's face. "I didn't dwell on it while we were together. I didn't bring it up, even once. I treasured the time we had together for what it was and he did the same, but that doesn't change reality, either. In a matter of an hour, two at the most, he'll be forced to bend over and take some other man's cock up his ass, and I can't do a damn thing about it."

"Yes, you can," Caleb said. "You can get back to work on that fan. Or better yet, you can let us do that and you can work on whatever invention you've got stashed in the basement since I know that's 'the big one'. Crying over spilt milk isn't going to help Lucio. Hard work and your genius will."

Gabriel took a deep breath. "Come downstairs with me, both of you. Maybe you can see what I'm missing."

GABRIEL stood at the casement of his window, staring up at the clearing sky. He thought he could feel a hint of coolness on the breeze, making him hope fall was on the way, or if not that, at least a storm to clear the air and break the heat for awhile. Slowly he stripped, trying to catch every bit of a breeze on his overheated skin. He imagined having Lucio there with him, coming up beside him equally naked, wrapping his arms around Gabriel in invitation. His cock swelled with interest. Sliding his hand down his body, Gabriel closed his eyes and gave free rein to the fantasy, stroking himself languidly as he imagined Lucio touching him as he had touched Lucio that afternoon. It would have been so easy to ask Lucio to return the favor, and he knew Lucio would have done it, but it would have been out of a sense of obligation or habit still rather than because he simply couldn't wait a moment longer. Gabriel didn't want to be an obligation or a habit. He wanted to be an addiction, a haven, a ravening need that Lucio could not ignore a moment longer.

As if to mock him, his thoughts conjured an image of Lucio with the faceless Lord Endicott. He had no problem imagining what Lucio would look like naked, though he suspected his imagination might not do justice to the real thing, and bent over a couch, his head turned so he could look over his shoulder at the man behind him. Lucio's face was closed as he batted his eyelashes flirtatiously and wriggled his buttocks in eager invitation. Gabriel wanted to believe the gestures were an act to satisfy his customer, but a part of him would always fear it was real. He opened his eyes, trying to force the images aside, but his inner demons had the bit in their teeth now, supplanting that image with one of the faceless lord plunging between the creamy cheeks while Lucio bucked and moaned and begged for more.

"Stop it," Gabriel shouted, although there was no one to hear. He scrubbed at his face with his hands, no longer aroused. Pushing away from the window, he paced the room, fighting his anger and resentment. Caleb had told him, Cressida had told him repeatedly, that he had to let this go or he would drive Lucio away. He couldn't hope to have Lucio in his life if he couldn't accept Lucio's life. He could work to change it for the future, but he had to accept its reality for now. If only he could figure out how to do that.

He wanted to. He would love to be able to brush the thought of Lucio with another man aside as if it had no importance or relevance whatsoever, but he was not an aristocrat, used to thinking of sexual pleasure as another convenience. He believed in love and fidelity and happily ever after, no matter how long or short a time that happiness lasted. His parents had only spent ten years together before an accident took both their lives, but Gabriel remembered watching them together, seeing how they loved each other. When Caleb's parents had taken him in, orphaned, grieving, and alone in the workhouse where he knew no one and had no idea how to survive, he'd seen a different example of love, the quiet, enduring kind that never seemed to explode into passion the way his parents' had done, but that provided a bedrock of support for Caleb and his siblings as well as for Gabriel.

Nothing in his experience had prepared him for loving a companion. The thought brought him up short, and something his father had always said came back to him: *When you love someone, you do whatever it takes to make your beloved happy.* He had very little left from his parents, but he had their example and his father's advice. Caleb and Andrew had already promised to help him earn the money to buy Lucio's contract, however much the idea of buying Lucio bothered him. He'd made that commitment. Now he had to make the rest. Climbing into to bed, he resolved to be as supportive of Lucio's life as he could. He didn't want to hear details if he could help it, but he would ask Lucio how his day or week had been since they last saw each other. He would listen to whatever Lucio chose to share, and he would not let any reaction on his part show on his face or in his voice. He *would* make Lucio happy.

LUCIO leaned his head against the window frame, staring out at the stars and wondering what Gabriel was doing, if the inventor was thinking of him, and if he was, if he thought of him fondly. His backside stung a little from the vigorous pounding Lord Endicott had given him, but he knew from experience that he would be fine by morning. The evening had been as hellish as he feared, trying to pretend an interest in the somewhat paunchy older man when all he wanted was to be with Gabriel, but his training had kicked in, and he had said and done all the right things.

The epiphany had come about the time Lord Endicott finished stretching him, however inadequately, and started pounding into him. He knew what it felt like to be loved now, even if Gabriel hadn't put those words on it yet. Surely no one could touch him the way Gabriel had done without some degree of love. Closing his eyes, he could recall with perfect clarity the sensation of Gabriel's coarse hands on his body, Gabriel's lips kissing him so tenderly. The novelty of finding release, of *wanting* release. Nothing Lord Endicott or the others did to him roused him. It was mechanical, automatic. It was his job, nothing more. He had known that already. It had been repeated ad nauseam since he was a child, hiding in Cressida's bedroom and dreaming of a man who would see past it. They had put aside those dreams when they returned from their first guests, but the memory of those whispered secrets made him smile. Tonight he had realized something his trainers had never told him. The aristocrat might touch his body, but it didn't have anything to do with Lucio. If anyone was sullied by what Lord Endicott was doing, it was the aristocrat, not Lucio. Lucio had no choice in the matter. Lord Endicott had chosen to be there. Given the choice, Lucio would be in Gabriel's arms. That put any dishonor firmly on the aristocrat's shoulders, not on Lucio's. He only hoped he could express that surety in a way Gabriel could understand and accept, because he had realized something on the way home from Nicholasville that afternoon.

He loved Gabriel.

"BLACKSTONE! It's been a while. We thought perhaps you had forgotten about us."

Gabriel summoned a smile for Bill Beacham, one of the leaders of the Caste Equality movement. "Hello, Beacham. No, I haven't forgotten. I've just been busy."

"And what had you so busy you missed three meetings?" Elijah Wakefield, another of the political activists, asked. "You've always had time for us before."

"Work," Gabriel replied, not ready to talk about Lucio, even here where his desire to free Lucio from his situation would be understood and accepted. His feelings for the companion were too new and precious to share. "I made something for an aristocrat who was pleased enough with my work to recommend me to some of his friends. I've been swamped ever since."

"Sounds like he's gotten too good for us," Wakefield teased.

"No," Gabriel replied quickly. "It's nothing like that, but I need the money from the commissions. I have employees to pay and debts to reimburse." *And Lucio.* "If anything, I'm even more determined to be part of the movement. I... I met a companion, two, actually, through Lord Stuart. Watching the way the aristocrats treated them made me sick to my stomach. I believed the system had to change before I met them, but now I'm more determined than ever."

"It's rare to actually meet a companion if you aren't a paying customer," Beacham said, his interest clearly piqued. "Their time is so structured, from what I've been able to find out."

This was safe. This was fact, not his feelings for Lucio. He could talk about what Cressida had told him, even what Lucio had said, without getting into his feelings for the beautiful man who dominated his thoughts. "Incredibly regimented," Gabriel agreed. "One of them wanted to purchase a fan from me and had to check out and check back in to come see me to place the order. Our discussion ran longer than he planned, and he was worried about the consequences of returning late. He might as well be in prison!"

"That's awful," Wakefield chimed in. "Although it says something that he had the money to make any purchase."

"He said it was from tips customers gave him," Gabriel replied. "He sees nothing of the money the customers pay for his time. That all goes to his 'upkeep'. Like he was some kind of animal."

"You said you met two companions. Where did you meet the other one?"

"At Lord Stuart's ball," Gabriel said.

"Wait. What were you doing at Stuart's ball?" Dominic Moberly, the third leader of the Caste Equality movement, demanded.

"He invited me," Gabriel replied. "He wanted to thank me for the invention I made for him, so he invited me to his niece's birthday ball."

"That's quite a thank you," Beacham said with a low whistle. "I mean yes, you're merchant caste, not labor or guardian, but you aren't an aristocrat."

"Nor did he try to say I was," Gabriel replied. "He was very clear in his introductions, as to both who I was and why he had invited me."

"How did that go over?" Wakefield asked.

"I've been so busy I missed the last three meetings," Gabriel reminded them. "It's apparently all the rage at the moment to have a Blackstone machine. I've got enough commissions to keep me busy for six months, and that's if nothing more comes in."

"Lucky dog. So tell me about Stuart."

"He's not opposed to shaking things up a bit," Gabriel said, thinking of the seating arrangements at the dinner before the ball, "but he's still an aristocrat who, to judge by the way he treated his companion at the ball, hasn't necessarily considered life outside his caste."

"What do you mean?"

Gabriel shrugged, not really wanting to think about what he had witnessed—much less what he hadn't—between Lord Stuart and Lucio, but it was too late now. "Little things," Gabriel said. "The way he was always touching the man, groping him really. I mean, not obscenely, but far more than he would have ever touched another aristocrat. The other companion, Miss Cressida, said no one would have thought anything of

Lord Stuart doing anything short of stripping him naked and taking him on the table."

"That's obscene."

"Apparently not when the one being exposed is a companion," Gabriel said bitterly. "Lord Stuart wasn't anywhere near that bad, in public at least. I don't know what they did in private." Not all of it, anyway. The puffiness around Lucio's lips after he'd been called away was telling, and Gabriel knew it hadn't come from the swift kisses they'd shared. The thought still turned his stomach, but he pushed that aside for now.

"If Stuart invited you to a ball, do you think he'd be willing to talk to us?" Wakefield asked.

"I hinted at it when he brought up the ball," Gabriel said. "He made a comment about the aristocrats being inbred and needing fresh blood. He equivocated, talking about his nieces and nephews and not doing anything to hurt their position in society, but when I probed a little, he told me the ball was my chance to prove my worth. We could call on him. I don't think he'd send us away, even if he didn't agree to help."

"How soon can we go?" Wakefield asked eagerly.

Gabriel thought about his schedule, the work he needed to do, and Lucio's promise to visit during the weekend. "Monday morning," he proposed. "You could come to the workshop around ten, and we could call on him from there."

"Is it really a good idea to bring ourselves that strongly to the attention of an aristocrat?" Moberly asked.

"A sympathetic aristocrat," Gabriel reminded them. "He already knew about us, anyway. Not who we are personally, but he knew about the movement. We have to take risks if we're going to bring about change. Isn't that what you're always telling me?"

"Well, yes, but—"

"No buts," Gabriel interrupted. "I have no idea how long my current popularity will last. We should take advantage of it while we can, because society is a fickle thing."

18

"YOU had visitors while you were out," Caleb said when Gabriel got back from the Caste Equality meeting.

"Who?"

"A Lord Endicott who requested a fan for his house," Caleb said, holding up a piece of paper. "I didn't quote him a price and he didn't ask."

"Good," Gabriel said, his face tightening as he thought of the man who had taken Lucio from him on Thursday. He would have to be subtle about it, but the fact that each fan was tailored to the size of the room and the customer's specifications meant Gabriel could have his revenge. Lord Endicott might not ever know it, but he would pay for using Lucio, and the extra gold would hasten the day when Gabriel could free Lucio from the pleasure palace. "I'll visit him early next week and give him the price and an estimated time of completion. You said visitors. Who else came by?"

Caleb looked away. "Lucio."

Gabriel's stomach dropped. He had missed the chance to see his lover. "What did he say?"

"When he realized you weren't here and that we couldn't say when you'd be back, he left right away," Caleb said, "but he said to tell you he was free tomorrow from ten to one and that he would come back then. He hoped you would be available."

"If I'd known he was coming today, I would have stayed home," Gabriel said.

"He knows that," Caleb promised. "He said he had a cancellation and used the chance to come sooner than he'd planned and that he didn't expect you to do nothing but sit around and wait for him. He left this as well."

Caleb handed Gabriel an envelope with a suspicious lump in it. Gabriel opened it, a gold ring falling out into his hand.

"What's that?" Caleb asked.

"The fruits of his labor," Gabriel replied, trying to push aside the bitterness. "He's smuggling out the tips his clients give him so that I can use them toward his contract. Each time I see him, he gives me something to hold in trust until I can get enough to rescue him."

"How much will that cost?" Caleb asked, his voice curious.

"I have no idea," Gabriel replied honestly, "but it doesn't matter. I'll work and save until I have enough."

"You really care about him, don't you?"

Gabriel nodded. "I think… I think I'm falling in love with him."

"Then we'd better get back to work," Caleb said. "I don't know what a companion's contract costs, but I know it's a lot more than the price of a fan or two. How much are you charging for them?"

"Forty," Gabriel replied, "unless it was for a much larger room."

Caleb's eyes narrowed. "Make it sixty."

"Sixty? That's way too much."

"No, it's not," Caleb said, "not when you're the only one making them and they're this much in demand. Materials alone cost you between twenty-five to thirty and you have to pay Andrew and me. And you have to eat. You aren't making enough on each one to set anything aside for Lucio, either to visit him or to buy his contract."

"So what do I tell the ones who've already discussed price with me?" Gabriel asked.

"Tell them the materials were more expensive than you expected or tell them the construction was more complicated than you thought it would be," Caleb said. "Or sell the first few for the quoted price and raise it for everyone else. They're too proud to discuss money with each other. They'll never know that one of them paid a different price than another."

"The ones for a bigger room cost more anyway," Gabriel said slowly. "I could always tell them that we had to change the size of the fan given the size of the room they wanted it for."

"Make the bigger ones eighty or even a hundred," Caleb directed. "They have the money to pay for it and you have a need."

"Yes," Gabriel said, thinking of Lucio's face when he cried because he had to leave Gabriel's arms and go to someone else's bed. "Yes, I have a need. We'll need something else. Something to whet their interest when everyone has a fan. Something we can start working on quietly now and present ready for purchase, at least the first one, so that we can keep their business and their interest."

"Did you have something in mind?" Caleb asked.

"No. I was hoping you might."

"What do I know of aristocrats?" Caleb said with a laugh. "I see them on the rare occasion they come into the shop. Ask Lucio. He knows their lives. He knows what would appeal to them, either functionally or for show."

Gabriel smiled, not only at the thought of seeing Lucio but at the fact that Caleb would make the suggestion. A month ago, Caleb wouldn't have given a companion the credit for having a thought in his head besides how to please his guests. Gabriel's rants or, more likely, Lucio himself had succeeded in convincing Caleb otherwise. "I'll do that."

"How did your meeting go this morning?"

"You could come with me and find out," Gabriel said hopefully, but Caleb shook his head. "It went well," Gabriel continued, answering the question. "I'm going to take Wakefield with me to meet Lord Stuart on Monday. I'm hoping his fire will interest the old man and we'll finally have some aristocratic support."

"You realize the chance you're taking," Caleb said. "If you end up in prison for this, you won't be able to help Lucio."

"Yes, but if I don't do it, things will never change, and Lucio will never be anything more than a pleasure slave. He might be mine rather than on sale to the highest bidder, but he won't have any more freedom than he does now."

"Of course he will," Caleb exclaimed. "You'd never treat him that way!"

"No, I wouldn't," Gabriel agreed, "but he'd still be my property. I'd still have a piece of paper proclaiming my ownership, and I'd have to produce that paper any time someone questioned what a companion was doing away from the pleasure palaces. People might not question an aristocrat, but nobody expects a merchant to own a companion. I'd have to carry the contract with me any time Lucio left the house. I'll do it if that's the price of having him at my side, but that's demeaning to him. I'd rather see things change so he doesn't have to belong to anyone. Even me."

"Just be careful," Caleb entreated. "Andrew and I would be pretty much destitute without you."

"You'd keep the workshop going," Gabriel said. "Even if you didn't come up with anything new, you could keep making the fans and selling those. That would keep a roof over your heads and food on your table even if it didn't make you rich."

"But nobody wants a fan by Deahl or Lambert," Caleb reminded him. "They want a fan by Blackstone. If you're disgraced, we all lose out."

"I'll be careful," Gabriel promised. "I have a future to dream about now, a concrete one, and I'm not going to throw that away."

GABRIEL felt quite ridiculous as he paced the front of the workshop the next morning, attired in the visiting suit David Reading, the tailor down the street, had made for him, but he wanted to look his best for Lucio. He had gotten up early and heated water for a bath, thinking of Lucio's chance comment the night of their first meeting about heated water. He hoped Lucio would not be disappointed when he realized how few conveniences Gabriel had in his life. He might be capable of making all the machines necessary for those conveniences, but he had to sell them to live. Now, scrubbed clean and terribly aware of the empty room behind him, he felt like a nervous bridegroom—or perhaps not even that. More like a nervous suitor showing his beloved the reality of his life and hoping his chosen would not reject him because of it.

Gabriel had come to the conclusion since his last meeting with Lucio that he wanted the companion in his life, however that worked out, which meant making sure Lucio understood exactly what he would be giving up if he chose to become Gabriel's. Gabriel imagined Lucio would say something about it not being his choice, that if Gabriel bought his contract, he would come, but Gabriel didn't want to take that choice away from his lover. He wanted Lucio's agreement to the life they could have together.

The chime on the door drew his attention, Lucio coming through as casually dressed as Gabriel had ever seen him. Immediately Gabriel locked the door and flipped the sign to "Closed." "Come in the back," Gabriel urged, not wanting to kiss Lucio where any passerby on the street could see them. Lucio might say he was used to people watching him, but this was not business, and Gabriel refused to treat Lucio the way his guests did.

Lucio followed him into the back room.

"Your friends aren't here?"

"I gave them the morning off," Gabriel said. "I didn't want anyone or anything to disturb us."

Lucio's grin grew mischievous. "Did you have plans for the morning?"

Gabriel felt his cheeks redden. "Indulging your every whim," he said impetuously. "I want to kiss you again, but only if you want it."

"Silly man," Lucio scolded, stepping into Gabriel's embrace and kissing him thoroughly. "Of course I want you to kiss me."

"Business first," Gabriel said. "Your fan should be ready by the end of the week."

"I'll need a second one," Lucio said. "I promised Cressida one too."

"Will the handlers let you see to that, or will they allow her come?"

"They might make her come with me, but she would leave us alone once she was here," Lucio said.

"What else could I make for you?" Gabriel asked. "Or more importantly, what else could I make that will catch the interest of the aristocrats? The fans have been a huge success, but eventually everyone will have one, and I need something else to catch and hold their attention."

Lucio thought for a moment. "Nothing jumps to mind, but I will think about it and have a suggestion for you when I come to pick up my fan." He reached in his pocket and pulled out another piece of jewelry. "And here's my business taken care of. You are keeping them safe, are you not?"

"I spoke with Doctor Headley, my neighbor and friend. He recommended a jeweler who would give me a fair price," Gabriel said. "The gold from the others is safely in the bank, waiting for me to add to it. Lucio...." His voice broke as he tried to master his emotions. "I need you to see what my life is like. I want you to share it with me. I want to buy your contract and bring you here to be my lover and my partner, but it is not the life you are used to."

"No," Lucio agreed, "it is not. I won't have to worry about keeping my appearance perfect and my skin unblemished. I won't have to worry about keeping a calendar and making sure I have enough time to bathe between appointments. I won't have to worry that my new guest might be abusive and hurt me. I won't have to worry about disappointing a guest and being punished for it. If fewer luxuries are the price I pay for that, I'd say it's a small price indeed."

Gabriel flinched at the description of Lucio's life, but he had to be sure. "Look around. Come upstairs with me and see what my home is like. Make sure you can accept that. If you can, then nothing will stop me from making our dream a reality, no matter how long I have to wait or how hard I have to work."

Gabriel swore his shoes caught on every uneven board on the floor as they walked through the kitchen, highlighting the roughness of his dwelling. He flinched as he looked at the wooden staircase, the boards only smoothed by the tread of feet and the brush of hands along their surfaces. He gestured for Lucio to precede him up the stairs, keenly aware of the creak of the wood as they climbed. Another time he would have admired the perfect form of the man in front of him, but his apprehension precluded such thoughts. His bedroom, which he hoped Lucio would soon call his own, filled the full area of the loft, its size the only redeeming feature as far as Gabriel could see. The furniture was utilitarian, nothing more, the straw mattress over the leather webbing a far cry from what Lucio was undoubtedly used to. Lucio, however, seemed to have no hesitation, wandering around the room and studying it carefully. His fingers trailed over the handmade quilt, one of the few things Gabriel had from his grandmother.

"I think I could be very happy here," Lucio said slowly. "Not a bar or a lock or bit of cold marble in sight. Just a warm, welcoming room where I can lie down with my lover and find a respite from the world."

Gabriel's eyes closed with relief. He held out his hand, reaching for Lucio. "I love you," he said softly. "I think I realized it when I watched you walk away from me on Thursday, but I couldn't very well call you back to tell you then."

Lucio smiled softly, his dark eyes luminous in his pale face. "I love you as well. I knew it when I got home Thursday night. I will always hate anyone else touching me, but I realized something else as I lay in bed alone wishing I was with you."

"What was that?" Gabriel asked. The thrill of hearing that Lucio loved him was offset by the mention of Lucio with someone else.

"I realized that there is no dishonor to me in my profession. I didn't choose it. I didn't choose my clients. They are the ones dirtied by what they do to me, not me," Lucio said. "If I chose to sneak out and meet someone else the way I meet you, if I chose to cheat on you that way, it would touch on my honor, but what happens because of my job isn't about me at all. Only when you touch me, love me, is it about me."

"And when I touch you, it is only about you," Gabriel swore. "Your pleasure is what matters to me."

"I know," Lucio assured him. "Will you accept that your pleasure matters to me as well?"

Gabriel swallowed hard, not sure what it would do to him to have Lucio's smooth hands on his body. "As long as you promise me you will never do anything because you think I want it rather than because you want to do it to me."

"I swear," Lucio said, taking both of Gabriel's hands in his and placing them over his heart, "that there will never be anything but truth between us."

Overcome with emotion, Gabriel lifted their joined hands to his lips, kissing Lucio's knuckles tenderly. "Will you lie down with me?" he asked softly. "I want the smell of your hair on my pillow and the memory of you in my arms when I fall asleep at night. We don't have to do anything."

Lucio shook his head with a shy smile. "You cannot truly expect me to do nothing but lie beside you after the way you touched me in the inn," he teased, backing toward the bed and drawing Gabriel with him. "I need the surety, the purity of your touch. I need to feel to the depths of my being that you love me in spite of what I am."

Gabriel caught Lucio in his arms, pulling him close. "I hate what your job forces you to do, but there is nothing about *you* that I would change." He toed off his shoes and removed his jacket, leaving his shirt and trousers in place. It would be easy to strip away the barriers between them and fall onto the bed in a passionate heap, but Gabriel was not sure he was ready for that, much less that Lucio was. Instead, he sat on the bed, fully clothed, leaving the quilt in place, and patted the space beside him. Lucio mirrored him, removing his shoes and his coat before taking the offered seat. When Gabriel hesitated still, Lucio reclined across the bed, tugging on Gabriel's arm until Gabriel stretched out next to him.

"I don't sleep with my guests as a rule," Lucio said when Gabriel was comfortable. "None of them wants to keep me. Lying here like this is as much a novelty to me as kissing you."

"Another thing that belongs only to me, then," Gabriel said, reminded of the sense of innocence he had gotten on Thursday as they kissed and as he touched Lucio.

"My heart, my kisses, my rest, and anything else they will let me offer you," Lucio swore.

"I will be happy with anything you can give me," Gabriel promised.

"Good," Lucio said, pushing on Gabriel's shoulder until he rolled to his back. "Then you will be thrilled with his." His hand ran over the linen of Gabriel's shirt, caressing him through the fabric.

Gabriel caught his hand. "This isn't what I had in mind when I asked you to lie down with me."

"I know," Lucio replied, "but it is what I want."

19

LUCIO pushed up onto one elbow and stared down at the man whose bed he shared. His entire body tingled at the thought of where he was and what he was doing. He was nervous, knowing this was far more important that simply pleasing a guest, but he hoped—maybe—that this would be easier. He didn't have to pretend an interest he didn't feel. He didn't have to do something because a guest wanted it when he would rather have done something else. He could touch Gabriel however he wanted.

And oh, how he wanted! Gabriel's chest was broad beneath his linen shirt. Giving in to temptation, Lucio traced that breadth with eager fingers, feeling the firm muscle beneath the shirt, proof of Gabriel's active life. He flattened his palm, kneading the hard planes as he explored. He could hear the change in Gabriel's breathing, but his lover did nothing to direct his movements, nothing to speed him up or slow him down. Eagerly Lucio reached for the cravat at the base of Gabriel's neck. "May I?" he asked, hand hovering over the length of cloth.

In answer, Gabriel drew Lucio's face back to his for a kiss. Lucio gave it willingly, his tongue sliding over Gabriel's lips and into his mouth, exploring every crevice and cranny. Once again he tasted coffee, making him smile against Gabriel's mouth. Lifting his head finally, he looked down at the man beneath him, sure his expression betrayed the wealth of emotions surging through him. "You didn't answer my question."

"You may do anything you'd like," Gabriel replied. "And you may stop at any time you like."

"You keep saying that," Lucio joked, despite his appreciation of the consideration behind the words. "I have the man I love in bed with me, and he keeps telling me not to do things to him. There is something wrong with this picture."

Gabriel chuckled. "I'm not a martyr," he said, "but I want you to feel free to be yourself and to do what you want."

"I am," Lucio assured him, his fingers tugging at the cravat to loosen it so he could open the shirt that hid Gabriel from him. The darker color of the merchant's face faded to a pale cream beneath his shirt, the line of contrast fascinating Lucio. He lowered his head and licked along the line, smug satisfaction filling him at the inarticulate sound Gabriel made. Lucio slid his hand beneath the cloth of Gabriel's shirt, finding hot skin and stroking across it. Gabriel's chest was covered in a light pelt of hair, the wiry texture tantalizing his fingertips. More aristocrats than not had smooth chests, whether by nature or by design. Lucio liked the proof of Gabriel's unpretentiousness.

Remembering how carefully Gabriel had searched out his sensitive places, Lucio did not move directly to Gabriel's nipples, choosing instead to linger on his collarbone and the hollow at the base of his neck. He licked along the protrusion of bone, absorbing the taste of Gabriel's skin. He had never bothered before, but now he wanted every sense imbued with some memory of Gabriel so that when he was alone or with a guest, he would have it to draw on for comfort. Gabriel seemed willing to oblige him, lying back and giving him the freedom to explore. A part of Lucio felt guilty that he was so focused on his own explorations rather than on Gabriel's pleasure, but a glance at Gabriel's face revealed an eager bliss that encouraged him to continue.

Gabriel's nipples peeked through the dusting of hair on his chest, but Lucio left them untouched. He knew what it did to a man to pay attention to the little buds. He wanted to experience everything else, all the things his guests had no patience to allow him.

Gabriel, on the other hand, seemed made of patience as he lay there unmoving, allowing Lucio to explore his body, licking and nibbling, inhaling his scent. Lucio studied his face for a moment, but Gabriel nodded at him encouragingly. "Whatever you want."

Lucio hesitated at the waist of Gabriel's trousers, not sure if he was ready to take that next step.

"I'm a man, not a rutting animal," Gabriel said, echoing words he had said to Lucio before and bringing a smile to the companion's face.

"I know you're not," Lucio assured him. "I trust you to keep your promise and not take anything I'm not ready to give, but I also have to decide what I'm ready to take."

"Come up here," Gabriel urged.

Lucio slid back up on the bed, relaxing into Gabriel's arms when the inventor tugged on his sleeve. Without thought, he turned his head for a kiss, knowing without a doubt Gabriel's lips would be there to meet his. The kiss was as sweet and tender as any they had shared, making Lucio realize that even with the provocation of his earlier caresses—he knew Gabriel was aroused because he could feel the hard shaft against his hip—his lover would stay in control and keep their interactions as light and tender as he needed them to be.

He suddenly needed to see, to touch, to wallow in the scent and taste and texture of Gabriel's skin. He knew it was selfish, but he would find a way to repay the other man when he was done. Pushing up on his elbow, he stroked Gabriel's hair, the reddish streaks less noticeable in the relative dimness of the room. He wondered randomly if they faded completely in the winter. The thought disappeared as quickly as it came because other delights beckoned. Taking a deep breath, he slid his hand down Gabriel's chest again to the fastening on his trousers. "May I?"

"You may do—"

"Whatever I like," Lucio finished in tandem with Gabriel. "Thank you."

"I love you," Gabriel reminded him, sending another thrill through Lucio at hearing those words. "No thanks are necessary."

Lucio fairly beamed up at Gabriel as he opened his lover's trousers and pushed them down, baring long, muscled legs to his gaze and touch. His eyes darted away from the engorged erection, not ready to deal with that outside of his profession. He knew exactly how to touch it to bring pleasure, but he feared doing so would cheapen his feelings for the man whose bed he currently shared. Instead, he turned his attentions to the length of Gabriel's legs, starting at his feet and working his way up, licking and nuzzling and reveling in the roughness of the coating of hair beneath his fingers and tongue, the scent of Gabriel's arousal on the air—arousal he had induced without doing anything his trainers had taught him. He rubbed his smooth cheek against Gabriel's thigh, wanting to cover himself in his lover.

The hitch of breath above him drew his attention back to Gabriel and the selfishness of his own actions. "I'm sorry," he apologized, reaching for Gabriel's shaft. "I shouldn't have been so selfish."

Gabriel caught his hand before it connected, lifting it to his lips and kissing the knuckles gently. "You aren't being selfish. You have no idea how good you're making me feel." He glanced down at his thick erection. "Or maybe you do. I want exactly what you're doing to me, Lucio, because *you* want what you're doing to me, and that makes it the most wonderful, arousing, fulfilling experience of my life."

Lucio searched Gabriel's face, sure his lover had to be teasing him. He knew what aroused men. He had spent the last eight years of his life perfecting those skills, but Gabriel didn't seem to need any of them. "I'm so used to men who take their pleasure from me or demand I give them pleasure in certain ways. I don't know how to act with you."

"Don't act," Gabriel said. "Be yourself." His hand stroked over his cock slowly. "You aren't blind. You see what you've done to me by being in my bed even fully dressed as you are. Having you here touching me in any way is so much more than I believed possible, and then to hear you say that you love me on top of it—you could stop right now and I would be a happy man."

"I don't want to stop," Lucio admitted hoarsely.

"Then keep doing whatever you want to do."

Lucio swallowed around the lump in his throat. "Turn over?" he requested.

Immediately Gabriel rolled to his stomach, hitching a pillow beneath his hips and spreading his legs slightly. Lucio stifled a moan at the sight of his lover lying there, stretched out for his enjoyment. His hands trembled as they settled on the broad expanse of Gabriel's back, finding tense muscles and kneading at them. This, too, had been part of his training, but it was a part his guests rarely utilized, and the impulse to care for Gabriel now had nothing to do with his trainers' suggestions on how to lull a guest into a relaxed mood.

No aristocrat Lucio had ever known had a body to match Gabriel's, not like this. Their bodies were too often soft from days of indolence. Not Gabriel's. The muscles in his back and arms proclaimed a life of hard work, a physique Lucio envied. He worked his way lower, past Gabriel's rib cage to the small of his back. The pillow beneath Gabriel's hips pushed his buttocks up as if asking for attention, but he moved past them. Perhaps he would work up the courage to return, but for now, he massaged his way down Gabriel's legs instead, lingering any time his ministrations drew a moan or a hiss from his lover's lips. He wanted to make Gabriel feel as good as he felt in the freedom of the moment without turning it truly sexual.

Finally having reached Gabriel's feet, he could delay no longer. He either had to work up the nerve to stroke or suck Gabriel to climax or he had to deal with being as selfish a bastard as the aristocrats who fucked him and left him alone.

Gabriel's eyes glittered when he rolled to his back again at the touch of Lucio's hand on his hip. Lucio recognized the look. Mostly. Because while Gabriel's gaze was as admiring and as lustful as any aristocrat's, Lucio also saw the love in Gabriel's eyes, an emotion he had never seen on any other face. He reached tentatively for Gabriel's cock.

"No," Gabriel said, catching his hand. "Not when you have that look on your face."

"But I can hardly leave you like this," Lucio protested, eyes fixed on the leaking shaft. "I won't do to you what they do to me."

Gabriel's free hand circled his erection. "You won't," he promised. "Having your eyes on me as I come will be more than enough."

Lucio's breath caught in his throat as he realized what Gabriel was proposing. Eyes never leaving the arresting sight of the thick flesh sliding through the channel created by Gabriel's fist, Lucio nodded. The foreskin slid back and forth in time with Gabriel's movements, the pink tip peeking out of its protective shield and then disappearing again, leaving Lucio breathless with excitement as he waited for the next glimpse. His body throbbed as he watched Gabriel pleasure himself, making him wish he had worked up the courage to put his hand on Gabriel's cock.

Unable to stop himself, he reached out and ran his finger over the slit when it next came into view. Gabriel gasped, but Lucio did not look up to meet him, his gaze fixed on the decadent image of that hooded tip slipping in and out of Gabriel's fist as he lifted his finger to his lips, tasting the salty fluid.

Seconds later, Gabriel cried out, his erection twitching and spilling all over his hand. He slumped back against the pillows, panting. Without even thinking, Lucio grabbed Gabriel's hand, lifting it to his lips.

"Don't," Gabriel said. "You don't have to do that for me. I'm not one of your guests."

"I know you aren't," Lucio said. "I don't do this for my guests unless they order me to. The only 'order' you've ever given me is to do what feels good to me." He licked the length of one finger. "This feels good to me."

GABRIEL couldn't stop the groan that escaped as Lucio's hot mouth closed over one of his fingers, sucking from the base past each knuckle to the tip of the digit. He had clenched his jaw and his fists and every muscle in his body to stay still while Lucio explored him, recognizing the companion's avoidance of any area his clients might demand he service. Gabriel hadn't cared about the lack of attention to his nipples or his cock or his bottom. He hadn't needed that to get so hard it hurt. All he'd needed was the knowledge that Lucio was in his bed touching him voluntarily.

Now, though, Lucio's actions couldn't be mistaken for anything but provocative, yet he'd chosen to do them even after Gabriel tried to draw away. His eyes wanted to close, but he forced them to stay open, to watch every second of Lucio's attentions as his lover laved each of his fingers and then turned his attention to the palm of Gabriel's hand, cleaning it with little kittenish lick that set off new charges of desire in Gabriel's cock. There was something incredibly decadent about lying in bed naked while Lucio knelt next to him fully clothed. Gabriel suspected he should have felt uncomfortable with his nudity, but he had only one concern: Lucio's comfort. If Lucio wanted him undressed, Gabriel would undress, no matter how Lucio was clothed.

He waited anxiously to see what Lucio would do when he finished cleaning Gabriel's hand. He got his answer when Lucio stretched out beside him, his head pillowed on Gabriel's shoulder and his fingers tangling in Gabriel's chest hair.

"Every time I'm with you, you help me discover new things about myself," Lucio confided.

"I'm glad," Gabriel said, heart beating a little faster at the admission. "I want there to be special things between us."

"There are," Lucio promised, kissing Gabriel softly, the contact over before Gabriel could search out his flavor on Lucio's tongue. "Our kisses, being together without having sex or at least without feeling like we have to have sex, talking about things. You taking the time to care about my pleasure and my feelings. Nothing about our time together reminds me of my guests. Truly. Even now, doing something to you that I have done to some of them, it's not the same. With them, it's empty gestures. With you, it's about how much I love you and want to make you feel good. About how much I want a connection with you."

"I want the same connection," Gabriel replied, turning to kiss Lucio more deeply. Their lips clung for long moments, derailing Gabriel's train of thought temporarily. When they finally pulled away to breathe, it took him several heartbeats to remember what he'd intended to say. "That's why I stopped you from tugging me. You weren't doing it because of the connection between us. I could see your expression change when you reached for me, and I didn't want that. I wanted the eagerness and the wonder to stay on your face, not resignation. Not where I'm concerned."

"I'm glad you stopped me," Lucio said softly. "I'd have done it. I know how, and it's not like it isn't something I've done before, but it wouldn't have been the same. Watching you, though.... I've never seen anything like it."

"I don't believe that," Gabriel said.

"I've seen men touch themselves," Lucio agreed, "but always for their pleasure, not for mine. When you were... seeing to yourself, I felt like it was all for me, like you were teasing me with your gestures." He tilted his head back so he could meet Gabriel's eyes. "How did you make something that should have been all about you all about me?"

Gabriel kissed the tip of Lucio's nose, then his full, smooth lips. "Because when I was touching myself, I was thinking about you. About touching you, being touched by you, wanting you so much it hurts when you're away. I've never felt anything like this with anyone, no matter how serious or casual our encounter was. That's what makes it different."

"Next time I want to be the one to touch you," Lucio said.

"If you still feel that way next time, I won't say no," Gabriel promised, pulse pounding at the thought of Lucio's smooth palm closing around him. "I want everything we could possibly do to each other, but only when you want it too. That's what will keep what we share different from what happens with your guests. Nothing will ever happen between us that we don't both want."

"I love you," Lucio said, blinking rapidly.

Gabriel pulled Lucio even closer, burying his face in Lucio's fragrant black hair. He clung to those words like a lifeline, knowing Lucio would leave in a matter of hours and go back to his profession and the beds of other men. It wouldn't be like this, though. There would be no tender kisses or whispered words of love. Those were for him and him alone. "I love you too. How long can you stay?"

"Until one," Lucio replied. "I hoped maybe you'd let me help on your flying chair. I want to learn."

"Really?" Gabriel asked. "I'd be glad to show you. Caleb and Andrew have started helping me with it a little too. I finally feel like we might be making some progress."

Lucio sat up, running his hand down Gabriel's side. "Then get cleaned up and come on. I only have so much time, you know."

The teasing reminded Gabriel of Lucio's impending departure, but he pasted a smile on his face and did as Lucio ordered, wiping himself clean with a damp rag and pulling on his work clothes instead of the ones Lucio had taken off of him. Leading the way down the stairs, he pulled the tarp off his masterpiece and set to work.

"ARE you ready to go?" Wakefield asked, arriving at Gabriel's workshop promptly at ten o'clock Monday morning.

"As ready as I'll ever be," Gabriel replied. He had not seen Lord Stuart since the ball and the night the aristocrat had bedded Lucio. Gabriel reminded himself of what Lucio had said about it not touching him anymore, but Gabriel could not let it go so easily. If there had been any other way to introduce the two men without involving himself, Gabriel would have taken it, but he had to play his part.

They took a cab to the quieter, posher section of town where Lord Stuart lived. Wakefield gaped out the window at the size of the houses.

"You'd better get that wide-eyed amazement off your face or Lord Stuart will never take you seriously," Gabriel warned. "You look like you're about twelve at the most."

Wakefield scowled at him, making Gabriel laugh.

The cab stopped in front of Lord Stuart's townhouse and let them out. The butler recognized Gabriel and showed them into the same drawing room where Gabriel had met with Lord Stuart to negotiate the price of his pet.

"Blackstone!" Lord Stuart said, rising and coming to shake Gabriel's hand. "And you've brought a companion with you, I see. He's nearly as pretty as Cressida."

"I'm no companion!" Wakefield interrupted indignantly, stepping forward and drawing Lord Stuart's attention. "You're so set in your ways that you assume any beautiful man or woman is a companion. I happen to be a guardian."

"A guardian?" Lord Stuart repeated. "You don't look big enough to guard anything."

"Lord Ian Stuart, meet Elijah Wakefield, guardian," Gabriel said. Elijah extended his hand, the sword tattoo a clear indication of his caste.

"I stand corrected," Lord Stuart said with a slight bow of his head toward Wakefield. "So what brings you here today with a guardian in tow?"

"Mister Wakefield expressed an interest in talking with you," Gabriel explained.

"That was when you told me he was different from the average aristocrat," Wakefield muttered, though Lord Stuart could clearly hear him. "He's as bad as the rest, assuming I'm a companion because I have big eyes and a slender body. He didn't even wait for an introduction."

"Perhaps you would care to take your pique out on me?" Lord Stuart said. "Blackstone is hardly to blame for my shortcomings."

"Very well," Wakefield said, turning to Lord Stuart, blue eyes flashing. "Where do you get off making assumptions about my caste based on my looks?"

"You have to know you are not a typical guardian," Lord Stuart replied. "I'm surely not the first person to be surprised."

"No, although people usually have the good grace to look at my tattoo before jumping to conclusions," Wakefield said. "And your mistake only highlights how illogical our caste system is. When I go to businesses that advertise for a guardian, they often laugh me out into the street. No matter that I am fully trained. They look at me and have the same reaction you did. How can I possibly be a guardian with the face and body of a companion? Yet I must make my living this way because no other path is open to me. How am I to support a family if I cannot get a job because I cannot train for a profession more suited to my size and temperament?"

"What would you do if you could?" Lord Stuart asked. "You have already thought about this, obviously."

"I would teach," Wakefield said immediately. "I would open a school for all children, not simply for aristocratic children, and I would make sure they had access to the knowledge and skills to choose a trade that suited them."

"You make it sound as if only aristocrats can be educated," Lord Stuart said, "but I know your friend Blackstone graduated from university, something many aristocrats never do."

"And yet he is stuck in a struggling lab dependent on the whims of the aristocrats," Wakefield scoffed. "Where is the justice in that?"

"Where is the justice in Lucio or Cressida being forced to sell their bodies when they might have preferred some other path?" Gabriel echoed, thinking of Lucio's visits to his workshop. "Did you know Lucio is interested in machines?"

"But he's a...."

"Don't say it," Gabriel argued when the aristocrat trailed off. "His caste controls the living he makes, but it doesn't control his mind. He's as well educated as either of us. He could work in my lab in a heartbeat if he was allowed."

Lord Stuart looked at Gabriel sharply. "Interesting that you should know him so well."

"He's a customer of mine," Gabriel said, hiding his unease. "He has ordered several things from me since we met last week at your ball."

"That isn't the point," Wakefield said, drawing Lord Stuart's attention away from Gabriel again. "The point is that he is forced into one life when he would prefer another. He is a human being just like you or me."

"Of course he is," Lord Stuart said, "and a most enjoyable one. We have spend many hours in pleasant conversation, but—"

"But nothing," Gabriel snapped. He had managed to keep his temper under control up until now, but to hear Lord Stuart dismiss Lucio so casually was more than Gabriel could bear. "You're being deliberately obtuse, you and all the aristocrats. The caste system is flawed at its very core, and it's time for a change."

"Your Caste Equality movement, Blackstone?" Lord Stuart asked sardonically.

"You gave me a chance," Gabriel said. "I thought you might be willing to listen to a little more now that I didn't make a complete fool of myself."

"What do you want from me?"

"Your vote in the election," Wakefield said immediately, "and any suggestion for other aristocrats we might likewise approach. Our candidate, Paul Ashbrook, is the distant cousin of an aristocrat, even if his branch of the family has neither title nor land, so he is eligible to run for office, but we must find support for him to enter the government. We want peaceful change, but we will have change one way or another. The time is at hand. So you have to ask yourself, Lord Stuart, whether you'll be the harbinger of a new society or if you'll be left behind in the ruins of the old."

"That's quite a fiery rhetoric, young man," Lord Stuart said, his eyes admiring. Gabriel stifled a grin as he watched Lord Stuart's reaction. He knew the man was susceptible to a beautiful face. It seemed that now Wakefield's fire had won him over. "So how do you see an old man like me fitting into this new world?"

"You aren't old," Wakefield said immediately, surprising Gabriel even more. Was Wakefield as intrigued as Lord Stuart? Surely not. "And you could fit in however you please. That's the beauty of losing the barriers. No one would be required to change caste. If Blackstone wants to stay on as an inventor, he can, but I wouldn't be trapped in a life I'm not fit to lead."

"And someone like Lucio or Cressida, since Blackstone brought them up?"

"They could stay where they are just as easily," Wakefield said, "if they are content with the lives they lead. If they want to learn to do something else, they could as well. They would lose the benefits of living in the pleasure palace, with its luxuries and meals and the rest. They would have to find some other way to earn their living, but they could if they chose."

"And if someone wanted that life of luxury?"

Gabriel barely resisted the urge to roll his eyes at their description. Lucio's life *was* luxurious on the surface. Only beneath was it miserable.

"If they were already a companion, they could stay," Wakefield replied, "and it they weren't, they could apply to become one."

"Companions are trained for years," Lord Stuart reminded him.

"Then they could sign a contract of a certain number of years of service in return for the training," Wakefield replied. "At least it would be their choice. We're not proposing the end to any institution, only the right for people to choose which path their lives will follow. No more tattoos, no more taboos. Merely people picking the livelihood that makes them happy. For an aristocrat, little would actually change. You could still hire someone to guard your house or to cook your meals. You would simply choose from people who wanted to do those jobs instead of people forced into them by the accident of their births."

"You could still order an invention by Blackstone," Gabriel said with a smile, "only I would be free to visit the clubs where I might meet other patrons instead of relying on your generosity to introduce me."

"You could still spend an evening with a companion," Wakefield added, "only it would be someone who had chosen to be there instead of someone being forced into that."

"Can you imagine?" Gabriel said slowly. "Can you imagine how you would feel if I told you that if you didn't spend the next three hours pleasing a man of my choosing, you wouldn't eat tonight? Can you imagine me taking you into a room and stripping you because I felt like it?"

"They're trained to enjoy sex," Lord Stuart protested.

Gabriel barked out a laugh. "They're trained to make you believe it. Have you ever seen Lucio's face when he comes?"

"He's a companion."

"He's a man!" Gabriel bowed sharply and strode to the door. "Wakefield, stay as long as you'd like. I can't listen to this anymore. Lord Stuart, you missed the most beautiful sight you could ever have known." The door slammed shut behind him.

AS WORKED up as Gabriel was, he knew he would never be able to concentrate at the workshop. He strode down the street until he saw the home of Lord Endicott. He was not sure meeting the man with his emotions in turmoil was a good idea, but he was already here, and it was a waste of gold to take a cab home and come back later. Opening the gate, he knocked on the door.

"Is Lord Endicott receiving?" he asked when a butler opened the door.

"Who is calling?"

Gabriel offered his calling card to the butler. "He called on me on Friday, but I was unavailable at the time, and he did not say when I should return his call."

"I will let him know you're here," the butler said, disappearing inside.

A moment later, he reappeared. "I will show you in."

Gabriel followed the butler down the hall and waited as the man announced him. He walked in to see three gentlemen sitting in the drawing room. One of them rose and offered a hand. "Welcome, Blackstone, and thank you for returning my visit."

"A pleasure, my Lord," Gabriel said, shaking the offered hand. "My assistants said you were interested in a fan. If I could perhaps see the room it will go in, I could give you a better idea of price and when we could have it for you. We do build each fan custom for the room where it will be used."

"This room, I think," Lord Endicott said. "I spend most of my time here, whether with guests or on my own."

And it showed, Gabriel thought uncharitably, seeing the man's rounding belly and chalky skin. He looked like he could benefit from a turn or a few around the square once a day. He relaxed somewhat. If this was his competition for Lucio's time, he didn't have to worry about losing his lover. "Do you want to continue this discussion in front of your guests?"

"Perhaps we should step into my office," Endicott agreed. "If you'll excuse me for a moment, gentlemen?"

Lord Endicott led Gabriel into the office. "Now, about the price."

"For a room that size, it would be one hundred five gold," Gabriel said, unrepentantly adding to Lord Endicott's price. If the man had the money to purchase Lucio's time, he had the money to pay extra for Gabriel's inventions. "Half up front and the other half when we deliver the fan."

"And when will that be?" Lord Endicott asked, opening the desk and pulling out a purse.

"Once we have the first payment, we can buy the materials we need. You should have it by the end of the week."

"That fast?"

"It would be faster, but others paid before you," Gabriel explained. "Those who are interested but haven't paid yet will lose their places to you since I have your first payment."

"Well, by all means, take it," Lord Endicott said, counting out the coins and handing them to Gabriel. "I'll draw the balance from the bank and have it ready before Friday so there's no delay."

"I'll send word when it's done and you can send someone to take delivery," Gabriel replied. "Or we can arrange delivery and bill you for it."

"Do that," Lord Endicott said. "That will be easier."

"If there's anything else I can do for you, my Lord, my workshop is at your disposal."

"There is one thing," Lord Endicott said. "I know it's not the season yet, but even with the fireplaces, my study gets cold in the winter, and I have a bit of gout. If you had something that could help keep it warm, I would be most grateful."

"I could probably come up with something," Gabriel said, his thoughts already racing. "Let me experiment a bit, and I'll contact you when I have a prototype and a price."

"I look forward to hearing from you," Lord Endicott said, shaking Gabriel's hand again.

Gabriel almost felt guilty for adding the extra gold as he left and hailed a cab for home, but he reminded himself of the look on Lucio's face when he brought up Lord Endicott at the inn. The aristocrat might be no worse than any other aristocrat, but he had purchased Lucio's time, and that was black mark against him in Gabriel's eyes.

"BACK so soon, Lucio?" Andrew joked as Lucio came into the workshop on Monday afternoon.

"I couldn't stay away," Lucio quipped in return, holding the door for Cressida. To his surprise, the handlers had not blinked an eye when he explained where they were going and why. "Is Gabriel in?"

"No, but he should be back any minute," Andrew replied. "He went to speak with Lord Stuart. He said he'd be back by noon, and as you can see, he's five minutes late already." He looked from Lucio to Cressida and bowed awkwardly in her direction. "Ma'am." Lucio was sure if Andrew had been wearing a hat, it would have been in his hands at the moment.

"I think I like inventors," Cressida said, her face still hidden by the hood of her cloak. "They're far more polite than aristocrats where I'm concerned." She looked around the room for a place to sit.

Andrew sprang from behind the counter, nearly tripping over his feet in his haste to dust off the seat of the chair Lucio remembered from his first visit. "You can sit here if you'd like, ma'am. I'm sure Gabe... er, Mister Blackstone will be back soon."

"Mister Lambert, this is my friend Cressida. Cressida, meet Andrew Lambert, one of Gabriel's assistants," Lucio said when Cressida was settled.

"Nice to meet you, Mister Lambert," Cressida said, pushing back the hood of her cloak.

Lucio stifled a grin at the befuddled look on Andrew's face as he stared at her. "My pleasure, ma'am," he stuttered. "Can I... can I get you anything?"

"A fan, I hope," Cressida said. "Lucio told me about his, and I'm insanely jealous."

"That's easy as pie, ma'am," Andrew promised. "You just tell us what size room and we'll have one for you within a day or two. We're getting good at making them fast. Once we got all the schematics worked out for Lucio's, duplicating it was easy."

The door chimed again and all three of them turned to look. "Lucio!"

Lucio smiled, crossing to Gabriel's side. In deference to the others in the room, he did not kiss his lover the way he wanted, but he did slide his hand into Gabriel's, the mere clasp of Gabriel's hand almost as welcome a reassurance. "I brought Cressida to place her order," he said by way of explanation. "Andrew has been keeping us company."

"And you made them sit out here?" Gabriel chided. "Where are your manners, Andrew? We'll be more comfortable in the kitchen. You won't mind escorting Miss Cressida?"

Cressida rapped Gabriel's free arm with her fan. "Stop calling me that," she scolded. "I know you well enough that we can do without the formality."

"Ma'am," Andrew said, offering his arm in an awkward imitation of courtly fashion. Cressida didn't scold him for it, Lucio noticed. Courtly gestures could be taught. Consideration could not.

Lucio held back a bit, allowing the door to swing shut after Andrew and Cressida. He leaned up for a quick kiss. "I couldn't stay away, not when I had an excuse to come back."

"I'm not complaining," Gabriel said, kissing Lucio in turn, "but I doubt we'll have much private time with Caleb and Andrew here and Cressida as well."

"I know," Lucio said, "but it wasn't about having the time in private as much as it was about being with you, seeing you working and happy and mine."

"I am yours," Gabriel promised. "Come on, the others are waiting for us."

Lucio nearly laughed when he and Gabriel walked into the kitchen. Cressida sat at the table—in Gabriel's seat, he noticed—and Caleb and Andrew were tripping over each other to bring her something to drink and a plate of something to nibble on. "Careful there, or she'll start thinking she's royalty or something," he teased.

Cressida glared at him, the expression so much sharper than usual that he subsided, leaving Andrew and Caleb to fawn over her. Instead, he gave his attention to Gabriel, the real reason he was there anyway. "Here," he said, pulling a heavy purse out of his pocket. "I managed to smuggle out all the gold I've accumulated."

"Won't you need some of that?" Gabriel asked.

Lucio shook his head. "The only thing I need gold for is something like indulging myself with the fan I bought from you. If I do need something, I'll sell one of the jewels I have left, but I was able to get this out today, and it's a fairly substantial sum. There's probably close to ten thousand there, in larger coins, of course."

Gabriel looked at Lucio in surprise, taking the purse and pocketing it. "Are you sure?"

Lucio squeezed Gabriel's hand. "I'm sure."

"I don't think I've ever seen that much money before," Gabriel admitted. "I'll take it to the bank this afternoon. I don't want anything to happen to it."

"I don't know what my contract will cost, but I want to do my part toward paying for it," Lucio said.

"With this, what you've already given me, and what I've managed to put away from the fans I've sold already, we'll have close to fifteen thousand gold," Gabriel told him. "Now I just have to find out how much more we have to save."

"However much it is, we'll keep working and saving until we have it," Lucio insisted. "It might take longer than we'd like, but we'll find a way to make it happen."

21

THE chime of the front door, a much more frequent occurrence in the weeks since Lord Stuart's ball, brought Gabriel into the front of the workshop, wiping his hands on his leather apron in case his client wanted to shake hands.

"Cressida, Lucio!" he said with a smile when he saw who graced his home. "I keep telling you to come to the back door. You're hardly customers anymore to wait out here on my arrival."

"And I keep telling you that ladies never use the back door," Cressida replied with a wink. "Lucio can slink around back if he wants, but I will come in the front."

"She's feeling uppity this morning," Lucio teased. "Her guest last night was generous."

"Extremely generous," Cressida said, jingling her purse. "I'm in the mood to reward myself."

"And coming here is a reward?" Gabriel asked.

Cressida's smile softened. "Coming here is the best reward of all."

Gabriel met Lucio's eyes and smiled, lifting the counter so they could come into the back. The moment Cressida entered the workroom, Gabriel could hear Caleb's and Andrew's exclamations and welcomes. He leaned down to kiss Lucio softly. "We'll give them a minute."

Lucio leaned into Gabriel's embrace, the familiarity such a balm to Gabriel's heart. "You mean we'll take a minute for ourselves?"

"That too," Gabriel agreed, resting his cheek against Lucio's and inhaling the fresh scent of his lover's hair.

Lucio smiled and turned his head for another kiss. "I can try to get away without her more often, but she enjoys these breaks so much too."

"Of course you should bring her with you when she can come," Gabriel said. "She's as much a part of our funny little family as any of us by now."

It was true too. In the past month, Cressida had visited at least twice for every three times Lucio came to see him, not counting the occasions when he had purchased Lucio's time, and Gabriel could see how much lighter her footsteps were when she left. He suspected it was much like Lucio. No one here expected anything of her but the pleasure of her company, and no one judged her for the tattoo on her hand. Not to mention that Caleb and Andrew still worshipped the ground she walked on. They had gotten past the tongue-tied babbling of the first meeting, but the abject adoration in their eyes had yet to fade. Gabriel wondered how they thought that could work given their own relationship, but so far they seemed content to love each other and put Cressida on a pedestal.

"I've missed our quiet times together," Lucio admitted.

"I have too," Gabriel said. "If you can't slip away without Cressida in the next few days, I'll take a little gold and buy some more of your time."

"I hate that you have to do that," Lucio said with a sigh, "both because I hate having the money between us and because it's that much less toward my contract, but I can never predict when I'll be allowed to leave and whether Cressida will want to come with me. Today I told them we had an appointment at the milliner's to order new hats."

"I don't like the idea of paying for your time either," Gabriel said, "but if it means we have the privacy to love each other, it's worth it. I'm making more money than I ever dreamed possible now that Lord Stuart's patronage has brought me to the attention of the aristocracy. I had an order yesterday for twenty fans, one for each room in a very large house. That's a thousand gold coins toward your contract right there. I'm tempted to hire another assistant so I can speed up production because the demand is definitely there."

"How is Lord Stuart?" Lucio asked, his voice curious. "He hasn't purchased any more of my time since his ball. Come to think of it, I haven't heard anyone else mention visiting with him either."

"I have the impression," Gabriel confided, "that he is rather taken with a colleague of mine from the Caste Equality movement. That could be why he has stopped patronizing the pleasure palaces."

"That would be a real coup for the movement," Lucio said with a low whistle. Gabriel had shared enough of the rest of his life over the past month to give Lucio an idea of the agenda and timeline for the movement. Gabriel only hoped things would work out between Wakefield and Lord Stuart so they wouldn't lose the aristocrat's support.

"It would be," Gabriel agreed. "We should go make sure Caleb and Andrew aren't making fools of themselves."

They walked into the other room, only to find it empty, but laughter in the kitchen drew them into the small room. Cressida sat in the chair that had become hers, Caleb having scrounged an extra chair from somewhere—Gabriel found it prudent not to ask from where—so that they all had a place to sit when she came to visit. Andrew had put water on for tea, and Caleb was setting out little cakes. "My kitchen never used to be this busy," Gabriel teased, pulling out a chair for Lucio and taking the seat next to him.

"Are you complaining?" Lucio asked.

"Not at all," Gabriel replied, squeezing Lucio's hand under the table. "I wouldn't change a thing."

That wasn't completely true. If he could, he would rid Cressida and Lucio of the rules hanging over their heads that forced them to leave the sanctuary of his kitchen and return to the pleasure palace and the guests who would use them and discard them. He reminded himself of the progress the Caste Equality movement had made recently. Paul Ashbrook's name was officially on the ballot for the next election, and Wakefield regularly came in with names of new aristocrats to contact. Gabriel wasn't sure how successful those contacts were since he preferred to let Wakefield and Beacham handle them, but Wakefield certainly seemed pleased.

Lucio's thumb brushed back and forth across the palm of Gabriel's hand, sending little frissons of pleasure up his arm. That was one change he wouldn't undo. Lucio had blossomed under his patience and affection, his hesitations nearly gone so that when he and Gabriel had time alone together, they enjoyed each other's bodies in a myriad of ways. Gabriel had still not broached the subject of penetration because he knew that was Lucio's least favorite part of his time with his guests, but he knew the flavor of Lucio's cock now, as Lucio had learned his. The pleasure of that night still heated his blood whenever he thought about it.

He thought about it often.

If the rest never happened, Gabriel would not complain. He had so many pieces of Lucio that no one else had ever known. He could live without that one with no regrets.

"So what else have you been working on since our last visit?" Lucio asked Caleb and Andrew. "Gabriel mentioned the order for twenty fans."

"We've finished at least that many before we got the new order," Caleb said. "And Lord Endicott decided he liked his heater, so we'll probably start getting orders for more of those in a week or two. It isn't quite cool enough to need it yet, although the heat seems to have broken for good, but once he has the most comfortable room in the city, others will follow suit."

"We also had a request for a mechanical lift," Gabriel said. "Something to use in a dumbwaiter for heavy trays and the like."

"Fans and heaters and all this utilitarian stuff," Cressida fussed as the five of them sat at Gabriel's kitchen table. "What you really need is something to appeal to the ladies."

"Like what?" Gabriel asked. He had grown used to Cressida's blunt nature at the same time he had come to appreciate her intelligence.

"And why?" Caleb added.

"Because aristocratic ladies have as much money to spend or more than their husbands, and they're far more likely to spend it on something decorative than on something functional," Cressida explained. "The men deal with the practicalities. The women want to make their homes beautiful. The fans have some appeal because they add to the comfort of the room, but it's not the same thing."

"So I'll ask again," Gabriel said. "Like what?" He had no doubt Cressida was right in her logic, but he knew even less about aristocratic ladies than about the gentlemen. If Cressida had a suggestion, he was sure he could make the product, but he wouldn't know where to begin.

"Can you make a music box?" Cressida asked.

"Probably, but other people already make those. Why would I want to duplicate their products? What would make the ladies want to buy mine?" Gabriel replied.

"I keep thinking about Lord Stuart's dog," Cressida said slowly. "She is a marvel to behold. If you could use some of that same idea to put moving figures, perhaps dancers, on a music box, that would be what made yours different."

"We had a hard enough time making the gears small enough for Roxie," Andrew said. "What you're suggesting would require even smaller parts."

"That doesn't mean we can't do it," Caleb disagreed. Gabriel hid his smile. Caleb and Andrew might have gotten over their initial babbling where Cressida was concerned, but the desire to impress her, particularly for Caleb, had not faded.

"No, it doesn't," Gabriel agreed. "We'd have to refine our tools even more, but we can do it. It will take some time and work."

"You know," Lucio said slowly, "that's the same problem you have with the flying chair. Everything is too large. If you can make the music box work, those same small gears and pistons could work for the chair."

"Except that moving a mechanical figurine requires a lot less power than lifting a chair," Caleb reminded him.

"Yes," Gabriel said, "but I think Lucio might be onto something. If we can attach the small gear to a larger one so that it turns faster…. This might work!"

His mind racing, Gabriel hurried down the stairs, hearing footsteps behind him. He had no idea who would follow him, but it didn't matter. After months of fighting with this problem, he could suddenly see the configuration of gears and levers that would allow him to decrease the size of the engine. He grabbed the tarp and tossed it aside, revealing the chair and the half-completed engine. Pulling the engine out into the center of the room, he tore into it, ripping out gears and pistons. He looked around, searching for the smallest gear in the room.

"What do you need?" Caleb asked.

"The gear we used for Roxie's head," Gabriel replied, "or something about that size."

"There's one upstairs," Caleb said, disappearing up the stairs again.

"Andrew," Gabriel said, "get a belt and some of the small levers."

"What's he doing?" Gabriel heard Cressida ask Lucio, but he ignored them both. He needed to get the mechanism assembled while it was clear in his mind. Caleb and Andrew returned moments later with the materials he had sent them to fetch. He laid it all out on the floor, mentally calculating vectors and torque and acceleration.

"He's working," Lucio said in answer to Cressida's question.

"This is why he's the boss," Caleb added as Gabriel continued to change the placement of the gears and levers and belts. "He sees things, conceptualizes things that the rest of us don't see. Once he puts something together, once he gives me a plan, I can build anything you want me to, but he doesn't have a plan. Not a set one. He's putting the pieces together in his head and coming up with something entirely new."

LUCIO watched as Gabriel worked. He could almost see the wheels turning in the inventor's mind as he fiddled with this piece and that. His heart pounded as he waited for the verdict of success or the decision to try something else. Gabriel had eyes for nothing other than the metal in front of him, but Lucio found he didn't mind. This was a side of his lover he had never truly seen until now. Gabriel had shown him the workshop, explained what he was doing, but it wasn't the same. This wasn't discussion. This was creation. He took a step forward, careful not to block the light from the one lantern in the room, but wanting to see Gabriel's face.

The expression on his lover's countenance took his breath away. The concentration paired with an excitement Lucio had only seen in their most intimate moments sent a thrill through his body. He swallowed down his reaction, not wanting to shock Andrew or Caleb. He suspected he couldn't shock Cressida. Finally Gabriel looked up, meeting his gaze with eyes so bright, so hot that Lucio swore he'd go up in smoke right there. "I have to actually assemble it and test it, but I think this will work. Using the smallest gears here and transferring the mechanical energy through progressively larger ones means I can start with a smaller engine and still have the greater power output on the other side."

"Do it now," Lucio urged. "Put it together right now and see if it will turn the rotors on the chair."

"This isn't a five-minute job," Gabriel said with a shake of his head. "I don't want to waste the time you're here working."

Lucio shook his head. "It's not a waste. If this works, it's our ticket to freedom. Tell me what to do. Tell Caleb and Andrew what to do, but let us help you get it done."

"You do that," Cressida said. "I'll make more tea. I can already tell this is going to be thirsty work."

Lucio smiled at her quickly, but his real focus was Gabriel. "With the price you could charge for one of these, it wouldn't take but a few to buy my contract. Please, Gabriel. Let me go back to the pleasure palace today with the hope that it's truly close to the last time."

"Nothing ever works perfectly the first time," Gabriel warned. "Even if it turns the rotors, that doesn't mean the chair is ready to sell. There are other issues that have to be resolved too."

"But they're small ones compared to the engine," Lucio confirmed. "You told me that the first time you showed me the chair. If you could get the engine small enough, you said, the rest would be a matter of tinkering until it all came together."

"Yes," Gabriel said, rising and taking Lucio's hands, "but that tinkering could still take months."

"Months instead of years," Lucio insisted, clinging to Gabriel's grasp. "Please. Give me that much hope."

"We'll see what we can do," Gabriel said finally. "I can't make promises, but we'll try."

"That's all I can ask," Lucio said, stepping back to let Caleb and Andrew join Gabriel to work.

An hour and much cursing later, Gabriel rocked back on his heels and looked at the contraption on the floor. Piece by piece, the gears and levers and belts had disappeared into one larger whole. Carefully Gabriel and Caleb picked it up and moved it to the chair, attaching it to the legs so the small engine would remain beneath the seat as the contraption lifted off the ground. "Let's hook it up and make sure everything is connected correctly before we try turning the rotors," Gabriel said.

Caleb nodded and they worked in easy silence to attach the gear system to the motor. "Fire it up," Caleb said, taking a step back. "It's your invention. You should be the one to make it work."

Lucio held his breath, reaching for Cressida's hand to help steady him as they waited to see what would happen. The engine creaked noisily to life as Gabriel fed it coal for steam. Slowly, the new mechanism started to turn. Gabriel added more coal, and the engine hissed. He tightened a clamp here and a fitting there, and the shaft that would ultimately attach to the rotors spun faster. Lucio had no idea what Gabriel would consider success, but it seemed to him to be working. "Well?" he asked, unable to wait any longer.

"Well, we'll have to take it outside, attach the rest, and see what happens," Gabriel said, pushing to his feet, "but the small engine is turning the rotor shaft at high speed. If adding the rotors doesn't slow it down too much, it might actually work."

Lucio threw himself into Gabriel's arms, pressing kisses all over his face, heedless of their audience. "We have to celebrate," he said. "We have to do something to mark this occasion."

The clock in the workshop chimed the hour, dampening his high spirits. "I don't have a guest tonight," he whispered to Gabriel, not wanting the others to hear. "Buy the slot, and we'll celebrate then. Buy the whole night if they'll let you. I want to sleep in your arms and wake up with you in the morning."

GABRIEL shared a cab with Lucio and Cressida back to the pleasure palace. He let the two companions out and directed the driver to take him to the other side of the square before descending himself. The last thing he wanted was for the handlers to see him with Lucio and Cressida outside of an appointment and make it more difficult for him to purchase Lucio's time later.

He walked back across the square and into the pleasure palace. "Good afternoon, Mister Blackstone," the clerk at the desk said. "You'll be wanting Lucio again, I assume."

"Yes," Gabriel said, "tonight if possible."

"Your luck is something else," the clerk said with a shake of his head. "His calendar is free for tonight, although we may be less able on such short notice to fulfill any special requirements as far as dress is concerned."

"No special requests," Gabriel said. If he had his way, they wouldn't be wearing any clothes at all just as soon as they got home. "I'll pick him up at seven and return him in the morning."

"He has a ten o'clock guest tomorrow," the clerk warned. "He needs to be back here by seven in order to be ready."

It was earlier than Gabriel had hoped but more time than he had ever had with Lucio before. "That can be arranged. One hundred gold for the night, correct?"

The clerk swallowed. "Well, sir, normally…."

Gabriel pulled out his purse and withdrew two large coins. "One hundred gold for the night."

The clerk nodded and penciled in Gabriel's name. "We'll have him ready for you at seven."

PROMPTLY at seven, Gabriel stepped back into the pleasure palace, wearing the suit Lord Stuart had purchased for him. He had debated what to wear, but he could hardly pick Lucio up wearing his leathers when he told the clerk they were going out for the evening. They might not stop Lucio from leaving with him, but he didn't want to make anyone suspicious of his intentions in Lucio's regard. They had enough problems as it was.

The moment they were alone in the cab, Lucio undid Gabriel's cravat. "Lucio," Gabriel chided, "we aren't home yet."

"But we're going home," Lucio reminded him. "You gave the driver your address, which means that even if we don't go straight to bed, we'll still be alone. And if we're alone, you don't need this stuffy cravat."

"What if I wanted to look my best for you?" Gabriel said, undeniably aroused by the slowly emerging forward side of Lucio.

"You look your best when you aren't wearing anything at all," Lucio said, stroking Gabriel's chest through the waistcoat and shirt.

Gabriel groaned at the provocative words. "Who are you and what have you done with my sweet, shy Lucio?" he teased.

"I'm still your Lucio," the companion said, kissing along the line of Gabriel's jaw, "but watching you work today opened a valve inside me. All the fears that were holding me back have disappeared. I want us to make love tonight with no holds barred."

Gabriel drew a shuddering breath. "I've dreamt of that," he admitted. "I wouldn't have pressured you into anything because I don't ever want that between us, but I've dreamt of making love with you, just as I've dreamt of sleeping with you in my arms. Tonight will be a dream come true."

"For both of us," Lucio said, kissing Gabriel urgently. Gabriel responded in kind, licking and nibbling at Lucio's lips until the companion crawled into his lap trying to get closer.

The cab stopped in front of Gabriel's workshop, forcing them to separate momentarily. Gabriel paid the driver and led Lucio around to the back of the house and through the side door, the one reserved for family and friends. "Take me upstairs," Lucio pleaded when Gabriel shut the door behind them.

Gabriel cradled Lucio's cheeks in his palms, meeting the dark eyes and studying what he saw there. "I told you I dreamt of making love with you," Gabriel said slowly, "but I didn't tell you what I dreamed. Do you want to know?"

"I want to know everything about you," Lucio replied.

"I dreamed of feeling you inside me," Gabriel said. "I dreamed of lying on my back with my legs thrown over your shoulders as you pounded into me until I couldn't walk tomorrow without feeling you."

"I've never…." Lucio took a deep breath and started again. "I've never done that with any of my guests. The men all want to fuck me, and the women either want my mouth and hands or they use a strap-on. No one has ever let me inside them."

"Another thing only we will share," Gabriel said softly. "If you agree."

"I agree," Lucio said, his laugh joyous as he threw his arms around Gabriel's neck. "I never imagined it could happen, but now that you've offered it to me, I can't think of anything I want more."

"Then it's time to go upstairs."

They barely made it to the top of the stairs before Lucio started pulling at Gabriel's clothing. Gabriel helped him so the suit wouldn't be ruined and then ignored Lucio's wandering hands as he attacked Lucio's clothes in turn.

There should have been nothing new about the sensation of standing there together, bodies brushing, because this was not the first time they had been naked together, but Gabriel gasped, grasping for control the moment Lucio's cock brushed against his. Fortunately, Lucio seemed to have retained his, backing Gabriel toward the bed and urging him to lie down across the quilt. "Will you let me make love to you?" Lucio asked. "Will you lie here like you did the first time we shared your bed and let me do all the things I didn't do then?"

Gabriel swallowed roughly, his body aching already. "As long as you don't linger too long," he said huskily. "I don't know how long I can wait."

"If you come before I'm ready, I'll simply have to get you worked up again," Lucio teased. "You know I know how."

Gabriel knew the truth of that statement. More than once, Lucio had brought him to climax only to rouse him a second time with his knowing hands and eager mouth. The thought only added to his desire. He clenched his fists in the quilt to keep from reaching for Lucio and guiding his head or hands where Gabriel wanted them to go. Lucio knew his preferences by now. Gabriel didn't need to direct. He closed his eyes, hoping that would make the waiting easier.

Lucio's breath tickled his chest, ghosting across his nipple only to move away, down toward his cock, teasing the head but not connecting with it either. "Lucio," Gabriel pleaded. "Please."

"Please what?" Lucio said, his voice as seductive as Gabriel had ever heard it. "What do you want me to do to you, lover?"

Gabriel shook his head. He had resisted the urge to issue even a suggestion when he knew Lucio's customers ordered him around all the time. He wouldn't ruin this moment by breaking that habit now.

"Talk to me," Lucio said, ignoring Gabriel's gesture. "You said you'd dreamt of this moment. Tell me what you dreamed. I want to make those dreams come true."

"I won't order you around," Gabriel protested. "They do that, not me."

Lucio straddled Gabriel's waist, his backside brushing Gabriel's cock. "You aren't giving me orders," he disagreed. "You're sharing your fantasy with your lover. If I choose to help you live out that fantasy, that's my choice. They don't give me a choice."

Gabriel still felt like Lucio was splitting straws, but he couldn't resist the plea in Lucio's eyes. "As much as I love what you do to me with your hands, it's your mouth that fascinates me," he admitted. "From the first time you kissed me, I haven't been able to get it out of my mind."

"So then I should lick and kiss you all over," Lucio purred. "Is that what you want?"

"For a start." Gabriel gasped as Lucio's lips captured one nipple, sucking on it eagerly. His back arched into the caress, his hands tangling in Lucio's long black hair. He wanted to speak, to encourage, but his voice deserted him except for inarticulate cries. That seemed to be all the encouragement Lucio needed because he lingered, alternating between hard pulls with his tongue and gentle nips with his teeth until Gabriel was writhing beneath him, struggling to catch his breath. When he finally released the puckered teat, Gabriel collapsed back onto the bed, panting hard.

"I think you liked that," Lucio said, all but purring with satisfaction. "Should I do the other side? Or maybe I should find somewhere else to suck on?"

"Other side," Gabriel rasped, even as he hoped to feel Lucio's mouth all over his body before the night was over. Lucio obliged immediately, repeating the mind-blowing caress to his chest until Gabriel thought he'd scream with the pleasure of it. The smug look on Lucio's face when he finally lifted his head made Gabriel wonder if he had. Unable to speak, Gabriel urged Lucio's head lower. His lover moved easily, lips trailing over the lines of muscle until they reached his navel. Lucio's tongue darted out then, probing the indention lasciviously, making Gabriel ache to feel that same caress elsewhere. His guardian muscle clenched in anticipation.

Finally, Lucio moved lower, looking up to meet Gabriel's eyes as he lifted the tip of the inventor's cock to his lips. Gabriel groaned as Lucio's pink tongue darted past his lips to tease the weeping slit. Moments later, he bucked up as he felt the full length of his shaft engulfed in wet heat. He tried to resist, but Lucio's hands urged him to move, and within seconds he found a rhythm that let him fuck his lover's mouth. He could feel his release boiling in his balls, rising up within him, when Lucio pulled back. Gabriel cried out in protest.

"Trust me," Lucio said, his fingers clamping down around the base of Gabriel's cock. "Hold back a little longer while I prepare you. I want you too much. I'm not sure I can wait for you to be ready a second time."

Gabriel nodded, struggling for control. When he thought he had found it again, he spread his legs, pulling them up to his chest so he was completely open to Lucio's attentions. He wanted to feel Lucio rimming him, but neither of them had the control for that right now. Perhaps later. After all, they had all night.

Lucio's fingers probing at his entrance nearly proved Gabriel's undoing. It had been so long since anyone had touched him that way. He hissed at the stretch, consciously reminding himself to relax. The sensation of that long digit moving inside him took his mind off the slight burn, making it easier to give in and beg for more. Lucio gave it to him, sliding a second finger in next to the first, and then moments later, a third as well.

"Now," Gabriel begged, "before you make me come with your fingers alone."

Lucio's groan matched Gabriel's. He withdrew his fingers and slicked his cock with oil from a vial Gabriel had never seen before, but he gave it no more thought when the head of Lucio's cock pressed against his entrance. He planted his feet on the mattress so he could push up to meet it, feeling it pop past the ring of muscle and slide inside him. Lucio caught Gabriel's knees with his arms, lifting them up so Gabriel's calves rested on his shoulders. The angle allowed him to slide even deeper, eliciting another groan from deep in Gabriel's chest. Gabriel untangled one hand from the sheets and reached for Lucio's, twining their fingers together as Lucio slid all the way home inside him. "Love... you," he gasped.

"Love you too," Lucio replied, his voice trembling. Slowly he started to move.

Gabriel understood his hesitation, but he needed more than this careful in and out. He needed the slap of flesh against flesh, the feeling of Lucio's cock boring so deep into him that he would feel it for days or more. "Harder."

Lucio hesitated, continuing the same cautious rhythm, but he looked up and met Gabriel's eyes instead of staring at the place where they were joined. "I promise I'll tell you if it hurts in any way," Gabriel said, guessing at the cause of Lucio's fears, "but I want to feel you let go. Please, Luc."

"Don't close your eyes," Lucio said as he thrust a little harder. "I have to see that I'm not hurting you."

Gabriel kept his gaze fixed on Lucio's face after that, despite the nearly overwhelming temptation to close his eyes to better savor the sensation of Lucio finally pounding into him the way he wanted. If Lucio needed to see his eyes in order to continue the glorious thrust and withdraw, Gabriel would give it to him gladly.

As on edge as he already was, it didn't take long for Gabriel's release to hit him, pushed out of him by the tip of Lucio's cock prodding his gland. Another spurt escaped with each pass until Gabriel thought he would pass out from the sheer ecstasy of the prolonged release. Finally he felt the hot surge of Lucio's pleasure within him. Lucio collapsed forward onto his chest, releasing Gabriel's legs. Carefully, so as not to dislodge Lucio from inside him, Gabriel lowered his legs to a more comfortable position, wrapped around the back of Lucio's thighs as his arms encircled Lucio's back, keeping them tangled together for as long as possible.

LUCIO was sure his heart would beat right of his chest, so hard was it pounding. He had found release in Gabriel's arms often enough not to be surprised at being able to climax, but he had never imagined the sensation of being surrounded by his lover as he was now. Not simply Gabriel's arms and legs wrapped around him, holding him close, but his body as well, open to accept Lucio inside him. Slowly he lifted his head to meet

Gabriel's blue eyes. "If it always feels like that, I'm not sure I'll ever leave your bed."

"It's never felt like that before," Gabriel replied. "It's different because we love each other."

"Will it feel that good next time?" Lucio asked, hoping the answer would be yes.

"We'll have to try and find out," Gabriel said with a grin. "We have all night."

"I don't want to leave you sore," Lucio cautioned, thinking of nights when one of his guests had used him multiple times.

"It won't be like that," Gabriel said, as if he could read Lucio's thoughts. "Even if I am tender in the morning, there won't be any regret. I'll spend the day or days until it fades remembering what we did together to make me feel that way, and it will only make me that much more eager to see you again so we can start all over. I love you, and that changes everything you think you know about sex. This isn't sex. It's making love."

"As someone who's had his fill of sex, I can see that it's a very different thing," Lucio agreed, shifting slightly. "I should clean us up."

"Why?" Gabriel asked, his arms tightening. "If you're uncomfortable, we can move. If you're cold, we can pull the quilt over us, but I want to lie here in bed covered in the scent and feel of you."

"We'll be sticky later," Lucio warned.

"So we'll clean up later," Gabriel said. "You're so used to trying to erase what happened as soon as it's over. You're used to feeling dirtied by their spend on your body. Do you really feel dirtied by what we just did?"

"No!" Lucio exclaimed. "Absolutely not! Please don't think that."

"I don't," Gabriel promised soothingly. "But if there's nothing dirty about what we just did, then there's no reason to hide the evidence of it. We can lie here in bed and let the stickiness, the pull of hair stuck together, remind us of what we shared and maybe even get us in the mood for the next round. I really do want to feel you after you leave."

Lucio consciously pushed aside his training and let himself relax into Gabriel's arms, his shaft slipping free of its berth. He shifted, feeling his skin stick to Gabriel's belly, but instead of getting up or leaning down to lick him clean, Lucio made himself relax and think of what they had shared, consciously overcoming years of training. He *wanted* to give

Gabriel pleasure, and this was proof that he had succeeded. The stickiness on his cock was proof of his own pleasure, an even more amazing concept. Taking a deep breath and smelling the musk of their release, he relaxed onto Gabriel's shoulder. "How much have we saved up?"

"Between your money and the jewels you brought and what I've been able to save, we have almost twenty-five thousand gold," Gabriel said. "Have you been able to find out how much we need?"

Lucio shook his head. "I can't ask directly, and I haven't figured out a way to ask indirectly. It would be more than that, I'm sure. I bring in close to that amount in a year, with the number of guests I see, even if they have to spend some of that on feeding and clothing me. I fear that's only a fraction of what we'll need, and I've brought almost all I had saved."

"Then I'll keep working," Gabriel said firmly. "We'll test the flying chair over the next few weeks, and once it's ready to go, I'll earn money far more quickly than I've ever done before. I promise it won't be long before we can be together like this every night."

GABRIEL whistled his way through the next few days, smiling even as he winced every time he sat down. He and Lucio had made love twice more before Lucio had to return to the pleasure palace, each time even more intense than the last. Caleb and Andrew had teased him mercilessly the next morning, but he hadn't even cared. He was in love; nothing else mattered.

"When are you going to see Lucio again?" Caleb asked on the third day after the night Gabriel and Lucio spent together.

"I don't know," Gabriel said with more equanimity than he had ever felt in that regard before. "He'll come when he can, and if he hasn't come to see me by this weekend, I'll take a little money out and arrange to see him."

"You seem far more relaxed about this than you were," Caleb observed.

Gabriel shrugged. "I can't change it until I have the money, but that won't be as long as I'd feared. Not with the flying chair almost ready to test."

"That's not what you were saying a month ago," Caleb reminded him.

"And you told me to stop being an idiot," Gabriel replied. "I took your advice."

Caleb didn't look convinced, but he let it go, for which Gabriel was grateful. He didn't know how to explain to Caleb what had changed. It still bothered him to think of Lucio being used by an unknown number of customers when they were apart, but he had come to the realization that what they did to Lucio bore no resemblance to what he and Lucio shared. The aristocrats used Lucio's body for release. Gabriel and Lucio made love. That distinction made all the difference in the world for his peace of mind. He still longed for the day when he wouldn't have to share even Lucio's body with anyone else, but as long as he knew he held Lucio's heart, the rest faded in significance. No one else kissed Lucio. No one else took the time to caress him, to love him. No one else felt Lucio's fingers preparing him carefully or Lucio's tongue slipping inside him. No one else felt Lucio topping him so tenderly and yet so thoroughly.

"I'm going to work on the flying chair," Gabriel said, changing the subject. It wasn't that he didn't want to talk about Lucio, but Caleb didn't really seem to understand and Gabriel didn't want to spend the time explaining it to him.

An hour later, he heard footsteps on the stairs. He looked up, expecting to see Caleb or Andrew coming down to check on him. Instead of their heavy boots, he found Lucio's dressier shoes. "I didn't expect to see you today," Gabriel said, meeting Lucio at the foot of the steps and embracing him. "How long can you stay?"

"Only an hour or so," Lucio said. "I have a ball tonight that I must get ready for."

"Lord Stuart again?" Gabriel asked.

"Not this time," Lucio said. "Lady Bentley. She's a connection of Lord Stuart's, I believe, although I can't always keep the aristocrats straight in my head. She enjoys having pretty young things on her arm in public."

Gabriel didn't ask what she preferred in private. He didn't need that level of detail.

"It won't be as enjoyable as the last ball I attended," Lucio said with a smile, "since you won't be there to meet me in secret, but it should also be less work than the last one."

"That's good," Gabriel agreed. "Do you want to see what I've gotten done since your last visit?"

"Of course!" Lucio replied. "That's part of why I came."

"Only part?" Gabriel teased.

"I had to make sure you were well after the other night," Lucio replied, more serious than not as he ran his hand down Gabriel's back to settle on his buttocks.

"I am perfectly well," Gabriel promised, shivering a little at the touch of his lover's hand. "Still feeling you a little, exactly as I wanted. I have never felt as loved as I have since then, even when you weren't here."

"If you say things like that, we aren't likely to spend much time working on your invention," Lucio warned. "I haven't been able to stop thinking about what it felt to lie with you. There isn't time today because I don't want to rush, but I can't wait until we can do it again."

"There's something to be said for rushing sometimes," Gabriel replied, flushing with warmth at the idea of Lucio bending him over the worktable or pushing him up against the wall and taking him. "Not in being callous or uncaring, but in needing so powerfully that you simply can't wait."

"And if Caleb or Andrew or Cressida decides to come down and see what we're working on?" Lucio asked. "I've been ordered by my guests to have sex in public, but I don't want to share making love with you with anyone."

There it was again, Gabriel realized. That casual reference that once would have sent him into fits of jealous rage that now was little more than a twinge. He still hated the thought of Lucio being used that way, but it didn't touch them. "Then we'll have to find a time when they aren't around," Gabriel said huskily, "because I'm not going to be able to work down here now without imagining you taking me against the wall or over the bench in your haste."

Lucio's fair skin flushed in the dim light, tempting Gabriel to bar the door and beg Lucio to make love to him, the others be damned. He refrained, barely, by reminding himself that he wanted to show Lucio the improvements in the chair.

"Come see what I've done," he said, trying to defuse the moment.

Lucio caught his hand, pulling him into a tight embrace. "The next time I visit," Lucio said, his voice so low Gabriel could barely hear him, "I'm going to hold you to that. I'll be dreaming about it until then."

Gabriel swayed in Lucio's embrace, the need so strong it nearly took him to his knees. He steadied himself against the banister. "We have to stop this, or we're going to end up making love despite everyone upstairs."

"They think we're making love anyway," Lucio said.

"Not helping," Gabriel groaned, stealing a quick kiss before pulling away. "I've got the motor hooked up to the rotors."

He led Lucio over to the flying chair, explaining the mechanism that attached the engine to the overhead rotors and how their rotation would create a lift that would allow the chair to fly. "Then this one, in the back," Gabriel said, "provides the forward propulsion."

"What's this?" Lucio asked, indicating a stick that rose in front of the seat.

"That's the steering rod," Gabriel explained. "It's attached to a rudder in the back that works much the same as a rudder on a boat, changing the course of the flying chair by changing its position in the air."

"But air isn't nearly as resistant as water," Lucio said. "Will it still work?"

"It should," Gabriel said, "but it's one of the things we have to test. Now that everything is hooked up, all we have to do is wait for a calm day. My hope is to eventually stabilize it enough that we can still use it on a windy day, but until I know that it works at all, I'd rather start in ideal conditions."

"That makes sense," Lucio said, walking around the chair. "So when it's in the air, the chair will essentially hang from the spinning arms above the driver's head?"

"Yes," Gabriel said. "The spinning of the rotors will create the lift needed to get the chair off the ground. Think of it as a hot air balloon and basket only self-propelled and controllable instead of being subject to the prevailing winds for direction."

"I want to be here when you test it," Lucio said.

"I'd love to have you here," Gabriel agreed, "but there's the little problem of your schedule being almost as unpredictable as the weather."

"Please, Gabriel," Lucio said. "The first few tests will be dangerous until you're sure it works. I need to be here if something happens."

"Even if it means the chair isn't ready as soon?" Gabriel asked, thinking of the money he needed to buy Lucio's contract. "The longer we delay testing it, the longer it will be until I can sell it, and that means the longer until I can buy your contract."

"I know," Lucio said, arms going around Gabriel's waist again, "and I want that more than ever, but if something were to happen to you, I'd have no way of knowing, for days or even weeks if I can't get away. It's worth it to me to spend a little longer in the pleasure palace if I can know that you're safe."

Gabriel wasn't entirely sure he agreed with that, but he could see how much it meant to Lucio, so he nodded. "I won't test it the first time without you."

"Thank you," Lucio said, kissing Gabriel's cheek. Gabriel turned his head, meeting Lucio's lips for a real kiss. When they parted, Lucio looked back at the chair. "I had a couple of thoughts about the flying chair actually, if you're interested."

"Of course I'm interested," Gabriel said. "What were you thinking about?"

"Well, it's aesthetics mostly," Lucio warned. "I don't have the mechanical knowledge to do much in that area, but I was thinking that once you get the prototype done and ready to show, it would be far more appealing visually if you had some kind of cover for the engine so it wasn't visible from the outside. And maybe some kind of bubble around the chair. The ladies would never be able to use it right now because their skirts would go flying."

"Along with the rest of them?" Gabriel laughed, but he could already see what Lucio was describing in his mind's eye. "I could do the box around engine in thin metal plates so it wouldn't add much to the weight or be a fire hazard, but that wouldn't work for the bubble. The bubble would almost need to be glass so you could see through it, but that seems dangerous as well. If there were a crash, the broken glass could do as much damage as the impact itself."

"Maybe it's not such a good idea after all," Lucio said with a sigh. "I never claimed to be an inventor."

"No," Gabriel said, turning to face Lucio, "it's a good thought. We'll simply have to think about how to make it work, or what else we can do to address the issue without creating new problems." He looked back at the chair again. "Perhaps if the bubble only covered the lower half of the body so the view was unimpaired but a lady's skirts would be enclosed. The wind would still be in their faces, but a pair of goggles would protect their eyes and a scarf could protect their skin if they were worried about the exposure."

"And around their hair as well," Lucio said with a nod. "Yes, I think that could work."

"Then go get some of those metal sheets over there and help me start fashioning something," Gabriel ordered. "It was your idea. You're going to make it a reality."

Eyes lighting up, Lucio hurried across the room to the pile of materials Gabriel had indicated.

"Wait," Gabriel called, pulling a pair of gloves off his belt. "Wear these. You don't want your hands to get cut up. The handlers might not let you visit again."

Lucio slid on the protective leather and brought two of the metal pieces over to Gabriel. "What do I do now?"

Gabriel showed Lucio how to measure and cut the metal, leaving it up to the companion to decide on the correct sizes. In the eyes of society, Lucio would be dependent on Gabriel for everything once Gabriel purchased his contract, but Gabriel had no intention of leaving Lucio with nothing to do but wait for him to return to bed. Lucio deserved the chance to have a new life, a new profession if he wanted it.

He kept an eye on Lucio's progress as he puttered around the flying chair, tinkering with gears and pulleys and belts that needed no adjustments so that Lucio would not feel like Gabriel was hovering over him.

Eventually, Lucio had five pieces of different shapes cut out. "Now how do I put them together?"

Gabriel showed him, delighting in the enthusiasm Lucio showed as he pounded the rivets into place and slowly brought his vision to life. When nearly the whole hour had passed, Lucio stepped back so Gabriel could see the completed project. "What do you think?"

Gabriel circled around the cube that sat on the floor, checking both the design and the execution. The top, bottom and three sides were metal, but the fourth side was open, allowing the box to go around the pilot's legs. "We'll have to cover the edges on this end so they don't cut the pilot," Gabriel said, thinking out loud, as he tried to imagine adding Lucio's creation to the existing flying chair. "A rounded piece of wooden trim all the way around the opening would do it. Or I could leave the trim off the bottom and attach it to the box around the engine, although then we'd have to figure out a way to make the front detachable so people could climb in and out and to channel the heat from the steam away from the pilot's legs."

"Could you put hinges on the front seam?" Lucio asked. "Then you could—"

"Lucio!" Cressida's voice interrupted them before Lucio could finish. "We need to go or we'll be late."

"Damn it," Lucio cursed. "Why does the time always go so fast when we're together and so slow when we're apart?"

Gabriel pulled Lucio into his arms, holding his lover's slender body close and kissing him tenderly. "Not much longer," he promised. "We'll get this working and selling and then nothing will ever separate us again."

"It can't happen soon enough," Lucio said. "It gets harder each day to pretend to an enthusiasm that I've never felt with them. When it was all pretend, at least I didn't have anything to compare it to. Now that I know what it should feel like, it's even more of a charade."

"Do you regret it?" Gabriel asked, praying the answer was no. He didn't want to make Lucio's life any more difficult than it already was, but the thought of Lucio regretting their intimacy tore at him.

"No!" Lucio exclaimed. "Oh, Gabriel, don't ever think that. The only thing I regret is having to leave you each time. I'll never regret what we do in the time we do have together."

"Soon," was all Gabriel could say, even knowing it did nothing to help Lucio now. "Have a good time at the ball. Hopefully Lady Bentley will be kind to you."

Lucio shrugged. "She'll show me off at the ball, and then she'll want me to pleasure her orally until she finds her release. Sometimes she uses a dildo on me at the same time. It depends on how she's feeling. It won't be too bad."

Gabriel grimaced, hiding the expression in Lucio's hair. He could have done without the last bit of information, but he took a deep breath and let it go. Their salvation was sitting on his cellar floor right behind them. He simply had to finish it.

As if sensing the change in mood, Lucio nudged Gabriel's chin until he lifted his head. "It won't be bad," he repeated, "and I'll come home and lie in my bed and think of you as the fan you made me blows cool air through the room. I'll think of working with you today and what our lives will be like later, when I'm free of this. I'll curl up in my bed, wishing you were there, and imagine all the things I would do to you if you were there with me or if I were here with you. I'll fall asleep with a smile on my face because you love me. Whatever she asks me to do, it's nothing compared to the fact that you love me."

"I do love you," Gabriel said fervently. "With all my heart and all my mind and all my body."

Lucio slipped a hand between them and stroked Gabriel's cock. "Not *all* your body. Not yet anyway, but that will happen in time too."

"Only when you're ready."

"I know," Lucio said with a soft smile. "That's how I know, truly know that you love me. Anyone else would have pressured me into it already, saying it's something I do all the time so why not now. You've never been that way. It's the reason I fell in love with you."

Gabriel flushed, uncomfortable with the praise. "You're more than your profession. A blind man could see that. It's my good fortune that most of your customers are too stupid to see the treasure you are."

"They see what they want to see," Lucio replied philosophically. "You didn't have any preconceived notions, so you could see me as I am."

"Lucio! The cab is here and waiting."

"I have to go," Lucio said sadly.

"I'll walk you out," Gabriel replied, not wanting to let Lucio go a second sooner than he had to. Keeping Lucio's hand firmly in his as they climbed the steps, Gabriel resolved to spend a portion of any time he and Lucio had together in the workshop. Even when they were making love, Lucio had not been as relaxed as he was today.

Caleb and Andrew stood at the door of the workshop, watching as Cressida climbed into the carriage. Gabriel handed Lucio in as well, lifting a hand in farewell as they pulled away.

"Did you have a good visit?" Caleb asked as they walked back inside.

Gabriel nodded. "You should see what Lucio came up with for the chair. He has the mind of an inventor even if he doesn't have the training. Did you have a good visit with Cressida?"

Both men flushed, to Gabriel's surprise. "Is there something you want to tell me?"

Andrew shook his head, but Caleb hesitated only a moment before replying, "You're not the only one with a soft spot for a companion, it would seem."

Gabriel raised an eyebrow, looking at Andrew for confirmation. The fact that his friend wouldn't look at him was answer enough. "I'm not a hypocrite, but be careful, please? I don't want to see either of you hurt."

"She's not for us," Caleb said with a shake of his head. "We know that. It's enough to be able to see her when she comes to visit with Lucio and to know she thinks of us kindly."

Gabriel doubted that would be enough for long, but he had his own relationship woes. He wouldn't borrow trouble from Caleb and Andrew if he could help it.

"Show us what Lucio came up with," Andrew said, deflecting Gabriel's attention from Cressida and back to his current project.

"He sees things we don't because he's used to being around aristocrats," Gabriel explained as they went downstairs again. "It would never have occurred to me to worry about a lady's skirts. Lucio not only saw the problem; he came up with a solution."

"He'll be a welcome addition once we get him out of there," Caleb agreed, looking at the shell Lucio had made. "That's decent work for someone with no training."

Gabriel smiled, relaxing again at his friends' acceptance. Lucio could truly build a life here once they freed him from his old life.

29

LUCIO stared at the note in his hand and the other notations on his calendar, dread turning his stomach. He had begun to hope that Lady Merydith had forgotten about her threats at Lord Stuart's ball nearly six weeks ago, but now her name was on his calendar along with the note in his hand and then the entire week after was blacked out, indicating his total unavailability. They knew he wouldn't be able to work after she was done with him, this hardly being the first time she had purchased a companion's time, but they were sending him to her anyway.

"Lucio?"

Lucio looked up to see Cressida in his doorway. "Sorry," he said, tucking the note into his desk. "I'm not quite ready yet."

"We have an afternoon free to spend with Gabriel and you're not ready yet? What's wrong?" Cressida demanded, coming into the room.

"Go ahead," Lucio said. "Tell him I couldn't get away. I can't see him right now."

"What was in that note to have you passing up a chance to see Gabriel?"

Lucio handed it to her silently.

"Oh, fuck," she said, her eyes darting back and forth between Lucio and the paper. "Why would they do this to you? What are they punishing you for?"

"I don't think they did it," Lucio said. "The night of Lord Stuart's ball, I had words with Lady Merydith. She felt I was not being obsequious enough with the other aristocrats and promised to take me down a peg or two. It seems she's finally keeping her promise."

"What are you going to do?" Cressida asked.

"What can I do?" Lucio countered. "She's paid whatever price they demanded because she's on the calendar and a week is blacked out afterward."

"You have to tell Gabriel the truth," Cressida insisted.

"I can't," Lucio said. "It's bad enough for him knowing that I'm still seeing guests. I can't ask him to casually accept that my guest next week will probably hurt me so badly I can't work for a week. That's too much."

"Seriously, what are you going to do?" Cressida asked. "Hide from him until it's over?"

"I don't know," Lucio said honestly, "but until I do, I can't go see him. He won't know I skipped a visit, because my schedule is anything but predictable. Even if you go, all you have to do is tell him I couldn't get away. He'll assume I'm working and won't ask beyond that."

Cressida frowned at him. "You're making a mistake. I just want you to know that."

"My mistake was angering Lady Merydith," Lucio disagreed. "Since I can't undo that, I'll pay the price and live with the consequences. Hopefully if I'm submissive enough, she won't mark me permanently. Or if she does, it will hopefully be somewhere discreet enough not to disconcert my other guests."

"This is two weeks away," Cressida pointed out. "You won't be able to avoid Gabriel for all that time because if you try, he'll come here looking for you and spend his and your hard-earned money to buy your time when you could have spent it with him for free."

"I know that," Lucio snapped. "I just need day or two to get past the idea of what's going to happen to me so I can pretend nothing's wrong. Then I'll go see him again, and he'll be none the wiser."

"Until you come home and he sees you afterward," Cressida reminded him. "What will you tell him then?"

"That a guest lost her temper and took it out on me," Lucio replied. "He doesn't need to know I had any warning. He's so happy right now. He's finally making progress on the flying chair, and once he has it working, it will just be a matter of selling a few before we'll have enough money for him to buy my contract. I don't want to ruin his good mood over something neither of us can change. Even if he sold the first flying chair today, he wouldn't be able to build and sell enough to buy my contract before I go to Lady Merydith's. There's no way out of this, and troubling him with it doesn't change anything."

"It's not about changing anything," Cressida said softly. "It's about sharing the hard times as well as the good ones with the one you love."

"Not this time," Lucio said with a shake of his head. "This is a burden I have to bear alone. If you go to visit today, tell Gabriel I'll come the day after tomorrow. I have some free time then."

"He'll still love you, no matter what she does to you."

Tears sprang to Lucio's eyes. "I know. That's what scares me most."

Cressida shook her head and withdrew, leaving Lucio alone. He locked the door behind her, something he almost never did. He grasped his head in his hands as he fought the tears of anger and frustration that threatened and collapsed on the bed. They were so close. In a matter of months they would be free, and now this happened. He stared at the window, wondering if he could force the screen and get out, but where would he go? Without a contract to prove Gabriel's ownership of him, he would never be safe, and if he was captured and returned to the pleasure palace, he would lose the few privileges he had. He might lose them anyway if Lady Merydith hurt him too badly, but at least then he wouldn't be a prisoner and would be able to see Gabriel still until they had the money to purchase his contract. He had heard tales of the fate of companions who tried to escape the pleasure palaces, and none of them were pleasant. At the very least he would lose all his freedoms within the palace as well as the ability to leave on certain errands during his free time. At the worst, he could be killed.

No, however badly Lady Merydith treated him, it could be endured.

LUCIO woke on Saturday morning two weeks later, his stomach so tied in knots he couldn't swallow the first bite of breakfast. The smell of the bacon, an aroma he usually enjoyed, made him nauseous. He had been pleased not to have any guests before Lady Merydith demanded his presence at five o'clock that evening, but suddenly the long hours until then seemed to press far too heavily on him. He had talked with a few of the other companions who had known Lady Merydith's attentions, wanting to have an idea of what to expect. They had confirmed some of his fears and eased others. She liked the whip, they warned him, although she was talented enough with it not to break the skin so it wouldn't leave scars. She would almost certainly burn him, enough to make him scream without marking him permanently. And she would fuck him. Repeatedly. Until the mere thought of her doing it again hurt. His body would heal, the other companions assured him, but no one seemed able to promise him that his heart would survive.

He needed to see Gabriel. He needed the fresh memory of Gabriel's loving touch to hold onto through the night. If he could focus on that, he could let his mind drift safely while his body endured Lady Merydith's sadistic pleasures. Dressing quickly, he tucked the last few pieces of jewelry and the gold he had received as a tip from a pleased guest earlier in the week into his pockets and informed the handler at the door that he was going for a walk. The handler looked like he might argue, but Lucio brushed past him and into the street as if he did this all the time. He hailed a cab as soon as he was out of sight of the pleasure palace, directing the driver to Gabriel's workshop. He only hoped Caleb and Andrew would be understanding and leave them alone for a few hours.

When he arrived, the front windows were still dark, so he paid the driver and walked around to the back door. He found Gabriel still at breakfast. "Lucio, what are—"

Lucio cut the words off with a hard kiss. He didn't want to talk, to wait, to think. He wanted Gabriel to take him upstairs and claim him, body and soul.

Gabriel returned the kiss, but Lucio could tell he was still focused on the question of why Lucio was here. Determined to distract his lover and get what he wanted, Lucio used every skill he possessed to bring Gabriel's mind to the here and now, rubbing against the inventor like a cat in heat as he started working at the fastenings on Gabriel's clothes.

"Lucio!" Gabriel protested, tearing his mouth free.

"Are you going to take me upstairs or would you rather fuck me on the table?" Lucio asked, ignoring the protest as he pushed Gabriel's shirt free from his chest and fell on it like a starving man at a banquet, licking and sucking on the hair-dusted skin.

"I'm not going to fuck you at all," Gabriel insisted.

Lucio ignored the question of semantics, pushing down Gabriel's trousers as he dropped to his knees, drawing the hardening shaft into his mouth. Releasing it for a moment, he looked up at Gabriel with determined eyes. "Call it what you want. I want to feel you inside me before I leave here today. I need to know what it's like with a lover rather than a guest."

Lucio could read the question in Gabriel's eyes, but he ignored it in favor of encouraging Gabriel's cock to stiffen more quickly. He needed this, and he needed it now.

Gabriel's hands tangled suddenly in his hair, pulling him away and urging him to stand. "What's going on? Why are you like this today?"

Lucio flinched, eyes closing as if he could hide from reality by hiding from Gabriel's gaze. He had managed to avoid mentioning Lady Merydith when he visited the workshop over the past two weeks, but he could not maintain the charade any longer. "Please trust me," Lucio said after a moment. "I need this to get through tonight."

"What happens tonight?" Gabriel demanded.

"I don't know for sure," Lucio answered, "but I have a new guest, one with a reputation for being especially callous. I'll endure it the way I've endured everything else since I started working as a companion, but having the memory of you inside me would make it so much easier to bear."

Gabriel hesitated so long that Lucio took a deep breath, ready to press his argument, when the inventor nodded sharply. "If we do this, we do it my way," he warned. "You'll lie back on the bed and let me make love to you properly."

"Yes," Lucio said, his voice desperate. "That's what I want."

"Go upstairs and get in bed," Gabriel directed, the words going directly to Lucio's groin. "I'm going to put my dishes away and then I'll join you."

The order and the delay both surprised Lucio, but he climbed the stairs, already loosening his clothes. Alone in Gabriel's room, the room he dreamed of someday sharing, Lucio finished undressing, taking the time to fold his clothes and set them neatly on the dresser. Gabriel's room was always immaculate except when Lucio strewed their clothes everywhere. Somehow it didn't seem right to leave his garments lying on the floor this time, when he had the time to fold them. Shivering a little in the cool morning air, he slipped beneath the covers and waited for Gabriel to join him.

He could hear the dishes clattering in the kitchen as Gabriel rinsed them in the sink, the incredibly domestic sounds helping him relax. It might still be temporary, but this was not a job. He was in his lover's home, in his lover's bed, while his lover tended to his chores. And when his lover came upstairs, they would make love. Taking a deep breath, he inhaled Gabriel's scent on the quilt, letting it wrap around his senses and comfort him. He could do nothing about the future, either tonight or in the longer term, but he could relish every second of this time with Gabriel.

A step creaked beneath Gabriel's tread, bringing a smile to Lucio's face, the first one that had felt real since receiving Lady Merydith's summons. His lover was coming to join him. His lover was coming to make love to him.

When he stepped into the room, Gabriel was already gloriously naked, having taken off the trousers Lucio had pushed down rather than pulling them back up. He set the clothes on the dresser next to Lucio's, the quiet intimacy of the sight far more compelling than Lucio could have expected. Like he belonged there. He resisted the urge to jump from the bed and rush into Gabriel's arms. Gabriel would come to him. He had promised. All Lucio had to do was wait and savor the anticipation.

"Put your hands on the headboard," Gabriel directed, indicating the brass frame with a wave of his hand. "You're mine this morning, and you're going to lie there and let me love you. That means no distracting me."

Lucio shivered a little, afraid he would spend much of tonight with his arms equally bound, but this was Gabriel giving him orders now, and he had nothing to fear in this bed. Lifting his arms over his head, he found a comfortable grip around the metal rungs and waited to see what Gabriel would do next.

His answer came moments later when Gabriel knelt on the bed next to him and kissed him tenderly. All the tension in Lucio's body fled at that first loving touch. He parted his lips, offering his mouth to Gabriel as he would never do to anyone else.

He thought he had grown accustomed to the feel of Gabriel's roughened hands on his body, to how different it felt from when his guests touched him, but suddenly it was all new again, either because he could not touch in return or because Gabriel had been holding back on him. Whatever the cause, he gasped and writhed beneath the tender caresses as Gabriel worshipped every inch of his torso, licking and kissing and caressing until Lucio was wild with need.

When the hot mouth closed over the head of his cock, sucking on it lightly, he screamed, his entire body clenching as he flooded Gabriel's mouth. His lover seemed unfazed, licking and sucking until Lucio had nothing left to give. Panting still from his climax, Lucio lifted his head to watch as Gabriel licked lower, over his sac and then behind. His head fell back to the pillow, the new sensations leaving him trembling again. Gabriel had fellated him before, but Lucio had never let him go beyond that, and Gabriel had respected that line.

No more.

When Gabriel's lips closed over his rosette, sucking at it lightly, Lucio cried out. His guests used his hole, but they didn't pleasure him as they did it. Gabriel, on the other hand, seemed determined to lavish as much pleasure on the little section of skin as possible. Lucio's head tossed on the bed, his hair tangling around his face and obscuring his vision. He wanted to push it aside, but he didn't want to move his hands. Then Gabriel's tongue speared his entrance, and he forgot about his hair and seeing and everything other than the amazing sensations evoked by his lover's mouth. "Gabe...."

Gabriel didn't reply. He simply worked his tongue deeper and faster into Lucio's body, sending spasms of ecstasy through the companion's overloaded system. Then his mouth was gone, two long, thick fingers in its place, probing deeper inside him than Gabriel's tongue could reach, finding the spot inside him that made him cry out and rubbing back and forth across it until Lucio nearly screamed with every pass. "Now, Gabriel," he sobbed, his voice breaking in his need.

"Not yet," Gabriel said. "If tonight will be as bad as you fear, then this morning must be wonderful beyond your wildest imaginings. Trust me a little longer."

Lucio subsided, giving in to Gabriel's request as Gabriel had always given in to him. He could feel his sac tightening as another climax built inside him, but he held back as much as he could, giving Gabriel control of the moment. The wicked fingers worked inside him until he was mindless with need, his cock spurting with every pass against his gland. Finally Gabriel's fingers withdrew, and the inventor moved between Lucio's legs, stroking a hand over his cock to spread the oil on his fingers. Lucio tensed automatically, but Gabriel's hand settled hot and heavy on his belly. "Relax," Gabriel ordered. "I'm not going to hurt you."

Lucio knew Gabriel meant the words to reassure him, but he couldn't bite back a sharp laugh. "I've lost track of how many people have said that to me."

"I love you," Gabriel said. "How many people have said that?"

"Just you," Lucio replied, his voice softening. "Just you."

"Then you know I'm not going to hurt you," Gabriel said, "because it would hurt me to know I was causing you any pain. Relax for me now?"

His fingers teased Lucio's entrance again, reminding him how good it had felt with Gabriel's fingers inside him. He consciously relaxed, even when he felt the tip of Gabriel's cock probing his entrance. The tip popped through, stretching the muscle as Lucio had known it would. Nothing about having a cock up his ass should have been unfamiliar after eight years as a companion, but Lucio knew he would never confuse Gabriel with any guest because no guest had ever filled him so slowly or so perfectly. No guest had ever rubbed over his sweet spot until he tossed on the bed with need. No guest had ever reached for his cock, stroking it in time with his thrusts the way Gabriel did.

No guest had ever made him come the way Gabriel did.

No guest had ever cradled him in his arms and stroked the hair out of his face or lowered his head to kiss him as he whispered, "I love you."

No, Lucio would never confuse any guest for his lover, no matter how many more years he had to spend as a companion.

"FEELING better?" Gabriel asked when Lucio's breathing calmed. He felt the immediate return of tension and cursed himself for bringing it up, but he had to know what had prompted his lover's odd behavior.

"Yes," Lucio replied, his voice firm, but Gabriel was not convinced.

"Why are you so sure tonight will be worse than any other night?"

Lucio buried his face against Gabriel's neck. "Please don't make me talk about this. I don't want to lie in your bed and think about her."

Her. Not that it really told Gabriel much, but at least he knew that the source of Lucio's fear was a woman. "Our bed," he corrected, even knowing it was more wishful thinking than anything else at this point. "I can't help you if I don't know what the problem is."

"You can't help me anyway," Lucio said sadly. "Even if you went right now and somehow convinced them to sell you my contract with the money we have saved up, they'd still make me go tonight because they've already taken her money, and it's too late to cancel or send someone else in my place. I just have to get through it."

"You're scaring me," Gabriel admitted slowly. "You're talking about your guest tonight like you're in danger, and that worries me. Will you please tell me what's really going on?"

"Most of my guests use my body for their own pleasure and leave it at that," Lucio said. Gabriel flinched despite his promise to himself not to let any reaction to Lucio's reality color their interactions. Lucio didn't seem to notice, fortunately. "A few guests, however, take their pleasure by causing pain to the companions they've purchased for the evening. It's something we're trained to deal with, but that doesn't make it any easier to think about. I came here to forget about it for a few hours. Can we please talk about something else now?"

Gabriel didn't want to let it go, the idea of Lucio being hurt deliberately enough to set a spark to his anger, but he bit it down. He couldn't do anything about it no matter how much he wanted to simply lock Lucio in his basement and keep him safe. That would be considered stealing since he didn't own Lucio's contract, and no judge would accept his excuse of protecting the man he loved. Not in the current political climate. If the Caste Equality movement was successful and Ashbrook was elected, perhaps, but not now. Not yet. He considered appealing to Lord Stuart for assistance, but Lucio had said he would be forced to go to his guest tonight no matter what happened because she had already paid. "I won't mention it again, but promise me you'll come to me as soon as you can so I'll know you aren't truly injured."

"It may be a few days," Lucio said, "depending on the handlers and what state I'm in, but I'll come as soon as I can."

"That's all I can ask for," Gabriel replied, wondering if the handlers would give him news of Lucio if he went and asked. Somehow he doubted it.

THE bumping of the carriage over the cobblestone roads was pure torture on Lucio's battered body. He tried to keep track of the streets, but his head pounded, and he was drifting in and out of consciousness. Every inch of his body ached, from his throbbing head to the soles of his feet. He had no idea how he was going to get inside the pleasure palace when the carriage reached its destination because he was quite sure he couldn't walk. He only hoped the driver didn't simply dump him on the sidewalk and drive off. He lifted a trembling, bloodied hand to his face, trying to clear his vision a little. He wiped at the muck on his face, not entirely sure what it was. Dirt, for sure, blood, and spend, but it stank worse than that. Even once he cleared that away, his vision was blurred by the swelling. He was sure she had blacked both his eyes. He didn't even want to think about the rest.

"D'ya need a hand there, lad?"

Lucio lifted his head to peer toward the door of the carriage. The driver stood there, hand extended. "Yes, thank you," Lucio replied, his voice cracking from dehydration and the screams of the night. "Although I'm a bit of a mess at the moment."

"Her Ladyship was a bit rougher even than usual," the driver commented. "You ain't the first sorry chum I seen when she were done with 'em, but they ain't usually quite as bad off as you seem to be. Come on with ye. Let's get ye inside where they can see to ye proper-like."

Lucio took the offered hand, groaning when the pressure of the man's assistance pulled on his strained shoulders. He managed to get out of the coach and up the stairs to the entrance. A sharp cry drew his attention, but he hid his face when he realized it was Cressida. She ignored his attempts at disappearing, thanking the driver profusely and sliding her shoulder under his other arm as she pulled open the door.

With her help and the driver's, Lucio managed to reach a chair before he collapsed, but he had no idea how he would navigate the steps to his bedroom. His balance was simply too precarious.

Cressida came to his rescue, recruiting two of the other companions to lift the chair and carry it up the stairs to his room, setting it down as close to the tub as possible. He flinched beneath the pity in their gazes, but it wasn't like he could hide what had happened. Once they had gone, leaving Lucio alone with Cressida, she set to work stripping him, little sounds of distress escaping her at each new abuse she uncovered. Lucio wished he could have spared her the sight, but he needed her help. He couldn't take care of himself at the moment.

"What did she do to you?" Cressida exclaimed when she finally had him undressed and was helping him into the bath.

"What didn't she do?" Lucio replied bitterly. The hot water stung, but he needed to be clean again, if only so he could take stock of his injuries. "She started with a beating and went from there. I don't think she broke my nose, but I'm pretty sure she cracked at least one rib."

"You need a doctor," Cressida counseled as she washed the blood and dirt from his body.

"I don't have the money for one," Lucio said. "I took the last I had to Gabriel yesterday morning."

"Forget about the money," Cressida spat. "I may not have what you stored up, but I can pay for a doctor."

"I don't want a doctor," Lucio repeated. "I only want Gabriel. We can tell them you're taking me to a doctor, I don't care, but I have to see Gabriel. I have to let him know I'm all right."

"All right?" Cressida shrieked. "You call this all right?"

"No," Lucio said with a hoarse laugh, "but I promised him I'd come to him as soon as I could. He has a friend who's a doctor. Maybe a better one than the quacks they call for us here."

Cressida stared at him for a long time. "Fine. Let's see how you feel after your bath. If you can walk, I'll take you."

"Even if I can't," Lucio insisted, the need to see Gabriel, to feel a loving touch, nearly overwhelming. "Even if they have to carry me back out to the carriage, I need to see him. I need to know that even like this, he'll want me."

"If you weren't already beaten black and blue, I'd thrash you within an inch of your life," Cressida muttered. "Of course he'll still want you. You'll be lucky if he lets you come back after this."

Lucio smiled, feeling his awareness deserting him. "Maybe he won't."

CRESSIDA tutted as she washed Lucio's insensate body, muttering under her breath as she took an inventory of the marks on his skin. Bruises were already forming beneath the surface along the same lines as the red marks that came from either a cane or a switch. She couldn't do anything about those, but she carefully cleaned the broken skin on his chest, wondering how many other marks adorned his back and buttocks. She could see blood in the water, but she didn't know if it was fresh or left over from before. "Bitch," she spat. "Who abuses another person this way?"

Lucio didn't reply, but she hadn't expected one. While he was unconscious, she pushed him sideways so she could reach his back. It was covered with even more red stripes than his chest. She didn't even want to look at his backside, but what she saw was far worse. Blood still seeped into the water. "Wake up, Lucio," she said, shaking his shoulder. "I need you to wake up."

Lucio's eyelids fluttered open, but his gaze remained vacant. "You need a doctor," she said bluntly. "You're bleeding. If you can get dressed, I'll get you to Gabriel's and hope his friend can help you."

Lucio struggled to rise, nearly falling. Cressida's arms went around him. "Your dress," he mumbled, trying to keep from getting her wet.

"Don't be ridiculous," Cressida scolded. "It's already ruined from your bloody suit anyway. Sit there on the chair while I find an old suit. The one you were wearing is rags, but it's too dirty to put back on you. We'll have to find another one it won't hurt to get bloody."

Lucio collapsed onto the chair, the impact sending jolts of pain into his gut, but he stifled the groan, not wanting to worry Cressida. She returned moments later with his oldest suit and helped him dress. "Can you walk downstairs?" she asked. "I can't carry you, and I'm not sure who's around and awake at this hour to help us. You know the handlers won't."

"We'll have to go slowly, but I'll try," Lucio said, levering himself to his feet with a pained grunt. "If it means I get to see Gabriel on the other end of it, I'll do what it takes."

Cressida put her arm around his waist. Lucio hissed at the pain, but it was either that or risk falling, and that would hurt far worse than the pressure of her arm on the welts on his back. He winced as each step put weight on his abused feet, but his legs held, the bath and the conversation having revived him enough that he could manage to put one foot in front of the other to the top of the stairs. He grabbed the banister to steady himself as they started their descent. He suspected the palms of his hands were the only intact part of his body. Lady Merydith had brutally taken a cane to the soles of his feet, but she hadn't attacked his hands.

Finally they made it to the main entrance. "Where are you going?" the handler at the desk demanded.

"To see a doctor," Cressida snapped. "Can't you see he's hurt?"

"We can summon a doctor," the man began.

"I'd rather go to a doctor I trust," Lucio rasped, "than to one who will bleed me even more."

The handler, a new one whose name Lucio still didn't know, looked around as if to see if anyone else was watching. "Take as long as you need. I'll clear her schedule so she can stay with you today. Just let me know where you are so I don't get in trouble."

Lucio nodded gratefully. "As soon as I hear what the doctor says, we'll send word."

The handler helped them out the door, hailing a cab for them and lifting Lucio inside. "Will you be all right?"

"We'll be fine," Cressida assured him. "Thank you."

The handler stepped back, and Cressida gave the street next to Gabriel's as a destination. "Why are we going there?" Lucio asked.

"Because I didn't want the handler hearing the real address," Cressida replied. "I don't know whether Gabriel's friend will see you or will be able to help you, but this way you can safely stay with Gabriel even if he can't."

Lucio wasn't sure he followed the logic, but then his thoughts were still incredibly fuzzy. It was easier to drift, unthinking, and let Cressida take control. When they reached the original destination, Cressida leaned out and explained to the driver that she had been mistaken and would he please take them to the correct address. Lucio could hear the driver grumbling, but he couldn't make out the words. He was far more concerned about the wetness he could feel growing beneath him. Apparently the jolting ride had started the bleeding again. He needed to get into a bed and soon.

"Don't move," Cressida ordered when they reached their destination. "I'll get Gabriel."

"Go to the back door," Lucio said, his head spinning again. He propped his head against the cushions and waited, fighting to stay conscious until he could see Gabriel. Vaguely he heard voices in the background, and then Gabriel's face appeared in the doorway. Lucio summoned a smile as much as his chapped, cracked lips would allow. "I survived," he slurred, lurching toward Gabriel's outstretched arms. Everything went black around him.

"WHAT happened to him?" Gabriel demanded, turning to Cressida, his eyes panicked as he lifted Lucio out of the carriage.

"Lady Merydith," Cressida said curtly, paying the driver and sending him on his way. "He said you had a friend who's a doctor. I'll sit with Lucio while you fetch him. He's bleeding."

Gabriel filed the name away for later, although it wasn't familiar to him at the moment. It would be, though. He would find a way to take revenge for Lucio's injuries eventually. In the meantime, he carried Lucio up the stairs to his bedroom. "Are you sure you can stay with him while I fetch Doctor Headley?"

"Go," Cressida said. "I have a few hours at least before I have to be back."

Gabriel scrambled down the stairs and out the door, his feet pounding on the cobblestones as he ran for Bernard's office. He found the doctor in and still at his breakfast. "Gabriel?"

"Please, Bernard, can you come? A friend of mine is hurt badly," Gabriel said, struggling to catch his breath.

"I'll get my bag," Bernard said, rising immediately and disappearing into the other room momentarily. He returned, pulling his coat on, and motioned for Gabriel to precede him out of the house. "What happened to him?"

"I don't know exactly," Gabriel replied, "but he looks like he was beaten, and I think he was…." Gabriel had to stop and clear his throat before he could continue. "I think he was raped."

Bernard's eyes widened. "That's not something you hear every day. Should we send for a guardian? Perhaps your friend Wakefield from the Caste Equality movement?"

"It won't do any good," Gabriel said bitterly. "Lucio is a companion. It won't matter what happened to him if a paying customer did it."

"It might not matter in a court, but it matters to me," Bernard said, his face pinched. "It will matter to Wakefield and the others at the Caste Equality movement. If your friend is willing, it could be made to matter to a lot of people."

"That's his decision," Gabriel said. "He's been through enough already. I won't pressure him into anything he isn't comfortable doing."

Bernard nodded. "I'll respect your decisions, but if he decides to make a stink about it, I'll be ready."

"He's upstairs," Gabriel said when they reached his house. "His friend Cressida is sitting with him. He was unconscious when I left. He fainted in the coach. She might have a better idea of what happened to him since she was the one who brought him to me."

"We'll see what she says," Bernard agreed, following Gabriel into the bedroom. He let out a low whistle when he got a good glimpse of Lucio. "You weren't kidding when you said he'd been beaten up. I'm Doctor Headley, young lady. And you are?"

"Cressida, sir," Cressida said, rising from her perch at Lucio's bedside. "I'm a friend of Lucio's."

"And of mine," Gabriel added.

"So what can you tell me, Miss Cressida?" Bernard asked.

"Not much, sir," Cressida said. "I happened to arrive back at the pleasure palace this morning at the same time Lucio did. He could barely walk and was only sometimes making sense when he talked. I got him into a bath, but I could tell he needed more attention than that. I wanted to call a doctor, but the handlers make us pay for our own medical expenses, and Lucio doesn't have any gold."

"So you brought him here," Bernard concluded.

"He said Gabriel—that is, Mister Blackstone, knew a doctor who might be able to help him," Cressida explained. "I don't know what you can do, but he's bleeding, sir."

"Let's get him undressed then and take a look," Bernard said. "Gabriel, perhaps you should wait downstairs."

Gabriel shook his head. "No, I want to help."

"Gabriel," Cressida said softly, drawing his attention away from Lucio, "do you really want to see him like this?"

"I love him," Gabriel said, heedless of Bernard's presence in the room. "I won't leave him."

"Then lift his shoulders," Bernard directed. "We're wasting time."

Between the three of them, they stripped Lucio. Gabriel winced at every new welt and bruise, but he held his tongue, only his tightly clenched jaw betraying his turmoil. He had to hold it together for Lucio's sake. He could kill someone later.

"You did well, bathing him," Bernard told Cressida. "Most of these cuts and abrasions are shallow. As long as they stay clean, they'll heal without problem and probably without scars. I'm more concerned about the bleeding. There are surface tears, but it seems to be coming from deeper than that, where I can't get to it to stitch it up."

"So what do we do?" Gabriel asked, heart clenching at the thought of Lucio bleeding to death.

"*We* don't do anything," Bernard said, digging around in his bag. "You and Miss Cressida go downstairs now while I prepare this mixture of agrimony and yarrow. It will help stop the bleeding, whether it's on the surface or inside him."

"I don't want to leave him," Gabriel protested.

"Give me ten minutes to finish taking care of him and you can come back up," Bernard assured Gabriel. Unhappy still, Gabriel nodded and offered Cressida his arm, leading her down the steps to the kitchen.

"Your friend seems competent," she observed when they took their accustomed seats around the table.

"He does his best," Gabriel replied, "but I've heard him complain many times about all the things he can't help. I only hope this isn't one of those times."

"We'll just have to keep a close watch on Lucio," Cressida declared.

"How long can you stay?" Gabriel asked, hating the thought of having to return Lucio to the pleasure palace in this condition.

"The handler at the door cleared my schedule for the rest of the day," Cressida replied, "and Lucio's was already blacked out for the entire week."

"They knew this would happen?" Gabriel bellowed, incensed that the handlers would prepare for this outcome but do nothing to prevent it.

Cressida shrugged. "She paid the fee they demanded. As long as she didn't kill him, she's within her bounds."

"And if he can't work anymore because of it?" Gabriel demanded.

"Then you'll be able to buy him cheap," Cressida quipped.

"That's not funny," Gabriel growled, rising to pace the room. "How can anyone think what happened last night is acceptable?"

"They don't know about it, mostly," Cressida reminded him. "Lady Merydith and her ilk don't play those kinds of games with people who might complain. They choose people with no power as their victims and then they pay the handlers to cover it up."

"Have you ever been hurt that way?" Gabriel asked.

"Not as badly as Lucio was, no," Cressida said, "but I've never seen anyone come back, even from Lady Merydith's, as badly off as Lucio is now. It's like she had a grudge against him for some reason."

"I've done what I can for now," Bernard interrupted, joining them at the table. "I'll come back this evening to change the poultice I used and to see if he's awake yet. If he wakes up, Gabriel, try to get him to eat some broth and drink as much water as you can get in him. Keep him awake as long as you can. I'm worried about the repeated loss of consciousness and the fact that he wasn't always making sense when he was awake. It suggests an injury to his head, although I saw no evidence of any trauma other than the black eyes."

"Excuse me, Doctor Headley," Cressida said, her voice as small as Gabriel had ever heard it. "Without some reason for him to stay where he is, the handlers will expect him back in a few hours."

"Absolutely not!" Gabriel shouted.

"I would agree," Bernard said, "although not for the same reasons, I imagine. He shouldn't be moved until he has recovered his wits."

"Could you tell the handlers that?" Cressida asked. "Perhaps even imply that he's under your direct care so they won't come looking for him? Otherwise they'll take him back, and I don't know if they'll let even you come visit. They certainly won't let Gabriel come."

"I would be happy to explain certain facts to them," Bernard said, his face tight. "Certain things should not be allowed, and the state of the young man upstairs in that bed is one of them."

"Thank you," Gabriel said with a sigh of relief.

"It won't be indefinite," Bernard said, "but I can probably buy you a day or two. If he isn't on the mend by then, he may never wake up."

Gabriel's heart fell. "He was awake earlier. Surely that's a good sign."

"It is," Bernard agreed, "but you need to be aware of the possibilities. I have other patients to check in on, but I'll come back later to see how he fares. Can you wait for me to return and take you home, Miss Cressida? I intend to explain Lucio's absence in ways they will not misunderstand."

"I don't have to be back until tonight," Cressida replied.

"Thank you," Gabriel said again, rising and shaking Bernard's hand. "For everything."

"You're welcome," Bernard said, tipping his hat to Cressida.

AFTER Bernard left, Cressida turned to Gabriel. "Take a chair upstairs and sit with him. I'll wait down here."

"You can come up," Gabriel said halfheartedly, but Cressida shook her head.

"He doesn't need me. He needs you. I'd be in the way."

With a nod, Gabriel took one of the chairs and climbed the stairs slowly, afraid to return to Lucio's side. It tore at him that anyone would choose to treat another person the way Lady Merydith had treated Lucio. When he reached his room, he stopped and simply stared at Lucio in his bed.

He had dreamed of having Lucio there, but not like this. Never like this. The beloved face was battered, both eyes swollen nearly shut, and his lips cracked and bruised, making Gabriel wonder what Lady Merydith had shoved in Lucio's mouth. Moving to sit on the edge of the bed, Gabriel reached for Lucio's hand, holding it gently as he stared at the ligature marks on Lucio's wrists, proof that he had been tightly bound for some portion of the evening. His chest was covered with welts and red splotches that looked like the little burns Gabriel got on his hands sometimes when a valve gave and steam came shooting out. He flinched to think of something being applied repeatedly to Lucio's body to create that odd pattern of marks.

Lucio's back was even worse, some of the welts open and bleeding instead of merely red lines across his skin. Gabriel wanted to touch, to comfort, but he was afraid he would only make the pain worse. From what he could see, only Lucio's hands had escaped some kind of torture during the night. Tenderly he rubbed his thumb back and forth across Lucio's palm, letting the repetition soothe his nerves. He had no idea if any of it was getting through to Lucio, but he had to believe he felt Gabriel's presence at his side or he would go crazy with the waiting.

He heard voices in the kitchen as he held vigil, Cressida's light tones in counterpoint to Caleb's and Andrew's basses. He should go down and greet them, but he couldn't tear himself away, even to find out what they were doing here on their day off. He didn't think he'd be able to move until Lucio opened his eyes again.

"Gabriel?"

Caleb's voice interrupted Gabriel's thoughts, but he didn't look away as he answered. "I'm here."

"Can we come up?"

Gabriel hesitated, not sure Lucio would want them to see him this way, but in the end, he made sure the quilt hid all but Lucio's face and gave his permission.

"How's he doing?" Caleb asked softly as he stepped across the threshold into the room.

"He's been better," Gabriel said with a choked sob. "Bernard said we have to hope he wakes up soon."

"He will," Caleb said. "He has too much to live for."

Gabriel snorted in disbelief. "This is what his life has done to him, and you think he has something to live for?"

"This is what an abusive aristocrat did to him," Caleb disagreed. "His life, his real life, is here with you, and I'll say it again. I see the way he looks at you. He doesn't need any other reason to fight."

"I hope you're right."

"I'm right," Caleb said, his voice so assured that Gabriel didn't argue anymore. "I'm going to keep Miss Cressida company while we wait. Talk to him, Gabriel. It doesn't even matter about what. Let him know you're here and waiting for him."

Gabriel swallowed roughly, not sure he could make his voice work through the welter of emotion that closed his throat. He coughed a couple of times and did his best. "Can you hear me, Lucio?" he said softly. "Somewhere in there, wherever you are, can you hear what I'm saying to you? If you can, remember that I love you and that no matter what she did to you, I still want you. Even now, even like this, you're the most beautiful thing I've ever seen, and I dream about the day when you won't have to get up and leave my bed to return to that other life."

Taking a deep breath to steady his voice, Gabriel leaned forward and brushed his lips against Lucio's cheek below the bruising around his eyes, where he hoped the contact would bring pleasure rather than pain. He could feel the slightest hint of stubble on the usually smooth skin, the thought enough to tear a sob from him. Lucio was always so meticulous in his appearance. He would have shaved immediately before he left yesterday. For him to already have the stubble on his cheek this way, he must have been at the bitch's mercy since late afternoon the day before, and from what Cressida had said, she had only taken the time to bathe Lucio before bringing him to Gabriel's. "I don't know how yet," Gabriel swore softly, "but I will find a way to make her pay for what she did to you."

"Tell Lord Stuart what happened."

Cressida's voice surprised Gabriel. He straightened and turned to look at her.

"I'm sorry. I didn't mean to overhear, but I made tea and thought you might like some," Cressida explained. "But since I did hear, if you truly want to make her pay for this, tell Lord Stuart what happened, or even better, bring him here to see Lucio."

"Why Lord Stuart?" Gabriel asked.

"Because he has a soft spot for his 'pretty boy'," Cressida said. "He's more generous with Lucio than with any of the other companions, even if he doesn't always ask for him. If anyone in the aristocracy will help—and it will take an aristocrat to affect Lady Merydith in any real way—it will be Lord Stuart."

"Perhaps once Lucio is awake and can tell him what happened," Gabriel said. "Right now it would be our guesses against her word."

"It is a matter of record that she purchased his time last night," Cressida reminded Gabriel. "Unless she then gave him to someone else, she did this."

"I don't understand how she could want to hurt him this way," Gabriel said, reaching for Lucio's hand again, his eyes drifting back to the beloved face.

"He said she felt like he'd slighted her at Lord Stuart's ball," Cressida answered. "He didn't say any more than that, but perhaps this was a result of that."

Gabriel's stomach churned. Had he been part of Lucio's decisions that night? "This is my fault, then."

"No!" Cressida said, grabbing his free hand so he turned to face her. "This is Lady Merydith's fault. We don't know that it had anything to do with that night, but even if it did, her reputation precedes her. Lucio is not the first companion she's abused, merely the first one she's abused this badly."

Gabriel swallowed hard, trying to push aside the guilt. "I should have found a way to buy his contract sooner. I could have taken a loan or something."

"You are determined to wallow in this, aren't you?" Cressida scolded. "Fine. I'll leave you to feel guilty. I'm going to send a message to Lord Stuart. At least it's something productive."

Gabriel let her go. He had no problem with quietly taking revenge on Lady Merydith without talking to Lucio first, but he wouldn't contact Wakefield or any of the other Caste Equality movement people until Lucio was awake and could give his consent. If Gabriel had his way—and he suspected Wakefield and Beacham would feel the same way—they would use Lucio's situation to highlight the problems with the caste system and the desperate need for change.

He heard footsteps on the stairs again and glanced over to see Andrew enter the room. "Have you come with more advice?" he asked, his voice bitter.

"No," Andrew said, pulling the chair Gabriel had carried upstairs over to the edge of the bed.

"No tea?"

"No," Andrew replied, sitting down and staring at Lucio's face.

The silence stretched between them, and Gabriel let it, surprisingly comforted by Andrew's quiet presence. Caleb and Cressida had both come with comfort and advice, which Gabriel appreciated, but this was different. Andrew wasn't trying to reassure him that everything would work out. He wasn't trying to convince Gabriel to take action. He was simply holding vigil at Gabriel's side.

"I never really understood why you felt so strongly about the Caste Equality movement," Andrew said eventually.

Gabriel looked at the clock, surprised to see that nearly thirty minutes had passed.

"I do now," Andrew added before falling into silence again.

"I'm glad," Gabriel said, letting the conversation trail off again.

After another long stretch of silence, Andrew rose and patted Gabriel on the shoulder. "You should lie down next to him. If I were in Lucio's shoes, I'd want Caleb's arms around me, and if I were in your shoes, I'd want Caleb close enough that I could feel his heart beating beneath my hand."

Andrew left without waiting for a reply.

Tears prickled in Gabriel's eyes as he removed his shoes and jacket so he could follow Andrew's advice, the best he had gotten all day. He slid beneath the covers, not entirely sure how to hold Lucio without hurting him, but Andrew was right. Gabriel needed the comfort even if none of it got through to Lucio.

A MUFFLED groan woke Gabriel from the light doze he had fallen into, lying next to Lucio. Afraid to hope, he pushed up on one elbow so he could look down at Lucio's face. The swelling around his eyes made it difficult to tell, but Gabriel thought Lucio was trying to open his eyes. "Relax," Gabriel murmured in his ear, reaching for Lucio's hand again. "You're safe. I won't let anyone hurt you."

"Gabe…."

"I'm here," Gabriel said, squeezing Lucio's hand. "You're at my house in my bed where you belong."

"Hurts."

"I know it does, beloved, and I wish there was more I could do to help," Gabriel said, "but Bernard, Doctor Headley, didn't leave anything for me to give you. He did say you could have something to drink if you're thirsty."

"Tea?" Lucio croaked hopefully.

"I'll see if there's any made," Gabriel said. "If not, I can put a pot on and give you some water for now. Will you be all right for a moment while I go downstairs?"

"Hurry."

"I will," Gabriel promised, starting to lean forward to kiss Lucio, but the sight of his abused lips stopped him. "I want to kiss you, but I'm afraid it will hurt you."

"Hurts anyway," Lucio slurred, trying to lift his head for a kiss. Gabriel pressed him back against the pillows, bringing his mouth to Lucio's, a tender brush of lips that even so drew a hiss from Lucio.

"I'm sorry," Gabriel said, lifting his head immediately.

"I'm not," Lucio replied. "Tea now?"

"Yes," Gabriel promised, rising and starting toward the kitchen. "I'll be right back."

When he got downstairs, he found Caleb and Andrew still sitting at the table. "Cressida left?" he asked.

Caleb nodded. "Bernard came back and picked her up. He said he'd be back later since you were sleeping as well."

"Lucio's awake. He wants something to drink. Is there tea?"

"On the stove," Andrew said. "It should still be hot."

Gabriel poured two cups, carrying them carefully upstairs. "Can you sit up?" he asked Lucio, setting the cups on the dresser so he could help Lucio.

"I think so."

Gabriel hovered at Lucio's side, trying to figure out how to help without putting pressure on Lucio's injuries. Ultimately, though, he had to put his arm around Lucio's shoulders and grit his teeth against the sound of pain as he propped the pillows up behind his lover's back. "Relax," Gabriel urged once he had Lucio settled again. He fetched the tea and lifted it to Lucio's lips. "Slow sips. It's hot."

Lucio took a few sips before letting his head drop back against the pillows.

"Don't fall back asleep on me," Gabriel begged, afraid that if Lucio lost consciousness again, he wouldn't wake back up.

"I'm not asleep," Lucio said, his voice less rough after the warmth of the tea. "Just resting my head. How did I get here?"

"Cressida brought you," Gabriel said. "Don't you remember?"

"Everything's fuzzy," Lucio admitted. "I remember some things, but others are a complete blank. Is she still here?"

"No," Gabriel said. "Bernard took her back a little while ago. He was going to tell the handlers you couldn't be moved and had to stay under his care."

"I don't have to go back?"

"Not right away," Gabriel promised. "Not until you're well enough."

"Thank you," Lucio said softly.

"For what?"

"I survived last night by thinking of making love with you yesterday morning," Lucio said. "She might have broken my body, but because I have you, she couldn't break my soul."

Gabriel's eyes closed against the image evoked by Lucio's words. "She didn't break your body," he said hoarsely. "You're here, alive and talking, and Bernard said you would heal given enough time."

Lucio's eyes drifted closed. Gabriel started to rouse him again, but Lucio's eyelids continued to flutter, his breathing hitching from time to time, reassuring Gabriel he was merely asleep, not unconscious again.

When Lucio woke again the middle of the night, Gabriel brought him water and helped him shift to a more comfortable position. Lucio was asleep again in seconds, leaving Gabriel to hold him and dream of a future when this would be their reality every night.

WHEN Lucio woke a second time, he stammered out an embarrassing need to use the chamber pot. Gabriel jumped out of bed and brought it, helping Lucio stand for the few moments it took to relieve himself. "Don't fall back asleep yet," Gabriel said. "Bernard said we needed to keep your cuts clean, and you're covered in sweat. Let me help clean you up a little."

Lucio nodded, bracing himself on the edge of the bed. Gabriel returned moments later with a cool cloth, wiping it over Lucio's bruised face first and then down over the rest of his body. "Why would she do this to you?"

Lucio shrugged, trying to block the memory of the night from his mind completely. "I don't know. She's known for it among the companions, but I don't think she's ever hurt anyone this badly before. She saw me at Lord Stuart's ball and said he was too gentle with me. Maybe she thought I was too high in the instep? She hurled insults at me the entire time, but nothing that would explain her virulence."

Finished with the ablutions, Gabriel pulled out a spare nightshirt. "Can you put this on? You'll be warmer that way."

Lucio lifted his arms slowly for Gabriel to help pull the garment over his head, but that took the last of his strength. He sagged back onto the pillows. "I need to sleep now."

Gabriel helped him get settled, spooning up behind him. Lucio took a deep breath and clung to the security of his lover's embrace with all his heart. The echoes of Lady Merydith's taunts followed him into his dreams.

"How long do you think the handlers will let you stay?" Gabriel asked the next morning as he brought breakfast for Lucio. He had made scrambled eggs, keeping them very moist and soft so Lucio would be able to chew and swallow them. His jaws were not blackened like his eyes were, but Gabriel was not sure how much other abuse his mouth had endured.

"I have a week," Lucio told him. "Whatever she paid them, it was enough to black out a week of my time, but once that is over, I'll have to go back to work, no matter what shape I'm in."

"Even if you aren't healed?"

"My guests won't be happy about it," Lucio agreed, "but if I'm lucky, they'll settle for not tipping me until I'm back to full beauty again. If I'm not lucky, they'll find other companions, and I'll lose my position within the pleasure palace."

"You were beaten within an inch of your life with their full knowledge, and they won't even give you the time you need to heal," Gabriel said with an indignant shake of his head. "If people knew what your life was really like, there would be far more indignation on your behalf."

"You're thinking about your friends in the Caste Equality movement," Lucio said.

"Of course I am," Gabriel said. "This is exactly the kind of situation people aren't aware of but that makes the message of the Caste Equality movement so much more important. People need to know how the system can be—is being—abused. That's what will persuade them to change their minds and change the system."

"You can tell them about me if you think it will help, but I can't be a part of it. Not while I still live in the pleasure palace and rely on the handlers for everything. It would be far too easy for them to slip something in my food or else stop feeding me altogether if I'm seen to make too much of a fuss."

"That's inhumane!" Gabriel protested.

"That's the point," Lucio said with a sigh. "We aren't human in their eyes, not really. We're high-class, high-priced livestock they use for their own profit and discard when they're done with us."

"I won't tell them your name," Gabriel decided, not wanting to put Lucio at risk, "but people need to know what you're suffering."

Lucio coughed a little and shifted on the bed, rubbing his backside. "Did the doctor do something to me? I feel funny."

"He said you were bleeding inside," Gabriel explained. "He made a poultice to stop the bleeding. He wouldn't let me stay so I don't know exactly where he put it, but he must have smeared it up inside you."

"If it helps me heal, I'll live with the odd feeling," Lucio said. "I've never heard of a doctor doing anything like that before."

"Bernard stays up with all the latest studies," Gabriel said. "He prides himself on knowing even the most recent research. If anyone can help you recover quickly, it will be him."

"I can't pay him," Lucio warned Gabriel. "I gave you the last of my gold and jewelry yesterday morning. Needless to say, Lady Merydith didn't give me a tip."

"He didn't even ask about payment," Gabriel said, "but if it comes up, I'll pay him. Whatever he charges, it's little enough compared to having you here and alive."

Lucio patted the bed next to him. "Will you lie with me? I know it's a dream destined to end, but I want to spend the next few days here with you and pretend I don't have to go back."

"Anything you want," Gabriel said, coming back to the bed and Lucio's side. He sat with his back against the headboard, smiling as Lucio turned into his embrace. "I love you."

"I love you too," Lucio said, burying his face against Gabriel's shoulder. "I'm sorry you have to see me like this."

Gabriel shook his head, kissing the top of Lucio's head tenderly. "I'm sorry you're hurt like this," he said, "but I'm not sorry you're here. I'll never be sorry you're here with me."

27

GABRIEL wasn't terribly surprised to see Lord Stuart in his workshop later in the day. He was somewhat surprised to see Wakefield there with the aristocrat, but he chose not to ask for an explanation. They would give him one or not, as they pleased.

"I received an unsigned note that suggested I call on you," Lord Stuart said. "It said the matter was urgent without explaining why."

"I think Cressida worried about it being read and traced back to her," Gabriel said. "She took a terrible risk sending for you."

"And why would Cressida send me a note to call on you?" Lord Stuart asked.

"Because she hoped you would care enough about Lucio to be outraged when you see him," Gabriel explained.

"That is no explanation," Lord Stuart said.

Gabriel sighed. "If you can overlook a merchant's dwelling, you should come upstairs. Everything will make sense then."

Lord Stuart gestured for Gabriel to lead the way. Gabriel mounted the steps to his bedroom, relieved he had thought to dress Lucio in one of his night shirts. At least the companion would have some illusion of modesty. If Lord Stuart insisted on seeing the extent of Lucio's injuries, they could always remove the shirt then.

"Lucio?" Gabriel called as he neared the top. "You have a visitor."

"What is Lucio doing here?" Lord Stuart asked. Gabriel didn't answer, simply stepping aside so the aristocrat could see Lucio's battered face. The curse that escaped the older man made clear his thoughts on the matter.

"What happened, pretty boy?" Lord Stuart asked, crossing the room and taking the seat by the bed.

"Please don't call him that," Gabriel requested, trying to keep his voice level at the reminder of all the intimacies Lucio had shared with the aristocrat. "I realize you're used to thinking of him that way, but you aren't his guest here, to take that kind of liberty with him."

"It's all right, Gabriel," Lucio said, his voice stronger than that morning but still far weaker than usual. "He doesn't mean anything by it. Not that I'm very pretty at the moment."

"Neither of you has answered my question," Lord Stuart reminded them. "I don't care which of you does, but someone will explain this to me. Now."

"Lady Merydith summoned me to her estate on Saturday evening," Lucio said. "She sent me home Sunday morning looking like this."

"Have you reported her?" Wakefield demanded.

"You're a guardian, Wakefield," Gabriel reminded him. "You know that as long as she paid for Lucio's time, there's nothing the guardians can do about the way she treated him."

"I can get my brothers and give her a good scare," Wakefield muttered. "Nobody should be treated like this."

"I would agree," Lord Stuart said, his eyes still fixed on Lucio's face. "Leave Lady Merydith to me. I may not be able to restore your looks, but I can make her life far less pleasant from now on."

"Thank you," Gabriel said. "It rankled that I couldn't do anything to make her pay for this."

"Which brings me to my next question," Lord Stuart said, turning from Lucio to Gabriel. "What is going on here?"

"Noth—" Lucio began, but Gabriel shook his head.

"I'm taking care of the man I love," Gabriel said, bracing for the explosion that was sure to follow.

He was completely unprepared for the laughter that came instead. "Good for you," Lord Stuart said. "I didn't have this end in mind when I introduced you to Cressida, but I'm glad Lucio has found someone to care for him. He doesn't deserve to be at the mercy of anyone with a big enough purse."

Lord Stuart turned back to Lucio, eyeing him speculatively. "That seems an awful lot of damage for one woman to inflict," he observed. "Is there something you haven't told me?"

Gabriel fought the urge to retch. He almost wished he could leave so he wouldn't have to hear Lucio's answer, but he wouldn't abandon his lover that way. Whatever had happened, they would deal with it together.

Lucio looked away, refusing to meet Lord Stuart's gaze.

"Lucio?" Lord Stuart pressed. "Tell me the truth."

"I don't know who they were," Lucio said, his voice so soft Gabriel could barely hear it. "They wore masks and stayed in the shadows. There were five of them, I think, although it was hard to tell in the candlelight and with the masks on. She told them what to do, and they did it."

Lord Stuart's eyes narrowed. "I shall see what I can find out, although it may be nothing. One way or another, Lady Merydith will not have a place in polite society after I'm done with her."

"Don't mention my name," Lucio pleaded. "I still have to work, and if others are worried about being ruined because of me, I'll lose guests, and if I do that, I'll lose status."

"I won't mention your name," Lord Stuart agreed. "Has this happened before to others, do you know?"

"Not this bad, to my knowledge," Lucio replied, "but then again, the handlers try to cover up things like this, even between companions. They can't hide it completely—I knew she would be cruel before I ever went there—but they may be able to hide the severity of it."

"Then I will assume this is not the first time she has left someone in such a pitiable state," Lord Stuart said. "It's not as if she will present a companion to contradict my tale, or that anyone would believe a companion over me if she did."

"I won't use your name either," Wakefield promised, "but I will make sure people are aware of how poorly companions can be treated. A lot of people who don't know one see it as a life of luxury in exchange for very little work. They don't understand the risk involved. They will, though. We'll make sure of it."

"Why are you doing this?" Lucio asked. "Neither of you has any reason to help me this way."

"Because right is right and wrong is wrong, regardless of who is involved," Wakefield said firmly. "No aristocrat would consent to be treated this way. Therefore you should not have to be treated this way."

"Consent is not an issue when you're a companion," Lucio said bitterly. "We do what we're told and hope for the best."

"You truly couldn't have refused her?" Wakefield asked.

Lucio shook his head. "No one ever asks a companion's opinion or cares about a companion's pleasure. We're tools to be used by those who

purchase our time and then sent away when we've served our purpose."
He reached for Gabriel's hand. "Gabriel is the only person other than my
fellow companions who has ever seen me as anything more than that."

Lord Stuart flushed at the implicit criticism in Lucio's words, but he
did not deny the accusation, even when Wakefield looked at him for
confirmation.

"Some things are simply not right," Wakefield muttered.

"And your tireless campaigning on that subject is bearing fruit," Lord
Stuart said. "It will take time still, but things will change. I saw it even
before I met you, though not as clearly as I see it now. We must all do our
part to speed that along."

Lord Stuart took Lucio's other hand, squeezing it gently. "I apologize
for all the times I looked at you and didn't see you. Wakefield and your
Mister Blackstone have opened my eyes to things I had never before
noticed. If I can be of assistance to you, please don't hesitate to call upon
me. I would be pleased to see you in a better position. Elijah, we should
leave Lucio to rest now."

Lord Stuart rose and escorted Wakefield out of the bedroom, leaving
Gabriel and Lucio alone and staring at each other. "Are they...?" Lucio
asked.

"Your guess is as good as mine," Gabriel replied, "but it would
certainly appear that way. They seem an odd couple on the surface, but I
can see how they could be good for each other. Wakefield is passionate,
fiery, but impulsive. I can see Lord Stuart providing some caution and
wisdom to his exuberance."

"And Wakefield's firebrand attitude could certainly offer some
rejuvenation to Lord Stuart, who is not as young as he used to be," Lucio
agreed. "I hope they will be happy, whatever is between them. Lord Stuart
has been generous with me more than once. I grow weary. I think I should
rest again."

"Sleep," Gabriel said, helping Lucio scoot down on the bed. "I'll make
sure you aren't disturbed."

Lucio's eyes had already closed when Gabriel leaned over and pressed
a tender kiss to his forehead.

"HOW'S our patient today?" Bernard asked, coming into the workshop through the back door.

"Asleep right now," Gabriel replied. "We had visitors this morning, and that wore him out."

"We won't wake him right away, then," Bernard said. "Is he eating some?"

"A little," Gabriel said. "We had eggs for breakfast, but it still hurts him to chew. He said they avoided striking his mouth or jaws, but the pressure of biting down hurts his black eyes."

"Eggs are good for him," Bernard said. "Until he can handle meat, you should keep making them for him. They'll help restore his strength."

"What else can I do for him?" Gabriel asked. "Anything. It doesn't matter how small. I want him well again."

"Don't let him overdo," Bernard said. "More than anything, he needs rest and quiet to heal. If he's anything like most of my patients, the pain will fade a little tomorrow or the next day and he'll want to be up and moving around, but he risks restarting the bleeding if he does that."

"I'll see that he stays in bed," Gabriel promised.

"Are you lovers?" Bernard asked bluntly.

"Yes," Gabriel replied. "Why?"

"Because the last thing he needs for some time is anything anywhere near his rectum," Bernard said. "He needs to heal completely before you return to intercourse, or he risks tearing open the healing wounds. Each time he does that, he sets his recovery back again."

"Then you need to tell his handlers that as well," Gabriel said. "I would never force anything on him, but they may not have the same consideration. They sent him to the bitch to begin with." At another time, in another place, Gabriel might have chosen his words more carefully, but Bernard had seen the damage done to Lucio. He would understand why Gabriel had no patience for mincing words.

"I'll speak with them," Bernard said. "I intend to escort him home when the time comes and make my professional opinion on a number of matters very clear to them."

"Gabriel?"

"It sounds like he's awake," Bernard said. "If you don't mind, I'll go up and talk to him alone for a few minutes about his injuries and his prognosis. I know you want to come, but some things are best left between doctor and patient."

"I'll wait down here," Gabriel agreed, despite wanting to insist on going up with Bernard. He suspected Bernard would press Lucio for answers about all that had happened to him, answers Gabriel did not really want to hear. "Call me if you need me."

LUCIO was surprised to see the doctor answer his call instead of Gabriel. "Where's Gabriel?"

"Downstairs, pacing the kitchen because I wanted to talk to you alone," Bernard replied.

"Is something wrong?" Lucio asked nervously.

"No more than there was before," Bernard replied. "I thought perhaps you might want to talk to someone who isn't your lover about what happened. I don't imagine you want Gabriel knowing the details of what was done to you, but you need to tell someone."

"I usually talk to my friend Cressida," Lucio said, "but she is at the pleasure palace and I'm here."

"Anything you say to me will remain between us," Bernard assured him. "I won't say anything to Gabriel about it."

Lucio nodded. "You can probably guess most of it from the marks on my body. Like all companions, I was trained in the art of pain as well as the art of pleasure, but I have never been brutalized the way Lady Merydith did. Whips, canes, paddles, she used them all on every part of my body she could abuse with them. There were others there as well who took turns using me while she beat me. I shudder to think of the amount of fluid they spilled down my throat, in my ass, and on my skin. And the entire time they did, Lady Merydith hurt me."

"What did she burn you with?" Bernard asked.

"Candle wax," Lucio replied. "She said she was decorating me, to make me a fitting offering. I don't think the flame ever touched my skin, but the wax was more than hot enough to leave marks. Obviously. And when the men were exhausted, she started looking for other things to fuck me with."

"To rape you with," Bernard corrected. "I know what you're taught about consent and the fact that once the money changes hands, the choice is no longer yours, but some things are beyond the pale. You were tortured. There's no other word for it. You don't have to say it to anyone else, but this once, to me, call it what it is."

Lucio took a deep breath, trying to push down the bile that rose in his throat at the doctor's blunt assessment of the situation. "I...." He choked on the words, clearing his throat and reaching for the glass of water on the table by the bed. Taking a couple of sips, he tried again. "I...."

"You were tortured," Bernard repeated slowly.

Lucio nodded, tears flowing down his cheeks from his swollen eyes as he let the reality of what had happened roll through him. "I was tortured," he said, his voice breaking on the words. "They sold me to her for the night, knowing I would be tortured."

"Good for you," Bernard said, patting Lucio gently on the shoulder. "Now that you've said it, now that you believe it, you can begin to heal. I've already talked to Gabriel, not that I was truly worried about him. You cannot have intercourse until you are completely healed or you risk a setback or worse."

"They blacked my schedule out until Saturday," Lucio told Bernard. "On Sunday, I have to go back to work if I want to eat."

"We'll see about that," Bernard said. "If they do that to you, they risk you dying, either from bleeding or from infection. Surely the cost of a few days' income is not worth the possibility of losing you and your income for all future clients."

Lucio shrugged. "I don't know what drives their decisions, but I know if I can't work, I don't eat. If I have a hole in my schedule, that's one thing, but if I tell them I can't work, I have to pay for my own food instead of having it given to me as part of my job, and I have no money to pay for food or anything else. That's why Cressida brought me here in the first place. I couldn't pay for a doctor."

"We shall see about that," Bernard said gruffly.

"Please," Lucio pleaded. "Don't meddle. In a matter of a few months, Gabriel will have the money to buy my contract, and then it won't matter anymore."

"It will matter a great deal if you die between now and then," Bernard disagreed. "I have a few choice things to say to your handlers."

Lucio gave up arguing. Bernard could say what he wanted. Lucio would do as he had always done and obey their orders because the last thing he needed was to get the reputation as a troublemaker. At the moment he enjoyed more freedom than most of the other companions because of his favored status within the pleasure palace. If he lost that, it would be harder to see Gabriel without his lover purchasing his time, and that would delay the day when Gabriel could buy his contract and they could be together permanently. That was the last thing he wanted.

"Can I come up now?"

Lucio glanced anxiously at Bernard, not sure what the doctor had said to keep Gabriel downstairs in the first place, but he needed the comfort of his lover's arms around him.

"Yes, come ahead," Bernard called down.

Lucio smiled at the sound of Gabriel almost racing up the stairs. He opened his arms for his lover, clinging to Gabriel's strong shoulders with all the strength in his arms.

"I'll see myself out," Bernard said. Neither man looked up.

"I love you," Gabriel said roughly. "No matter what she did to you, no matter what secrets you told Bernard, nothing will change that."

A soft sob escaped as the tears Lucio had stilled came back with renewed force. Gabriel pulled him closer.

Lucio buried his face in the crook of Gabriel's neck and wept.

ON TUESDAY, Lucio was so sick of lying in bed that Gabriel reluctantly agreed to help him get up. The companion was still unsteady on his feet so Gabriel put a couple of pillows on the wooden chair and helped Lucio onto it.

"Sit there and rest," Gabriel instructed, pulling the sheets off the bed. "You'll sleep better on clean sheets."

"I'm sick and tired of sleeping," Lucio complained. "I want to get well. I have these precious days I can actually spend with you, and I'm trapped in bed. I want to help in the workshop."

"I know, beloved," Gabriel said soothingly, setting the sheets on the straw mattress that he had not yet switched for the heavier feather mattress he used in the winter. "But you're stronger than you were yesterday, and that was better than the day before. It will just take time."

"Time I don't have," Lucio muttered. "It's already Tuesday. I have to go back to work on Sunday. I don't know if I can."

"We'll worry about that on Friday," Gabriel said, not wanting to contemplate Lucio leaving or the risk to his health if he returned to work too soon. "Right now you need to concentrate on getting well."

Lucio doubted ignoring the issue would make it any easier to deal with on Friday, but Gabriel was right that they couldn't do anything to change it between now and then. He could make himself sick thinking about it, or he could relax and enjoy the time with Gabriel, even if he was too weak to do much more than sit in bed and let his lover tend to him.

Gabriel disappeared down the stairs with the soiled sheets in his hands, leaving Lucio alone for a few moments. Tentatively, he shifted on the chair, trying to determine how well he was healing. The first movement didn't bother him, but the second one sent pain shooting up through his belly. Cursing under his breath, he panted until the cramps eased. He had the answer to that question, then. He couldn't see the welts on his back, but he reached behind him, running his hands over the nightshirt to see how much tenderness remained.

"What are you doing?" Gabriel asked when he came back into the bedroom carrying clean sheets.

"Trying to see how much damage remains," Lucio replied. "I know you said to worry about it on Friday, but I have to take stock, to see what liabilities I'll have when I go back to work."

"Let me remake the bed and then I'll help you," Gabriel proposed. "I can see what you can't."

"Will you be honest about what you see?" Lucio asked. He didn't think Gabriel would lie to him out of malice, but he needed a realistic assessment of the marks on his body to know what reaction he would get from his guests on Sunday.

"I promise."

Lucio relaxed on the chair as much as he could, wishing idly for the cushioned arm chair in his bedroom at the pleasure palace. The moment the thought crossed his mind, he felt guilty for it. Gabriel had bent over backward to care for him. The lack of amenities owed directly to Gabriel's determination to save every piece of gold he could so he could buy Lucio's contract sooner. Once Lucio lived there, they could use some of the money from Gabriel's inventions to add small indulgences to their rooms.

That brought another thought to mind. "What will I do after you buy my contract? I can't sit around idly waiting for you to be ready to bed me."

"I'd hoped you would want to work with me in the workshop," Gabriel said, finishing with the sheets and sitting on the edge of the bed facing Lucio. "But if there's something you'd rather do, that's up to you. I know the paper will say that I own you, but it won't be that way between us."

Lucio hadn't truly thought it would be, but he hadn't thought beyond the hurdle of getting free of the pleasure palace to the rest of his life. "I would love to work with you in the workshop," he said. "The afternoons we've spent together there have been some of the happiest of my life, surpassed only by the night we spent together in your bed."

Gabriel shook his head. "Our bed," he insisted. "For as long as you desire to be here with me, even if it is only a dream still, this will be our bed."

"You shouldn't say such things to me," Lucio said, his voice rough with emotion. "Going back will be hard enough as it is."

"If we left now, we could be so far away they would never find us before they realized you were missing," Gabriel offered.

Lucio held out his hand. "Until the first time a guardian questioned what a companion was doing out alone with only a merchant. You wouldn't have my contract, and I'd be forcibly returned to the pleasure palace, and you'd be thrown in prison. That would leave us no hope of being together."

"It's a risk I'd be willing to take," Gabriel said softly. "I won't pressure you, but I would deem any risk worth it if it would keep you safe."

If it would keep him safe, Lucio would have taken the risk, but he feared the consequences of being caught more than he feared a few more months at the pleasure palace. "Help me take this shirt off and tell me how bad I look," he said, changing the subject.

Gabriel helped him undress. Lucio shivered at the air on his skin. It wasn't even particularly cool, but every inch of flesh seemed far more sensitive than normal still. The burns and welts on his legs and belly seemed less pronounced than they had on Sunday, the only real chance he had gotten to look at them. They were still visible, but not nearly as obvious. The ligature marks on his wrists were also fading. If he continued to heal at this rate, they would be gone by Friday. Though his memories of the night at Lady Merydith's hands were somewhat hazy, he feared his back and buttocks had borne the brunt of her abuse. "What does my back look like?"

"It's looked better," Gabriel joked. Lucio glared at him. "There are still six raised marks, but the scabs are gone. They look now like the others did when you arrived on Sunday."

"So all I really have to worry about is whether my insides have healed enough to let a guest bed me," Lucio said.

"Your face is still pretty battered," Gabriel said. "Not as swollen, but the bruising is still very dark. If the guest intends to take you out in society at all, he or she will be sorely disappointed."

"Then he or she will have to be disappointed," Lucio said with a sigh. "I can't make my body heal any faster than it already is."

"I know," Gabriel said soothingly. "Lie back down. The more you rest, the faster you'll heal."

Lucio sighed and let Gabriel help him to his feet and back into bed. He was sick of resting, but he knew the inventor was right. Perhaps tomorrow he'd feel well enough to sit downstairs for a few minutes. The change of scenery would be good for him.

"ARE you sure you want to try this?" Gabriel asked.

"I'm sure," Lucio said, fastening the buttons on a pair of Gabriel's trousers. They were loose on him, but they were better than the pair he had worn upon his arrival. He doubted the blood would ever come out of those. "I'm tired of being cooped up. I know I'm not strong enough to go for a walk or even for a ride, but even going downstairs will be better than feeling confined any longer."

"I could get Caleb or Andrew to come help me carry the chair down the stairs so you don't have to walk," Gabriel offered, but Lucio shook his head.

"I need to regain my strength. It's Wednesday. I only have a few days left. If I can't even walk down the stairs, how am I supposed to return to my job?"

Lucio flinched a little at the sour expression on Gabriel's face, any sign of displeasure from those around him setting off the need to soothe it away. He took a deep breath and reminded himself that Gabriel was not a guest and never would be a typical one, demanding Lucio cater to his every whim and never do anything that might upset him.

"If I had my way, you wouldn't return," Gabriel muttered.

Lucio pretended not to hear. He didn't want to argue with Gabriel over something they couldn't change. "Give me your arm? I'm not sure I can navigate the steps alone."

Gabriel put his arm around Lucio's waist immediately, steadying and supporting him. They moved slowly across the room and down the steps. More than once, Lucio would have fallen without Gabriel's help, but he persevered, determined to join Caleb and Andrew for their midday meal instead of eating from a tray like an invalid.

The two assistants rose to greet him when he reached the bottom of the steps, bringing a smile to Lucio's face. He had so few friends in the pleasure palace, the rivalry instilled by the handlers who wanted the companions to compete for the attention of the aristocrats having made it nearly impossible to relax around others of his caste. Cressida was the notable exception, but they had been friends since childhood, long before that kind of rivalry made any sense to them. Having friends here, in his new life, made it all the sweeter.

"How are you?" Lucio asked them as he braced himself to endure the claps on the shoulder that would surely come.

They came as predicted, but with much less force than usual. "We're well," Andrew said, "but how are you feeling?"

"Better," Lucio said, overstating the case a little perhaps, but he didn't want Caleb and Andrew to worry about him. Gabriel worried enough for all four of them. "Not back to full strength yet, obviously, but a few good meals will put me to rights."

"I don't know that our cooking qualifies as good," Caleb joked, "but it's filling at least."

"I'm sure it's wonderful," Lucio insisted. Even if it wasn't, he would never let them know that, not when they'd taken the time to make sure he had a hot meal at lunch instead of a few bits of cold meat stuck between two slices of bread, which was what Gabriel usually ate.

Andrew served a bowl of steaming stew and set it in front of Lucio before serving everyone else. Lucio blew on it gingerly, not wanting to burn his tongue. It wasn't the most refined dish he had ever tasted, but it was hearty and filling and exactly what he needed. He focused on eating, dimly aware of the conversation around him, but too hungry to take part. When he had scraped every bit of food out of the bowl, Andrew's laughter drew his attention.

"I think he liked it," Andrew said.

"Would you like some more?" Caleb offered. "There's still some left."

Lucio took stock for a moment. "No, I don't think so, but it was delicious. How are things going down here this week?"

"We haven't taken any new orders," Andrew said, "because with Gabriel spending so much time with you, we're a bit behind on our current ones, but now that you're doing better, we should be able to get back on schedule."

"I'm sorry," Lucio said, looking from Andrew to Gabriel. "I didn't mean to mess things up."

"You didn't!" all three men exclaimed.

"Andrew and I don't begrudge the time Gabriel's been spending upstairs," Caleb said. "You were sick. That came first. No one's going to come pounding on our door because we finish a project on Thursday instead of on Tuesday, and even if they do, we'll tell them technical difficulties slowed us down. Besides, if I know Gabriel, he'll work like a fiend after you go back so he's too tired at night to do anything but fall asleep with his clothes on."

Lucio turned back to Gabriel again. "Do you really do that when I'm not here?"

Gabriel nodded.

"Why?"

"Because if I don't, I have time to wonder where you are and what you're doing," Gabriel said. "I don't let myself think about it during the day or when we're together, but at night, alone in my bed and missing you, it's hard not to think about it."

"As long as you don't wear yourself out so much that you get hurt because of it," Lucio said. He wanted to chide Gabriel for agonizing over something they couldn't change, but he knew if their positions were reversed, he would have the same difficulty letting it go. He had made his own peace with his situation thanks to Gabriel, but he couldn't force Gabriel into that same mindset. "Remember that no matter where I am or what I'm doing, I'm thinking of you at the same time. Maybe that will help you rest more easily."

Gabriel didn't look convinced, but Lucio didn't push the matter with Caleb and Andrew sitting there looking on. If they were going to argue, he didn't want an audience. "Is there anything I can do to help? I can't do any heavy lifting, but I could do smaller things."

"We could set him up at one of the work benches and let him assemble the gear mechanism for the fan," Andrew said to Caleb and Gabriel. "It isn't hard, and he wouldn't need to get up. If he does that, I can work on the casings. The rivets are all in, but they need to be forged."

"Could you really show me?" Lucio asked eagerly. "I don't know how long I'll be able to stay upright, but I do want to help, especially since Gabriel's been neglecting his work because of me."

"Of course I'll show you," Andrew said. "Come in the other room, and I'll get you all set up."

Lucio wavered a little on his feet as he rose, but he brushed Gabriel's hand away, hoping the stew had strengthened him enough he could walk to the other room on his own. He still wouldn't attempt to negotiate the steps alone, but he wanted to do this if he could. Gabriel hovered at his elbow, but he let Lucio try it on his own. To Lucio's delight, he made it all the way into the workshop by himself. "I *am* getting stronger," he said determinedly.

"Have a seat here," Andrew said, indicating the bench he usually worked at. "I've got one halfway finished so I'll show you what I've done and then how to finish the rest."

Lucio stared at the complicated collection of gears and pulleys in front of him, hoping he wasn't making a mistake in offering to help, but he refused to back out now. Gabriel had offered him a place in his workshop, and Lucio intended to earn it. Starting today.

Andrew walked him through the process of laying out the gears and pulleys and then connecting them with the appropriate belts. "Once you have that done, we'll thread it through a casing, put a motor on one end and the fan blades on the other, and then send it off to its happy owner."

"Will you watch while I do the first one?" Lucio asked. "I don't want to mess it up."

"You don't have to worry about that," Caleb said. "We always test them, even when we build them, before we put them in the casing to make sure everything is working properly. If you have something reversed or out of place, we'll catch it and fix it then. We have to tinker with things all the time."

"Go ahead," Andrew said. "I'll watch you do one on your own."

Concentrating on remembering all the steps, Lucio assembled the mechanism, threading belts through pulleys, hanging gears on pins. Finally he got it done and looked up to Andrew for approval.

"We'll make an inventor out of you yet," Andrew said with a smile. "You keep doing exactly what you just did, and if you need help, ask Caleb or Gabriel. I'm going out to the forge."

"What does he do in the forge?" Lucio asked when Andrew had left.

"He heats the rivets in the joints of the casing," Gabriel said. "When they cool down, they shrink, and that holds the joints tightly in place. We didn't do that with the carriage you built for the flying chair because I wanted to test it and make sure the size worked before we fired it, but I wouldn't sell it without doing that because I wouldn't want a rivet to come loose and something to come apart because of it."

"Can I learn how to do that too?" Lucio asked.

"Not at the moment," Gabriel said, "but if you want to learn once you come to live with me, I'm sure Andrew would show you how."

"It's hot, dirty work," Caleb warned, "and he ends up with burns on his hands as often as not."

"Once I'm out of the pleasure palace, that won't matter," Lucio said. "Gabriel won't care if I have burns on my hands because it will be proof that we're working together for real instead of only on those occasions when I can steal away for an afternoon."

"I'll still care," Gabriel replied, "but not because I want you to be perfect. I'll never be happy about knowing you're hurt."

Caleb snorted. "A few red patches from sparks hardly count as hurt. If Lucio's going to be an inventor, you'll have to get used to him bearing the same nicks and bruises as you do, and you can't make him feel bad for it. You wouldn't treat me that way, so don't treat him that way."

"I'm not in love with you," Gabriel reminded him, making Lucio chuckle.

"Maybe not, but you can't stop him from being your equal or you'll both regret it later."

29

"CRESSIDA, I'm surprised to see you," Lucio said with a smile as Cressida walked into the workshop where he sat, assembling more gear sets for the fans. He rose and hugged her, leading her into the kitchen where they could talk in private. Not that he had many secrets from the other three, but he had some questions to ask Cressida that he wasn't ready for Gabriel to hear.

"I wanted to check on you," Cressida said when they sat down at the table. "How are you doing? Your face looks a little better."

"That seems to be the worst of it now," Lucio replied, "other than my ass, anyway."

"When are you coming back?" Cressida asked.

"Saturday," Lucio replied. "Doctor Headley said he would come with me and make it clear to the handlers the risks of me going back to work so soon. It might not do any good, but at least they can't say they didn't know."

"I looked at your schedule before I came," Cressida said. "You have a guest for Sunday afternoon. I didn't see anyone for the morning or evening."

"Did you see who it was?" Lucio asked.

"Lord Palmer," Cressida replied. "It looked like he only reserved a couple of hours."

"He's not my favorite guest by any means," Lucio said, "but it could be worse. He usually prefers fellatio to anal sex, which is good because I'm not healed enough for that yet."

"Your face isn't exactly healed enough for fellatio," Cressida pointed out.

"They didn't hurt my mouth," Lucio said. "I may not be pretty to look at, but I can still suck a man dry."

"Been practicing on Gabriel?" Cressida teased.

"No," Lucio said. "I've been practicing being an inventor. I find that far more rewarding."

"I'm happy for you," Cressida said, squeezing Lucio's hand. "I hope everything works out for both of you."

"So do I," Lucio said. "It's everything we dreamed of and resigned ourselves to never having. A real life, Cressi. Can you imagine it?"

"It's easy to imagine it for you," Cressida replied. "I see the way he looks at you, the way he cares for you when you're here. He didn't hesitate when I showed up here with you on Sunday. He pulled you into his arms and rearranged his life for you."

"He wants me to run away with him," Lucio confided. "A part of me wants to agree, but I'm afraid of what will happen if we aren't successful."

"It's a huge risk," Cressida agreed. "Don't blame him for thinking of it, though. He's never lived our lives. He doesn't have any way of understanding the risks. All he sees is a chance to be with you all the time, a way not to have to share you with anyone else. He doesn't realize that if you were caught, you could be killed."

"They probably wouldn't kill me right away," Lucio said. "They'd breed me first so they wouldn't lose that chance. Then they'd think about killing me."

Neither of them said it, but Lucio knew Cressida was thinking the same thing. If he was sent to the breeding barns in disgrace, he would be fair game for the handlers there. He would die in the end, but they'd make his life a living hell first.

"It will only be a few more months until he has the money to buy my contract," Lucio said. "I can wait that much longer."

"What do you want me to say if the handlers ask how you're doing?" Cressida asked. "I told them I was going to the doctor's to check on you."

"Tell them I'll be back on Saturday," Lucio said. "I'll deal with the rest then. They aren't going to reschedule a guest because you tell them I'm still injured. They probably won't even if the doctor tells them, but they'll never take your word for it without seeing me."

"I could try," Cressida offered. "Even if they don't change anything, at least they can't say your arrival is the first they've heard of how badly you're still hurt."

"That's up to you," Lucio said. "Let's talk about other things. Do you want to see what I've been working on the last few days?"

Cressida smiled indulgently. "You obviously want to show me, so let's go take a look."

"You just want to spend some time with Caleb and Andrew," Lucio teased.

"Is there a problem with that?" Cressida asked, her voice as cool as Lucio had ever heard it.

"No, of course not," Lucio said. "I didn't realize you were serious."

"I don't know what I am," Cressida said, "but I know I've been treated better in this little workshop than I have been anywhere else, and that's something to treasure."

"It is," Lucio agreed. "Come on. We'll get Andrew to explain what I'm doing since all I do is follow the model he set out for me."

They returned to the other room. Lucio went to Gabriel's side, giving him a reassuring squeeze around the waist. "Everything is fine," he whispered. "I needed to talk to Cressida for a bit. That's all."

"You'll tell me what she said later?"

"The important parts, yes," Lucio promised. "I'm sure you have no interest in the latest *on-dit*."

"No, probably not," Gabriel agreed.

"I promised Cressida I'd show her what I've been working on," Lucio said, pulling away and going back to his workbench. "Andrew, come tell Cressida what all this is for."

Immediately Andrew appeared at their side, explaining the entire mechanism in far more detail than Lucio was able to follow. He suspected Cressida was similarly lost, but her smile never wavered as she listened intently to the lecture. Lucio glanced across the room at Caleb. He was not entirely sure of the relationship between them, but they almost always arrived and left together. Caleb's face was serene, even a bit indulgent as he looked at Andrew and Cressida, reassuring Lucio that even if Cressida's interest was not returned, she was not causing problems between the two men. The last thing Lucio wanted was to do anything that might disrupt the friendly ease of the workshop or to be the one who brought a disruptive element into anyone's lives.

FRIDAY came and went in the same studied quiet, everyone doing their best to forget that Lucio would have to leave on Saturday. When Caleb and Andrew had said their good-nights and left, Gabriel pulled Lucio into his arms. "I don't want you to go back tomorrow."

"I don't want to go back," Lucio said, "but if I don't, there will be hell to pay, and I can't bring that down on your head. I can't ask you to live the life of a fugitive when we'll have the money we need soon. Let the week we've had together motivate you to work harder, and I'll do the same."

"You'll do no such thing," Gabriel interrupted. "You'll turn down every job you can until you're completely well. It's not worth the risk to your health to take more customers. They don't tip you that well. The flying chair will be ready to test the next time you can visit or I can purchase your time. Once we know it works, I'll show it to Lord Stuart and hope he'll arrange a more public event for me to show it off to society. For something like the flying chair, I can charge twenty thousand gold easily. Even if I have to sell ten or fifteen of them to get the money we need, it won't take that long to build them, and I can get you out."

"I want to help," Lucio insisted.

"You have helped," Gabriel reminded him. "You've given me every piece of gold you've saved up over eight years, and then you came here and helped with the flying chair and with the fans. Believe me, you've helped. And if you weren't hurt, I wouldn't argue so hard against it, but you heard what Bernard said. If you're injured again, it will take even longer to heal. I don't want to lose you now that I've found you."

Lucio laid his head against Gabriel's shoulder. "You won't lose me. I'll be as careful as possible. I promise."

Gabriel feared "as careful as possible" wouldn't be enough, but he didn't want to ruin their last night together with an argument. "Come to bed. I want to hold you for one more night."

Lucio undressed slowly, giving Gabriel plenty of time to wish for more than the night would surely bring. The first few nights, when Lucio was all but unconscious and too weak even to move, it had been easy to sleep next to him and hold him close without wanting more, but the last two nights had been more difficult. Only the bruising on Lucio's face remained now as a visible sign of what he had endured, although Gabriel could still see the occasional hitch in his step because of the internal injuries. While the sight of Lucio's blackened eyes still enraged him, it did nothing to stifle his desire for his lover.

Gabriel disrobed as well, tossing his clothes on top of Lucio's on the dresser, a casual mixing of garments that he wanted so badly to represent the mixing of their lives, and slid between the sheets, holding the top sheet up in invitation. Lucio climbed in bed next to him and curled into his embrace.

"Hold me tight tonight," Lucio said softly. "Hold me like you'll never let me go."

Gabriel didn't repeat his offer of running away. They had gone over that ground already. Instead he pulled Lucio tightly against him from knee to chest, tucking Lucio's head against his shoulder and pressing a gentle kiss to the top of his head.

Lucio turned his head and kissed Gabriel's collarbone as he settled comfortably against his lover. Gabriel let out a deep breath as he let the simple pleasure of the moment roll through him. He closed his eyes, expecting to fall asleep as they had at this juncture for the past five nights.

Lucio, however, seemed to have other ideas, his hand beginning to move over Gabriel's skin. Gabriel's breath caught in his throat. He hissed as the questing fingers brushed across one nipple. "What are you doing?"

Lucio laughed throatily. "Did you really just ask me that?"

"Lucio, we can't—"

"I can't take you inside me," Lucio interrupted, "but there's no reason why we can't do other things. I have to go back tomorrow. Let me play tonight. Please?"

Gabriel took a deep breath, steadying himself and shoring up his control. "Whatever you want."

Lucio leaned up and kissed him. "You always say that to me. Will you ever do what you want?"

Gabriel chuckled. "That's the beauty of it. When you do what you want, I get what I want too."

"Well, in that case," Lucio teased, lowering his head and licking across Gabriel's nipple, "I'll enjoy tonight even more."

Gabriel forced himself to lie back and give Lucio free rein. Always before, he had questioned whether Lucio truly wanted each new thing he tried, but he pushed that impulse aside. He would simply lie still and let Lucio play. The result would undoubtedly steal his wits, but it would be worth it to have this new memory of Lucio.

Lucio's lips closed around the taut bud, sucking lightly. Gabriel groaned and stroked Lucio's hair, not guiding so much as simply touching, steeping every sense in Lucio. The moment he shifted on the bed, Lucio's lips moved to the other side of his chest, nibbling and sucking with the perfect blend of pressure and tenderness to set Gabriel on edge without pushing him over. He had the traitorous thought that he was benefiting from Lucio's training, but he pushed it aside. Lucio might be calling on that expertise, but he was doing it because he wanted to, not because he felt required to in any way.

Then Lucio moved lower, licking along Gabriel's ribs to the line of hair that bisected his abdomen, following it lower and lower until he nuzzled the wiry hair at the base of Gabriel's cock. Gabriel groaned as he fought the desire to guide Lucio's mouth to his erection. He bit his lip when Lucio's lips moved away, tracing the crease where his hip and thigh joined and then lower, his chin nudging Gabriel's sac.

"I love the way you smell," Lucio said, his breath whispering across Gabriel's sensitive flesh. "My guests all smell of perfumes and oils, as if they needed to hide. You smell real, like sweat and hard work and desire."

"With good reason," Gabriel choked out as Lucio licked across his scrotum. He grabbed the headboard with both hands, trying to ground himself as he parted his legs, giving Lucio permission to do whatever he wanted. Gabriel only hoped he would do it soon.

Lucio chuckled, the sound vibrating through Gabriel's skin. Suddenly desperate, Gabriel reached for his shaft, intending to speed the process along, but Lucio intercepted him, kissing the palm of his hand and pushing it upward again. "My turn tonight," he reminded Gabriel. "I won't leave you hurting, but you promised me tonight to do as I please."

"I didn't know you planned on torturing me," Gabriel replied. The moment the words were out of his mouth, he wished he could call them back. Lucio flinched and pulled away, his shoulders shaking with suppressed sobs.

Cursing under his breath, Gabriel sat up, wrapping his arms around Lucio's shoulders. "I am so sorry, beloved," he whispered, peppering tender kisses over Lucio's neck and shoulders. "It was a careless turn of phrase, not an accusation. I love you, and I know you love me and would never hurt me."

Lucio turned in Gabriel's arms, burying his face against Gabriel's chest. "Let it out," Gabriel urged, stroking Lucio's back. "Let it go."

Finally Lucio's sobs eased to soft sniffles. Gabriel rocked them on the bed, offering comfort in every way he knew how. When Lucio finally lifted his head, Gabriel wiped away the tear tracks from his pale cheeks. "I'm sorry," he said again. "I didn't mean to speak so rashly. Will you forgive me?"

"If you'll forgive me for ruining our last night together," Lucio said, his voice rough from his tears.

"You didn't ruin anything," Gabriel insisted. "You're still here in my arms, aren't you?" Lucio nodded. "That's all I expected when we came upstairs tonight, to hold you as I've done this past week. Anything else is a bonus."

"I wanted to make you feel good," Lucio said. "To show you I appreciated how much you've taken care of me this week."

"You don't have to make love to me to do that," Gabriel reminded him. "A simple thank you will suffice. I'm not a guest, for whom every transaction is sexual."

"Which is why I keep making mistakes," Lucio explained. "I don't know how to act sometimes because everything is so different with you."

"You were doing fine until I messed things up," Gabriel said. "Don't worry about it so much. If it feels right to you, I can assure you I will enjoy it."

"So can I finish what I started?" Lucio asked, his voice shy. "Without unfortunate comments this time?"

"If you want to," Gabriel said, trying not to sound overly eager. Lucio needed to be able to say no if that was what he wanted.

"Do you want me to?" Lucio pressed.

"I will never say no to your hands on my body, beloved," Gabriel swore. "I may want you to go faster, which is what I should have said earlier. I may want to feel you touching other parts of me, but I will never say no."

"Then in that case," Lucio said, pushing Gabriel back on the bed and moving between his legs.

He didn't finish his sentence, but Gabriel had no chance to ask what he intended because he swept down on Gabriel's cock, sucking the softened length into his mouth. Gabriel cried out in surprise and delight, bucking up into the moist cavern. He tried to still the movement of his hips, but Lucio stole every bit of his control, sucking and swallowing around his shaft until it had reached full hardness again.

Far more quickly than he would have liked, Gabriel felt his climax welling up inside him. He grabbed the base of his shaft, squeezing it tightly, but Lucio pushed his hand away, lifting his head only long enough to urge Gabriel to find his release before sinking back down on the thick shaft.

Giving up on staving off his climax, Gabriel closed his eyes and let Lucio sweep him into rapture. The sucking pressure didn't ease, prolonging his orgasm until the sensation teetered on the edge of pain. Before it could cross that line, Lucio lifted his head, licking his way up Gabriel's stomach until he lay completely atop the inventor's body.

Gabriel reached between them, only to find the stickiness that proclaimed Lucio's pleasure as well. "I don't get to return the favor?" Gabriel teased.

"Another time," Lucio promised. "It felt so right being with you this way that I couldn't hold back."

"I love you," Gabriel said, rolling to the side and snuggling Lucio against him.

Lucio nestled into his arms, rolling onto his side so they were spooned together. "Don't wiggle around too much," Gabriel warned. "You'll give me ideas I can't follow through on."

"Not tonight," Lucio agreed sadly, "but as soon as I'm well, I'll find a way to come back and you can follow through on any ideas you want."

"I'm looking forward to it already," Gabriel said. He hated the thought that Lucio would leave tomorrow, but he would bide his time. They would be together soon and nothing would ever separate them again.

30

LUCIO dressed slowly, deliberately avoiding any glance at the mirror. He would have to stand in front of it eventually unless he asked Cressida to tie his cravat, but he would put that off as long as he could. He didn't want to see the bruises still marring his face. The handlers had been totally unimpressed by Doctor Headley's impassioned insistence that sending him back to work now could threaten his health. He had to work in order to eat, and since he had no gold left to contribute to his own upkeep in the event of not being able to work, he had no choice but to accede to their demands.

Doctor Headley had stomped off, muttering dire imprecations, but Lucio hadn't bothered. It would do no good. Resignation was the far easier option.

Finished with all he could do without the mirror, Lucio crossed the room, wincing at the discoloration around his eyes. Ignoring that for the moment, he tied his cravat and then looked at the assortment of powders and creams on the dresser. He rarely used them, the natural paleness of his skin more pleasing to the eye and the touch than any makeup would be, but today that was not the case. The bruises had faded from dark black to a purplish-green that was not at all appealing. With a sigh, he opened the containers and set to work, hoping he could make his face presentable enough for Lord Palmer.

When he finally set down the brushes, he doubted he had succeeded, but at least he had hidden some of the bruising and lightened the rest. He was not his usual radiant self, but it was the best he could do. Lord Palmer had not given any indication of wanting to take Lucio out in society, so perhaps the aristocrat would be satisfied with fucking Lucio's mouth in the privacy of his home and then sending him back.

Taking a deep breath and checking to make sure he did not have powder on his jacket, Lucio descended to the foyer to wait for his guest.

"You shouldn't have upset Her Ladyship," the handler at the front desk sneered. "You're lucky they didn't send you to the breeding barns and be done with it."

"The bruises will heal," Lucio reminded him, unable to stop himself from arguing. He hadn't done anything to merit the abuse Lady Merydith had heaped upon him. "There aren't any scars. With enough time, I'll be as good as new."

"Time you don't have if your guests won't wait for you," the handler retorted. "I wouldn't pay for you looking like that."

"You couldn't afford me no matter what I looked like," Lucio snapped, knowing he would probably regret the words but unable to keep his temper leashed any longer.

"I should double your guest load for that," the handler growled, "but I'll let it go on one condition."

"What condition?" Lucio asked warily.

"When you get back from bedding Lord Palmer, come up to my quarters for an hour," the handler said, rubbing himself beneath the desk. "I'm sure I can find a better use for your pretty lips than mouthing off."

Lucio's stomach sank. A week ago none of the handlers would have dared suggest such a thing. It seemed his status within the pleasure palace had already taken a hit. If the alternative was seeing twice as many guests, he wasn't sure he had a choice. He would survive the encounter with Lord Palmer because the aristocrat had never had any interest in Lucio's ass. Most of his guests didn't share that preference. He could beg them to be gentle with him, explain what had happened and what could happen if they weren't, but the more guests he had to see, the greater the chance of him sustaining a real injury.

"When Lord Palmer sends me back," Lucio agreed.

The front door opened, and a liveried servant walked in. "Lord Palmer sent me to fetch his companion," the man said.

"That would be me," Lucio said, putting on his best smile and ignoring the leer of the handler at the desk as he followed the servant out to the carriage. To his surprise, Lord Palmer waited inside. "Good afternoon, my Lord," Lucio said. "I didn't expect you to come for me yourself."

"I was out already," Lord Palmer explained curtly. "Step back outside a moment."

Puzzled, Lucio did as the aristocrat directed.

"What is wrong with your face?" Lord Palmer demanded.

"I had an accident," Lucio replied. "I have a few bruises, nothing serious. Nothing to keep us from enjoying our afternoon together."

"I didn't pay top price to have to look at your battered face," Lord Palmer disagreed. "Go back inside. I will have an explanation for this."

Lucio cringed but did as he was told, following Lord Palmer back into the pleasure palace.

"What is the meaning of this?" Lord Palmer demanded of the handler behind the desk. "I paid thirty gold for an afternoon with a beautiful companion, and you send me this bruised thing instead."

Lucio shrank back against the column, the words hitting him hard as he saw all his fears realized. The handler shot him an evil look. "We apologize, my Lord. I didn't make the arrangements for you, so I assumed you had specifically requested Lucio. I can arrange another companion for you. Perhaps Desdemona would suit you?"

"I have no interest in females," Lord Palmer said. "I paid the thirty gold for Lucio because I know he's worth it. Usually. I have no intention of paying that price for a companion whose talents I don't know."

"Alonso?" the handler suggested. "He has the afternoon free. I could have him ready for you in fifteen minutes."

"If I must wait on top of everything else, you'll send a second companion with him to make up for my lost time," Lord Palmer insisted.

The handler nodded, flipping frantically through the book. "Of course, my Lord. I shall find someone else as well and send them both to you as quick as may be."

"Good." Lord Palmer turned to look at Lucio. "It is nothing personal, you understand. I pay for perfection when I seek a companion. When your face has returned to its former beauty, I'm sure I will visit you again."

"Thank you, my Lord," Lucio said because he knew the response was expected. The moment Lord Palmer looked away, Lucio slunk toward the door, hoping to escape while the handler was still trying to make arrangements for the aristocrat. He needed to talk to Cressida.

He had gotten almost to the door when a hard hand landed on his shoulder. "Not so fast, boy," the handler said. "You have a promise to keep, remember? You're probably off to the breeding barns anyway, but if I tell them you were rude to me, it'll be a whipping on top of it."

"I hadn't forgotten," Lucio said. "I was going to relieve myself so I could give you my undivided attention."

The handler looked unconvinced, but he released Lucio's arm. "Five minutes," he growled. "If you aren't back by then, it's the whipping post for you."

Lucio fled toward Cressida's room as fast as he could. Not bothering to knock, he barged in, calling her name.

"I'm in the tub," Cressida called back.

"Lord Palmer refused me," he recounted quickly, joining her in the bathroom. "I'm going to try to bribe the handler at the desk to keep it quiet, but if it doesn't work, I may be sent to the breeding barns. They won't keep me here if no one will purchase my time. If that happens, tell Gabriel he has to hurry."

"I will," Cressida promised, reaching for his hand. "Be careful with the handler. They aren't the most considerate of men."

"I have to go. He gave me five minutes before I had to be back or he'd report me for insolence," Lucio said, leaning over and kissing Cressida's forehead swiftly. "If the worst happens, tell Gabriel I love him."

GABRIEL stood in the middle of the crowd at the Sunday rally for the Caste Equality movement's candidate, Paul Ashbrook. He had met with the movement's organizers after Lucio left the day before, providing all the details he could of Lucio's abuse and even of his normal life, to help provide a rallying cry for the movement. Ashbrook had agreed not to use Lucio's or Cressida's names so as not to further complicate their lives. Gabriel only hoped he kept his promise. Already he itched to check on Lucio, but he had to let a few days pass or he risked drawing unwanted attention to them. Lucio had promised to visit as soon as his schedule allowed, but Gabriel feared the handlers would be less lenient after Lucio had slipped their control for an entire week. He would wait until Thursday, but if he hadn't heard from Lucio by then, he would insist on purchasing an hour of Lucio's time, if only so they could test the flying chair.

Ashbrook took the stage to vigorous applause and cheers. Gabriel could see guardians in uniform around the edge of the square, but in the past, they had only interfered if the rally turned violent. Gabriel hoped that would not be the case today. He did not want anything to interfere with Ashbrook's message.

"Ladies and gentlemen," Ashbrook began, his voice carrying over the square, "thank you for coming today. I appreciate your support and hope to always be worthy of your faith in me."

Gabriel applauded with everyone else.

"The subject of our rally today is something that has only recently come to my attention and that I'm sure many of you are as unaware of as I was," Ashbrook continued. "Most of us have little chance to make the acquaintance of any of the pleasure caste since we have other uses for our hard-earned wages than buying the time of a companion. Because of that, most of us have probably never realized the true extent of the dangers they live with on a daily basis."

Gabriel let the rest of the speech wash over him. He knew what Ashbrook intended to say because he had listened to the speech the day before. Instead he looked around the crowd, trying to gauge people's reactions to Ashbrook's revelations. He could see disbelief on most of the faces as the candidate began. Companions might be the lowest caste, but they were guaranteed shelter, given an education and clothing, and lived in apparent comfort compared to many of the labor caste especially. The farmers and drivers and others of the caste had little patience for anything concerning the companions.

Ashbrook was a persuasive orator, though, and as he outlined the harsher realities of a companion's life, how they were denied food if they could not work on a particular day, how they had no say in the disposition of their bodies or their time, Gabriel could see people's expressions beginning to change. When Ashbrook added to the list by talking about Lucio's situation and how he had been so cruelly tortured by a guest with no recourse, the crowd burst out in angry shouts of indignation, their chant of "No more tattoos, no more taboos" growing nearly deafening.

Gabriel tensed, seeing the guardians standing far more at attention than they had been earlier, but they made no move to interfere with the crowd. Gabriel wondered if they, too, were falling victim to Ashbrook's rhetoric. Gabriel hoped so. They needed people from every caste on their side if they were going to institute the kind of systemic change needed to help not only Lucio but every companion who was dissatisfied with his or her job.

Shouts near the front of the crowd drew everyone's attention, including that of the guardians. A few of them advanced slowly toward the crowd as the shouts grew louder, fists waving in the air along with the placards many of the demonstrators carried. Gabriel backed away, not wanting to get caught in any violence. One of the tenets of the Caste Equality movement was change by political rather than violent means, but not everyone who attended the rallies subscribed to those methods.

The sudden crash of breaking glass caused an explosion of shouts, people starting to scatter as they fled the guardians and the escalating violence. Gabriel moved to the far side of the square, hovering there as he waited to see what would happen. Not that he could help Ashbrook or the other organizers if the guardians tried to arrest them, but at least he would know how much damage the outburst of violence had done to the movement.

He caught a glimpse of people being pushed into the reinforced wagons the guardians used to transport prisoners, but none of them seemed to be wearing the purple and white cockades the chief activists always wore on their lapels. He breathed a sigh of relief as the remnants of the crowd dispersed rapidly and without additional incident. Gabriel retreated as well, heading toward the headquarters of the Caste Equality movement, where he hoped someone would have a better idea than he did of what had happened.

To his relief, all his friends had already reassembled when he reached the building where they met. "There you are, Blackstone," Wakefield said, shaking Gabriel's hand. "I saw you when the rally first started and then I didn't see you after that."

"I moved deeper into the crowd," Gabriel replied. "I wanted to see what kind of reaction the speech was getting, not just from the militants up front but from the people who stopped to see what was going on."

"And?" Ashbrook prompted. "What kind of reaction did it get?"

"Very positive," Gabriel said. "They were somewhat hostile at first. They all have this idea of companions living in the lap of luxury, second only to aristocrats in their comforts. By the time you were done, they realized those luxuries don't make up for the hardships in their lives. What happened up front? I couldn't see."

"We got the same kind of reaction near the grandstand that you saw in the back," Beacham reported, "but as they started shouting, someone got hit in the face with a placard, which started a shouting match and then a shoving match. One man fell into a shop window and shattered the glass, which is when the guardians stepped in. Fortunately Ashbrook had his carriage right there so we could get him out of the square quickly and safely. The last thing we need is for our candidate to end up in prison."

"How is your friend?" Ashbrook asked. "Any news?"

"None," Gabriel said, "and I don't expect to have any before Wednesday or Thursday. I only hope nothing happens to him."

"They won't tell you anything if you ask," Wakefield agreed, "but they might tell a guardian and an aristocrat. I could see what I can find out."

"Not yet," Gabriel said, no matter how he was tempted to accept Wakefield's offer. "He was so worried about being the subject of worse scrutiny because of everything that happened. If I haven't heard from him a few days, I'll try, and if I can't find anything out then, I'll take you up on your generous offer."

"If you speak with him, tell him of the success of today's rally," Ashbrook suggested. "It might hearten him somewhat. We don't want him to lose hope of a better future, not when I know we are close to seeing that future realized."

Gabriel nodded in agreement, although he suspected most of Ashbrook's reassurances were empty political rhetoric rather than real expectations. He scolded himself silently for being cynical, but while he desperately yearned for the changes Ashbrook and the Caste Equality movement were proposing, he had been disillusioned too many times in his life to blindly accept that this time would be materially different, in the short term anyway.

"When can we schedule the next rally?" Beacham said, turning the conversation back to business. "We gained some ground today in people's sympathies. We don't want them to forget our message. The sooner we get back out there, the better."

The conversation swirled on around Gabriel, leaving him to his dour thoughts. Before Lucio had left yesterday, he had confided the preferences of his guest for this afternoon, trying to reassure Gabriel that he could make it through the day and perhaps even beyond with his other charms. Gabriel hoped Lucio was right, because the thought of him lying somewhere bleeding scared Gabriel more than anything had done since he learned that his parents had died.

Perhaps he would not wait for Thursday after all. Cressida said she had not given his name to the handlers when she told them where Lucio was, and they were used to him coming in every few weeks and purchasing an hour or two of Lucio's time. They wouldn't think it at all odd if he did the same thing now so he could check on his lover. He'd wait until Tuesday in case Lucio could get away on his own, but no longer than that. He had to know Lucio was safe.

31

LUCIO spat on the floor of his new accommodation, trying to get the sour taste of the handler's cock out of his mouth. The man must have alerted the others to his situation while he was talking to Cressida because as soon as he left the handler's quarters, he was summoned before the chief handler and informed that his current inability to work left them with no choice but to use his talents in other ways. He would be consigned to the breeding barns until all the marks from his time with Lady Merydith had healed, and then, if there was still demand for his time among the guests, he would be given the chance to regain some of his previous status.

He paced the confines of the small room, the sawdust on the floor barely covering the caked dirt beneath it. The straw pallet in the corner was clearly supposed to be his bed, but he doubted he would find much rest there. He almost regretted asking Cressida to tell Gabriel where he was. He hoped Gabriel never knew what kind of conditions he was reduced to. Not that any of this was Gabriel's fault, but Lucio knew his lover would find a way to feel guilty about it anyway, if only because he hadn't earned the money fast enough to buy Lucio's contract before this all happened.

The door to his room opened and a brawny man walked in. "Strip."

Lucio swallowed roughly, but he didn't dare disobey. When he was naked, the man indicated he should turn around with a wave of his hand. Once again, Lucio obeyed.

"I can see why they'd want you to stand stud service," the man said. "Even with the bruises, you're a looker. I'll see who we have in the other stalls who will match your pedigree. You can get dressed again. We won't start the breeding until tomorrow."

"Am I allowed out of the room?" Lucio asked.

The man laughed. "The door isn't locked, if that's what you're asking, but you've got a barn full of handlers who spend all day breeding studs like you to sweet little mares and can't touch any of the girls. You, on the other hand, are fair game. The choice is yours."

Lucio had no reply to that, but he resolved to jam the door during the night if he could. He needed to heal, not be used by all the handlers in the barn.

The handler looked him over once more and turned to leave, pausing before he shut the door behind him. "Oh, yes, the boys are going to enjoy having you around. You're nearly as pretty as the girls."

"Wait!" Lucio called. The handler turned back. "What's your name?"

"Smith," the handler replied. "Why do you want to know?"

Taking a deep breath and reminding himself he had to survive long enough for Gabriel to buy his contract, Lucio put a sway in his hips as he approached the door where Smith still stood. He walked his fingers up the man's arm, playing with the collar of his shirt. "I don't suppose we could work something out, Mister Smith," he purred. "I give you whatever you want, and you make sure the others leave me alone? I've been told I'm the best in the business, and I'd be at your disposal the entire time I'm here."

The handler looked at Lucio speculatively. "They said your ass was too torn up for a proper fucking."

"My last guest was a little overzealous," Lucio agreed, "but there's nothing wrong with my mouth or my hands. You'll never get another chance like this one. Are you really so fond of the others that you'd pass up my willing cooperation so you can share me with them?"

Smith took a step into the room and pushed on Lucio's shoulders. "Convince me you're worth it, boy."

Lucio took a deep breath and prepared to give the best blow job of his life.

LUCIO stared at the door as it closed, shutting him in the stall. He was covered in spend again, the handler having chosen to decorate his face rather than coming down his throat. Slowly he pushed to his feet, his insides cramping at the movement. He kept hoping he had healed enough to be done with the pain, but odd movements still caused the wrenching sensation inside him. He found a pail of water on one side of the room. He suspected it was supposed to be for drinking rather than for cleaning up, but he had to get the mess off his skin. He wouldn't be able to rest otherwise. He dipped the end of his cravat in the water and wiped his face clean as best he could. He couldn't do much about his hair, but at least he no longer had the smell in his nostrils. Sinking down on the pallet, he summoned the memory of climbing the stairs to Gabriel's room on Friday night, of lying in his lover's arms and kissing him.

If he closed his eyes, he could still feel the tenderness of Gabriel's hands on his hair rather than the demanding jerks of the handlers' hands. He could still hear the husky whispers as Gabriel lavished praise on him rather than the insults heaped on his head by the handlers who saw him as nothing more than a commodity. He could still smell Gabriel's honest sweat rather than the stink of the handlers' unwashed skin. He could still see the rapture on Gabriel's face rather than obscene lust. He could still taste the saltiness of Gabriel's essence rather than the sour flavor of the men who had used him that day.

He focused on those memories rather than on his worries about what the next day would bring. He couldn't change it, whatever it was, not as a virtual prisoner in the breeding barn. He could only hope for the best and pray that Cressida would get his message to Gabriel and that Gabriel would find a way to get him out sooner rather than later. Smith had been satisfied with his mouth tonight. He had no way of knowing how long that would last.

POUNDING on the door roused Gabriel from bed with the sun the next morning. Puzzled, he drew his dressing gown around him and descended the stairs to the back door. To his surprise, Cressida stood on the other side. "Cressida, what's wrong?"

"They've taken Lucio," Cressida said breathlessly. "He told me yesterday it might happen, but then I had guests. By the time I got back, he was already gone."

"Taken him where?" Gabriel asked.

"To the barns," Cressida said. "A guest refused him yesterday because of the bruises, and the handlers used that as an excuse to send him to the breeding barns to stand stud there."

Gabriel shook his head, trying to clear away the remnants of sleep. "Slow down. I don't understand."

"Companions aren't simply born," Cressida explained impatiently. "The handlers study our physical traits and match us up for maximum effect. They breed us like a farmer breeds his livestock. Lucio has been sent to stand stud, hopefully only until he heals enough to work again."

"What does that mean for our plans?" Gabriel asked, trying to take in everything Cressida told him.

"It depends on the handlers at the barns," Cressida replied. "If they merely make him stand stud service and actually let him heal, he could be back in the pleasure palace in a couple of weeks, but I've heard stories of the handlers using the companions who are there for their own pleasure, the men anyway. They don't want to risk the breeding by using the women."

"So he's even more at risk now than he was before," Gabriel guessed, mind racing.

"I don't know," Cressida said, "but I fear that may be the case. He came to me yesterday and asked me to tell you that he loved you."

Gabriel swallowed hard. "If you see him, tell him I love him as well and that I'm doing everything I can to help him. I don't know what I can do, but I'll explore every avenue open to me."

"I probably won't see him unless he returns to the pleasure palace," Cressida said, "but I'll pass on the message if I get the chance. You must hurry, Gabriel. I don't want to see anything happen to him."

"Neither do I," Gabriel promised. "Go back now before you're missed. It's too early for me to start calling on people, but there's one thing I can do even at this hour. Don't give up hope yet."

Cressida kissed his cheek and ran back to the waiting carriage. Gabriel rushed up the stairs to dress in his warmest clothes. If all went as planned, he would need them.

Wrapping his scarf around his neck, he went down to the basement. The flying chair sat on a wheeled cart, waiting for the right time to test it. He had hoped to have Lucio at his side when he did it, but that was no longer an option. Resolutely, he opened the door from the cellar to the garden behind the workshop and dragged the cart up the ramp. He was closing the doors behind him when Caleb and Andrew appeared through the workshop.

"What are you doing?" Andrew asked. "I thought you wanted to wait for Lucio to test it."

"I did," Gabriel said, "but that's not going to happen, and time is suddenly very much an issue. Help strap me in here. Everything rides now on the flying chair working. We do nothing else in the workshop until it's ready to demonstrate to Lord Stuart."

Caleb and Andrew helped Gabriel move the flying chair from the cart. Gabriel took the pilot's seat, strapping the belt around his waist to hold him in place. Caleb and Andrew latched the front cockpit in place to protect Gabriel's legs. "Ready?" Caleb asked.

"Ready," Gabriel replied, pulling his goggles into place. Caleb started the motor behind him, the gears turning slowly. Above Gabriel's head, the rotors started to spin. The chair vibrated beneath him as the machinery gained speed, but it didn't lift off the ground, much to Gabriel's dismay. He turned the handle to open the valve that would send more steam to the engine. The volume increased, making him hope it would be enough. He tilted the rudder, holding his breath as the lift from the overhead rotors raised the chair a couple inches off the ground. He steered it forward slowly, hoping it would maintain its altitude.

Then the engine puttered and the chair jolted back to the ground.

"Damn it," Gabriel muttered, waiting for Caleb and Andrew to come unlatch the cockpit so he could see if there was any damage to the chair.

"It worked," Andrew exclaimed.

"Barely," Gabriel groused.

"Stop that," Caleb said, rapping Gabriel's shoulder sharply. "It worked. We still have work to do, but you built a device that will lift that chair off the ground and allow it to be directed around the garden. We can tinker with the details now, but the basic idea is a success."

Gabriel pulled his watch out, checking the time. "I need to call on Lord Stuart and on Mister Ashbrook. I don't know if either of them can help me, but I have to ask."

"Help you with what?"

"Help me get Lucio out now."

Andrew looked like he was about to ask what had changed that made the matter suddenly so urgent, but Caleb caught his eye and shook his head. They would ask later, when Gabriel was not so distraught.

"Go do what you need to do," Caleb said. "I watched the flight. I think I see a couple of things we can improve quickly and easily. We'll work on that while you're gone."

"Thank you," Gabriel said, going inside to change his clothes.

Dressed to go out in society, Gabriel headed to the Caste Equality movement headquarters first, hoping his friends there would be able to help him.

Only Bill Beacham was there when he arrived.

"Blackstone," Beacham said, rising and shaking Gabriel's hand. "What are you doing here so early?"

"The companion I told you about before has been punished for not being able to work," Gabriel explained. "I've been saving up to buy his contract, but I'm out of time. I'm afraid he won't survive much longer if I don't get him out of there."

"You need gold?" Beacham verified.

Gabriel nodded.

"How much?"

"I don't know," Gabriel said. "I asked once, but they wouldn't tell me how much his contract cost, only saying it was too much for a merchant like me. I came here hoping Mister Ashbrook would be in and would be willing to help."

"He has family obligations this week," Beacham said. "I don't expect to see him again until next Monday at the earliest."

"I can't wait that long," Gabriel said. "I have about fifty thousand gold saved up, and I have a new invention that's almost ready. I could pay back any loan."

"Find out how much you need," Beacham said. "We don't have a whole lot in the coffers at the moment. We spent it on the ads in the newspapers, but we can lend you what we have."

"Thank you," Gabriel said, putting his hat back on and taking his leave. He would hope to have better luck with Lord Stuart.

He found the aristocrat still at breakfast, Wakefield joining him at table.

"What brings you to call so early on a Monday morning?" Lord Stuart asked, offering Gabriel a seat.

"Lucio is in danger," Gabriel said bluntly, "and I can't help him by myself."

Lord Stuart's teacup clattered as he set it on the saucer. "Tell me what's going on."

Gabriel related everything Cressida had told him as well as his own unsuccessful attempt last week to find out how much it would cost to buy Lucio's contract. "I have fifty thousand gold that I can retrieve from the bank immediately, but I'm sure that won't be enough. The problem is I don't know how much more I need. I've almost finished work on a new invention, a flying chair. We were able to fly it around the garden this morning, although it will need more work before it can be more than a novelty. I'd hoped to have it ready to sell so I could use the gold from that to make up the difference, but we've run out of time."

"Don't worry about that now," Lord Stuart said. "The first thing we have to find out is how much it will cost to get Lucio out. They wouldn't tell you, but they will tell me, or I will have the guardians in to insist."

"Do you really think the guardians will come?" Gabriel asked.

Wakefield laughed, drawing Gabriel's attention. "I may not look as impressive as many of my caste, but I do have a guardian's uniform, and I'm perfectly happy to assist. The handlers won't know that I'm not currently working for the city."

"I'll owe you a debt I can never repay," Gabriel swore.

"I have an idea about that too," Lord Stuart said, "but before we discuss that, we need more information. Go home and work on your invention. The sooner you get it ready to present to society, the better for everyone. Wakefield and I will see what we can discover and join you there in a few hours."

"Are you sure?" Gabriel asked. "I could come with you."

"You could," Lord Stuart agreed, "but the handlers know you now, and they know you've only expressed interest in Lucio. They'll increase the price if they think I'm asking on your behalf simply because they can. I, on the other hand, have spent time with a variety of companions in the past, and I have been absent for some weeks now, so they will be interested in bringing back my business. You did me a great favor when you introduced me to Mister Wakefield. Let me return that favor by helping you now."

Gabriel wanted to argue, but he saw the sense in Lord Stuart's words. "Thank you," he said instead, bowing as he took his leave.

When he returned home, Caleb and Andrew met him at the door. "Any news?"

"Lord Stuart has agreed to help gather information," Gabriel said. "He promised to come here later today once he had time to visit the pleasure palace and see what he could learn. In the meantime, he wants us to work on the flying chair."

"Put your leathers back on, then," Caleb said, "because we're ready to try another flight."

Gabriel dressed again, for the third time that day, a bitter laugh escaping him as he thought that Lucio's days must have often been spent that way. Sitting down hard on the bed, he reached for the pillow Lucio had used while he was there, lifting it to his nose so he could smell the fading scent of Lucio's hair on the rough cotton. "I don't know how yet, but we will get you out," he whispered to the empty room, hoping Lucio, wherever he was, would feel his love and reassurance.

"Gabriel?"

"I'll be right down," Gabriel called, taking a deep breath and trying to pull himself together again. Lucio needed him to work on the flying chair. His bout of self-pity could wait for tonight when it was too dark to work anymore.

Putting his scarf back around his neck, he went down to see what Caleb and Andrew had done while he was gone.

SEVERAL hours later, Lord Stuart arrived at the workshop. Gabriel started to ask about Lucio, but Lord Stuart held up his hand. "Show me this invention you were talking about."

Irritated at the change of topics, but knowing he could not afford to lose Lord Stuart's support, Gabriel led the aristocrat into the garden. "We just finished some adjustments," he explained as Caleb closed the casing on the engine again. "We've managed to keep it in the air for over three minutes and to steer it, but we still haven't gotten it very high off the ground."

Lord Stuart walked all the way around the contraption before stepping back to stand by the wall. "Let's see how it works."

Gabriel sat down and fastened the belt as Andrew latched the cockpit and Caleb started the engine. Gabriel put it in gear and watched the rotors start to turn. A few moments later, the flying chair hovered off the ground again. Using the steering shaft, Gabriel sent the chair buzzing around the garden. Pressing the pedal for a little more power, he tried for more altitude, succeeding in getting the chair even with the height of the garden wall before the engine sputtered in protest. Carefully, he lowered it back to the ground. "Each time we try it, we get better results," Gabriel said.

"Good," Lord Stuart declared. "I have news for you, then. Let us sit inside and discuss business over a cup of tea like civilized men."

Gabriel unfastened the belt and waited while Andrew unlatched the cockpit. He shook his head when his friends would have followed him into the kitchen. Whatever Lord Stuart had to say, Gabriel preferred to hear it alone. "Were you able to find anything out at the pleasure palace?"

"Tea first," Lord Stuart insisted.

Gabriel bit back his impatience, heating water on the stove and serving Lord Stuart, keenly aware of the difference in the quality of his dishes and the china Lord Stuart had used that morning.

Lord Stuart took a sip of his tea and set down the cup. "The handlers did their best not to talk to me," he began, "but I insisted, and ultimately they gave in. I am, after all, an aristocrat. After much negotiation, they agreed to sell me Lucio's contract for one hundred twenty-five thousand gold."

"It will be months before I can afford that," Gabriel said in dismay. "From what he and Cressida have told me, I'm not sure he'll still be alive by then."

"You misunderstand," Lord Stuart said. "They sold me his contract."

"What? Why?" Gabriel asked.

"Because as you surely realize, they wouldn't have sold his contract to you for any price," Lord Stuart explained. "In their minds, only aristocrats can buy a companion's contract, and you will never be mistaken for one, no matter how nicely we dress you up, and because, as you said, Lucio might not last until you had the money."

"So what happens now?" Gabriel asked, jealousy eating at him. "And where is he?"

"He is still at the breeding barn, unfortunately," Lord Stuart said. "One of the ways I negotiated down his price was by agreeing to let them keep him for a month for stud service. I insisted in turn that none of the handlers touch him while he's there. As for what happens now, I have a proposition for you. I have no interest in owning a companion, Lucio or any other, as I find my time and appetites much in demand elsewhere. I do, however, have an interest in your business and in the money it will make for both of us. So here is what I propose. In exchange for thirty thousand gold and a fifteen percent interest in your workshop, I will sign Lucio's contract over to you the moment he is free of the pleasure palace. I would do it sooner, but I don't want to give them any excuse to invalidate our agreement or to doubt that I will inflict significant damage on them if anyone has touched Lucio outside of the stud service."

"Will we be able to see him in that time to make sure they keep their promises?" Gabriel asked, his mind reeling from everything Lord Stuart had told him.

"I plan to insist on seeing him once a week," Lord Stuart replied. "I highly doubt they will let you go with me, but I promise to bring back news of his well-being. Does this mean we have an agreement?"

"Yes!" Gabriel said. "I'm sorry. I should have said that to begin with. What do you need me to do to make it legal?"

"I'll have my solicitor draw up all the documents along with a transfer of Lucio's contract," Lord Stuart said. "I suggest we wait to sign all the papers until he is free and clear and with us again. After all, if something goes wrong, you will want the money to invest in your business rather than having it tied up with me."

"As you wish," Gabriel agreed, his heart clenching at the thought of anything going wrong. He didn't even want to think about what could go wrong, not when they were finally so close to realizing his dream. "I suppose this means I should get back to work on the flying chair. You'll want to see a return on your investment."

"I will," Lord Stuart replied, "but I do understand that genius takes time. I don't expect you to have a new invention every week or every month. What I expect is for you to do your best work. You'll have a family to support before long."

"Not soon enough," Gabriel replied. "Although sooner than I could have hoped possible without your help," he added, realizing how ungrateful the first comment sounded.

"I'm glad I could be of assistance. I've always had a soft spot for Lucio," Lord Stuart admitted. "At one point, I thought of buying him for myself, but now I'm glad I didn't. Even as badly hurt as he was the last time I saw him, he was so clearly happy with you. He deserves that."

Gabriel wondered how much of Lord Stuart's words were due to Wakefield's influence and how much had been there before, but he didn't ask. It was enough that the aristocrat felt that way now. "Thank you," he said, rising and offering his hand. "For whatever it's worth, you'll always be welcome here."

"It's worth a great deal," Lord Stuart said, "and once Lucio is recovered from his ordeal, I shall expect to see both of you in my salon again. We'll never shake up the complacency of the aristocracy and bring about real change if my peers aren't forced to see the value of the other castes."

"I won't have Lucio demeaned," Gabriel warned.

"He won't be," Lord Stuart promised. "He'll be your companion, not merely for the evening but for always. I know he is much more than that to you, but even if my peers never understand that, they will realize he is unavailable and will not approach him. If they do, you will have every right to protest loudly and publicly, and I assure you society's opinion will side with you."

"If Lady Merydith dares to show her face—"

"She won't," Lord Stuart interrupted. "Not in my salon, certainly, because she will never be admitted there, but not in most of polite society either. No one would fault her for hiring a companion when so many of us have done the same, but there is a difference between enjoying a little rough sex and abusing someone so badly they could have died from the injuries. The majority of my peers realize this, even if the lady did not. Her word, her credit, and her custom are no longer welcome in large parts of the city."

"Thank you," Gabriel said. "I could wish worse fates on her, but I will be satisfied with the one you've arranged."

"I'll leave you to your work now," Lord Stuart said. "Unfortunately I already have a commitment for this afternoon, but I will insist on seeing Lucio tomorrow, both to check on his health and to assure him of his imminent change in fortunes. It's only a matter of patience now, my boy."

Gabriel might have taken umbrage at the epithet, but Lord Stuart was far closer to the age Gabriel's parents would have been had they still been alive than he was to Gabriel's own age, and the debt of gratitude he owed the aristocrat outweighed many such comments. He walked Lord Stuart out to his carriage, lifting a hand in farewell.

"What did he say?" Caleb asked as soon as Gabriel walked back inside.

"I don't even know where to start," Gabriel replied, sitting back down at the table and pouring another glass of tea. "It's like all my dreams just came true, all in one fell swoop. Lucio will be here in a month, Lord Stuart wants to invest in the workshop in repayment for helping Lucio, and that leaves me money left over from what I'd saved to buy Lucio's contract to expand, maybe even to hire another assistant or two. I'm afraid to believe it's happening."

"Don't look a gift horse in the mouth and all that," Andrew said. "Time to put a little spit and polish on the place if we're going to have aristocrats hanging out in our front room."

Gabriel laughed, shaking his head in wonder at his good fortune. "We'll have Cressida come in and tell us what we need to do. For now, though, we have a flying chair to perfect because that's going to make us the kind of money that will impress Lord Stuart and convince him he made the right decision in investing in us."

"GET dressed. You have a visitor."

Lucio looked at Smith in surprise. The man had visited him again Monday morning before dosing him with saffron and sending him from stall to stall to stand stud for the girls in each one. The drug had finally burned out of his system, leaving him limp and achy from the number of times he had come. The handlers had sent him back to his own stall, and Lucio had expected another visit from his protector, but he had spent the night in relative peace, only to be roused this morning, dosed again, and sent back to work.

The interruption came as a surprise, but he did not question it, hurrying back to his stall to pull on his clothes. He brushed ineffectively at the dust on the black linen, but nothing short of a thorough cleaning would restore them to their previous elegance. It was all he had, though, so it would have to do.

He stepped back into the aisle and waited for Smith or one of the other handlers to take him to see his visitor. Moments later, Smith reappeared. "You're still a mess, but His Lordship will have to pay a whole lot more than he did if he wants a better stable for you."

Lucio frowned, the handler's words making no sense whatsoever. He didn't ask, though. He would find out soon enough, he hoped. He followed Smith through the barn to the office. The handler shoved him inside and shut the door.

"Good afternoon, Lucio."

"Lord Ian?" Lucio asked. "What are you doing here?"

"Coming to check on you," Lord Stuart replied. "Your Mister Blackstone came to me in a panic yesterday because you had been forced back to work too soon and then sent here because your guest refused you. He seemed to fear you wouldn't survive if you had to stay here long."

Heart warmed by the show of Gabriel's concern, Lucio smiled. "He worries too much."

"And you love him for it," Lord Stuart said, returning Lucio's smile. "Have a seat, pretty boy. I have news for you."

Lucio took the seat across from Lord Stuart. "News, my Lord?"

"I'll get to that in a minute. First, tell me how they're treating you."

Lucio flushed. "I made a deal with one of the handlers the first night I was here. I would give him the benefit of all my talents and training if he would keep the others away from me. So far it has worked."

"When was the last time he took advantage of your offer?" Lord Stuart asked, his voice as dangerous as Lucio had ever heard it.

"Yesterday morning. Why?"

"Because none of the handlers are to touch you other than as part of the stud service," Lord Stuart explained. "You still have a month to serve here—there was nothing I could do about that—but your talents, as you called them, are no longer available to the highest bidder."

"How did Gabriel get the money that fast?" Lucio asked. "He bought my contract, right?"

"Not quite," Lord Stuart said. "The handlers wouldn't even talk to him about the price of your contract, much less about actually purchasing it. I bought it instead."

Lucio's face fell. "I shall do my best to be of service, my Lord."

"No," Lord Stuart said with a chuckle, "you won't, because the moment you are safely free of this place, I will sell your contract on to Blackstone. I cannot do it sooner because Blackstone's influence will not keep them from abusing you the way mine will, but our current arrangement is only a temporary one, I promise. I have gotten them to agree to a visit once a week. Blackstone can't come with me, but I can carry any messages back and forth, and I can make sure you're being treated well."

"Some clean clothes would not go amiss," Lucio said, looking down at himself. "Even if I only wear them during the night in my own stall, I hate being dirty."

"I will try to bring some next week," Lord Stuart said.

"May I ask you a question?" Lucio said, thinking of the saffron and his body's reaction to it the day before.

"Of course, pretty boy," Lord Stuart replied. "What is it?"

"They're dosing me with saffron," Lucio said. "I'd never taken it before, but I know you do sometimes. Is it safe for me to have it every day?"

"Probably," Lord Stuart said, "but I'll talk to them about limiting how much they give you. How much did they give you yesterday?"

"They dosed me four times," Lucio said. "With breakfast, about halfway through the morning, with lunch, and about halfway through the afternoon. I don't know how many girls are here in all, but they had me service eight yesterday. My whole body ached by the time I was done."

Lord Stuart frowned. "You're not bleeding again, are you?"

"No, I'm fine," Lucio assured him. "Just exhausted."

"I'm not surprised," Lord Stuart said. "I can't make any promises, but since you are technically my property on loan to them for the month, I should have some leverage to convince them to use you a little more reasonably. How many girls have you seen this morning?"

"Three," Lucio said. "I was on my way to the fourth when they sent me to dress so I could come see you."

"You've had a second dose of saffron?"

"Yes, before I visited the third girl."

"You'll need to come again to work that out of your system," Lord Stuart said, "so we'll allow one more visit for today. And then after today, only one dose of saffron and no more than three visits with the ladies. They'll get better results with their breeding that way, not to mention taking fewer risks with your health. The saffron might give you an erection and the sensation of a climax, but it doesn't force your body to produce seed any faster. You were shooting blanks the last several visits yesterday."

"Thank you," Lucio said. "I'm not sure I could keep that pace for a month."

"I'll speak with them," Lord Stuart promised. "And a day of rest on Sunday. Now, I can stay for a few more minutes, so you should take this and write a note to your lover. He is most worried about you."

"You won't tell him anything other than that I'm not being abused, will you?" Lucio pleaded. "He has a hard enough time with my life without knowing the sordid details."

"Then answer all his questions in your letter so I won't have to lie to him," Lord Stuart said. It wasn't exactly an answer, but Lucio suspected it was the best he was going to get. Taking the paper and the quill from Lord Stuart, he concentrated on pouring out his love and devotion while giving as little detail about his current situation as possible. He didn't want Gabriel to worry or to be unnecessarily jealous.

"Time to get back to work, stud," Smith said, sticking his head in the doorway. "We've got mares waiting for you."

"About that," Lord Stuart said, gesturing for Lucio to continue his letter. "I have a few concerns about how much you are using my companion. Let's go for a little walk while Lucio finishes his correspondence. There will be a few changes for the rest of the time he's with you."

Lucio breathed a sigh of relief as the door closed behind the two men. He could feel the saffron working in his blood, making it hard for him to concentrate around the need to come, but he had to finish his letter to Gabriel first. He pressed hard on his twitching cock, thoughts of Gabriel making it even more unruly than the saffron alone had done. He considered slipping his hand inside his trousers and finding relief that way, but he had no idea how the handlers would react to that, and he didn't want to be dosed again. He would simply have to control himself for now. Forcing his mind back to the letter, he channeled his need into the words, smiling as he imagined Gabriel reading it in the privacy of his—their, he corrected himself—bedroom. This could be fun.

33

ALONE in his empty bed, Gabriel took out the letter Lord Stuart had delivered to him that afternoon, along with the assurance that Lucio had looked better than the last time Lord Stuart had seen him and that he was not being molested by the handlers. The aristocrat had not lingered, but Gabriel had not truly expected him to. The letter was already an unexpected boon, but he had tucked it safely inside his pocket to read when he was alone and could savor every word.

My beloved Gabriel,

Gabriel smiled at seeing his own term for Lucio on the paper. He stroked his finger across it, wishing he could stroke Lucio's skin instead, but this would have to do for now.

I am sitting here putting pen to paper in shock and amazement. I cannot believe the news Lord Stuart brought me today. One month until we are reunited, and then nothing will ever separate us again. The days will drag, I know, but the hope of that moment will carry me through.

I miss you already, even more than during our other separations because having spent the past week in your life, in your bed, I know the joys that can be ours when we are finally together again.

I think of you at night, alone in my room. I remember all the things we have done together, in your workshop, but especially in your bedroom. I know, you are chiding me for saying your bedroom instead of our bedroom, and it will be mine soon, beloved. Not soon enough, but sooner than we could have dreamed. And when it is our bedroom, I will keep you there for days, until I have indulged every dream, every fantasy I have had in the time we must spend apart.

You will think me wicked for writing these things down, but I cannot seem to help myself. I want to feel your skin against mine, to kiss you and feel you kiss me. I dream about the delight of your tongue in my mouth as you claim me. I have never told you this because one does not speak of such things, even when one is a companion, but when you kiss me that way, your tongue tangling with mine, I cannot think. I can barely breathe. I would do anything for you in those moments. Your kisses alone have made me your slave. And when you have thoroughly stolen my wits, I dream of everything else I want you to do to me.

You are always so careful with me, making sure I am comfortable with what we do together, and I love you for it because I know it means you care for me as deeply as I care for you, but we are past that now, beloved. There is nothing you could do to me in love that I wouldn't want to feel.

Do you want to know what you do to me in my dreams? I can almost see you shaking your head, but you aren't here to stop me from putting the words on paper, so I will tell you. You put aside all your hesitations and make love to me with the same decisiveness and determination I see in you when you're working on an invention. I want that same focus turned on me. I want you to press me into the sheets and ravish me.

I know you, though, and I know you won't do anything I don't want. I'm telling you now, darling Gabriel, this is what I want. In my dreams, you straddle me, your weight on me so I sink into the mattress, held in place by your body. You kiss me until I can't breathe, and then you kiss me some more. When finally I am hard and begging, bucking up into your weight to find some friction for my poor, neglected cock, you slide down. Not as far as I want, but to my chest at least, your stomach pressing against my shaft now, the hair there tickling in a most erotic way. You start at my neck, licking and sucking until you've raised a bruise that everyone will see. They'll smile and whisper behind their fans that I'm a very lucky man to have someone who loves me that well.

When you're done there, you'll work your way lower until you find my nipples. I never knew I was sensitive there until you showed me. Now I'm insatiable. You lick and nip and pinch and twist until I'm writhing on the bed beneath you, sobbing in my need. I think I want you to move on, but you know better. You know what I need better than I do, keeping me right there, on the cusp of release until I explode from that and the pressure of your belly riding my cock.

Only then do you lick your way lower, finding the cream on my stomach and licking me clean. Your tongue rasps against my skin, arousing me again without needing anything else, and you don't stop there. You slide lower, once again ignoring my poor cock. You have other targets in mind, pressing my legs wide with your shoulders, my calves draped down your back. You lick your way over my sac, sucking it into your mouth, rolling the nodules inside with your tongue, driving me wild with need once more. I reach beneath myself, spreading myself even wider, offering my darkest secrets to you. For once, you don't make me wait, your thumb pressing against me as you continue to suck on my sac.

My heels must hurt you, the way they're driving into your back, but you don't move them or give any sign of anything other than complete concentration on your task as your thumb teases my muscle until it relaxes in invitation. The moment you feel my surrender, your mouth moves, your tongue plundering what your thumb has tantalized. I cry out, but you don't stop. You know it's a cry of need, not of protest. I am hungry for you, for your tongue, your fingers, your cock. I need something inside me and the teasing is almost too much now.

You know that as you know everything else about me, pushing up onto your knees, the movement folding me back in on myself so my body is lifted to you, open to you. When you slide inside me finally, I nearly faint from the pleasure. You fill me perfectly, rubbing against my sweet spot with every thrust until I am thrashing on the bed with the need to come. I reach for my cock, intending to see to myself, but you catch my hand, pinning it above my head, giving me a little swat for my daring. Not enough to hurt, just to remind me who is in charge. I moan, overcome by your dominance. Your cock keeps nudging that spot within me, prodding me toward release, each pass sending more of my seed onto my stomach, until I can take it no more and I release, untouched, exactly as you intended. Seconds later, I feel you flood me with the proof of your own need. We collapse onto the bed, still joined, your arms tight around me, and I know the people who will see the mark the next day and be jealous have every reason to be.

I am well loved.

I have to go now, beloved. I will write to you again if I can. If you write back, do not sign the letter. I will know it's from you even without your name.

Until we are together again, remember that I am yours.

Lucio

Gabriel set the letter on the bed beside him, wiping at the tears that coursed down his cheeks. His entire body ached with unfulfilled need, as he imagined Lucio had intended, but it was his heart that demanded his attention first. Lucio's faith and devotion humbled him. He had no idea how he had earned such love, but he swore to do his best to always be worthy of it.

Closing his eyes, he summoned the memory of Lucio's face aglow with rapture. With that image in mind, he slipped his hand beneath the quilt on the bed and worked his nightshirt up until he could encircle his erection. Lucio's words had done their job, and it took only a few tugs and the thought of his lover's beautiful body to push him over the edge. He wiped his hand on the covers, then lifted the letter to his lips, kissing it reverently before setting it on the table next to his bed, where he could read it again in the morning or tomorrow evening and begin to think of a reply.

FINISHING his lunch, Lucio accepted his daily dose of saffron. Lord Stuart had been as good as his word, bargaining or threatening, he didn't know which, until the handlers had eased up on the number of times they forced Lucio to stand stud in a day. He saw one girl in the morning, followed by lunch, a dose of saffron, and two more in the afternoon. Even that, day after day, left him exhausted, but not as much as he'd been at the end of the first day. Although he had seen multiple guests per day while he was working, he had never been expected to find release as part of that service, much less multiple times, nor had he been recovering from torture on a barely adequate diet in a room where he could find little rest. He was looking forward to tomorrow and a chance to rest. Lord Stuart had promised to return on Sunday, Lucio's day off, for another visit, and Lucio hoped for a letter from Gabriel as well. He had started composing another letter to his lover in his head, but he wanted to read Gabriel's reply first if at all possible.

The handler in charge, not Smith today, but another one Lucio didn't recognize, led him back out of his room and through the barn to the last stall. He opened the door and shoved Lucio unceremoniously inside. Lucio rolled his eyes at the treatment. He wasn't going to fight them, not when he knew it was only a question of biding his time before he could leave permanently.

A horrified cry escaped when he turned to greet the girl in the stall. "No," he whispered, taking a step toward Cressida. "What are you doing here?"

Cressida looked up at him with tearful eyes. "They said you were leaving soon and that this was their only chance to breed their two best companions. Why are you leaving?"

Lucio pulled Cressida into his arms, holding her close as he pressed a tender kiss to her temple. "Gabriel bought my contract," he whispered, not wanting the handlers to hear if any were outside the stall. "On the condition that I spend a month in the breeding barns first. In three weeks, all my dreams will come true."

"And all mine will die," Cressida said. "They'll throw us together every day until they know I'm pregnant. The time is right for it. Not only will I lose my best friend, but I'll be confined here for nine months, and by then all my guests will have forgotten about me. Even if I go back to the pleasure palace after it's over, I'll have to start all over without the allure of a nubile teenager to attract new guests. I'll be back here in a matter of weeks, a broodmare for the rest of my life."

"I'm sorry, Cressida," Lucio apologized, stroking her hair. "I wish there was something I could do."

"There isn't," Cressida said with a muffled sigh, "so get it over with already. The sooner you poke me, the sooner I can try to sleep and pretend this isn't happening."

Lucio shook his head. "I can't change the outcome," he said slowly, tipping her head so her eyes met his, "but you're my best friend. I care too much about you to simply use you that way. Let me make it good for you. Gabriel showed me how."

"Gabriel showed you how to make love to a woman?" Cressida teased. "I didn't think that was his style."

"Gabriel showed me how to take care of a lover," Lucio corrected, thinking of the afternoon they had spent together at the inn in Nicholasville. "I may not be in love with you the way I am with him, but I do love you. If we have to do this, we'll do it right." He brushed her hair from her forehead tenderly. "I can't kiss you because I promised Gabriel I would never kiss anyone but him, but I promise I will make this as pleasurable for you as possible."

Cressida leaned her forehead against his. "You will be the only one who ever has."

The saffron burning in Lucio's blood made it easier than it should have been to adjust to the delicate shape of Cressida's body in his arms, to the light floral scent she preferred, to her skin, as smooth and silky as his own. She melted beneath his tender caresses the same way he had melted into Gabriel's hands on his own skin, proof of how starved she was for affection. He wished he could give her more than simple affection—she deserved to be loved for the wonderful woman she was—but his heart belonged to Gabriel. He would have to settle for genuine caring and what pleasure his hands and lips could bring.

He'd had enough female guests to know how to caress a woman's breasts, but with Cressida, he lingered out of a desire to bring her pleasure rather than the need to make a guest climax so he could go home. She shifted on his lap, her pale thighs rubbing against his engorged cock, adding to the arousal raging inside him from the drug.

Carefully he laid her back on the pallet, staying close and touching her constantly, little caresses intended to calm and soothe her. Her eyes opened, dark against her fair skin, and he could see arousal in them. Smiling softly, he tweaked one of her nipples before slipping his hand between her thighs to test the wetness there. He sought and found the little nubbin that would see to her pleasure, rubbing his thumb over it with the same patient determination Gabriel had shown when he fingered Lucio's gland. Cressida's mouth formed a perfect little O of surprise as he pleasured her with all the expertise he had learned as a companion and all the tenderness he had learned at Gabriel's hands.

She cried out, her eyes closing as he worked a finger inside her, pleasuring her inside and out. He caught himself leaning forward to kiss her, but he had promised Gabriel, and even under the circumstances, he would not ask his lover to accept that infidelity. Bad enough that he was truly making love to Cressida instead of simply bedding her like he'd done all the others. He wouldn't make matters worse by kissing her.

Pulse pounding from the saffron and the wanton cries, he moved onto his knees between her legs. "Look at me now, Cressi," he said softly.

Her eyes opened, soft and unfocused, a look for a lover. It tore at Lucio that she would only know this with him instead of with someone who could truly love her as she deserved, but he would give her this at least in case her fears were realized. When he pushed inside her, he bent and gathered her to his chest, holding her tightly as he thrust, his actions nearly out of his control. He fought the impending climax until he felt her tremble beneath him, only then giving in to his need. When the shuddering pulses faded, he withdrew carefully, stroking her cheek. Her eyes opened again, tears wetting the lashes.

"Don't cry, Cressi," he begged, pulling her tightly against him. "We'll find a way through this, I promise."

"Don't make promises you can't keep," she said, dashing angrily at her tears. "You got your happy ending, and I'm glad for you. Truly I am, but I'll never have that chance, and now I won't have you to keep me company either. Forgive me if I feel like crying a little."

Lucio rocked her against him until the handler pounded on the door, demanding he finish up because he had another mare to service.

"See?" Cressida said as Lucio rose to do his duty. "That's all I am to them now. It's all I'll ever be again."

Lucio didn't speak aloud the promise that sprang to his lips for fear of not being able to keep it, but he would find a way to get her out if it was the last thing he did.

34

"ONE more week," Lord Stuart said, pocketing the letter Lucio gave him. "The next time I come to visit, it will be to take you home."

"It cannot come soon enough," Lucio said, fingering the letter Lord Stuart had brought to him that he would read in the privacy of his room as soon as he was alone again. He rose, embracing the aristocrat impulsively. "Thank you again. For everything."

"You're more than welcome, pretty boy," Lord Stuart said, patting Lucio's shoulder. "I'm glad I could be of service to both you and Blackstone. Read his letter. It's full of news this week."

"As soon as I'm back in my room."

"What are you waiting for, then?" Lord Stuart teased. "Go on. I know the way out."

Smiling, Lucio hurried back to his room, pulling out the precious link to Gabriel the moment the door closed behind him.

My beloved Lucio,

The letters always started the same way.

I hope my letter finds you well and in good spirits. I am counting the days until you are done with your service and can come home to me for good. I received your last letter and read it with great delight. I don't have your way with words, though, so you will have to wait for our reunion for me to return the sentiments you expressed.

Lucio chuckled. Gabriel's letters had all been so circumspect. Part of that, he was sure, was the fear of them being found and used against Lucio. Part of it as well was Gabriel's innate reserve, especially where matters of the heart, or in this case of the body, were concerned. Lucio found the timidity, so in contrast with Gabriel's decisiveness in his workshop, alluring. He would have to cure his lover of that, though. Reserve was fine in public. In private, Lucio wanted none of it.

We have finally perfected the flying chair to the point that I piloted it out of the garden and over the house to land in the street, to the

*amazement of all who saw it. It still needs work to go from a novelty item
to something truly useful, but Lord Stuart says the time has come to
introduce the Blackstone chair to society. He has planned a garden party
for the week after you have joined us so you can be there for the spectacle
as well. I'm sorry you missed the first test flight, but I refused to have you
miss the first public demonstration. Fortunately Lord Stuart seems willing
to indulge me where you are concerned. I suspect I have Mister Wakefield
to thank for that, but I don't think it polite to ask, and they have not said.
Perhaps at the garden party you can observe them and tell me what you
think.*

    *Caleb and Andrew are bereft, for with your absence from the
workshop, Cressida's visits have tapered off and ended completely as well.
They have mentioned several times that they hope she will visit more
regularly once you are living here. You haven't mentioned her in your
letters, but then you have mentioned very little that would be fit for polite
company. Do you have any news of her? Caleb and Andrew will be eager
to hear it if you do.*

Lucio closed his eyes, all his delight in Gabriel's success turning to
dread at the mention of Cressida. He did indeed have news of her, but not
any that would meet with approval from the denizens of Gabriel's
workshop. He had gone to visit her the previous morning, dosed with
saffron, as he had every day since he had first encountered her in the
breeding barn. After they had fulfilled their duty, Cressida had tearfully
admitted that her menses should have started two days before and was still
notably absent. Lucio knew little enough about such things, but Cressida
insisted her body had always been frightfully regular and that its tardiness
now was a sure sign that the breeding had been successful. Lucio had cried
with her, for the child who would be born into the same caste as its parents
and for the struggle Cressida's life would become because of her
pregnancy. Forcing his thoughts away from what he could not change,
Lucio returned to the letter in his hand.

    *The Caste Equality movement continues to gain ground in public
opinion, but we will not know until after the elections whether that will be
enough to allow any real change. Mister Ashbrook, our candidate, is
optimistic, but I wonder if he is not overly so. This is his first time on the
ballot. Even conservative candidates rarely win their first election. Still,
there is no harm in hoping, I suppose. Even if he loses, the message is
getting out, and we will have two years to continue our work before the*

*next election. When I think of all we've accomplished in six months, I have
to believe we will accomplish even more with more time.*

*You must think my letters incredibly prosaic next to yours. I wish I
could say what I know you want to hear, but other than telling you that I
miss you and think of you often, I haven't the words. I hold your letters
close to my heart, though, rereading them every night before I go to bed.*

Lucio chuckled. He had no problem conjuring up the image of Gabriel
lying in his bed, his cock in one hand, Lucio's letters in the other. Lucio
smiled at the thought, wondering if he could convince Gabriel to let him
read the letters aloud. Not right away. Lucio wouldn't be able to resist
touching long enough to watch Gabriel pleasure himself at first, but once
they'd been reunited for a few weeks… or months…. He licked his lips in
anticipation and glanced back at the letter. All that remained was the
closing remarks, Gabriel's avowal of love and the promise to be waiting as
soon as Lord Stuart brought him home next week.

Lucio tucked the letter in with the others, closing his eyes and letting
his thoughts drift. Always before, he had kept his mental ramblings to the
past, to actual encounters, not wanting to raise his hopes prematurely, but
now, with freedom only a week away, he let his thoughts turn finally to the
future and the life they would have together.

He had seen Gabriel during his one society appearance. The mention
of another one brought a smile to Lucio's face. He would be the one at
Gabriel's side this time, not Cressida, and he would make sure his lover
impressed all the shallow aristocrats with their emphasis on good breeding
and proper manners. Gabriel might not have an aristocratic pedigree, but
Lucio would coach him through the afternoon. The flying chair would do
the rest. Lucio could see it already, the surprise and then delight on the
aristocrats' faces as Gabriel flew his machine over their heads. They
would all want to try it, but Gabriel wouldn't let them. He would say they
needed to learn how to fly it first and that would require time and patience.
They would question whether this was some magic trick of Gabriel's,
some sleight of hand to trick them into parting with their money. Gabriel
would assure them it was not and offer to let Lord Stuart fly the chair to
show that it was possible to learn.

That assumed Gabriel would show Lord Stuart how to fly it between
now and then. If he had not planned to, Lucio would suggest it. He wanted
to learn as well, although he didn't know if there would be time to teach
both him and Lord Stuart before the garden party. If there was not, Lucio

would insist that Lord Stuart learn first. The aristocrats would be far more impressed by that.

Thinking of the party made Lucio wonder what other roles he would play in Gabriel's life. He hadn't the slightest idea how to cook, although Gabriel's cooking had been filling if simple fare, so that role would probably not fall to him. He supposed he could pick up after them, but he had never done more in terms of housework than that. All in all, though, he wouldn't make Gabriel a very good wife. He chuckled a little at the thought of himself in an apron and petticoats, trying to make a home for his husband to return to. Gabriel wouldn't expect that. He knew Lucio had none of those skills. He hadn't said it, but it had been understood in their conversation about the differences in their lives when Gabriel had insisted Lucio look around his house and see the simplicity. Wood instead of marble, a fireplace and bucket instead of heated water; none of those things mattered to Lucio. He only wanted to be a part of Gabriel's life. He hoped perhaps Gabriel could use him in the workshop as he had done during Lucio's convalescence. Fortunately the intervening weeks seemed to have allowed him to heal fully. He no longer hurt at odd moments and all the marks had faded from what he could see of his body. He could not tell if any remained on his back, but if they did, they were light indeed because he could feel no change in texture beneath his fingers and no pain when he moved or when he washed. Having regained his health, he would be able to do even more than he had done during the week he had stayed with Gabriel, as long as Gabriel was willing to teach him what needed to be done.

And if Gabriel wanted him only as someone to warm his bed, Lucio would learn to live with that. It would still be an improvement over the life he had now.

"HOW was he this week?" Gabriel asked the moment Lord Stuart appeared. "Is he well again?"

"He seemed that way to me," Lord Stuart replied, handing Gabriel Lucio's letter. "I gave him your letter and talked with him for a bit. He seemed in good spirits, very eager for next weekend."

"As am I," Gabriel said. "He wasn't walking stiffly?"

"If he is still hurting, he hides it very well," Lord Stuart said. "His gait appeared normal to me, although I could not see what marks might still lurk beneath his clothes. I doubted either of you cared to have me check on him to that degree."

"No, I can wait until he comes home," Gabriel agreed. Even knowing Lord Stuart was teasing him, Gabriel could not stop his reaction at the thought of the aristocrat—or anyone else—seeing Lucio unclothed, though he knew Lord Stuart was familiar with the sight. He pushed aside all thought of the women Lucio was being forced to bed in the hope of breeding the next generation of companions. The thought sickened him, for Lucio, for the women, and for the poor children who would come of it with no hope of a different future, but he would not hold it against Lucio when it had been no more his lover's doing than anything else in Lucio's life to date.

He could do nothing but keep working to change the system and hope that their labors bore fruit before those children were forced into an aristocrat's bed at far too early an age.

"Did he say anything else?" Gabriel asked.

"We speak only of inconsequential things so that anyone who overhears us cannot use what they hear against Lucio," Lord Stuart reminded him. "Anything of interest will be in your letter, not in what he said to me."

"I will read it before bed tonight," Gabriel said. "It helps me to sleep, feeling close to him that way."

"A few more days and you will be close to him," Lord Stuart said with a smile. "Now, we should discuss the debut of your flying chair. Lucio will have joined you by that time, but I doubt he will have much in the way of a wardrobe. I don't see the handlers sending on his current trousseau. I will alert Banks to expect you both on Monday afternoon."

"I had thought to purchase any new clothes we needed from a friend down the street," Gabriel said, thinking of David Reading. "Lucio is surely aware enough of the latest fashion to make sure we are appropriately attired."

"If you wish," Lord Stuart allowed, "but if you do not pass muster this time, it will be back to Banks for both of you."

"Fair enough," Gabriel agreed. "Is there anything else I need to do?"

"You need to keep the chair as much a secret as possible until then," Lord Stuart said. "I don't think any of your rivals could manage to produce a competitor between now and then, but we don't want to spoil the surprise for the guests. We want the moment of unveiling to be a true revelation. Some of your neighbors know what you've been up to since you managed to fly your chair into the street, but word of it has not yet reached my peers."

"I hardly have the kind of contacts who would go running to an aristocrat to reveal what I've made," Gabriel said with a laugh.

"You say that, but how many of my peers have purchased fans from you since you came to my niece's ball?" Lord Stuart asked. "And I heard Endicott saying just last week that you designed a portable heater for him. You are all the rage at the moment. They may not come actively looking for your flying chair, but they will jump on any rumor of a new invention."

"Would it really be that terrible if someone found out about it before the garden party?" Gabriel asked seriously. "I understand wanting the spectacle of the moment of unveiling, but realistically, if someone walked in while I was testing it, would it really be that awful for our prospects?"

"No, probably not," Lord Stuart admitted, "but I want you to have that moment of triumph and I thought you'd like to share it with Lucio."

"Of course I would!"

"It will be sweeter if it truly is a surprise for society," Lord Stuart explained. "If the secret is out, the excitement leading up to the moment you unveil the chair and fly it around the garden will be diminished or even absent, and it will be nothing more than another party, albeit with Lucio at your side."

35

"GET your things together. You're leaving," Smith said, barging into Lucio's quarters with a glare that nearly made Lucio cringe. He reminded himself Lord Stuart owned his contract now, not the handlers, and that Smith would face consequences if he damaged Lucio in any way. He rose from the pallet, Gabriel's letters already tucked securely in the pocket of his jacket.

"I'm ready."

Smith led him to the same office where Lucio had met with Lord Stuart each Sunday. Lucio had hoped Gabriel would be there as well, but only the aristocrat occupied the room. "Are you well?" Lord Stuart asked as soon as Lucio walked in.

"Quite well, my Lord," Lucio replied, "now that you are here."

"Then since everything is in order, I will have his contract now," Lord Stuart said.

Smith grumbled but produced the document. Lord Stuart read over it carefully, leaving Lucio squirming at being sold like a piece of meat. He could bear it because when this was over, he would be at Gabriel's side, but even so, the transaction bothered him.

"All seems to be in order," Lord Stuart said finally. "I look forward to many enjoyable hours."

"If he's any trouble, you can always send him back," Smith said. "We have our ways for dealing with troublesome ones."

"I'm sure he will be as delightful as he has ever been," Lord Stuart said with a wink for Lucio. "Now, if you will excuse us, I'm eager to get him home."

Smith glared at Lucio one more time, but Lucio ignored him, taking Lord Stuart's offered arm and leaving the breeding barn without a backward glance.

"Only a few more minutes," Lord Stuart said softly as they walked toward his carriage.

Lucio looked up at the aristocrat sharply, but before he could ask, they had reached the carriage. Lord Stuart opened the door and gestured for Lucio to climb in. He had barely put his foot on the last step when hands reached out from inside and pulled him into a tight embrace. All the tears Lucio had been holding back rushed to his eyes and down his cheeks as he wrapped his arms around Gabriel. He was vaguely aware of Lord Stuart climbing into the coach behind him and ordering the driver to head back to town, but his real focus remained on Gabriel, on the feel of his beloved in his arms once more, the smell of leather and sweat, the tender caress over his hair and down his back.

He wanted to lean up and kiss Gabriel, but he was not sure how his lover would feel about that with Lord Stuart right next to him. He got his answer when a hard hand lifted his chin and hot lips closed over his own. Lucio moaned into the kiss, trying to press even closer.

"Gently there," Lord Stuart chided from the other side of the carriage. "I know you have missed each other, but we have business still before I can return you to your home and you can be reunited properly."

"Can it not wait until tomorrow?" Gabriel asked.

"Do you really want to leave his contract in my hands even that long?" Lord Stuart asked. "Wouldn't it be better to have everything taken care of now and nothing but your life together before you?"

"Please, Gabriel," Lucio said, pulling back to look up into Gabriel's eyes. "I want to be yours in every way."

"All right," Gabriel conceded. "But the solicitor had better hurry. It's been too long since I last saw Lucio."

Lord Stuart chuckled. "Ah, the first flush of young love. It has been some years since I've felt that way about anyone, but not so long that I've forgotten completely. We will attend to our business and then I shall leave you at your home where you can have all the privacy two young lovers could desire."

Lucio didn't ask about Caleb and Andrew, but Gabriel didn't contradict Lord Stuart, making him hope that Caleb and Andrew would be elsewhere today. It was a Sunday, so hopefully they would be enjoying their day of rest at their own home. "Will your solicitor see us today?"

"I have made special arrangements," Lord Stuart assured them. "He is waiting for us now."

Lucio accepted the pronouncement and the reach of Lord Stuart's influence with a nod, turning his attention back to Gabriel. "Kiss me again."

Gabriel granted his wish immediately, his tongue surging between Lucio's lips in perfect imitation of the descriptions in Lucio's letters. Lucio stifled a moan, the kiss nowhere near enough to satisfy him after a month's separation. The rest would have to wait until their business could be concluded and they were alone in their room, though. He didn't doubt Lord Stuart would enjoy the show, but Lucio was no longer a paid companion. He didn't have to think about anyone's desires but Gabriel's ever again.

Soon enough, they arrived at the home of Lord Stuart's solicitor. The butler showed them in, and the solicitor rose to shake everyone's hands. "I have everything drawn up," the solicitor explained. "It only requires a few signatures and we'll be done."

"Make sure to explain to Mister Blackstone exactly what he's signing," Lord Stuart requested. "I know it's what we agreed upon, but I don't know how familiar he is with the legal jargon, and I don't want him to have questions later."

The solicitor held out the first document. "This is a transfer of contract for the companion named Lucio from Lord Ian Stuart to Mister Gabriel Blackstone," the lawyer explained. "It does not specify the monetary terms of that transfer because we address that in the investment contract. All I need is your signature as Lord Stuart has already signed it."

Lucio watched with bated breath as Gabriel signed on the indicated line. When he lifted the pen, Lucio sighed in relief. It was done. His life as a companion had ended, and his life as Gabriel's lover had finally begun.

"This other document is the investment contract," the solicitor went on. "In exchange for the contract of the companion Lucio, you, Mister Gabriel Blackstone, agree to transfer thirty thousand gold and fifteen percent of the profits from your workshop to Lord Ian Stuart. That percentage of any profit you earn will return to him at the end of each quarter, unless the two parties agree to leave that money in the workshop as an investment against future earnings."

"Wait, what does that last part mean?" Gabriel asked.

"It means I can decide at any time to have you take my percentage of the profits and reinvest it in new supplies, new tools, or anything else I deem the workshop needs to make it more profitable in the future," Lord

Stuart explained. "You do the same thing when you decide to buy new equipment rather than put money in the bank. I would have to approve the use of my portion of the income in that way, but if you can convince me something is necessary, I can return that money to you."

"Is that standard practice for an investor?" Gabriel asked the solicitor.

"It depends on the investor," the solicitor replied, "but it is standard practice for Lord Stuart's investments."

"You needn't worry you're taking advantage of me," Lord Stuart promised. "I am far more astute than most would give me credit for."

"I never doubted it," Gabriel said, making Lucio smile. Gabriel signed the contract and waited for Lord Stuart to do the same.

"I will have copies of the investment contract drawn up and delivered to you," the solicitor told Gabriel. "The companion contract is yours to take now since it is a one-time transaction."

"If everything is in order, then," Lord Stuart said, "we will leave you to your day off."

"Everything is in order," the solicitor said, shaking hands around the room again. "Good day, gentlemen."

They walked back toward Lord Stuart's carriage, Gabriel twining his fingers through Lucio's, a far more intimate gesture than what Lucio was used to in society. "Thank you again, Lord Stuart," Gabriel said when they reached the curb and the carriage. "Lucio and I will take a hansom from here."

"Are you sure I can't take you home?"

Gabriel shook his head. "You've been beyond generous with us already. We will call in a few days to discuss the final plans for the garden party, but we need some time to get used to being together. Think of it as our honeymoon, even if the difference in our castes precludes any legal union other than the one in my hand."

"Enjoy your honeymoon," Lord Stuart said, shaking their hands. "I'll expect you to call on me by Wednesday. We do have to finalize our plans."

Gabriel agreed and ushered Lucio down the street until they found a cab to take them home.

"I can't believe it's really happening," Lucio said, curling up against Gabriel's side once they were en route. "I'm really free."

"You are," Gabriel agreed. "You know... you do know that you aren't under any obligation to, well, to...."

"You just told Lord Stuart we were starting our honeymoon and now you tell me you aren't going to make love to me?" Lucio teased. "Did I miss something?"

Gabriel caught Lucio's hands. "Don't make jokes. I love you, and I want nothing more than to take you to bed and keep you there for a week, but I need you to understand how I interpret the contract in my pocket."

Lucio squeezed Gabriel's hands. "Oh, my love, I know it's nothing more than a piece of paper, a hoop we had to jump through in order to be together. I'm sure we will have plenty of discussions and probably disagreements as we start our life together, but I promised you there would never be anything but truth between us. If I don't want something you're doing to me, I will tell you, but you read my letters. Can you think of something you would want to do to me that I didn't already describe you doing in vivid detail?"

Gabriel shook his head.

"Then stop being noble and fuck me already."

"We aren't home yet," Gabriel protested.

"Some people have no imagination," Lucio joked. "It would be a simple matter to take down my trousers, open yours, and straddle you the rest of the way home. Think about it, beloved. Every bump of the road jolting you deeper inside me."

Gabriel swallowed hard, his Adam's apple bobbing in Lucio's face. Leaning forward, Lucio kissed the bump softly, caught in the web of desire of his own making. "Can you picture it?" he asked, his hand sliding down to Gabriel's trousers. "I can. I can feel you moving inside me already, claiming me for the first of many times."

"I don't have any oil with me," Gabriel protested.

Lucio looked up and smiled. "Then you'll have to take your time, won't you?"

Gabriel groaned as Lucio opened his trousers, drawing his cock out between the plackets. The sound sent shivers of delight through Lucio and made his entire body clench in anticipation. Using one hand to spread the fluid already leaking from the tip down the hard shaft, Lucio pulled his own trousers loose with the other, pushing them down to his ankles.

"Help me here," he directed, not wanting to lose his balance as he shuffled around until he could straddle Gabriel's thighs. His tongue traced Gabriel's lips. "So are you going to stretch me or do you want a show?" he purred.

Gabriel's lips crashed against Lucio's, silencing his provocative monologue, but Lucio didn't complain, not when Gabriel stroked him a couple of times, coating his fingers before reaching between his legs and probing the tight entrance. He relaxed into the touch, welcoming the long digits inside, relieved to feel only a slight burn as they penetrated rather than the searing pain he had known at Lady Merydith's hands. Whatever damage she had done seemed well healed.

Lucio rocked back against Gabriel's hand until the fingers were fully seated inside him. He lifted up, pulling away. "Now your cock."

"But I need—"

"You need to stop protesting and trust that I know what I'm doing," Lucio interrupted, positioning the tip of Gabriel's cock at his entrance and sinking down on it slowly. It stung, but the constantly seeping tip provided enough lubrication that he could work his way fully onto Gabriel's shaft. "Feels so good," he groaned. "I dreamed…."

"So did I," Gabriel whispered, pulling Lucio's head down for a kiss. As Lucio had predicted, the movement of the cab over the rough roads provided all the stimulation they needed, and far too quickly for Lucio's taste, he climaxed, followed almost immediately by the flood of Gabriel's release.

"That will take the edge off," Lucio said smugly, "so we can last longer for the next round."

"You're going to be the death of me, aren't you?" Gabriel asked, his gaze soft and vacant.

"But what a way to go," Lucio retorted. "We're nearly at your street. We should make ourselves presentable again."

"And whose fault is it that we aren't presentable?" Gabriel teased as Lucio lifted off him.

"Yours," Lucio said. "Most definitely yours."

"How is it my fault?" Gabriel asked. "You're the one who started undressing me."

"You're the one who is irresistible," Lucio explained, refastening his trousers. He couldn't stop the satisfied grin at the feeling of Gabriel's seed coating his bottom and upper thighs.

Gabriel shook his head as the cab rolled to a stop. "I can tell my life will never be boring with you around."

Lucio simply smiled and waited for Gabriel to pay the driver so they could go inside.

They walked around to the back door, stopping for a moment in the garden. "I can't believe it's working," Lucio said, running a hand over the cockpit of the flying chair. "Is there anything left to do on it?"

"It depends on what potential buyers want it to do," Gabriel said. "At the moment, it's a novelty. For someone to actually use it for transportation, I'll have to increase the range, but that can happen with time. Lord Stuart suggested I might want to look at the appearance of it as well. You made one suggestion already with the cockpit. Maybe you can help with other ideas."

"I'm sure I can," Lucio said, walking around the chair and looking at it critically. "I've been told I have an eye for aesthetics. I'd like to learn how to fly it at some point too."

"You don't want to do that now?" Gabriel teased.

Lucio shook his head. "Right now I want to go inside, climb the stairs to our bedroom, and make love with you in our bed. Unless you have a better idea?"

"No," Gabriel said hoarsely. "No other ideas."

Grinning, Lucio led Gabriel inside, stopping short when he saw Caleb and Andrew sitting at the kitchen table.

"Welcome home!" they said, clapping Gabriel on the shoulder and shaking Lucio's hand.

"We've missed you around here," Caleb said with a smile for Lucio. "Gabriel alternated between a long face and all but floating with joy. It'll be good to get rid of the long face permanently."

"I'll be happy to do my part," Lucio promised, wondering how quickly they could send Caleb and Andrew on their way without being inexcusably rude. "I wish I could have been here. It's been an eventful month for you all from what Gabriel said in his letters."

"It has," Andrew agreed. "Speaking of letters, we hoped you could tell us how to get a letter to Cressida. We haven't seen her since she came to tell us what had happened with you, and we didn't want to buy her time. We don't want her to think of us that way. Maybe now that you're here, she'll visit again sometimes?"

Lucio flinched at the memory of all that had happened with Cressida and his own role in it. "I don't know if we can get a letter to her or not," he said slowly. "She...." His voice broke at the thought of what her life had become and Gabriel's likely reaction to it.

"Is she hurt?" Caleb asked. "Surely she knows that she can come to us if she is."

"I'm sure she knows that," Lucio assured him. "She isn't hurt. She's... pregnant."

THE silence in the room after Lucio's pronouncement was deafening. Gabriel hurt for his lover, watching the way he seemed to fold in on himself. Gabriel waited for the rest of the story, an explanation, anything, but nothing came. After a few moments, Lucio murmured an excuse and went upstairs, his entire posture proclaiming his distress.

"What does that mean?" Caleb asked when Lucio was out of sight.

Gabriel did not make the joke that sprang immediately to mind. To judge by Lucio's reaction, the situation was far too serious for that. "I don't know," Gabriel said. "Why don't you two go home? We've all had a shock and it won't help any of us if Lucio feels crowded or hounded. I'll try to talk to him and see what I can learn. We can talk about it tomorrow."

"Could we talk to Lord Stuart again?" Andrew asked timidly. "He helped you save Lucio."

"I don't know," Gabriel repeated. "Let me see what Lucio has to say. We'll be better able to make decisions once we know more. Are you sure she's what you want? You've always seemed so happy together."

"It's not something we realized we were looking for," Caleb replied slowly, "but we both agree. We want her, even if it's only to admire her from afar."

Gabriel sighed. "I don't know what Lucio can tell me or what options there are, but you both helped me. I'll do my best to help you in return."

With a few more reassurances from Gabriel, Caleb and Andrew finally left. Locking the door behind them, Gabriel stared at the steps to his bedroom. He had no idea what he would find up there when he joined Lucio, but his dreams for an afternoon spent making love had already gone out the window. He just hoped Lucio's revelation had only spoiled their afternoon. Taking a deep breath, he climbed the stairs, finding Lucio standing at the window, his back to Gabriel, his shoulders slumped with far more despair than Gabriel had ever seen before. Crossing the room, he encircled Lucio's waist. "You want to tell me what's wrong?"

Lucio shook his head.

"I can't help if I don't know what's going on," Gabriel reminded him. "Women get pregnant all the time. Explain to me why it's such a problem for Cressida."

"Because she's a companion," Lucio said bitterly. "She won't be allowed to work for the next nine months so that nothing endangers the baby, which is nine months during which her regular guests will find new favorites. When she recovers from childbirth, she'll still have the marks of pregnancy on her body as she tries to return to work and hopefully rebuild a client base to support her. If she can, that will last for awhile. If she can't, which is far more likely, she'll be sent back to the breeding barns to act as a broodmare for as long as she can conceive. She's lost what little shred of humanity the handlers allow us, and now she'll have to watch the babies she carries for nine months be passed off to wet nurses and then trained as companions."

"That is unfortunate indeed," Gabriel agreed. "Caleb and Andrew would take her away from all that if we can find the money somehow."

"Why are you not angry at me?" Lucio said, turning to face Gabriel.

"Why would I be angry with you?" Gabriel asked, not following the turn of the conversation. "Cressida's predicament is hardly your fault."

"Hardly," Lucio said with a bark of biting laughter. "She wouldn't be pregnant if it weren't for me."

Gabriel took a deep breath, reminding himself that he'd known what Lucio had been forced to do in the breeding barn for the last month. He hadn't let himself dwell on it, but he had known. "Did you ask them to bring her there?"

"Of course not!" Lucio shouted. "How could you think that?"

"I don't," Gabriel said, struggling to keep his calm as the image of Cressida and Lucio together ate at him. "But you're acting like you think it."

"I didn't ask them to do it," Lucio said, "but it's still my fault. When Lord Stuart bought my contract, they saw the month they still had me as their last chance to breed their two top companions. If I'd been able to work when I came back to the pleasure palace, I wouldn't have been sent to the breeding barns, and Cressida wouldn't have either."

"It's not your fault," Gabriel insisted. "You didn't ask Lady Merydith to torture you the way she did. You didn't ask the handlers to give you too short a time to recover. You didn't ask them to send you the breeding barn.

And you didn't ask them to bring Cressida there as well. You are as much a victim in this as she is."

Lucio pulled away again, pacing the room in agitation. Gabriel let him go. Maybe if he worked off some of his emotions this way, he would be more rational when they continued the discussion. When Lucio's pacing finally stopped with him directly in front of Gabriel, his face radiated defiance. "I made love to her. I didn't kiss her—I promised I wouldn't kiss anyone but you—but I couldn't treat her as just another body. I couldn't do it."

Gabriel's eyes closed as the images he had been pushing down surged to the fore, the two beautiful bodies entwined, dark hair mingling as they leaned close. Bile rose in his throat, but he pushed it down. Lucio hadn't had a choice in the outcome, only in the execution, and of course his innate kindness would not let him treat Cressida poorly. His mind accepted it rationally, but his heart protested the thought of Lucio touching anyone else the way he touched Gabriel. "Once?"

"I wish it had only been once," Lucio said. "If it had, if they'd sent others to her as well, I could console myself with the thought that I probably wasn't responsible. Once a day. For over three weeks. She said I was the only person she saw the entire time besides the handler who brought her food and water. She's pregnant, and it's my fault."

Gabriel nodded, not knowing what else to say. After a moment, Lucio turned away again, returning to the window. Gabriel stared at his slumped back helplessly, but his own heart was in too much turmoil to console Lucio. Swallowing hard, he did what he always did when he didn't know what else to do: he headed to the basement to work.

HEARING Gabriel's footsteps on the stairs broke what little control Lucio had left. He sank to the floor, tears streaming down his face as the enormity of what he had done struck him again. In less than an hour, he had destroyed the tentative beginnings of his relationship with Gabriel because he hadn't had the heart to treat Cressida as he had treated all the other girls in the breeding barns. With them, it had been easy to be matter-of-fact, doing what needed to be done with skill so he didn't hurt them, but without affection or tenderness. He couldn't do that to Cressida. He loved her too much to do that to her. And in being true to his heart in her respect, he had forfeited Gabriel's regard.

He could hear Cressida now, scolding him for telling Gabriel more than the facts of the matter, but it was too late to take the words back, and he wasn't sure he would even if he could. He had cheated on Gabriel, and he'd known it when he did it, but he couldn't make himself regret it except in the impact it had on the moment at hand.

Pulling himself up off the floor, he weighed his options. He could return to the pleasure palace and hope they would allow him to see guests again rather than sending him back to the breeding barns. He could throw himself on Lord Stuart's mercy and beg for a roof over his head in exchange for whatever menial jobs the aristocrat could give him. He could beg a place with Caleb and Andrew if they forgave him for Cressida's predicament. Or he could hope Gabriel would find it in his heart to forgive him in time.

Lucio hoped the latter would come to pass, but he had to face reality and be prepared if Gabriel could not accept his choice. If Gabriel kicked him out, Lord Stuart would be his best choice, in part because it would keep him close in case Gabriel changed his mind without putting Caleb and Andrew in the position of being torn between him and Gabriel. If he went back to the pleasure palace, he would never see Gabriel again. That thought sent fresh tears streaming down his face. Hoping it would not come to that, he undressed slowly and climbed into Gabriel's bed. He hugged the pillow close and inhaled his lover's scent, concentrating on the stickiness between his thighs and all that represented. Within moments, he was asleep.

GABRIEL worked for several hours on the heater for a friend of Lord Endicott who had admired the first one Gabriel had made before hunger drove him back upstairs to the kitchen. His mind had calmed in that time, the comfort of his tools and machines giving him some perspective on the matter. He had seen the relationship between Lucio and Cressida, had likened it to his friendship with Caleb and Andrew. Not that he could imagine a situation in which he would be forced to bed his friends, but if it happened by some strange twist of fate, he would certainly do his best to make the proceedings as positive as possible for everyone involved. It stood to reason that Lucio would do the same, and Gabriel could hardly criticize him for making the best of a situation he would never have created on his own. It hurt, knowing Lucio had been put in that position, but it was not the betrayal it had first seemed.

"Lucio?" he called up the stairs, sure the companion would be hungry as well.

He received no answer. Worried now that Lucio had left while he was working, he took the stairs two at a time, reaching the top to find a vision from his most cherished dreams. Lucio lay asleep in his bed, curled around his pillow, clearly naked beneath the covers. Breathing a sigh of relief at not having ruined everything by walking away earlier, Gabriel crossed to the bed, stroking the hair back from Lucio's tear-stained cheeks. "I'm sorry, beloved," he whispered, bending to kiss Lucio's eyelids tenderly. "I didn't mean to make you cry."

Lucio's eyes fluttered open. "Gabriel?"

"I'm here, beloved. I needed to work, to think for a bit, but I'm here again now," Gabriel said. "I'm sorry I made you cry."

Lucio sat up slowly, rubbing at his eyes. "Why are you sorry?"

"Because I upset you," Gabriel said. "Because I was too shocked by what you told me to realize how badly you were hurting. I needed to take a step back and think it all through, but I shouldn't have left you alone."

"But I cheated on you," Lucio reminded him.

"No, you didn't," Gabriel insisted. "You made the best of a terrible situation, for yourself and for Cressida. Cheating would have been sneaking into her room in the pleasure palace to make love with her simply because you felt like it. You had no choice in what you did, and you chose how to do it in a way that reflected your friendship. I'm sorry you were in that situation, but I don't love you any less because of the choices you made."

"Really?" Lucio asked, his voice tearful still.

"Really," Gabriel promised. "I was going to make dinner. Do you want to dress and come eat?"

"Could I have a bath first?" Lucio asked. "Between making love in the carriage and crying myself into a frenzy, I feel a little less than presentable."

"It'll be a cold one," Gabriel warned. "I didn't set the buckets on to heat like I'd meant to when we got home. Or you can do a quick wash with a rag now and I'll heat the buckets for a real bath after dinner."

"That sounds lovely," Lucio said. "But only if you join me."

"There's an ewer with water in it on the sink in the bathing area," Gabriel said, "and plenty of clothes in the clothes press. Help yourself to whatever you need. This is your home now, and I want you to be comfortable here."

"I was afraid you'd change your mind," Lucio admitted. "I'd started thinking about what I would do if you didn't want me anymore."

"Don't ever worry about that," Gabriel said fervently. "We'll undoubtedly argue, but nothing you could say will change the way I feel about you deep inside. I may shout and rave and go pound on poor hapless machinery, but when I've calmed down, I'll still love you, and we'll talk like rational men and work things out."

"No matter what?"

"No matter what."

"I want to help in the workshop," Lucio said. "I don't want to be a drain on you."

"Clean up and get dressed," Gabriel said. "My clothes will be a little big on you, but yours are too filthy to wear. Get something out of the armoire for tonight. We have a lot to discuss over dinner, including what you'll need in terms of a wardrobe."

Lucio threw his arms around Gabriel. "This wasn't what I'd imagined when I thought of our reunion, but I'm glad it's out in the open and behind us now. I love you, and I never want to hurt you like that again."

"I love you too," Gabriel said. "I'm going to start dinner. Does roast chicken and vegetables suit?"

"After the slop they gave me in the breeding barn, anything you make will be a royal feast," Lucio said. "I'll be down to help in a few minutes. Cooking is something else you'll have to teach me."

Gabriel laughed. "I'll teach you to wash up after dinner. I don't mind cooking, but I hate doing the dishes."

"Then that will be my new specialty," Lucio said, climbing out of bed and giving Gabriel a delectable view of his backside as he disappeared into the bathing area to clean up. Gabriel's stomach growled, reminding him that he hadn't eaten since that morning and neither had Lucio. There would be time for bed sport later when their stomachs weren't likely to rumble at inconvenient times.

He set the chicken to roast and was cutting up potatoes when Lucio came downstairs a few minutes later, his face rosy from being scrubbed. He wore Gabriel's oldest pair of leathers that had gotten a little too small.

Gabriel kept meaning to see if David could adjust them and never had. They fit Lucio perfectly.

"You look good enough to eat," Gabriel said.

"You promised me chicken," Lucio said. "That will be much more filling."

Gabriel laughed, tamping down on the urge to forget about dinner and ravish Lucio on the kitchen table. "There is another knife in the drawer there and zucchini in the pantry. If you cut it thinly, it will go nicely with the chicken and potatoes."

Lucio smiled, only adding to Gabriel's desire. He did as Gabriel had said, though, pulling out the knife and the vegetables and carefully cutting them into thin slices. When everything was in the oven, Gabriel took his customary seat at the table and waited for Lucio to do the same.

"First and foremost," Gabriel said, taking Lucio's hand, "all that I have is yours. You don't need to hesitate or ask. If there's something you need and I have it, use it. I spoke the truth when I told Lord Stuart that I consider the contract in my drawer a formal commitment. I know it doesn't have that legal weight, but that's what it means to me."

"It means the same to me," Lucio said. "I have nothing to offer in return except my devotion and my willingness to be your partner in life. I'm not an inventor, but I have a pair of able hands and a willing mind. If you tell me how to be of assistance to you, I will do it."

"Tomorrow we will visit my friend David, who is a tailor," Gabriel said. "Lord Stuart is not entirely convinced he can outfit us for society, but he can certainly outfit you for the workshop."

"I have no money to pay him," Lucio reminded Gabriel.

"Yes, you do," Gabriel said. "Lord Stuart only took a fraction of the gold we'd saved for your contract since he asked for a percentage of the workshop's profit instead. We have more money in the bank than I have ever had in my life. Certainly enough to buy a few suits for you."

"Why would he do that?" Lucio asked in surprise.

"I think because he realized you'd given up everything to be with me," Gabriel said. "And because now we can use some of that gold to make improvements in the workshop that will ultimately earn him more money. He isn't in this for a month or a year. He's looking at a lifetime of profit."

"As are we if the chair goes over as well as we hope it will," Lucio said.

"Yes," Gabriel agreed. "The first thing I'm doing after we sell the first chair is putting in a system to heat the bath water. I don't want you to regret the luxuries you left behind."

Lucio took Gabriel's hands in his. "I spent the last month in a barn, living in a stall with dirt floors covered in sawdust, a straw pallet on the floor, a bucket for a chamber pot, and another for a tub. The only thing I left behind that I regret in any way is Cressida, and I don't delude myself that I can change her fate, however much I wish I could."

"You never know," Gabriel said. "If the flying chairs sell as well as I hope they will, we might be able to afford her contract in a year." He didn't mention the baby and neither, to his relief, did Lucio. That was more than Gabriel could take in at the moment.

37

THEY continued their discussion over dinner, their words punctuated with long, lingering looks, until that became its own seduction. Gabriel helped Lucio with the dishes, showing him where to put everything away. When they were done, Gabriel caught Lucio's hand, lifting it his lips. "Will you come upstairs with me?" he asked.

"Where else would I go?" Lucio asked, trying to lighten the moment.

"Wherever you wanted," Gabriel replied earnestly. "You are free to do whatever you want now."

"What I want is to go upstairs and make love with you," Lucio said firmly. "Our carriage ride notwithstanding, it has been far too long."

"It has," Gabriel agreed, much to Lucio's relief. They climbed the stairs together, Lucio nearly as nervous again as he had been the first time they had made that journey. Everything was different now. Everything was permanent now, and as much as he had yearned for this moment, the weight of it left him feeling unsettled.

Then Gabriel's arms closed around him, pulling him close, and Lucio felt his nerves calm. He might not know how to be anything but a companion, but he knew how to please a man, and he knew Gabriel would put the same effort into pleasing him. They might have to learn everything else about living together, but here in the bedroom, everything would work out fine. "Since I gave you little choice in the carriage this afternoon, you get to decide how we spend our evening."

Gabriel shook his head, but Lucio laid his finger on his lover's lips, stopping his rebuttal. "Do you remember the first letter I sent you? Do you remember what I said about always deferring to me?"

Gabriel nodded and kissed Lucio's finger. "You said there was nothing I could do to you in love that you wouldn't enjoy."

Lucio was surprised that Gabriel could quote the exact words he'd used. "I meant what I said. I don't want you to hold back. If you do something I don't like—I can't imagine what that would be, but if you do—or if you don't do something I want, I will tell you, but until I do, I want you to let go of your fears and make love to me the way you want to."

"You were quite explicit in what you thought that way should be," Gabriel said, kissing Lucio tenderly. "I was shocked."

"Is that what they're calling it these days?" Lucio teased back, rubbing against Gabriel's hardening cock. "I lay in bed that night after I sent it and imagined you reading it, touching yourself like you did the first time we shared a bed. Did you do that, Gabriel? Did you pleasure yourself to the thought of everything I wanted you to do to me?"

"You know I did," Gabriel said, his voice low and rough. "How could I not?"

Lucio smiled and kissed along the line of Gabriel's jaw. "What did you imagine? Did you imagine what I'd written or did you have some other fantasy that played out in your mind instead?"

"Both."

The wealth of need in Gabriel's tone left Lucio's knees trembling. "Then pick one, yours or mine, I care not, and act on it. Touch me before I go wild with the wanting of you."

"I am touching you," Gabriel reminded Lucio, tightening his embrace.

"Not the way I need you to."

"If I tell you my dearest wish right now, will you believe that it is truly what I want?" Gabriel asked.

"Don't tell me," Lucio said. "Show me."

Gabriel's hands flew over Lucio's body, stripping the shirt and trousers from him. "Lie down," Gabriel said, his voice a low growl that did unspeakable things to Lucio's insides. He hurried to the bed, flipping the covers off and lying down. He watched eagerly as Gabriel undressed as well. The sight of the golden skin appearing made his mouth water. He stroked his hand over his cock lazily, waiting for Gabriel to join him.

Gabriel caught Lucio's hand, squeezing it gently before setting it firmly on the bed next to them. "As lovely a sight as that is, it's not part of my fantasy."

"You were taking too long," Lucio complained in jest.

"I haven't even started taking my time," Gabriel replied, taking Lucio's lips in a torrid kiss. Lucio relaxed into the mattress—feather now, he noticed randomly—and gave complete control to Gabriel. To his delight, Gabriel took it, kissing him masterfully, with more command than he had ever shown before. Lucio wrapped his arms around Gabriel's neck and slid his thigh between his lover's, rutting against Gabriel's hip.

Gabriel's lips left his to slide down his neck, settling on the jointure of neck and shoulder to suck and bite. Lucio gasped when he realized Gabriel was playing out the scene he had described in his first letter. He tipped his head to the side, offering Gabriel uninhibited access to his neck as he would offer it to his body. He moaned as the pressure increased, squirming a little, not to get away, but because he simply could not lie still beneath the decadent sensations.

"Don't move," Gabriel rumbled. Lucio subsided on the bed, not wanting to do anything that might cause Gabriel to stop. The inventor's lips moved lower, latching on to one of Lucio's nipples, licking and sucking at the taut bud until Lucio cried out, begging exactly as he had said he would, and Gabriel responded exactly as Lucio had described, moving to the other side and ratcheting the tension higher and higher in Lucio's body until he could do nothing but pant and moan and plead.

Gabriel lifted his head, leaving Lucio momentarily bereft. "If you find your release now, will you be able to find it a second time? I want to share that moment with you later."

Lucio wanted to say yes, but the past month had left him wrung out to the point that the guards had increased the amount of saffron they gave him in the mornings. Granted, he shared a bed with Gabriel now rather than a pallet with a girl he didn't love, but he feared he would disappoint his lover. "I don't know."

"Then I should do other things," Gabriel said, dropping a tender kiss on each throbbing nipple before reaching for the vial of oil on the nightstand. He coated his fingers carefully, chuckling when Lucio spread his legs in invitation. "As arousing as that picture is, I had other things in mind for the moment."

"Like what?" Lucio asked, leaving his legs splayed in the hope that Gabriel's resolve would falter. He groaned when Gabriel's fingers disappeared behind his back.

"Like riding you until we both collapse," Gabriel replied.

Lucio wished he could see what Gabriel was doing, but before he could move or ask, Gabriel's hand found Lucio's cock, slicking it and lifting it. Lucio forced his eyes to stay open as Gabriel straddled him and sank down onto his eager shaft. The dual sensation of being pinned to the bed and yet inside his lover addled Lucio's wits, as Gabriel had surely intended, fulfilling Lucio's fantasy while at the same time drawing on one of the moments he had shared only with Gabriel. He pulled Gabriel's head down for a kiss, doing his own exploring this time as Gabriel moved above him. The tight heat of Gabriel's passage stole his breath, all awareness reduced to his cock sliding in and out of his lover's hole and his tongue sliding in and out of his lover's mouth.

The sudden rush of heat across his belly and the tightening of the sheath around him triggered Lucio's release as well, his hips stuttering up into Gabriel's body as he climaxed. Gabriel collapsed on top of him, his weight pressing Lucio deeper into the mattress. He made no move to roll Gabriel to the side or to fetch a rag to clean them up. They could be sticky. It would remind him of what they had shared.

What they would always share.

If his time with Cressida could not damage their relationship, nothing could, because now that he was free, he would never come even close to that kind of infidelity again.

GABRIEL was not surprised when Caleb and Andrew arrived well before their normal time the next morning. He simply cracked a few more eggs into the bowl and added them to breakfast. Lucio had not come down yet, though Gabriel did not imagine it would be long before he joined them in the kitchen as well.

"Did you find anything else out from Lucio?" Andrew asked almost as soon as they had said hello.

"A little," Gabriel replied. "He said Cressida would not be allowed to see guests while she was pregnant, to protect the baby." *The investment*, Gabriel thought bitterly, but he would not burden Caleb and Andrew with his cynicism. "He feared that after the baby was born, she would have trouble rebuilding her guest list and so would be sent back to the breeding barns indefinitely. He's as worried about her as you are, but none of us are exactly in a position to help her."

"So there's nothing we can do?" Caleb demanded. "There has to be something. We can't leave her there to rot."

"I didn't say that," Gabriel replied. "I said none of us can help her. I'm hoping Lord Stuart will play benefactor once more. I don't know what we can offer him in exchange except another chunk of the workshop, but

Cressida is important enough to Lucio and to you that I'm willing to make the offer if he's willing to accept it."

"Can we afford to keep the business running if we give him a larger portion of the profits?" Andrew asked. "You know I'm no good with numbers."

"One of the stipulations in the contract he already signed was the option for him to reinvest his portion of the profits instead of taking them in gold," Gabriel said. "If he does that from time to time, it should keep things balanced, even if he draws a larger percentage. The real question is whether he's willing. He'd said to call on Wednesday, but I don't want to wait that long now that we know about Cressida."

He didn't mention Lucio's description of his quarters, not wanting to further upset Caleb and Andrew, but he would be sure to mention them to Lord Stuart. If Cressida were languishing in her room in the pleasure palace, it would be one thing, but the conditions Lucio had described were deplorable, especially with winter approaching.

Lucio appeared on the stairs at that moment, silencing the discussion.

"What is on our schedule for today?" Lucio asked with a smile for Caleb and Andrew.

"Caleb and Andrew are going to finish up a few projects so they'll be ready for delivery on schedule," Gabriel said, "and you and I are going to pay a visit to Lord Stuart. I'm hoping he'll be willing to help Cressida."

Lucio's face brightened. "Really? You'd do that for me?"

"For you," Gabriel agreed, knowing he would do anything to make Lucio happy, "but also for Caleb and Andrew. They're worried about her too. I don't know what Lord Stuart will say, but there's no harm in asking. Even if all he does is find out the price of her contract for us. It might take time, but the flying chair will earn us the money we need. We might even be able to pay the handlers in installments so we can dictate some improvements for her in the meantime."

"That would be wonderful!"

"If it works out," Gabriel cautioned. "Lord Stuart hasn't agreed to be our go-between yet."

"We'll persuade him," Lucio said confidently. "And if he doesn't, maybe someone else from the Caste Equality movement would help?"

"They might," Gabriel said. "They were certainly willing to make good use of your abuse. Having Cressida's story to tell as well could add to the impact of their message."

Gabriel set the scrambled eggs on the table. "We'll go right after breakfast so we can catch Lord Stuart before he goes out for the day."

"I have nothing I can wear to call on an aristocrat," Lucio said suddenly. "Not even for a morning at-home."

"We aren't calling on an aristocrat," Gabriel said with a shake of his head. "We're going to meet with our partner, Lord Stuart. The leathers you're wearing will do until we can see David this afternoon and get you something that fits you properly. They're still better than what you were wearing when you got here yesterday."

"I know," Lucio said. "I'm not used to being dressed in anything but the latest style. I guess I have some adjusting to do."

"David is talented," Gabriel assured him. "He'll be able to make you what you need and want. And if he can't, Lord Stuart said he would recommend us to his own tailor. Yes, it will be an adjustment, not having a full wardrobe always at hand, but we'll make it work. I promise."

THEY found Lord Stuart still at breakfast when they arrived at his house an hour later. Gabriel didn't find that particularly surprising, nor was it all that unusual to find the aristocrat in his dressing gown. What did surprise him was Wakefield's presence at Lord Stuart's table, similarly attired. The moment the butler announced them, Wakefield rose to leave.

"Sit down, Elijah," Lord Stuart scolded. "I won't have you chased from the table in your own home, even by your own moral code."

"This isn't my home, Ian," Wakefield replied, flushing scarlet.

"Only because you won't unbend enough to accept my invitation," Lord Stuart retorted. "Please, Blackstone, Lucio, join us. Have you eaten yet?"

"We had breakfast," Gabriel said, trying not to boggle at the revelations the morning had brought. "But don't stop on our account. It's probably good that Wakefield is here, anyway. He might have some thoughts on what we wanted to discuss."

"Then you aren't here to talk about the garden party on Saturday."

Gabriel shook his head. "No, it's a little more serious than that."

"Well, out with it," Lord Stuart said when Gabriel didn't immediately continue. "I can't help if I don't know what the problem is."

"It's Cressida," Lucio said. "When they realized they were going to lose me, they sent her to the breeding barn. Their two top companions and all that. She's pregnant."

"I take it congratulations are not in order."

Lucio shook his head. "Her career is essentially over. They'll keep breeding her until she can't have any more children, and by then no one will want her anymore."

"What happens to companions when they get too old to appeal to aristocrats?" Wakefield asked. "You never see a companion much over thirty-five out in society."

"Mostly they're assigned to training the next generation," Lucio said. "Or else they end up doing servants' jobs around the pleasure palace."

"Not the most agreeable of fates," Lord Stuart concurred. "So what do you want from me?"

"We hoped you could find out the price of her contract," Gabriel said. "We'll have to save up for it like we did for Lucio's, but with the flying chair ready to go, it won't take us as long as it would have to save all of Lucio's fee."

"You're assuming they'll let you buy her contract," Lord Stuart reminded them. "They wouldn't let you buy Lucio's."

"Blackstone's gold is as good as any aristocrat's," Wakefield fumed. "It's ludicrous that he can't buy a companion if he wants one. They'll let him buy time for an evening. Why shouldn't they let him buy a contract? It's yet another example of the inherent inequalities between the castes and another reason why they should be abolished entirely."

"You won't get an argument from anyone in this room," Lord Stuart reminded him. "I may have been the first aristocrat to admit my sympathies, but I am not the only one who has them. We'll keep working for the system to change, but until it does, if the handlers will not discuss Cressida's contract with me, perhaps they will with another aristocrat sympathetic to the Caste Equality movement who could act as their go-between. As long as they have the money to pay for it."

"We aren't asking for a loan," Gabriel assured Lord Stuart. "Only for information right now so we can make plans."

"I'll see what I can find out," Lord Stuart agreed.

38

"I THINK I'm going to like my new clothes," Lucio said as they came out of Reading's Tailoring for Men. David had found a new suit for Lucio that fit him nearly perfectly, promising to have the rest ready for him before the weekend. "The leather is far more comfortable, not to mention more practical, than the 'fashionable' suits I wore in the pleasure palace." Not that he had spent all that much time wearing them most days. His guests usually had him out of them within minutes of his arrival. That life was behind him, he reminded himself resolutely. He could concentrate on the new one now.

"I told you David did good work," Gabriel said with an indulgent smile. Lucio knew Gabriel was laughing at him, but his spirits were too high to care. With Lord Stuart's willingness to help, the last of Lucio's concerns about his new life had melted away. Lord Stuart would find out what it would cost to buy Cressida's contract, they would work until they had the money, and then they would get her out of the breeding barn for good. Lucio didn't know if they would be in time to help the baby, but the baby wasn't real to him, not in any concrete sense. Cressida, on the other hand, had been his constant companion since they were little more than babes themselves.

"We'll see how the suits for the garden party turn out," Lucio said, although he had no doubt they would be up to snuff, given the quality of work he had seen in David's shop. They turned the corner onto Gabriel's street, and Lucio spied a carriage in front of the workshop. "Is that Lord Stuart's carriage?"

"It is," Gabriel said. "He must have news."

They hurried the rest of the way home, finding Lord Stuart in the outer room of the workshop, Wakefield with him. "What did they say?" Lucio asked.

"It's criminal," Wakefield muttered before Lord Stuart could reply.

The aristocrat hushed him and turned to Gabriel and Lucio. "I'm afraid I don't have good news," he told them. "The handlers refused to discuss a price for her contract. Any price. I thought perhaps it was because I had purchased another companion from them so recently, so I asked my niece to try, but she got the same answer. Cressida's contract is not for sale."

"It's criminal," Wakefield repeated. "It's slavery, pure and simple. The whole argument that the pleasure caste are not slaves is that the companions have a contract that can be purchased, a way out of the pleasure palace. This violates every tenet on which the caste is based."

"Unfortunately, none of those tenets is law," Lord Stuart said, "and so the decision cannot be appealed."

"What are we going to do?" Lucio asked, turning to Gabriel for support. "We can't leave her there."

"We'll take out ads in every newspaper in the city," Wakefield declared. "We'll make her our rallying cry. The public will put so much pressure on the handlers that they'll have to give in."

"How long will that take?" Lucio asked.

"More importantly," Gabriel said, "what will that do to Cressida and her safety while she's still under their control?"

"She's already confined to a stall in a barn barely large enough for two people," Lucio said bitterly. "What more could they do to her?"

"I don't know," Gabriel said. "You tell me. What more could they do to her if we use her name as part of our platform?"

Lucio's stomach churned. "They won't hurt her too badly because they want the baby she's carrying, so they won't beat her or anything like that."

"You were worried about being used by the handlers in the barns," Lord Stuart reminded Lucio. "Will they use her as revenge?"

"They might," Lucio replied, "but they could already be using her simply because she's there and they already know she's pregnant. They don't have to worry about messing up their breeding program because it already worked."

"You said she might be given a chance to regain her former clients after the baby was born," Gabriel said. "Will they take that away from her or would this pressure them into giving her that chance to prove they are reasonable?"

"There's nothing 'reasonable' about any of this," Lord Stuart scowled, "and there hasn't been since they refused to discuss a price for her contract."

"So what do we do?" Lucio asked again.

"Is there somewhere more private where we can talk?" Lord Stuart asked. "Anyone could walk in and interrupt us, and I don't care to share my thoughts with an audience."

"We could go down to the basement," Gabriel offered. "It's a workshop, but it's private. There are only two entrances. One of them is barred from the inside, and the other is through my kitchen. Caleb and Andrew won't let a customer wander down there by mistake."

"Let's go," Lord Stuart said. Gabriel led them through the main room of the workshop and into the basement. "Now that we're sure to be undisturbed, I think a little civil disobedience is in order."

"What do you mean?" Gabriel asked.

"We went to the handlers in good faith, to negotiate a price for Cressida's contract," Lord Stuart said, "and if they had named a price, you would have done your best to meet it in time, according to the tenets of the caste, as Elijah said. Since they have refused our good faith and since Cressida is in an untenable position, I propose we remedy it by unorthodox means."

"Unorthodox means?" Lucio repeated.

"You mean to steal her," Wakefield said, his eyes dancing. "But how?"

"Lucio can tell us all we need to know about the layout and the routine of the breeding barn where she's being kept," Lord Stuart reminded them. "No one expects that kind of problem so there is probably only one handler awake at night, if that, even. It shouldn't be too difficult to sneak in and sneak her out. What do you think, Lucio? Can we do it?"

"I don't know," Lucio said slowly, his thoughts racing. "We have no way of knowing if they've moved her since yesterday or if your inquiries today will cause them to move her. We could get into a lot of trouble with nothing to show for it."

"Or we could get Cressida out," Lord Stuart said.

"What will we do with her once she's out?" Gabriel asked. "They'll look for her, and you will be the first person they come to because you asked about her contract. When she isn't there, they'll think of Lucio next, knowing he and she were close, which will bring them here, maybe not right away, but before long. They'll search Caleb and Andrew's house because they're my employees. And it's not merely a question of getting away with it. She would have to stay hidden until the laws change, however long that might be."

"I have a thought about that," Lord Stuart said, "although I have to speak with Lady Bentley still. She is a cousin of mine, several times removed, enough of a connection that I feel comfortable approaching her without it being such a close connection that she would fall under scrutiny should the handlers decide I was responsible for the disappearance of their charge."

"I know Lady Bentley," Lucio said, thinking of the buxom red-headed aristocrat he had spent time with on occasion. "She was always kind to me. Do you think she could be persuaded to take Cressida in temporarily?"

"It won't be temporary," Gabriel said, "or at least it won't be short. It could be years before it's safe for Cressida to be out in society."

"But it wouldn't have to be years that she stayed with Lady Bentley, would it?" Lucio asked. "I mean, obviously for a few months until the search for her dies down, but couldn't she eventually move to Caleb and Andrew's place, for example? She'd have to keep her tattoo hidden and be careful about being seen, but Lady Bentley wouldn't have to keep her forever."

"All of that can be worked out," Lord Stuart interrupted. "The real question is whether you're willing to take the chance of getting caught. This won't be like the Caste Equality members who are arrested for overzealous protesting and spend a night or two, or a week or two, in prison. If we're caught, it could mean years."

"Right is right, and wrong is wrong," Wakefield said firmly. "And what the handlers have done to Cressida is wrong. It's up to us to make it right."

Lucio resisted the urge to look at Gabriel. He knew his lover would see the pleading in his eyes, but he didn't want this to be about them. It had to be about Cressida or it risked causing more friction between them down the road. "Let me think about it," Gabriel said finally. "We'll need a few days to plan if we decide to do it, so let me mull it over and I'll let you know tomorrow."

"Saturday night into Sunday would be the best time," Lucio volunteered. "There are fewer handlers in the breeding barn then because everyone wants to spend the day with their families. There are still a few handlers, but nothing like there would be during the week."

"Saturday is the garden party," Lord Stuart reminded them. "It could provide the perfect cover. We have the party, present the flying chair, and then celebrate late into the night at its success. If the guardians ask where we were, we have each other as alibis. You will provide an alibi for us even if you don't help, won't you, Blackstone?"

"Yes, I can do that," Gabriel agreed.

"Good," Lord Stuart said. "Now, we should talk about Saturday."

SATURDAY dawned clear and cool. As Gabriel shivered through his bath, he hoped the sun would warm the air by afternoon or none of Lord Stuart's guests would want to venture outside to see the flying chair, no matter how much Lord Stuart built it up as the latest rage. Then Lucio joined him and all thought of anything but his lover fled.

When they finally finished their bath and were dressing for the day, Gabriel marveled at the advantages of having a companion for a lover. Now that Lucio was his and his alone, he could appreciate the benefits of Lucio's training without the jealousy that had eaten at him before and enjoy the endlessly inventive variety of ways Lucio thought of to make love. Gabriel was quite sure he had never been as thoroughly loved as he had been this past week.

Catching Lucio's hand as the companion crossed the room to tie his cravat in front of the mirror, Gabriel pulled his lover into his arms. "I'll go with you tonight," he said. "It's important to you that we try to help Cressida, and that means it's important to me."

"Thank you," Lucio said, throwing his arms around Gabriel's neck. "I would have gone without you because I'm the only one who knows exactly where to find her, but a part of me would have always worried you disapproved or resented my friendship with Cressida. Now I don't have to worry."

Gabriel replied only with a tender kiss, refusing to allow his concerns show on his face or in his manner. He knew Lucio cared for Cressida the same way he cared for Caleb and Andrew, but she had a piece of him now that Gabriel would never have, a permanent link that nothing could ever sunder. Gabriel had never given any real thought to children of his own, given his preferences, but that didn't mean Lucio felt the same way. While he wanted to trust in Lucio's love, he couldn't completely stamp out the fear that he would lose part of his lover's heart to Cressida and the baby. It was a fear he would simply have to live with, though, because he couldn't stand by and let Cressida suffer out of jealousy that might never be realized.

"Finish getting dressed," Lucio said, bringing Gabriel back to the present, "and I'll tie your cravat for you."

"You don't think I can tie it myself?" Gabriel asked, feigning hurt.

"Of course you can," Lucio soothed. "It will just be easier for me since I can see what I'm doing."

Gabriel gave in and buttoned his shirt quickly so Lucio could adjust his cravat. When Lucio declared him presentable, Gabriel shrugged on his jacket as well and went downstairs to meet Caleb and Andrew, who would deliver the flying chair to Lord Stuart's so that Gabriel and Lucio would be presentable rather than covered in dust and grease and sweat from moving the chair. The two assistants got the contraption loaded onto a cart and set off for Lord Stuart's. Gabriel and Lucio would follow shortly.

"Are you ready for today?" Lucio asked, smoothing the jacket over Gabriel's shoulders.

"Probably not," Gabriel said with a short laugh. "I'm not at all comfortable in society. I don't know that I ever will be."

"I won't let you stumble," Lucio promised. "I may not be that much help to you in the workshop, but I can help you in society."

Gabriel pulled Lucio into his arms. "I'll accept your help in every arena it's offered," he said, dropping a quick kiss on Lucio's lips, "as long as you remember that it's your choice."

"I know that," Lucio assured Gabriel, "but what kind of lover, what kind of partner would I be if I didn't offer all the help that's mine to give? You went to great lengths to give us a future together. The least I can do is help make it as successful a future as possible. Besides, I rather like the idea of being out in society now that none of them can touch me. I'm yours alone now. They can look all they want, but I don't have to think about anyone but you."

"I can see that being very freeing," Gabriel said. "You never have to worry about any of them again except as potential customers for our inventions."

"I love it when you say things like that," Lucio commented.

"Like what?" Gabriel asked, not sure what he had said of any note.

"Our inventions," Lucio clarified. "*Our.* Like I truly am part of this."

"You truly are part of it," Gabriel insisted. "You may not have all the technical knowledge yet, but it's not just about what you know. You've helped build things. Now you're helping me sell them. That makes you as much a part of this as Caleb or Andrew or me. Shall we go impress everyone?"

"I'll be the envy of every man and woman there," Lucio said with a nod, resting his hand on Gabriel's sleeve as they left the house in search of a cab.

"And why is that?" Gabriel asked with a grin.

"Because I'll be the one on the arm of the man of the hour," Lucio replied. "They can come demanding your attention all they want. I don't have to demand it. I have it already."

"Simply by breathing, you have it," Gabriel agreed as they climbed into the cab and set out for Lord Stuart's.

They arrived in time for a late brunch. Wakefield was already there. Gabriel refrained from asking when he had arrived. "Are there any details we haven't discussed for this afternoon?"

"Everything is in place," Lord Stuart assured him. "My staff are quite competent and will have the luncheon ready to serve at two o'clock. Once everyone has eaten, we'll unveil the flying chair and give a demonstration. Probably around three thirty. Everyone will be on their way home by five to prepare for their evening's entertainment, whatever that might be, and then we have only to wait until dark to begin our own evening activities."

"Will there be room for one more in the carriage tonight?" Gabriel asked.

"So you came to your senses after all," Wakefield said. "I wondered if you would."

"We're taking a huge risk," Gabriel reminded them. "Someone needed to be cautious."

"It's a risk worth taking," Wakefield said with a shrug. "Lady Bentley has agreed to shelter Cressida for as long as we need, so it's purely a question of getting her out."

"She will be at the party this afternoon," Lord Stuart added. "She said she wanted to meet the people who were so determined to help a companion."

"I will be sure to thank her for her generosity," Lucio said. "She didn't have to help a companion either."

"It seems she knows Cressida," Lord Stuart said, "although she didn't say in what context they had met. She was quite happy to help out."

"I'm hoping she'll be interested in joining the Caste Equality movement," Wakefield said. "Given how easily she agreed to our plans, she seems a likely candidate for support."

"As well as a source of suggestions for other aristocrats who might share her sympathies?" Gabriel asked.

"Of course. The more people we bring around to our cause, the more likely we are to be successful in the elections and in the changes that must be made."

"I don't mind you sounding people out this afternoon," Lord Stuart told Wakefield, "but please remember that this is Blackstone's afternoon, not yours. Don't take the attention away from him."

"Not to mention that we don't want to draw undue attention to our interest in Cressida until after she is safely hidden away," Gabriel added. "We don't want the guardians looking at us too closely."

"They'll look anyway simply because Lord Stuart asked about her and because she and I were friends," Lucio said, "but we don't have to give them extra reasons to suspect us."

"It is nearly noon and people will start arriving before long," Lord Stuart said. "Shall we retire to the garden? I have set up several of the Blackstone heaters in tents for those who find the brisk fall air too cool for their tastes."

"So we advertise not only the flying chair, but my other inventions as well," Gabriel said with a smile. "Nicely done."

"It seemed the thing to do," Lord Stuart said. "We'll leave the servants to clean up in here while we make sure everything is in order outside."

They walked out into the garden, the sun having warmed the air considerably since that morning, although Gabriel would not have called it warm. Comfortably cool, perhaps. Fortunately there was almost no wind so there would be nothing to interfere with his flight. Wandering around the manicured garden, he found the flying chair covered by a large sheet. "We tested it a bit once we got it here to make sure nothing had gotten damaged in bringing it over," Caleb said. "It all started fine, and the rotors were picking up speed normally."

"Good," Gabriel said. "Are you sure you won't stay for the party?"

Caleb shook his head. "The aristocrats wouldn't know what to do with that many merchants in their midst. It'll throw them enough to have you and Lucio here. You'll let us know how the party goes?"

"Of course," Gabriel said, wishing he could tell Caleb and Andrew about their plans to help Cressida, but they had agreed that the fewer people who knew, the better. When the guardians came to the shop, as they certainly would once Cressida's disappearance was noted, the two men could answer honestly that they had no knowledge of her being taken or of her current whereabouts. They could tell Caleb and Andrew the truth later, after the guardians had given up their search for her.

"Shall we wait at the workshop?"

"I have no idea how late it will be before we finish up here," Gabriel demurred. "We'll come by your house and let you know."

"We'll be home. Enjoy the party."

Gabriel resisted the urge to double-check the flying chair. If Caleb said it was working, it was working. Wandering back to the others, he found them gathered in one of the tents. He stepped inside and was surprised that even with the flaps open on one side, the temperature inside was considerably warmer than outside. "This was a fabulous idea."

"It was Wakefield's idea," Lord Stuart said. "He saw one of the heaters in my house and commented that it would be nice if they could be used outside as well. There's no reason they can't be, as long as there is some way of keeping the heat from dissipating. The tents do that very nicely."

"Not to mention that they block the breeze," Lucio said. "You will be a hit today. I just know it."

"Lord Stuart," the butler said, appearing at the entrance to the tent, "your guests have started to arrive."

"Show them into the garden," Lord Stuart said. "We will greet them out here."

Lord Stuart led Gabriel outside to form the receiving line. Lucio stayed close to Gabriel's side. "Elijah," Lord Stuart said, his voice betraying his exasperation. "Come here where you belong."

"I don't need to stand in a receiving line all afternoon," Wakefield protested.

"I want to introduce you," Lord Stuart insisted. "Think of the publicity for the Caste Equality movement."

Wakefield pulled a face but took his place at Lord Stuart's side. "Don't blame me when people start looking at you oddly for having a guardian in your receiving line."

"If you'd let me tell them you were my lover, no one would look twice at your tattoo," Lord Stuart fussed, but Wakefield shook his head adamantly.

Gabriel smothered a smile. He had suspected for some time that Wakefield's interest in Lord Stuart had moved beyond Lord Stuart's potential ability to help the Caste Equality movement. He hoped they would both find happiness in their new relationship.

"Ah, Juliette," Lord Stuart said when the first guest came out into the garden. He embraced the lady, a buxom woman in her mid-thirties, perhaps, with flaming red hair and a ready smile. "So good of you to come."

"I couldn't very well miss your garden party when you sent out such an enticing invitation, Ian," the lady replied. "Introduce me to your guests, why don't you?"

"Lady Bentley, may I present Elijah Wakefield, guardian and activist in the Caste Equality movement?"

"I know you," Wakefield exclaimed, bending over Lady Bentley's hand politely. "I've seen you at some of our rallies."

"You have a good eye, young man," Lady Bentley said. "No one else has recognized me."

"Most people, even in the Caste Equality movement, still don't look past people's dress," Wakefield said with a scowl. "Now I understand why you were so willing to help with other projects."

Lord Stuart chuckled. "I should have known. You always did have an adventurous streak."

"Their message makes a lot of sense," Lady Bentley said, "but we aren't here to talk politics, and you have a guest I haven't met yet."

"Forgive me," Lord Stuart said. "This is Mister Blackstone, inventor extraordinaire, and his companion Lucio."

"Pleased to make your acquaintance, Mister Blackstone," Lady Bentley said, offering her hand.

"The pleasure is all mine, my Lady," Gabriel replied, bowing over her hand as Cressida had taught him. "I hope you'll see or hear something of interest today."

Lady Bentley laughed. "I have no doubt I will. And Lucio... you are looking well. I take it private life agrees with you."

"Infinitely, my Lady," Lucio said with a bow. "I have decided to become an inventor."

39

"WHAT a day!" Lucio exclaimed when the last guest had gone. "I knew the flying chair would catch people's fancy, but I didn't expect you to have five orders already, if only because I didn't think the aristocrats would discuss business at a party."

"We do occasionally bend our own rules," Lord Stuart chuckled. "You two are well on your way to being very rich men. Have you thought about what you're going to do with the money?"

"Install a system to heat the bath water," Gabriel replied immediately.

"Lucio?"

"Replace my wardrobe," Lucio replied. "Not with the same things, but with items suitable for my new life."

"If I might make a suggestion," Lord Stuart said, "you should look into acquiring a carriage as well. A horseless one is fine. As much in demand as you will be, always being dependent on hiring a cab could be difficult and expensive, not to mention that it is more fashionable to arrive in one's own carriage than in a hansom."

"We'll keep it in mind," Gabriel said. "Lucio, what time should we arrive at the breeding barn?"

"Not until at least ten," Lucio said. "That way most of the handlers will be gone or in bed for the night, with only the night watch still awake. Overpowering one man will be far easier than overpowering several."

Gabriel glanced at the clock. "So another four hours still. We should go tell Caleb and Andrew how the afternoon went and perhaps change into less formal clothes. If we get in any scrapes, I'd rather do it in my leathers than in my one good suit."

"That's the other thing you need to do with your money, then," Lord Stuart declared. "Expand your wardrobe as well. You can't wear the same suit to every party, and you may be sure this will not be the last one you're invited to attend."

Gabriel sighed. He would never keep Lucio from buying whatever clothes he needed to be comfortable in his new life, but Gabriel felt no need for such trappings. "I'll talk to my friend next week. Shall we meet back here at nine? That will give us time to change and eat before it's time to leave."

"Nine o'clock it is," Lord Stuart agreed.

TWO and a half hours later, having visited with Caleb and Andrew for few minutes and then come home to make love desperately, Lucio and Gabriel dressed again in their darkest clothes, wanting to be as invisible as possible in the hours to come. Gabriel switched his regular jacket for a black leather duster that made Lucio think all kinds of lascivious thoughts. If all went well tonight, he would greatly enjoy peeling it off his lover when they came home. First, though, they had to survive the next few hours.

"Are we ready?" Gabriel asked.

"As ready as I'll ever be," Lucio replied. "I know this is the right thing to do for Cressida, but I'm scared."

"That we'll get caught?"

Lucio nodded.

"It is a risk," Gabriel agreed. "Tonight and when they start searching for the culprits. We can still call it off."

"No," Lucio said. "I promised myself I'd find a way to help Cressida, and since the handlers refuse to sell her contract, this is the only choice left. But I don't want to lose you."

"I don't want to lose you either," Gabriel said. "We'll simply have to be careful and make sure we don't get caught. And if we get to the breeding barns and the situation isn't what we expected, we'll wait and try again later. We'll only get one chance to do it right, but that doesn't have to be tonight."

As much as Lucio wanted Cressida out of the breeding barns and somewhere safe, he knew Gabriel was right. If the barn wasn't as quiet tonight as he predicted it would be, they could come back another time and try then. As long as they didn't alarm the handlers, no one would be the wiser and they could wait for the most auspicious moment.

"We should go," Gabriel added. "We don't want to keep Lord Stuart and Wakefield waiting."

Lucio followed Gabriel out to the street. It took them several minutes to find an available cab, making Lucio think again about Lord Stuart's suggestion that they buy a carriage. "How much does a carriage cost? I never needed to think about those kinds of things in the pleasure palace. The handlers always arranged our transportation to meet our guests, and the guests arranged to send us home."

"I haven't the slightest idea," Gabriel replied as the cab carried them across town, "but we may find out before long. After we've installed the heating system and expanded our wardrobes appropriately. It's all well and good to imagine what we'll do with the gold, but until we have it in hand, we'd do well only to spend it in our minds. I've seen others fall into the trap of spending gold based on expected earnings only to have a sale fall through. I don't want to fall into debt that way."

"We'll be prudent," Lucio agreed. "We have Lord Stuart to keep us on the straight and narrow now."

"I don't know how involved he'll want to be in the day-to-day running of the business," Gabriel commented, "but we'll certainly have to account for our earnings at the end of the quarter when we give him his percentage of the profits."

"Should we offer something to Lady Bentley in return for her assistance?" Lucio asked.

"Lord Stuart made those arrangements," Gabriel answered. "If he feels she needs to be repaid for her help, he can see that it happens or bring it up to us."

"If you're sure," Lucio said, feeling guilty about involving everyone in what was essentially his problem. None of the others involved in the raid tonight had any real attachment to Cressida. Wakefield saw her as a means to an end. Gabriel was indulging him, as he suspected Lord Stuart was indulging Wakefield. Lady Bentley… he had no idea what had motivated Lady Bentley to agree besides her interest in the Caste Equality movement.

"If it will make you feel better, you can ask her about it tonight when we take Cressida to her house," Gabriel said. "As long as it's reasonable, we can do something."

"Thank you," Lucio said, throwing his arms around Gabriel. "I really will find a way to earn my keep around the workshop, and Cressida's as well."

"It's not about earning your keep," Gabriel said with a sigh. "Yes, you'll do your part to contribute to the workshop—you already have this week, and especially today at the garden party—but I'm not keeping a ledger with what you spend versus what you earn. I love you. Whatever you need, if we have the gold for it, you'll buy for yourself, the same as I buy what I need as long as we have the gold."

Lucio wanted to believe that was true, but he knew it would take time before he felt like he was more than a drag on Gabriel's purse. He let it go for now, though, because they had arrived at Lord Stuart's and they had other things to concentrate on.

Wakefield answered the door when they arrived. "Ian gave the servants the night off," he said. "That way they can say honestly that he and I were here when they left, and they won't have to lie for us. They won't be able to vouch for you arriving, but they won't be able to say you didn't, either. Anything that happened after eight o'clock will be an unknown for them until they arrive tomorrow morning to find us sleeping in our beds."

"Let's hope they find us in ours as well," Gabriel muttered.

"I pulled the carriage out. Fortunately Ian has a mechanical one because we don't want the attention the horse-drawn one would garner, and if we took it, someone would have to stay behind to watch the horses," Wakefield went on. "Here, put these on so no one will be able to identify our faces if they do see us."

Lucio looked down at the black kerchief Wakefield had given him. He felt rather silly tying it around his face like a highwayman, but Wakefield was right. They didn't want anyone to recognize them if they were sighted. "We should put one over Lord Stuart's hair as well," he suggested. "As distinguished as it makes him look, the white hair will catch every bit of moonlight and starlight."

"I have him all set," Wakefield assured them. "He's waiting for us in the garden."

They went through the house and back out into the night where Lord Stuart waited next to his carriage, his face and head completely obscured by masks and scarves. "Aren't we a disreputable-looking bunch?" Lord Stuart joked when the others joined him. "Shall we go? Time is passing."

Wakefield climbed into the driver's seat while everyone else moved to the interior of the carriage. Lord Stuart rapped on the roof when they were settled. "Let's go over the plan one more time," he said. "If all is normal, there should be one handler standing watch in the office for the night. If we can overpower him with a minimum of noise, we should then be able to enter the barn without difficulty."

"That's right," Lucio said. "I would occasionally walk the aisles at night to stretch my legs, and I never saw more than one handler on the weekends."

"Then it's simply a question of finding Cressida and taking her with us," Lord Stuart said.

Lucio nodded, not wanting to argue with the others about his addition to the plan. He knew they couldn't take all the women confined to the breeding barn with them, but he fully intended to give them the choice to flee if they wanted to. He suspected most would not, given the consequences if they were caught, but it would be their choice rather than Lucio doing nothing at all to help them.

Wakefield stopped the carriage well away from the breeding barn, not wanting the noise from the engine to alert the handler on duty. The four men slipped through the lanes on silent feet until they neared the breeding barn. The building was dark except for a single light that burned in the office.

"Everything looks quiet," Wakefield said. "This is it. If you aren't committed, now is the time to say so."

"Let's go," Lucio said after a quick glance at Gabriel revealed nothing but determination.

Lord Stuart nodded as well. They crept across the field around the barn, staying to the shadows as much as possible. Lucio wasn't sure if the nearly full moon was a blessing or a curse. It gave them light to see by, but it also made it harder to avoid being seen if anyone was looking. He saw no sign to suggest anyone was watching, but he couldn't entirely quell his nerves as he returned toward the site of his dreaded imprisonment.

Gabriel's hand settled on Lucio's back, almost as if the inventor could read his mind. Lucio took a deep breath and smiled before remembering the mask that would keep his lover from seeing his expression. He hoped Gabriel understood, because he wasn't going to risk speaking and having someone overhear. They snuck up to the window and peeked inside. Smith sat at the desk, his feet propped up, his chin on his chest as he snored loudly.

"Could they have made it any easier?" Wakefield whispered.

"He has no reason to expect tonight to be any different than every other night," Lord Stuart reminded them. "A little tap on the head to keep him asleep for a few hours, and we'll be in business."

"Stay here," Wakefield said. "I'll take care of him."

Lucio started to protest, but Gabriel silenced him with a restraining hand. "Wakefield is a guardian," Gabriel whispered, his voice so soft Lucio could barely hear it. "He knows where to hit him for maximum effect and minimum damage."

They watched with bated breath as Wakefield crept into the room and up behind the sleeping handler. With silent efficiency, Wakefield lifted one of the candlesticks and brought it down hard on the back of Smith's neck. The man fell sideways out of his chair into Wakefield's waiting arms. The guardian lowered him to the floor and tied his hands and feet quickly, stuffing a rag in his mouth as a gag. Turning back to the window, he motioned for the others to come in.

"Which room is Cressida in?" Gabriel whispered to Lucio.

Lucio gestured to the far aisle. The others followed him. "Let me go in first," Lucio said, pulling off his mask for a moment. "She's less likely to scream if she sees my face than if four masked men barge in on her."

The others nodded, so Lucio undid the latch and slid the door open, wincing at the creak of poorly oiled hinges. The scene that greeted his eyes was nearly as bad as he had feared. Cressida lay on the pallet, her dress pulled around her tightly for warmth. Its meager covering was no match for the cool of the autumn night, though. Pulling off his coat, Lucio knelt at her side, shaking her shoulder gently.

"No, please," Cressida murmured, still mostly asleep.

"Wake up, Cressi," Lucio whispered, heart breaking as the implications of the soft plea tore at his heart. "It's Lucio. We're going to get you out of here."

Cressida's eyes flew open. Lucio covered her mouth with his hand as he waited for her gaze to clear and recognition to set in. "Take my coat," Lucio said when she calmed down. "We're leaving now."

"They'll come after me," Cressida said.

"They won't find you," Lucio promised. "We have a safe place for you to stay. Will you trust me?"

Cressida hesitated a moment longer before rising unsteadily to her feet. Lucio fastened his coat more securely around her and helped her out of the stall. "Take her and start back to the carriage," Lucio told the others. "I have one more thing I have to do."

"Lucio," Gabriel said warningly.

"They have the right to make their own choice," Lucio insisted. "I know we can't take them all with us, but I can open the doors and give them the choice to stay or to flee."

"You're taking a huge risk," Lord Stuart said. "If any of them recognize you and tell the handlers…."

"They won't recognize me," Lucio said, putting the mask back over his face.

"Take mine too," Gabriel said. "Put it over your hair and forehead so only your eyes are visible. I wish you'd reconsider, but I won't stop you. Hurry, though. We have an appointment."

"I know," Lucio said. "I won't be long. Cressida, go with the others. I'll join you in a few minutes."

Cressida shivered as Gabriel lifted her into his arms. "The ground is rough," he explained. "I don't want you to hurt your feet."

Lucio smiled despite himself, beginning the task of opening the other stall doors. To each woman inside, he said simply, "You have tonight. The choice is yours."

He didn't wait to see what any of them decided. His lover awaited and he did not want to tarry.

The last stall open, he raced back across the field and down the lanes toward the carriage, uncaring if anyone saw him now. They had Cressida. They simply had to escape.

"Go," he said to Wakefield as he jumped into the carriage.

Gabriel pulled him immediately into his arms.

"I'm safe," Lucio murmured, removing the masks. "I opened the doors to the stalls. The women can decide what to do after that."

"You know most of them will stay where they are out of fear of what will happen if they're caught," Cressida told him.

"I know," Lucio said, "but I couldn't save you and not try to help them at least a little. It wasn't right."

"Elijah will keep trying to help them as well," Lord Stuart promised. "He's seen the breeding barns now. You may be quite sure the conditions he witnessed will feature in every speech he or any of the other Caste Equality activists give for the next few months. He doesn't take injustice lightly."

"What happens now?" Cressida asked. "Where are you taking me?"

"Lady Bentley has agreed to take you in for the foreseeable future," Lord Stuart told her. "She is a distant enough connection of mine that no one will think to look at her house for you. They'll certainly search mine and Gabriel's. You'll be safe with Lady Bentley until a more permanent solution can be found."

"What solution is there?" Cressida asked. "You can't buy my contract now that I'm missing."

"They wouldn't let us buy your contract in the first place," Lucio said. "That's why we came tonight."

Cressida had no reply for that, curling into Lucio's arms. Lucio held her gently, letting her cry on his shoulder.

40

GABRIEL wished he still had his mask when Cressida began to cry softly and Lucio cradled her so tenderly against him. He didn't want anyone to see the jealousy eating him at the sight of his lover holding someone else. He looked away, unable to watch a moment longer. The carriage bumped over the roads, taking them closer and closer to safety with each passing moment. They could not reach Lady Bentley's house fast enough as far as Gabriel was concerned. They would leave Cressida there, and he could take Lucio home and erase all thought of anyone but him from his lover's mind.

When they arrived at Lady Bentley's, Wakefield pulled the carriage around to the back entrance where they wouldn't be noticed from the street. They had no reason to suspect anyone was watching yet, but they had all agreed to do everything they could to pass unnoticed. "Stay here a moment longer," Lord Stuart directed. "Let me go alert the lady to our arrival."

He descended from the coach and knocked on the door. Moments later, Lady Bentley appeared in the doorway. Lord Stuart gestured for them to come in, so Gabriel climbed out of the carriage. "Hand her down to me," he told Lucio. "I'll carry her inside."

To his relief, Cressida clung to him the same way she had clung to Lucio, making Gabriel hope she needed comfort as opposed to needing Lucio. He carried her across the garden and into Lady Bentley's parlor.

"Oh, you poor thing," Lady Bentley exclaimed when she got a good look at the condition of Cressida's clothes and hair. "This won't do at all. Can you walk on your own or should I have your rescuer carry you up to your new room?"

"I can walk," Cressida said. "They thought to spare my feet since I don't have shoes."

Gabriel set Cressida down, keeping a hand on her waist until he was sure she was steady on her feet. "Thank you," she said, giving him a smile nearly as radiant as when he had first seen her. In the light of the parlor, he could finally see the state she was in, and his stomach turned. Her face was gaunt, her hair dirty and limp, and he could see bruises on her arms beneath her alabaster skin.

"You're welcome," he said. "Let Lady Bentley spoil you. We'll come check on you in a week or two when the hubbub over your disappearance dies down and we aren't worried about exposing you by visiting."

"In the meantime, I'm sure to see you out in society," Lady Bentley said. "I can pass news either way then. Now, you boys go make whatever appearances you have planned so no one suspects your involvement. I'm going to get this young lady a bath and some food and a warm bed. She looks like she could use all three."

"Before we go, my Lady," Lucio said, "is there any way we can repay you for—?"

"Nonsense," Lady Bentley interrupted. "I will have a lovely companion to help me pass my days and a babe to dote on in a few months. And I'll have the pleasure of knowing I helped thwart the system that abused her. That's more than enough repayment for me."

"Thank you," Lucio said, kissing Lady Bentley's hand. "If there is ever anything—"

"Yes, yes," Lady Bentley said, shooing them toward the door. "Go on now. Let me get Cressida settled."

Gabriel drew Lucio outside. "Do we need to be seen in public tonight?" he asked Lord Stuart. "At a restaurant or a club or some event?"

"We're hardly dressed for society," Wakefield reminded them.

"No, I think we will stick with our original story of having spent the evening at my house celebrating the success of the party today," Lord Stuart said. "We don't want to complicate our story."

"Then if you'll drop us off at home, we'll leave you to the rest of your celebration," Gabriel said, needing to have Lucio to himself again. "If anyone comments on seeing your carriage at the workshop tonight, we will explain that you offered it to us at the end of our evening rather than making us take a hansom."

"A story I will gladly back up," Lord Stuart said. "Let's go. The sooner we drop you off, the sooner we can enjoy the rest of our evening, eh, Elijah?"

Wakefield made a rude noise under his breath as he retook his seat, waiting for the other three to enter the carriage. The drive through the quiet streets passed mostly in silence, Gabriel fighting with his jealousy the whole way home. He didn't want to fight with Lucio, but he needed to erase Cressida's touch completely from Lucio's mind and body. He only hoped his lover would be amenable to being ravished.

When they reached the workshop, they thanked Lord Stuart and Wakefield and walked inside. The moment they crossed the threshold, Gabriel pulled Lucio into his arms, backing him against the counter. "You are mine," he growled, his lips crashing down on Lucio's.

Lucio moaned beneath the onslaught, his hands twining around Gabriel's neck in such obvious surrender that Gabriel abandoned all control. He stripped Lucio where he stood, his hands flying over the slender body until his lover wore nothing but moonlight. Gabriel lifted him until he could perch on the edge of the counter and lean back on his hands for support. The second he had Lucio settled, Gabriel worked his way down Lucio's neck and chest, attacking his nipples with unprecedented fervor. Lucio cried out, but he arched his chest, pushing up into the caress, egging Gabriel on. The memory of Lucio's first letter flitted through his mind, and Gabriel set out to make it a reality, nipping and biting and licking and sucking at Lucio's chest until he was trembling and begging, but Gabriel continued mercilessly until, with a broken sob, Lucio found his release. Gabriel slid his lips lower after that, attacking Lucio's navel with the same ferocity, licking away the evidence of his pleasure and hinting at all manner of untold pleasures on another orifice.

Glancing up at Lucio's face, barely visible in the dark room, Gabriel smiled to himself. Whatever thoughts had occupied Lucio's mind in the carriage, only pleasure remained now, pleasure Gabriel had bestowed on him. Determined to wring even more pleasure from his lover's body, he licked lower, cleaning Lucio's cock and then moving on, spreading his thighs wide with work-scarred hands, such a startling contrast to Lucio's perfect, pale skin, to attend to his sac and beyond. Lucio whimpered at the stimulation, but Gabriel ignored him, adding his spit-slick fingers to the equation, working them deep inside Lucio's relaxed passage until he could lavish attention on the bundle of nerves that drove his lover wild. He played with that spot until Lucio was fully hard again, crying out with each press of Gabriel's fingers. Rising to his feet with a last lick to Lucio's cock, Gabriel popped open the button on his trousers and pulled Lucio off the counter, spinning him around and kicking his feet wide. Lucio bent forward obligingly, pushing his buttocks back against Gabriel's cock in flagrant invitation.

It was all Gabriel needed. He pushed inside the inferno of his lover's body, groaning as Lucio's muscle stretched easily to receive him.

"Harder."

That one word, the first Lucio had uttered since they came inside, shattered what little remained of Gabriel's control. He pounded into the willing passage, racing toward the precipice. Every tendon on his body stood out in stark relief as he strove for rapture, finding it with a hoarse cry when Lucio clenched around him tightly. He collapsed forward, belatedly reaching for Lucio's cock, not wanting to leave his lover unassuaged. To his surprise, he found a fresh coating of spend on Lucio's softening cock.

"I didn't hurt you, did I?" Gabriel asked, pulling out carefully and turning Lucio in his arms.

"Not at all," Lucio said, leaning up to kiss Gabriel. "In fact, you could take me upstairs and do it again if you'd like."

Gabriel groaned at the thought even as the remnants of his jealousy fled in the wake of Lucio's patent eagerness to be in his arms in their bed. "I'm not sure I can start again so soon, but I'll take you upstairs and lie in your arms until I can."

"As long as you let me hurry that moment along," Lucio said flirtatiously, his hand sliding through the hair on Gabriel's chest. "I haven't forgotten everything I learned about rousing a man."

"You haven't forgotten anything, beloved," Gabriel said with a laugh, steering Lucio toward the stairs, "as witnessed by the number of times we've made love this week."

NOT unexpectedly, guardians pounded on the workshop door mid-morning as Gabriel and Lucio were enjoying a late breakfast. Gabriel gestured for Lucio to keep his seat, going to the door. "May I help you?"

"Mister Gabriel Blackstone?" the guardian asked.

"Yes, I'm Blackstone."

"We have some questions for you regarding the disappearance of a companion last night," the guardian said.

"I don't know that I can help you," Gabriel said, opening the door so they could come in. "The only companion I've had any contact with in the past month has been Lucio, and he isn't missing."

"Where were you last night from nine to midnight?" a second guardian demanded.

"We were at Lord Ian Stuart's house from before lunchtime yesterday morning until perhaps eleven thirty last night, with the exception of an hour from about six to seven when we came home to change clothes," Gabriel said. "I didn't check the time when we arrived home last night."

"Why would an aristocrat spend that much time with a merchant?"

"Because he admires my inventions and is an investor in my workshop," Gabriel replied. "He threw a party yesterday to celebrate my newest invention, and it was such a success that he invited us to stay and celebrate after all the guests left."

"I assume you have the companion's contract?"

"It's upstairs. Lucio, would you go get it for the guardians?"

Lucio nodded and went upstairs, trying to keep his pace as even and relaxed as possible. He couldn't believe how coolly Gabriel was handling the interrogation. The guardians had barely even looked at Lucio, and he was already trembling with nerves.

He retrieved the contract from the drawer where Gabriel had tucked it away for safekeeping. He hated its very existence, hated being reminded that regardless of how Gabriel felt about him, their relationship was reduced to this in the eyes of the law. Until the laws changed, though, he would try to be thankful Gabriel's name was on the paper and not someone else's.

Not able to think of an excuse to linger, Lucio went back downstairs, deliberately giving the contract to Gabriel rather than directly to the guardians.

"Here's the contract you wanted to see," Gabriel said, offering it to the guardians.

"How does a merchant in a place like this afford a companion?" the first guardian sneered.

"By choosing to spend my money on his contract rather than on luxuries for my home," Gabriel said.

"By being a brilliant inventor," Lucio said, resenting the slur to Gabriel's abilities. "He's invented a flying chair. We sold five of them yesterday at Lord Stuart's party alone. And what does any of this have to do with a missing companion?"

"The companion in question was a friend of yours when you still lived in the pleasure palace," the guardian replied. "We thought perhaps you might know what happened to her."

"I had many friends," Lucio replied. "I haven't seen any of them since Gabriel purchased my contract."

"Interesting that you don't say since Lord Stuart purchased your contract," the guardian commented. "Wasn't he the one who actually took you from the pleasure palace?"

"He was," Lucio replied, "but only because the handlers wouldn't sell my contract to Gabriel in the first place. Gabriel gave Lord Stuart the money. Again, what does this have to do with the missing companion?"

"When was the last time you saw the companion called Cressida?" the guardian asked.

"Last Saturday," Lucio said. "We were both in the breeding barn, and the handlers sent me to service her."

"What about you, Blackstone? When was the last time you saw her?"

"It's been at least a month," Gabriel said. "She came to tell me Lucio had been sent to the breeding barns and that I wouldn't be able to buy his time while he was there. I haven't seen her since."

"Then you won't mind if we look around," the guardian said.

"Feel free," Gabriel said with a wave of his hand. "It's a bit of a mess since we're an active workshop, but you're welcome to search the place. Just don't break anything."

"Do you work here alone?" one of the guardians asked as the other one began his search.

"No, I have two assistants," Gabriel replied. "Caleb Deahl and Andrew Lambert. They aren't here today because it's Sunday."

"Gabriel? Lucio?"

"Unless they drop in for a visit," Gabriel said with a rueful smile. "In the kitchen, Caleb."

Caleb and Andrew walked through the door into the kitchen. "We thought we'd come discuss—" He broke off at the sight of the guardian. "What's going on?"

"Cressida is apparently missing," Gabriel said. "The guardians hoped we could shed some light on her disappearance."

"Missing?" Andrew exclaimed. "What happened?"

"The guardians haven't seen fit to tell us," Gabriel said, "only to ask questions about when we last saw her and what we were doing yesterday."

"You were at Lord Stuart's all day yesterday," Caleb said. "I took the flying chair over in the morning and you met me there."

"And we stopped by to see you when we came home to change before going back to Lord Stuart's for the rest of the evening," Gabriel agreed.

"Please, sir," Caleb said, "will you tell us what happened?"

"You know the woman in question?" the guardian asked.

"Of course," Caleb replied. "She was a frequent visitor here at the workshop until about a month ago. She bought several of our inventions and would come sometimes with Lucio as well."

"She's not here," the second guardian declared, coming back into the kitchen. "I've searched the entire place."

"I think we should accompany these two men home," the first guardian said. "It seems they were also acquainted with the missing woman."

"What?" Caleb said. "Why?"

"Because someone stole her from the breeding barns last night and the handlers want her back," the guardian answered. "You knew her and seem to care what happened to her. You might have some part in her disappearance."

"That's ridiculous!" Caleb protested.

"Caleb," Andrew said soothingly, "we don't have anything to hide. We haven't seen her since the last time she came to the workshop. There's no harm in letting them search. They'll do so politely and then they'll leave us alone because we cooperated with them. We don't need to make a scene."

"Fine," Caleb said, "but it's ridiculous for them to spend time searching our house when they could be out searching for Cressida. She's pregnant, damn it. She needs somewhere safe and warm."

Lucio stifled a snort at Caleb's comment. The breeding barn hardly qualified as either as far as he was concerned. Fortunately she would have both of those things at Lady Bentley's house.

"Don't leave town, Blackstone," the guardian said as they followed Caleb and Andrew out to the street. "We may have more questions for you."

"I have no plans to travel at the moment," Gabriel replied. "I have too much work to do if I'm to fill the contracts I made yesterday."

The guardian glared at them one last time before leaving. The moment the door closed behind them, Lucio threw himself into Gabriel's arms. "I was so frightened I would say something wrong," he said, clinging to Gabriel's broad shoulders.

Gabriel stroked Lucio's hair gently. "You did fine. We did fine. They came and asked their questions. They searched the house. They didn't find anything. They may come back another time or two to see if they can shake anything else out of us, but Cressida isn't here and no one else saw us at the breeding barn. They can't prove anything and they can't arrest us without proof. It will be fine."

"I hope you're right," Lucio said. "They must have talked to Lord Stuart already if they knew you owned my contract instead of him."

"And I'm sure Lord Stuart told them very much the same thing we did," Gabriel said reassuringly. "We had the party. We left and came back. We stayed until after eleven, and then we came home. Cressida isn't at his house either so they didn't find anything if they dared to search. Come downstairs and let's start making a list of supplies we need to buy for the flying chairs. The more normally we act, the better in case anyone is watching still."

"Do you think they are?" Lucio asked nervously.

"Not really," Gabriel said, "but we really do need to do an inventory, and it will help take your mind off it. If we get everything done, maybe we can go back out to Nicholasville this afternoon."

"The guardian said not to leave town," Lucio reminded Gabriel.

"That isn't leaving town. That's going for a drive in the country," Gabriel said. "We'll be back this evening, and if they have a problem with it, maybe they'll spend time searching in Nicholasville rather than among Lord Stuart's connections."

SEVERAL hours later, about the time they finished the inventory, they heard a knock on the door again. "Relax," Gabriel said, seeing Lucio tense up immediately. "It could as easily be Caleb and Andrew as it could be the guardians. I locked the door before we came down here since there would be no one upstairs to mind the shop."

Lucio nodded and followed Gabriel upstairs to see who else had come to disturb their quiet Sunday. Wakefield stood at the door.

Gabriel smiled when he saw his friend. "Good to see you, Wakefield," he said, opening the door and inviting his fellow activist inside. "How are you today?"

"Doing well, all things considered," Wakefield said. "Have the guardians visited already?"

"A few hours ago," Gabriel said. "I assume you had a visit from them as well?"

"Roused us from our beds this morning," Wakefield complained. "No care at all for the fact that Lord Stuart is a gentleman, and an older one at that."

Both Gabriel and Lucio laughed at that. "He didn't seem older when I was trying to keep up with him last night," Gabriel said.

"And I rather suspect he didn't seem older when he was working off the adrenaline last night, either," Lucio joked. "I've spent time in his bed. I know what he's capable of."

Wakefield flushed a brilliant shade of red, only adding to Lucio's laughter. Gabriel found it harder to laugh, though. He knew he would have to get used to reminders of Lucio's past, but it was always a shock to hear Lucio speak so casually about it, particularly to the current lover of one of his former guests. "They obviously didn't find anything."

"Of course not," Wakefield said. "What was there to find? Lord Stuart has no companions under his roof, only a guardian and political activist."

"I'm sure that gave them pause," Gabriel said, imagining the guardians' reactions to finding Wakefield at Lord Stuart's that early in the morning.

"Yes," Wakefield said, "but it may have helped a little. I knew one of them from my days of training. I wouldn't say we were friends, but he recognized me and the questioning took on a slightly kinder tone after that. They eventually left us in peace."

"With orders not to leave town?" Gabriel joked.

"No," Wakefield said. "They didn't say anything like that to us. Did they tell you that?"

"Yes," Gabriel said. "They told us to stay available in case they had more questions. I fully expect to see them again a few more times before they're convinced we didn't have anything to do with it."

Wakefield scowled. "Yet another example of discrimination. Lord Stuart is a better suspect than either of you because he inquired about Cressida's contract, yet they made no attempt to keep him available after today. You, on the other hand, are fairly unlikely suspects except in Lucio's friendship with Cressida, and yet you were ordered not to leave town. Laws have to change."

"They will," Gabriel said. "It will take time and work, but the laws will change."

41

"LUCIO, have you seen Gabriel?" Caleb asked, coming back in to the workshop with a load of materials.

"No, he went to a Caste Equality rally. He said he'd be back in time for dinner," Lucio replied. "Why? What do you need?"

"I don't need anything, but there was a lot of commotion toward Mayfair Place," Caleb said. "I asked what was going on, and someone said the guardians had arrested a bunch of Caste Equality protestors. I was hoping Gabriel was here and not there."

"Arrested?" Lucio said, heart pounding in his chest. "What do we do? We have to get him out."

"I don't know if there's anything we can do," Caleb replied. "None of us has the clout to demand his release."

"Lord Stuart might," Lucio suggested. "He's helped us before."

"We can ask," Caleb said, "but you realize that if Gabriel was arrested, Wakefield probably was too. If Lord Stuart helps anyone, it will be his own lover, not yours."

"What about the shop?" Lucio said, knowing he was grasping at straws but needing some hope at least. "He needs Gabriel to run the shop so he gets paid."

"He's wealthy enough that he wouldn't notice even if he never saw a single piece of gold from us," Caleb reminded Lucio. "I'm not saying you shouldn't ask. I'm only saying you shouldn't get your hopes up too high."

"I should go change so I'm dressed for visiting," Lucio said, moving mechanically as he fell back on his training where appearances were concerned.

"Forget that," Caleb said, grabbing Lucio's shoulders and pushing him toward the door. "Lord Stuart won't care, and if he's worried about Wakefield, too, he probably won't even notice what you're wearing."

"Come with me," Lucio begged, clinging to Caleb's hand. "If something truly bad has happened...."

"Gabriel's fine," Caleb assured him. "He knows better than to fight the guardians. If they tried to arrest him, he went with them calmly so he wouldn't be injured. He'll be fine. It's a matter now of finding out where he was taken and what the sentence is, and then seeing if we can get it shortened or cancelled somehow. Let me tell Andrew what happened and I'll come with you. Go find a cab."

Lucio walked out to the street, his whole body stiff as he tried to hold himself together. He had relaxed in the past two weeks. The guardians had returned once more after their initial visit, but when they had still found no trace of Cressida, they had seemingly given up. Since then, he and Gabriel had started work on the heating system for the water, running pipes from the well to their bathtub. Gabriel had promised they would install the tank on Sunday so they would have hot water on demand. Under Gabriel's careful tutelage and Caleb's and Andrew's gruff instructions, he had started to feel like he was contributing to the workshop. Everything had been going as well as he had dreamed possible. And now this.

"Stop brooding," Caleb scolded, coming outside. "You'll make yourself sick and then Gabriel will have my head for worrying you. Pull it together, and let's see what Lord Stuart has to say."

Lucio did as Caleb said, pushing down the panic that threatened to strangle him. He could panic tonight alone in bed if that eventually transpired. Until then, he had to be strong and help Gabriel.

They reached Lord Stuart's home in time to meet him leaving. "I suppose you've heard the news," Lord Stuart said without preamble.

"We were hoping you could help," Lucio said.

"Do you know for certain he was arrested?"

"Not for certain," Caleb said, "but he went to the rally and hasn't returned."

Lord Stuart nodded, gesturing for them to join him in his carriage. The horse-drawn one this time, Lucio noted. All the better to remind the guardians of his status. "I don't know what I'll be able to do, for Elijah or for Blackstone, but I should be able to get information at least."

"This is because of what happened a couple of weeks ago, isn't it?" Lucio said softly. "With Cressida."

"That and the fact that the Caste Equality movement has increased their rhetoric on the situation of all companions," Lord Stuart agreed. "It was a risk the movement decided to take when they chose to add the details of her situation to their platform. It draws attention their way, both positive and negative. More people are attending the rallies than ever before, but it also casts suspicion on them in regard to Cressida's disappearance."

"Did they have anything to do with her disappearance?" Caleb asked suddenly. "Gabriel said Lucio had given them information about his situation and hers before he left, but it seems awfully convenient that they wouldn't start talking about her until she was out of the hands of the handlers."

"No," Lord Stuart said, "the Caste Equality movement had no knowledge of Cressida's disappearance until after the fact, and you'll notice if you listen to their speeches that they do not use her name nor make any reference to the fact that she is no longer trapped in the breeding barn because while she escaped, others were not so lucky."

Caleb's eyes narrowed. "You know more than you're telling me."

"It isn't my story to tell," Lord Stuart demurred, his eyes flickering toward Lucio momentarily.

"Lucio?"

Lucio wanted to tell Caleb the truth but they had said repeatedly that the fewer people who knew, the better. Deciding it didn't matter anymore now that the guardians had focused on the Caste Equality movement, he nodded. "She's safe with a former guest of mine," Lucio said. "I couldn't leave her there, but if you didn't know, you wouldn't have to lie to the guardians."

"You know we would have lied for her—for you—in a heartbeat."

"I know," Lucio said, "but Gabriel said—"

"Wait! Gabriel was involved too?"

"And Wakefield and myself," Lord Stuart confirmed. "And Lucio was correct that we felt it safer not to let anyone outside of the four of us know what we had planned. Your house was searched, too, I understand. As it was, the guardians saw nothing but confusion and dismay on your face at hearing that a woman you hold in some esteem had disappeared mysteriously. If you had known, you might have given away some hint, if only by not being as surprised as you should have been."

"So all this time, we've been worried for nothing?" Caleb demanded.

"Not for nothing," Lucio said with a firm shake of his head, glad for something to keep his mind off Gabriel for the time being. "We managed to steal her, but until the laws are changed to allow companions to leave that profession and enter some other, she remains in danger. If the guardians or the handlers find her, she will be sent back to the pleasure palace, if she isn't killed for running away as an example to discourage other companions from contemplating that escape."

"But she's safe where she is?" Caleb asked.

"She is," Lord Stuart assured them. "Lady Bentley is quite taken with her. She's introduced her to the servants as a cousin from the country who has come to stay with her during her confinement. A cousin who happens to have a mysterious skin ailment that disfigures her hands so she wears gloves at all times, even when she sleeps."

"Would it be possible, not right away, necessarily, for Andrew and me to see her?" Caleb asked. "We do hold her in very high esteem and would like to tell her that. We didn't dare before."

Lucio smiled. "She knows. Perhaps not the full extent of it, but she didn't come back to the workshop all those times simply to keep me company. As for when you can see her, I think it's best to let Lord Stuart and Lady Bentley make that decision."

"I will discuss it with her," Lord Stuart promised, "but we've arrived now. We have other, more pressing issues to concern us."

"Would it be acceptable for us to come in with you?" Lucio asked.

"I think the more people who express outrage over the arrests at a peaceful rally, the better," Lord Stuart said. "However, I would suggest you let me ask the actual questions."

Lucio and Caleb both nodded their agreement and followed Lord Stuart into the station where the city guardians worked. He removed his top hat, tucking it under his arm. "I will speak with the chief guardian," he declared.

"And who are you to make that kind of demand?" the guardian at the desk drawled.

Lord Stuart slammed his hands down on the desk, the first outward sign Lucio had seen of his distress over the situation. "Lord Ian Stuart and friends. Now you can announce us to the chief guardian or I can make a scene that will embarrass your entire caste for months."

"I'll see if Mister Campbell is available," the guardian said, rising immediately and disappearing deeper into the building. He reappeared a moment later. "Mister Campbell will see you now."

"I thought he would," Lord Stuart replied. "Come, gentlemen, let's see what kind of answers the chief guardian has for us."

They were shown into a finely appointed office, far nicer than anything Lucio had seen outside an aristocrat's house. "Lord Stuart and...."

"Friends," Lord Stuart said.

"And friends. What can I do for you today?"

"There seem to have been some arrests today," Lord Stuart observed.

"Ah, yes, the Caste Equality movement rabble-rousers," Mister Campbell agreed. "We arrested close to two hundred of them today."

"On what charges?" Lord Stuart demanded.

"Disturbing the peace, civil disobedience, slander."

"Slander?" Lord Stuart repeated.

"They accused the handlers of the Mayfair Place pleasure palace of various heinous, unfounded things."

"Unfounded?" Lucio spat. "Every word they say about the conditions we live in is true."

Mister Campbell turned his attention to Lucio. "And what is a companion doing away from the pleasure palace unsupervised?"

"I would hardly call him unsupervised," Lord Stuart said, "since he is standing right here, but he no longer lives in the pleasure palace, so that is none of your concern. I will see the names of those you arrested now, thank you."

"This is highly unusual!"

"So is arresting two hundred people at a peaceful demonstration," Lord Stuart reminded him. "And don't tell me it wasn't peaceful. We drove past Mayfair Place on the way here and there was no sign of any damage or violence anywhere on the square. The list of names?"

Mister Campbell scowled but drew a sheaf of papers from his desk. Lord Stuart took them and handed some to Lucio and some to Caleb. All three of them searched the lists, looking for either of the two names that mattered to them.

"Here's Gabriel," Caleb said softly after a few minutes.

Lucio bit back a cry, forcing himself to concentrate on the search for Wakefield's name. He found it a few moments later. "Here's Mister Wakefield."

Lord Stuart took both pages. "Inciting violence? I'll have you know I helped Mister Wakefield prepare his speech," he told Campbell coldly. "The only incitement was to vote for Mister Ashbrook in the election next month. You will drop that charge immediately."

"I have witnesses who—"

"Your witnesses be damned!" Lord Stuart roared. "You will drop that charge right now and tell me the sentence for this civil disobedience you claim he and Blackstone committed."

"A month in prison," Campbell said, cowering away from Lord Stuart's imposing presence.

Lord Stuart glared. "That is far too long for organizing a simple rally."

"It's standard procedure, my Lord," Campbell assured them. "I'm already breaking protocol by dropping the inciting violence charge."

"It is unacceptable," Lord Stuart repeated. "We will return with my solicitor and see what arrangements can be made. Do not think you will get away with this."

Without waiting for Campbell's reply, Lord Stuart turned on his heel and swept out of the room, Lucio and Caleb trailing behind him. Lucio wanted to ask what it all meant, besides Gabriel spending a month in prison, but Lord Stuart's expression dissuaded him. They had few enough benefactors as it was. He certainly didn't want to alienate Lord Stuart.

"Go home," Lord Stuart told Lucio and Caleb when they exited the building. "Do what you would do if this hadn't happened. I will do what I can, but at the worst, they will spend a month in prison. Blackstone will need a business to come back to. Do not disappoint him."

"We won't," Caleb said. Lucio looked at him gratefully, not sure he could have mustered the ability to speak without breaking into tears or begging for assistance that Lord Stuart could not give. Caleb took his elbow, steering him toward the horseless cabs that lined the square. Lucio went along placidly, too upset to do anything else.

When they were alone in the cab, Caleb turned to Lucio. "When we get back to the workshop, you have an hour to go upstairs and do whatever you need to do. Cry, scream, hit something, whatever it is. At the end of that hour, you're going to come back downstairs and help us figure out how to fulfill Gabriel's obligations for the next month. You're his partner now, which means you can make decisions in his stead."

"I couldn't," Lucio protested.

"You'll have to," Caleb said. "Andrew and I can't. We're his assistants. Our word doesn't have any weight where contracts are concerned."

"I'm a companion!" Lucio said. "I don't have even the weight of another merchant."

"You have Gabriel's faith in you," Caleb insisted. "We'll talk about it an hour after we get home. Andrew and I can do the work. That isn't the issue. You have to run the business."

"I don't know anything about business," Lucio said.

"But you know quite a lot about aristocrats," Caleb reminded him. "That will be what gets us through the next month if Lord Stuart can't help us. If you don't, no one will."

Lucio wanted to keep arguing, but he didn't know what else to say. He had already seen enough in the weeks he had been at the workshop to know that Caleb was right. He and Andrew were outstanding craftsmen, but they followed Gabriel's orders. Lucio had to pull it together and find a way to keep the business running until Gabriel got back. It didn't matter if he made the same decisions Gabriel would have made. It only mattered that he made sound decisions that kept the workshop stable and its reputation in place. He would gladly apologize to Gabriel for any mistakes when his lover returned to him. He simply had to make sure Gabriel had a home and a business to return to.

"I'll do it," he said to Caleb. "I may make a regular mess of it, but I'll do my best until Gabriel can come home and tell me how to do it right."

"You'll do fine," Caleb assured him as the cab pulled up in front of the workshop.

"Get Andrew and come join me in the kitchen," Lucio said. "I will have questions for which Gabriel would already know the answers. You and Andrew will have to provide them for me since he isn't here."

42

ANDREW knocked tentatively on the door to the palatial townhome. "This is the right address, isn't it?" he murmured to Caleb.

"This is the address Lucio gave us," Caleb whispered back as they waited for someone to answer.

A butler opened the door a few moments later, his gaze raking them from head to toe. "May I help you?"

"Begging your pardon, sir," Andrew said, "but we're friends of Lady Bentley's cousin. We hadn't heard any news from her in awhile and we wanted to see how she was doing."

"The city being new to her and all," Caleb added.

The butler opened the door enough that they could step inside. "Wait here while I speak with Lady Bentley," the butler ordered. "She is most protective of her cousin."

Caleb and Andrew waited as ordered. "I'm afraid to step on the rug for fear I'll get who knows what on it," Andrew whispered, looking down at his boots. "We don't belong here."

"We've come too far to back out now," Caleb insisted. "We'll see Lady Bentley, hopefully see Cressida, and then we can decide if we come back another time."

"Lady Bentley will see you," the butler said, returning to the hallway. "Your names, so I can announce you?"

"Caleb Deahl and Andrew Lambert," Caleb provided quickly.

"Misters Deahl and Lambert," the butler announced, opening the door so Caleb and Andrew could go inside.

They walked forward, reaching the threshold when the butler murmured, "Your hats."

Flushing beneath their sun-darkened skin, both men pulled their hats from their heads, standing awkwardly just inside the door as it closed behind them.

"My Lady," Caleb said with a slight bow, Andrew following suit awkwardly.

"So you are friends of my cousin, I hear," Lady Bentley said from her place on the chaise longue where she reclined comfortably. "Where did you meet her?"

Andrew looked at Caleb who nodded. "We met her through a mutual friend," Andrew explained. "At the workshop where we work."

"She has mentioned a workshop to me," Lady Bentley said. "She seemed fond of the time she spent there."

"She came with a friend of hers. He's now the partner of our employer," Caleb said eagerly. "Perhaps you've heard of him."

"No names," Lady Bentley ordered before Caleb could continue. "You must remember the circumstances under which my cousin came to be here."

"Yes, my Lady," Caleb said, shamefaced. "We'd never do anything that might harm her. We just wanted news of her. The last we had, well, you understand it wasn't good."

"I understand," Lady Bentley said. "I saw the state she was in when she arrived, much to my dismay. You may rest assured she is in good health and thriving now that she has joined me here in town. The only problem she cannot seem to overcome is the rash on her hands that forces her to wear gloves all the time, even when she sleeps."

"It is a curse," Andrew agreed, glancing down at the tattoo on his hand. "We can only hope the cure is not too far in the making."

"Indeed," Lady Bentley said. "So you have her news now. Was that all?"

"Please, my Lady," Caleb said, "could we see her? You needn't leave us alone with her, but it would do much to reassure us if we could see her smile again and know she has set aside the cares that weighed on her the last time we met."

"You are better at this than I expected," Lady Bentley said, rising from her couch. "Wait here a moment. I will have the butler summon Margaret."

Caleb and Andrew exchanged glances, but neither made any move to sit.

Lady Bentley returned shortly. "Please, sit," she instructed.

"Oh, we couldn't, my Lady," Andrew protested. "We're covered in dust and—"

"Sit," Lady Bentley repeated. "You are guests in my home, and I will not have you standing around like servants. The cushions can be cleaned if necessary."

Caleb and Andrew moved to the chairs on either side of Lady Bentley's couch, perching on the edges nervously. A few moments later, Cressida appeared in the doorway. "Miss Margaret Bentley," the butler announced.

Caleb and Andrew bounced to their feet immediately, though neither of them moved closer to Cressida.

She had no such hesitation, crossing the room swiftly to kiss each of them on the cheek. "Oh, I am so glad you came. I have been pining for news from home. Do you have some to give me?"

Caleb looked sideways at Lady Bentley.

"It's all right," Cressida assured them. "We maintain appearances in front of the staff, but Lady Bentley knows all there is to know about my past."

"Perhaps not all," Lady Bentley commented, "since I didn't know to expect your gentlemen callers today, but enough that you may speak freely and not worry I shall be shocked."

"Tell me the news," Cressida insisted. "How are Lucio and Gabriel?"

"Lucio is as well as can be expected," Andrew replied.

"What does that mean?" Cressida demanded. "He should be deliriously happy."

"He was until Gabriel was arrested two weeks ago," Caleb explained.

"Arrested? Why?"

"For participating in a Caste Equality rally," Caleb replied. "He will be home in two more weeks, and Lucio will be deliriously happy once more."

"Did you know about this?" Cressida asked Lady Bentley.

"I knew about the rally and the arrests," Lady Bentley replied. "I didn't know about your friend, only about Lord Stuart's lover, Mister Wakefield."

"What about you?" Andrew interrupted. "You look so different."

"Lady Bentley thought it best to change my appearance as much as possible," Cressida explained, reaching up to touch her now-reddish hair.

No one mentioned the slightly looser cut of her dress to hide the early stages of her pregnancy. "With short hair and a different color, I don't fit the description the handlers are circulating so the servants here don't become suspicious of me. Maybe someday I'll be able to let it grow back dark again, but this is a far better alternative than being caught and returned to the breeding barns or worse."

"You still look beautiful," Caleb said. "A tribute to your cousin and the pride of any man lucky enough to have you on his arm."

Cressida laughed. "You are as kind as ever. I have missed you both." She looked at Lady Bentley. "I know I can't call on them, but would it be permissible for them to call on me from time to time?"

Lady Bentley looked at Caleb and Andrew appraisingly. "No more than once a week, and always in the morning when we're less likely to have other guests. We cannot afford to rouse any suspicions, but yes, they may call again."

Cressida looked back at Caleb and Andrew and smiled. "It means so much to have friends," she said, squeezing each of their hands in turn. Caleb and Andrew blushed again, eyes looking anywhere but at Cressida, but their smiles never wavered.

"CALEB, will you have that heater finished by this afternoon?" Lucio asked, looking at the calendar he had hung on the wall of the workshop.

"I have to do a test on it, and then it should be ready," Caleb said.

"Good," Lucio replied with a nod. "Andrew, what's the status of Lord Palmer's flying chair?"

"I've got the engine seated," Andrew told him. "All I have to do is put on the casing over the engine and forge the cockpit closed."

"Very good," Lucio said. "It will be done ahead of schedule, it looks like. I'm off to meet with Lady Bicksley about a heater and possibly a music box. I'll be back in time for luncheon, I hope, but don't wait for me if you're hungry before then. Sometimes our clients invite me to stay for a meal. I think I'm even more of a conversation piece now than I was when I was working as a companion."

"It's a good thing for us," Caleb said. "We've never been so busy. Without you here to keep track of everything, we'd have run the business into the ground in no time."

"You wouldn't have," Lucio said. "You would have taken fewer commissions and worked on familiar projects until Gabriel got out of prison. All I did was help things along a bit. Now, I'd best be on my way. I don't want to keep Lady Bicksley waiting."

Lucio walked into the showroom of the workshop, pausing to brush some dust off the back of the couch he had insisted they buy so their customers would have a place to sit. He had organized the shelves as well, setting out a collection of inventions, large and small, designed to catch the attention of a visiting aristocrat. He called on many of them as well, but he always made sure they came by the workshop to see what the finished product would look like before taking a commission. It had earned them several extra commissions, customers intending to buy one item who looked at the display and ordered something else as well. He wanted to buy a table and a tea set so he could offer tea to the customers while they talked or browsed or waited their turn, but that would have to wait until a few more commissions were finished and paid in full. He didn't want to disappoint Gabriel upon his lover's return by having spent unwisely.

Glancing at his watch—Gabriel's watch, really, but Lucio had taken to wearing it over the past month—Lucio realized he was about to be late. Hurrying toward the door, he reached for the handle as the door opened. Stifling a sigh at having to deal with a customer before he left for Lady Bicksley's, Lucio put on his best smile, his eyes widening when he realized it wasn't a customer, but Gabriel come home a few days early.

"I've missed you!" Lucio exclaimed, throwing himself into Gabriel's arms. He could smell the stink of prison on his lover, but he ignored it. He was too happy to have Gabriel home again. "Come in the other room. Caleb and Andrew will want to see you."

"Not yet," Gabriel said, his voice gravelly. "Let me hold you a little longer first."

Lucio relaxed into Gabriel's embrace, cradling the gaunt body against his. The thinness worried him, but it could be remedied with time and good food. For now, he simply reveled in the feeling of having Gabriel's arms around him again. He had forced himself to think positively and to work toward this day, but alone at night in bed, it had been hard sometimes to keep that focus. Now, with Gabriel home again, it was all worth it because he had concrete success to show his lover. "Did they not feed you in prison?"

"Not much and nothing palatable," Gabriel replied. "I'll be glad for some real cooking again."

"There's rabbit stew left over from last night," Lucio offered. "I can reheat it for you if you want. Or I can make eggs—I learned that much while you were gone—and we have some bacon."

"Eggs would be good," Gabriel said, lifting his head from the crook of Lucio's shoulder. "After eating so little the past month, I probably shouldn't eat too much now. I don't want to make myself sick."

"Here," Lucio said, leading Gabriel to the couch. "Sit here for a moment. I was expected at Lady Bicksley's to discuss a commission, but I will send her a note begging off and asking to reschedule. As soon as that's sent off, we'll get some food in you, and then you can take a bath and sleep in our bed again."

"Couch?" Gabriel said, looking around the workshop. "What happened here?"

"Sit," Lucio said. "I promise to tell you everything as soon as I write this note."

Gabriel took a seat on the couch, looking around the workshop in bemusement as Lucio drew a sheet of paper from the drawer behind the counter and wrote a short note to Lady Bicksley, citing a family emergency and begging her indulgence to reschedule their meeting. Signing it with a flourish, Lucio stopped long enough to kiss Gabriel quickly before stepping out into the street and hailing one of the urchins who had taken to haunting the neighborhood now that the aristocrats came more frequently. Lucio had found most of them would run errands for him for a coin or two. Today was no exception, the lad running off in his hurry to deliver the message and earn his pay.

"Now," Lucio said, coming back inside, "I imagine you have questions."

"A few," Gabriel said with a shake of his head. "I barely recognize my own workshop."

"Only this room," Lucio promised. "I didn't change anything else, but we had people coming to browse and to shop, and I couldn't help all of them at once, and they had nowhere to wait other than a rickety chair covered in dust. So I found a couch for a reasonable price and had it delivered. Now that we have a place for them to sit, I've started asking our customers to come here to finalize any contracts. More times than not, they've bought something else while they're here from looking around at what we have to offer."

"I don't understand," Gabriel said with a shake of his head. "You've been running the business?"

"Someone had to," Lucio said. "Caleb and Andrew are great with the inventions, but they don't have the time, the patience, or the manners to deal with aristocrats all day, and I can't do their job either. It seemed like a reasonable way to keep the business earning money while you were gone."

"I'm amazed," Gabriel said. "How many commissions have you sold?"

"We'd have to look at the calendar," Lucio replied. "I don't try to keep track in my head. Everything is on the schedule."

"I don't recognize my own business anymore," Gabriel said with a laugh. "You are amazing! Show me the calendar. Show me everything!"

"As you eat," Lucio said firmly. "You're too thin. I want my Gabriel back again."

"All right," Gabriel said. "Let's go. But I want to hear everything."

Lucio led Gabriel into the back room of the workshop where Caleb and Andrew worked diligently. "Back alre—Gabriel!"

Lucio stepped to the side, watching with a smile as the friends reunited. Deciding to give them a moment alone, he slipped into the kitchen, loosening his cravat and removing his jacket so he could make Gabriel's breakfast. He hadn't mastered much in the kitchen despite Caleb's best attempts to teach him, but he had learned to fry up eggs without burning them. Fortunately, Caleb and Andrew had been willing to stay for dinner most nights and make sure he had an edible meal.

Gabriel came through the door a few minutes later as Lucio was serving the eggs. "Thank you."

"You're welcome," Lucio said. "It's just a few eggs."

"No," Gabriel insisted, "thank you for everything you've done for the workshop. Caleb and Andrew couldn't sing your praises highly enough. To hear them tell it, you singlehandedly rescued the workshop from ruin."

"Hardly," Lucio said, handing Gabriel his breakfast and taking a seat across from him at the table. Gabriel dug in immediately, making Lucio realize how hungry he really was. "I learned a bit about organization in the pleasure palace. I simply applied that to the workshop. Caleb or Andrew would tell me how long it would take to make the different inventions, and I would schedule them accordingly."

"And I hope you'll keep doing that now that I'm home," Gabriel said between bites. "The showroom, the calendar, the number of sales on there... I couldn't have done any better. I probably wouldn't have done nearly as well."

"Of course I'll keep doing whatever you need me to do," Lucio promised. "That will free you up to improve upon our current offerings or add to it with new inventions."

"You have it all planned out, don't you?"

Lucio flushed, feeling suddenly timid. He had grown accustomed to making decisions without consulting anyone over the past month because Caleb and Andrew never had an opinion and so he had stopped asking. "Is that acceptable?"

"It's far more than acceptable! It's perfect," Gabriel exclaimed. "I worried about how you would fit in around here. Not on a personal level, but how you would find your feet in the workshop when you didn't have any of the training that Caleb, Andrew, and I have. You've found the answer without me. As long as you know what the machines do once they're finished, you can sell them, schedule our production, and all the rest, something none of us are particularly good at."

Lucio smiled shyly. "I'm glad. I worried sometimes while you were gone that you'd resent the changes I was making."

Gabriel rose from his chair and pulled Lucio around the table and back into his arms. "If you have a thought for an improvement, make it happen," Gabriel said. "Caleb and Andrew showed me the calendar, what we've produced over the past month and what we have on order. Whatever you did, keep doing it. Whatever you think will make it better, do it. I'll be glad to discuss anything with you that you want to discuss, but you don't need my approval. You have it, unconditionally. You've proven yourself in countless ways."

Lucio relaxed finally for the first time in a month, knowing his decisions had been good ones. "If you're done eating, you should take a bath," he said, changing the subject. "Caleb hooked up the heater to the water tank."

"Only if you come upstairs with me," Gabriel said. "We've been apart too long. I don't want to let you out of my sight."

"Let me tell Caleb and Andrew to mind the shop and I'll join you," Lucio said. "Go on upstairs and start drawing the bath."

Gabriel kissed Lucio gently and did as the companion said, leaving Lucio alone for a moment. Lucio took a deep breath and let it out slowly, then another one.

Gabriel approved.

He hadn't realized how worried he had been about his lover's reaction until it was over. Pushing open the door enough to stick his head through, he told Caleb and Andrew where he was going. They shooed him back into the kitchen. Smiling at how fortunate he was to have such good friends, Lucio climbed the stairs in time to see Gabriel climb naked into the tub. His skin had gone pale from a month with no exposure to the sun, and he had bruises in places, but for the most part, he seemed sound. Lucio pulled his shirt and trousers off, leaving only his undergarments in place as he crossed to the tub. "Are you warm enough?" he asked. "I turned the heater off up here after I got dressed this morning."

"I'm fine," Gabriel said. "The hot water feels wonderful."

"Let's see if I can make you feel even more wonderful," Lucio purred. Before meeting Gabriel, a month with no sex would have been a dream come true, but in the short time they had been together, he had become addicted to making love. A month without that had been pure torture.

Gabriel looked at him askance. "Was there something you wanted?" he teased.

"Yes," Lucio said, his hand diving beneath the water in search of Gabriel's cock. "You inside me, as soon as you're clean. I washed the sheets two days ago. It wouldn't do to get all this dirt all over them."

"We'll get other things all over them instead?" Gabriel joked.

"Oh, I hope so," Lucio said fervently, stroking Gabriel's shaft until it hardened fully in his hand. "I dearly hope so."

Gabriel groaned, resting his head against the lip of the tub. "If you do much of that, I won't make it until we get to bed."

Lucio grinned and stroked a few more times. "I could always climb in there with you."

Gabriel shook his head. "As nice as that would be, I spent the entire month I was in prison dreaming of lying in bed with you once more. Hand me the rag so I can get clean."

"I'll do no such thing," Lucio said, picking up the washrag and soaping it up. "You aren't the only one who's spent the past month dreaming."

Gabriel relaxed back against the tub, his arms on either side so his entire body was open to Lucio's touch. Lucio took advantage of the position, running the rag and his hands over every inch of skin he could reach, wiping away dirt, soothing small hurts, and doing everything he could to make Gabriel feel good again after the month in prison. If his lover's quickened breathing and the state of his erection were any indication, he was succeeding. He urged Gabriel to tip his head back so he could wash the oil from the red-brown locks. Gabriel's hair had gotten long, but he could worry about that later. Right now he had a lover to welcome home.

Deciding Gabriel was clean enough for now, Lucio urged him to rise, drying him swiftly with a towel. Even with the weight he had lost, Gabriel was still incredibly beautiful to Lucio's eyes. His mouth watered at the thought of tasting his lover's skin again. Pushing Gabriel toward the bed, Lucio dealt quickly with the bath.

"You're wearing too much clothing," Gabriel said from the bed when Lucio turned back to him.

Lucio looked down at the undergarment that barely covered his groin. "Really?"

"Really," Gabriel said. "You aren't naked, and that's the way I've dreamed of you. Naked and in my arms."

Lucio smiled and removed the scrap of cloth, walking to the bed fully naked and fully aroused. "Like this?" he teased, sliding along Gabriel's body until he lay atop his lover, their bodies touching everywhere possible.

"Exactly like this," Gabriel replied, spreading his legs so Lucio slipped into the cradle of his hips.

"I thought we'd agreed that you would top tonight," Lucio teased, rocking his hips against Gabriel's.

Gabriel shook his head. "You suggested it. I didn't agree. Please, Luc. Make love to me."

Lucio stared down at his lover for a moment, helpless to refuse the heartfelt request. He resolved to make this the best homecoming possible.

He kept his touch light as he relearned Gabriel's body, lingering anytime the inventor gasped or moaned, drawing on the first time they had ever lain in their bed together to find and exploit the less obvious spots.

When they finally came together, Lucio held his breath against the pure pleasure of it. As much as he enjoyed all the ways they made love, this one held a special place in Lucio's heart because it was the way they had first made love.

After a month apart, neither of them had the patience to last long, the clenching of Gabriel's passage enough to set off Lucio's climax as well. Kissing Gabriel tenderly, Lucio rolled to the side, cradling his head against Gabriel's shoulder. He twirled his fingers through the ends of Gabriel's hair.

"Your hair's gotten long," Lucio commented. "With a bit of a trim, it will be quite dashing pulled back in a queue."

"I don't need to be dashing anymore," Gabriel murmured, eyes closed. "I have you to be dashing for me."

"Oh, no!" Lucio said. He knew how much Gabriel hated the demands society placed on his life and would gladly foist that responsibility off on someone else, but Lucio's devotion to his lover only went so far. "I'll deal with the customers in the shop and during the day one on one, but I refuse to go unescorted to any ball. I won't risk falling prey to someone like Lady Merydith ever again."

"Have you seen her?" Gabriel asked, looking at Lucio sharply.

"No," Lucio said, soothing Gabriel back onto the bed, "Lord Stuart was as good as his word on that count, but I was well-known in society before becoming an inventor, and not everyone realizes I am no longer available. I have no desire to be importuned by the ignorant."

"We could stay home," Gabriel suggested. "Then you wouldn't have to worry about that at all."

"And miss the chance to lure customers to the shop?" Lucio said. "We're better businessmen than that. If I arrive on your arm, no one will disturb me because they will know I'm taken."

"You could use my name," Gabriel offered. "Instead of being Lucio plain and simple, you should be Lucio or even Luc Blackstone. The fact that you have a surname would make it clear that you aren't a companion anymore."

Lucio smiled. Once he would have argued that he would always be a companion, but the past month had shown him how much more than that he could be, and Gabriel's return had not changed that.

Luc Blackstone.

He liked the sound of that. "So can we change the name of the workshop to Blackstone and Blackstone?"

"I'll speak with the painters tomorrow."

ARIEL TACHNA lives in southwestern Ohio with her husband, her daughter and son, and their cat. A native of the region, she has nonetheless lived all over the world, having fallen in love with both France, where she found her career and her husband, and India, where she dreams of retiring some day. She started writing when she was twelve and hasn't looked back since. A connoisseur of wine and horses, she's as comfortable on a farm as she is in the big cities of the world.

Visit Ariel's web site at http://www.arieltachna.com/ and her blog at http://arieltachna.livejournal.com/.

Historical Romance by ARIEL TACHNA

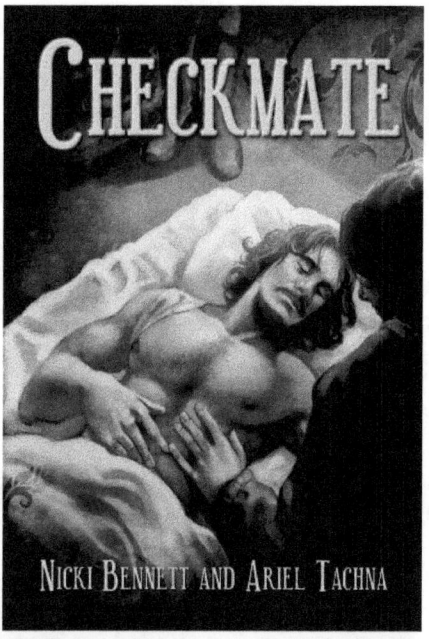